CW

BIR ZAMANLAR

TINA MUÑIZ STEIMLE

BIR ZAMANLAR

ONCE UPON A TIME: VOLUME 1

DEDICATION

To the love of my life.
To you Russ,
For loving me unconditionally.
For believing in all my dreams—no matter how crazy they were.

To my biggest cheerleader.
To you Monica, my loving daughter,
For believing in this book.
For being the strong wind at my back that helped me carry my dream to the finish line.

PALMETTO
PUBLISHING
Charleston, SC
www.PalmettoPublishing.com

© 2024 Tina Muñiz Steimle
All rights reserved.
No portion of this book may be reproduced,
stored in a retrieval system, or transmitted in
any form by any means–electronic, mechanical,
photocopy, recording, or other–except for
brief quotations in printed reviews,
without prior permission of the author.

Hardcover ISBN: 9798822943391
Paperback ISBN: 9798822943407
eBook ISBN: 9798822943414

TABLE OF CONTENTS

Character List ix
Prologue xiii
Chapter 1 The Beginning 1
Chapter 2 Loving Beautifully 4
Chapter 3 The Beginning of the Abyss 6
Chapter 4 Cascades of Silk and Ocean Blue 10
Chapter 5 Vague Sadness 16
Chapter 6 Mari's Discoveries 18
Chapter 7 Kurt's Aha Moment 26
Chapter 8 Baskets of Surprises 36
Chapter 9 Unforgettable Day 44
Chapter 10 Avocado, Tomato, Oregano, and Ham & Cheese 57
Chapter 11 Soul Compass 64
Chapter 12 Glee Club & Tap Lessons 69
Chapter 13 First and Second Rung 75
Chapter 14 LEGO Memories 89
Chapter 15 Pillow Dreams 92
Chapter 16 Mari-Car, Part One 94
Chapter 17 Mari-Car, Part Two 99
Chapter 18 Peter John 105
Chapter 19 Mari-Car Part Three 107
Chapter 20 Campus Life 110
Chapter 21 Ozan, Part One 118
Chapter 22 Kader {Fate} 120
Chapter 23 Two Pink Lines 127

Chapter 24 The Return 134
Chapter 25 Meryem Finds Herself 138
Chapter 26 Ozan Part Two 142
Chapter 27 Shock 151
Chapter 28 Brown-Eyed Beauty 156
Chapter 29 The Beginning and the End 161
Chapter 30 The Price of Victory 167
Chapter 31 Zoey's Legacy 169
Chapter 32 The Search 175
Chapter 33 The Heartbreak 177
Chapter 34 Forgiveness Begins 180
Chapter 35 Ozan, Part Three 187
Chapter 36 Scooter Strike 189
Chapter 37 Kader Strikes Again 193
Chapter 38 Thoughts Reflected 195
Chapter 39 Parting of Ways 201
Chapter 40 Mari-Car Denudates her Soul 204
Chapter 41 Betrayal 210
Chapter 42 Dr. Osman to the Rescue 215
Chapter 43 Ozan's Return 219
Chapter 44 Betrayal, Guilt, and Jealousy 227
Chapter 45 Ozan's Surprising Proposal 233
Chapter 46 Deniz-Mare Arrives in Milan 238
Chapter 47 Missing the Two of Us 243
Chapter 48 Ozan Falls in Love 245
Chapter 49 Growing Pains 251
Chapter 50 Brain Overload 253
Chapter 51 Peter John's Revelation 265
Chapter 52 Crash Course 270
Chapter 53 The First to Know 275

Chapter 54 Ozan Finds What's Been Missing 277
Chapter 55 Seni Seviyorum 282
Chapter 56 Do You Know How Beautiful You Are? 285
Chapter 57 Peter John Keeps His Promise 293
Chapter 58 Wrong Conclusion 299
Chapter 59 At a Loss for Words 305
Chapter 60 The Purest of Loves... 313
Chapter 61 Marriage Scare.. 322
Chapter 62 Mari's Admonition 325
Chapter 63 Allah'a ükür 334
Chapter 64 Migliaia di Minuti 342
Chapter 65 Kader Resurfaces 349
Chapter 66 The Costly Vineyard of Long Ago 352
Chapter 67 A Series of Damned Fine Lines 361
Chapter 68 One More Hoop to Jump Through 372
Chapter 69 Rare Gems 379
Chapter 70 First Touch 394
Chapter 71 If Only 404
Chapter 72 It's a Yes!.. 409
Chapter 73 Shocking Encounter 411
Chapter 74 Puzzling Behavior 416
Chapter 75 She's Giving Up 421
Chapter 76 In Search of a Reason 427
Chapter 77 Shocking Appearance 432
Chapter 78 Surprising "Friend" 439
Chapter 79 Luca Speaks Truth 444
Chapter 80 Unexpected Tenderness... 448
Chapter 81 A Sort of Knowing 450
Chapter 82 A Figment of Her Imagination? 454
Chapter 83 The Impossible Dream.. 460

Chapter 84 Excellent News 464
Chapter 85 Preposterous Proposal 472
Chapter 86 Iyi Ki Varsin 476
Chapter 87 Remembering the Early Days 481
Chapter 88 Yakamoz 488
Chapter 89 Mio Dio Aiutami! [My God Help Me!] 494
Chapter 90 The Plan 498
Chapter 91 The Bottle of Perrier Did It! 504
Chapter 92 If Allah Had Given Me a Love Like Yours 509
Chapter 93 Mi Niña Hermosa [My Beautiful Child] 513
Chapter 94 The Wooden Box 516
Chapter 95 Virgen de la Fuensanta 521
Chapter 96 If She Had Grown Up with the Abuelos 523
Chapter 97 The Sounds and Flavors of Childhood 525
Chapter 98 The Name That Revived Abuela's Pain..................... 528
Chapter 99 Tearful Almuerzo 537
Chapter 100 New Team Member 539
Chapter 101 He's Hot! 544
Chapter 102 Amça, I'm Screwed! 549
Chapter 103 A Favor for Ozan 559
Chapter 104 We've Made You Sad 562
Chapter 105 Impossible Choice 565
Chapter 106 We Fought with All Our Might to Keep You 582
Chapter 107 A Receptive Heart 584
Chapter 108 Mari Arrives in Istanbul 588
About the Author 593

CHARACTER LIST

María José García Cortés/Mari (18; 20s; mid 30s and older): A beautiful young girl who was brought to New York City by her parents from Murcia, Spain, at six months old. Her talent for fashion design was evident at an early age. Most of the events of the book take place from when Mari turns eighteen through her middle to late thirties.

Kurt Stewart (early to mid-20s): A handsome, blue-eyed, blond, student of architecture from North Carolina who left his native state to attend Columbia University. Mari and Kurt's love story becomes the underlying essence of this book.

María del Carmen Stewart García/Mari-Car (birth to early childhood; 18 and older): A beautiful, self-confident, very gregarious young lady and daughter of **Kurt** and **María José**. She is well-traveled and cultured and has attended prestigious private schools in New York City since preschool. Mari-Car follows in her father's footsteps and studies architecture.

José Felipe García Arias (late 20s and older man): A doting father to María José and a committed and loving husband to María Victoria. He brought his young family from Murcia, Spain, to New York City under mysterious circumstances.

María Victoria Cortés Fernández—Mavi (early 20s and older. A quiet, loving wife to José Felipe and doting mother to María José. A talented seamstress who encouraged and helped her daughter develop her career.

Peter John Stewart (early 20s): Mari-Car's handsome, blond, blue-eyed, outgoing cousin, best friend, and confidant. Born in South Carolina and raised in North Carolina, he is the only child of Kurt's older brother Peter and his wife Ashley. He and Mari-Car share an uncommon bond.

John Stewart (mid-40s and older): Father of Peter, Kurt, and Katherine. A quiet and unassuming man, but the backbone of the Stewart family.

Mary Stewart (mid-40s and older): Mother of Peter, Kurt, and Katherine. A devoted wife and mother but also very dedicated to her nursing profession.

Ozan Ulusoy/Ozan *Bey* (early 70s): Patriarch of the Ulusoy family and loving and dedicated grandfather to his grandchildren Ozan and Deniz-Mare. Generous toward those less fortunate, devoted to Allah, and respectful toward others.

Ceyda Ulusoy/Ceyda *Hanim* (late 60s): Wife of Ozan Ulusoy and authoritarian wealthy Turkish woman from one of Istanbul's most influential families. She is controlling and unforgiving of anyone who challenges her rules.

Dr. Osman Ulusoy (mid-20s; late 30s to early 40s): Youngest son of Ozan *Bey* and Ceyda *Hanim* Ulusoy. Brilliant cardiologist who, unable to withstand the severe, rule-bound home environment, left his family years before.

Dr. Zoey Clark (early to late 20s): Dedicated pediatrician and adored wife of Osman Ulusoy—her first and only love.

Mehmet Ulusoy (early 20s; mid to late 40s): Eldest son of Ceyda *Hanim* and Ozan *Bey*; distant father of Ozan and Deniz-Mare; estranged husband of Meryem.

Meryem (Yildirim) Ulusoy (early 20s; mid to late 30s and older): Married Mehmet Ulusoy very young. A dedicated mother and independent woman who fought family opposition and chose to finish her interrupted career in art history.

Ozan Ulusoy (20): Son of Mehmet and Meryem Ulusoy; born in Milan, Italy. Grows up under the strict rules of his grandmother Ceyda *Hanim* and the loving guidance of his grandfather Ozan *Bey*. He studies architecture in Milan, Italy.

PROLOGUE

A confused look emanated from piercing blue eyes that penetrated her wide-open dark ones; the two sets remained intensely fixed on each other. The look emitted by the striking azure eyes felt vaguely familiar. Her forearms rested on his chest as he lay flat on the cold, hard floor, wondering what had just taken place in what seemed like microseconds. One minute he was standing, stretching his neck to try to spot his passenger by following Ozan's description, and the next minute, he found himself in this awkward position.

María José was the first to break the uncomfortable, albeit intense, moment. "We cannot be too careful; you never know what these people will do."

Osman tried to look around, although he was barely able to raise his head. "What people?" he finally said in slightly accented English.

"The extremists," she replied, turning her head to look at the group of men in white robes and slippers that had made her so afraid just before she ran into the man that now lay beneath her.

María José had reluctantly agreed to come to Istanbul to attend a prestigious fashion show where she was granted a highly coveted spot to showcase her latest designs. As a fashion designer, she often attended events where her line of clothing was exhibited but felt uneasy when these took place in countries and cultures that felt unfamiliar to her.

Yağmur Gülsoy, her Middle East representative, was extremely talented, beautiful, and glamorous. Besides her native Turkish, she spoke fluent Arabic, English, and Italian. "A gem," María José considered her.

Yağmur represented María José throughout the major cities of Turkey, Jordan, and the United Arab Emirates (UAE), mainly Dubai. However, to María José's chagrin, at the last minute, Yağmur had backed out of her commitment to attend the Istanbul fashion show. "Family reasons," she had said. Yağmur's work had been nothing short of stellar so far, and María José wanted to give her her full support during this time of family need.

With her reputation on the line, María José's presence at the highly prestigious event was indispensable.

Recent family discoveries, however, had caused María José to be considerably more apprehensive about attending the Istanbul fashion show; on top of that, Mari-Car had begged her to allow Osman to pick her up at the airport. However, the feeling of impending doom had not abandoned her since she had left her grandparents' home in Murcia that morning, and during the almost seven-hour flight, she had worked herself up into a bundle of nerves. For the love of Mari-Car, she had told herself.

Her mother and grandmother had suggested that she pray various rosaries: the Rosary of the Blood of Jesus, the Rosary of the Holy Wounds, the Rosary to Saint Anthony. The latter, María José prayed on the flight with a lot of faith as, according to them, Saint Anthony found lost items, and she was sure she was losing her mind. But Mari-Car, or María del Carmen, as she was baptized, was all she had in this world: she was both the reason she was alive and her reason for continuing to live.

CHAPTER 1
THE BEGINNING

The sound of the screeching wheels as they swerved in and out of their lane, trying to avoid the oncoming car that suddenly came into view during the torrential rain, would never leave her mind. How many times did they roll after they hit the railings and went down the embankment? Five, six, ten? It didn't matter. When it was all said and done, her heart lay at the bottom of the hill.

Kurt had said that he felt claustrophobic driving in the blinding rain with his seat belt on. He'd said he was unable to concentrate and would remove it, "Just until we get out of the rain." María José barely acknowledged him; she was far away in her creative realm. But it turned out to be a deadly decision on Kurt's part.

For years, all the big "life questions" had invaded María José's mind daily; and, although with the passage of time, they made their appearance less frequently, they still tormented her. Was it really Kurt's time to die? Would he have survived, like she did, had he had his seat belt on? In that case, why did he suffer from claustrophobia? What happened to all those people who had survived worse accidents and did not have seat belts on? What if they had left five minutes earlier on that fateful day, instead of spending those minutes comforting Mari-Car, who did not want them to leave? Should they have listened to their little daughter? Had that been God trying to warn them? Instead of warning them, why didn't he just protect them?

In any case, fifteen years later fear remained in María José's heart and mind. It was an indefinable fear—hard to pinpoint but a constant companion. It had a sense of familiarity, and she had become accustomed to it, so at times, not having it close created anxiety and even a sense of longing.

Mari-Car had become the center of María José's life. It was for her daughter's sake that she had reached down beyond her own powers and found the strength to pursue her career in fashion design. Mari-Car was that motivational force that caused her to push on even when it was overwhelming to do so and to become one of the top clothes designers in the world.

María José and Kurt had dreamed of creating an architectural firm and fashion design center in New York's Garment District—or in Paris, near Sacré-Coeur. They loved the artistic feeling they got when they walked the eighteenth arrondissement. They dreamed, they created in the fertile creative fields of their minds, they designed, they planned…

Then Mari-Car had put a stop to that. Had "postponed" it, is what the ever-optimistic, carefree, always-loving Kurt called it. In retrospect, marriage was the only option. She, from an immigrant, upper-middle-class, Spanish family, the pride and joy of her parents, had put them in an uncomfortable situation. Mostly because she had only finished the first year of her four-year training.

They wanted their beloved daughter's future to be assured; they wanted her to be independent, able to stand on her own two feet so that if, *Dios libre*—God forbid—something were to happen to them, she would not have to depend on a man and could continue on and build a good life with her own God-given talents.

Kurt had almost finished his career, and his parents were less involved in his life decisions. They supported their son and welcomed their new daughter-in-law.

As for Kurt and María José, they shared an uncommon bond, as if they were the only two people in the world. For them, being in each other's presence was a constant desire—a need. Marriage was their destination; the *when* had been determined by Mari-Car.

CHAPTER 2
LOVING BEAUTIFULLY

The arrival of María del Carmen Stewart García put hundreds of miles on Kurt's parents' family car and caused their phone bill to go way up. Her eyes were undeniably their son's, as if the whole ocean resided in them. She had a sunny disposition, also Kurt's contribution. But the dark, silky locks were a gift from her mother.

Kurt received María del Carmen with open arms, soul, and mind. When she was born, he took her in his arms, looked at María José with tear-filled eyes, and whispered, "Thank you."

From the first day his Mari-Car arrived, he took over all the duties, with the obvious exception of breastfeeding. When Mari-Car woke up at night, Kurt brought her to her mother to be fed; when she was finished, he rocked her before putting her back in her cradle. He changed her, bathed her, carried her around against his chest in the baby wrap carrier. With his little daughter hidden in the cozy wrap, he did house chores, grocery shopping, and cooking.

María José looked at the father-daughter relationship in amazement and pondered in her heart how Kurt could love so beautifully. It almost scared her that she could be so lucky, and she wished that she lived in a world where her sort of life would last forever.

Although Kurt's parents believed their granddaughter would have a better upbringing if she were brought up in North Carolina, to the delight of the maternal grandparents, Kurt and María José decided that New York City was better for their careers as well as for Mari-Car's schooling.

They did give in to Kurt's parents' wish to let them pay for Mari-Car's private preschool. This would allow the young couple to continue their work and studies and still enjoy some financial freedom. María José's parents only insisted that the preschool be bilingual. Otherwise, life was lovely and loving for the young family.

CHAPTER 3
THE BEGINNING OF THE ABYSS

Doomsday hit unexpectedly, suddenly, insidiously. Hands-on dad Kurt had gone to Mari-Car's room. At three years old, she had just been moved to a toddler bed. He started the routine of running his fingers through her dark head while softly whispering, "Maaarii-Caar," in her ear. She turned on her side and continued sleeping until her dad scooped her up in his arms, brought her neck up to his lips, and showered her with kisses. He handed the child over to María José, or Mari, as he liked to call her.

As the girls got ready for the ordinary day that lay before them, Kurt went to fix breakfast.

The whistled tune of "You Are My Sunshine" interspersed with the whirring/humming sound of the juicer reached Mari and Mari-Car's ears; it added a familiar, pleasant feel to their morning routine, the kind of experience that, although simple, stayed with you and years later you recounted to your children.

They left their small apartment in Manhattan and drove to the preschool on that fateful, cloudy day in mid-October.

Heavy raindrops were beginning to fall as they neared the preschool. Usually, Mari-Car let go of both of her parents' hands and ran happily into the warm, waiting arms of her teacher, Ms. Scott. This morning, she held tightly to Kurt's and Mari's hands and whimpered as she clung tightly to her dad, wrapping her little legs around his waist and burying her face in his neck. Had that been a sign?

María José had racked her brain trying to figure that out and tortured herself for years for having missed the clue. From then on, she walked on eggshells every day for fear of missing a clue that might prevent a tragedy.

But they left Mari-Car at school after showering her with kisses and promising to pick her up earlier than usual that day. They continued on, driving Mari to the prestigious Fashion Institute before Kurt drove himself to the university. He had interrupted his thesis research when Mari got pregnant and gone to work part-time at an architectural firm in the city. In the mornings, he went to the university, where he worked with his professors putting the finishing touches on his thesis and tutoring undergraduate students.

Mari's creative juices were already at full throttle during her morning ride. She began to design in her mind long before she reached the halls of the design school. To the minutest detail, she already had the designs in her head. By the time she reached her design table at school and picked up her graphite pencil, her only job was to transfer what she had already conceived in her mind onto the white pad in front of her.

While in this design mode in the car, she barely noticed that in order to avoid traffic, Kurt had chosen to leave the city streets and take a two-lane back road. The rain had become harder, to the point of being blinding, but even then, cocooned in its sheets, her mind continued to design. Mari had entered a different world.

She came out of it abruptly when she felt her body making the same swerving movements as the car for what felt like interminable minutes, then finally hitting the railing on her side. Next, as if in a dream, she saw sky and ground, sky and ground—then ground.

Moments passed, or perhaps it was hours—Mari was neither able to judge the passing of time nor to process what had happened. She did notice that her door was jammed against the hard, leafy ground. But the driver's door was not; it was even open.

She methodically climbed out through the open door and looked up to the road. She saw mangled metal where the smooth railings had once protected and adorned the side of the road, and bare ground where blankets of colorful leaves had once decorated the embankment. But she did not see Kurt, and she became aware of that. The lump in her throat and the knot in the pit of her stomach told her a truth that she wished she had misunderstood.

Sirens, lights, voices. "Kurt," she whispered over and over, hoping her voice could be heard outside her head. She grabbed her right shoulder, felt great pain and confusion, then unconsciousness engulfed her.

The details had come out later: the brakes had failed; Kurt had been thrown out of the car; her right shoulder had dislocated, and she had broken her arm. The brakes, the shoulder, and the arm were fixed. The pain inside, however, would not be fixed so easily. In fact, fifteen years later, it had only dulled, not healed. It had changed her. The young, trusting, loving, optimistic Mari who saw the world as a beautiful, friendly receptive space where everything was possible and who tried to capture that beauty every day on her pad was no more. In fact, that former self now seemed like a distant memory. What remained was a fearful, distrustful, wary, cautious, fragile version of what once was.

That first year following the accident, she designed only in her head. She held Mari-Car tightly and kept her close, unable to let her go, even to school. They slept together at night, and their only outings were to her parents' townhouse and to Kurt's parents' small apartment.

His parents had temporarily moved to New York and rented the small space close by. They wanted to be near those who understood and felt what they themselves were feeling, because explaining it, even to friends back home in North Carolina, was an impossible task. For now, they felt more needed here, and so they stayed.

Everyone was fearful for Mari. She had become thin and frail, spoke little. No one knew what was going on inside her head. They feared that she would not be able to survive her loss; they feared that Mari-Car would be left without both parents.

But a lot was going on inside Mari's head. She designed, she planned for Mari-Car's future, for her future, and she thought about Kurt—his deep-blue eyes, which melted her the first moment they looked her way…

CHAPTER 4
CASCADES OF SILK AND OCEAN BLUE

She had thought about studying architecture and had gone to orientation week at Columbia University. Kurt was in his last year and was one of the career counselors.

Her parents had brought her to the campus, and Kurt, as he had been doing with the other families, greeted them outside the building and guided them into an available parking space. He proceeded to open the passenger door for María Victoria, Mari's mom.

He also attempted to open Mari's door while she tried opening it from the inside, so the door would not budge. Finally, he put both hands up in a sign of surrender, smiled big, and allowed her to open the door.

Her mane of long, thick, dark hair cascaded onto her face as she let one foot out of the car. She slid out, her back toward Kurt while she grabbed and dragged the backpack that had been lying next to her in the back seat of the family's small SUV. As she turned around and looked up, her hair glided back in place, and she was met by the pool of deep blue that never left her until… until…the day that her life was changed forever.

Mari was not quite eighteen, but as she looked up, standing before the deep-blue sea, she sensed something that reminded her of home. Or at least, that's the word that came to her mind for a fleeting moment.

Looking down at her and at a loss for words for the first time in his life, Kurt blurted out what he had been thinking: "Silk." He had been captivated by the dark locks that fell to cover Mari's face and the easiness with which she absentmindedly ran her slightly open hand through them to put them back in place, although to no avail.

"Blue; I like blue," were Mari's first words to Kurt. To his questioning look, she added, "I'm a designer. I mean, that's what I'll study—design, fashion design."

María Victoria and José Felipe reacted with amusement to their brief, nonsensical exchange. After all, their little girl was growing up, and it was only natural that admirers would soon be knocking at their door. A somber look crossed José Felipe's face as he thought they'd have to wait a while at that door.

Kurt nodded, regained his composure, and proceeded to lead them inside the building to join the other families waiting to be led on the tour of the beautiful campus, which Kurt conducted himself. Most were anxious to see the space where the architecture and design classes and lectures would be held, and they weren't disappointed.

Both parents and students were impressed with the courses of study as well as the physical setting of the undergraduate classes. Torrents of natural light invaded the spaces where the students designed and created.

Kurt explained that students in the undergraduate program would explore their creativity and design talents and eventually graduate with a liberal arts degree with a major in architecture. Then they could go on and pursue a master's degree in architecture at Columbia's Graduate School of Architecture, Planning and Preservation.

As a way of adding a more personal touch, Kurt shared that he was working on his doctoral thesis on green architecture, hoping to make an original contribution to the field by designing a multigenerational green home.

Upon hearing this revelation, one of the parents asked if he was married and to define "multigenerational" as it applied to building.

Kurt hoped that the heat that he felt inside did not reflect outwardly on his face as he went on to explain that no, he was not married, but hoped to be some day and live in a green home on a large enough geographical setting where both his parents and his future wife's parents could also live independently but close by.

He sure didn't mean to talk about his personal life; his ears felt hot and his tongue dry, which he quickly remedied by taking a swig of water from his thermos.

But the usually self-confident young man on this day felt self-conscious, an unfamiliar state that he did not know how to manage.

He had made presentations to faculty and students in large lecture halls, he had taught various classes to undergraduate students, he had made building proposals to the city manager and other local politicians at city hall, and he had met several times with the doctoral dissertation committee, first to make his thesis proposal and later to give updates on the progress and to receive feedback and answer questions. All these speeches, he had made with ease, enthusiasm, and even charm. Now he felt awkward giving a campus tour to a few families and some prospective undergraduate students. The right words had an even harder time coming whenever he glanced María José's way. She, on the other hand, seemed unaffected by his presence.

After a lovely luncheon, there was a break during which families and students could socialize and ask questions of the faculty members or simply go outdoors and enjoy a walk in the lovely surroundings.

After the break, everyone came together once again to listen to some of the experts in the broad field of architecture. This time, the parents sat in the back, and all the potential students gathered in the front of the hall.

María José was fascinated with the diversity of areas within architecture; she listened to each presentation with attentiveness and concentration. She was good at that—when she put her mind on something, the world around her faded away.

They heard from various professionals. The first one introduced herself as Sandra Miraflores, a young, enthusiastic woman, maybe in her late twenties, who had become a landscape architect. Mari's interest was piqued. She lived near Central Park, one of the most beautiful landscapes on the planet. Growing up, she had spent many hours getting lost in its greenery, tranquility, and beauty. She admired Calvert Vaux and Frederick Law Olmsted, who created such an oasis amid busyness and sometimes chaos. She would like that, she thought—to create beauty and peacefulness.

María José had lived a rather sheltered life and did not have many close friends, but she thought that Sandra, despite being older and at a different stage of life, could be an interesting person to get to know, especially because her bubbly personality balanced Mari's quiet, pensive one. She wasn't shy; in fact, she was naturally upbeat, confident, and optimistic. However, because of her creative nature, she often became engrossed in what her mind was designing at any particular moment, which of course was unseen by the observer and could be perceived as Mari being distant and uninterested.

The landscape architect was followed by professionals in urban planning and lighting. Finally came her favorite, a restoration architect. The young expert (she was surprised how young these experts were) enthusiastically explained how he restored historical buildings and the importance of preserving and reviving these structures. His name was Berk Stone. She thought it was an appropriate name for someone who restored buildings.

Mari's questions to Berk at the end of his presentation were endless: How do you become a restoration architect? How many years of study does it take? Is the job market for this work more substantial in the US or in Europe? Should one first become a conservation expert? Are more women interested in this field than men? How much history should one study?

Kurt did not miss the fact that the young, handsome restoration specialist looked at María José with interest as he passionately answered her questions. Damn! And his specialty had to be green design, thought Kurt, rolling his eyes; now it sounded boring.

Kurt felt an unexplained anger when María José spent time talking to the young architect after his lecture. What could they possibly be discussing? He seemed baffled, although he had no reasonable explanation for his reaction since his temperament was by nature affable and carefree.

After the presentations, it was time to say goodbye to the parents and welcome the students to the week of orientation. María José walked to the parking lot between her parents, arm in arm with both. Their watery eyes had not escaped her notice. She had seen them during each important event in her life: preschool graduation, confirmation, First Communion, eighth-grade graduation, *quinceañera*, high school graduation, and now college orientation week.

Their hugs were long and tight. As she was an only child, all their attention, care, resources, and hopes rested on her, and she felt their weight. Not in a bad way. She just knew that she had a big responsibility and did not want to disappoint them.

CHAPTER 5
VAGUE SADNESS

They hadn't been apart very much. Summer vacations, as far back as she remembers, were always spent as a family; they had visited almost every country in Europe. For sure all seventeen regions of Spain, her parents' homeland.

Her grandparents still lived in Murcia. It was one of her beloved places, not just because her doting grandparents lived there but because the place itself made her feel anchored somehow. The historical buildings spoke to her about family, forefathers—especially the Santa Iglesia Catedral de Santa María, or Catedral de Murcia, as it was also known.

Her mother had told her that she was the third generation of women in the family to bear the name of the holy church. Her grandmother was named María Dolores Fernández Campos; her mother, María Victoria Cortés Fernández; and she was María José García Cortés, carrying her father's and mother's first last names as was the tradition. She was the daughter of María Victoria Cortés Fernández and José Felipe García Arias.

María José had always wanted to know the reason her parents had left the "old country." She knew there was some sort of secret behind it, but both her mother and her grandmother avoided the issue.

She had tried to dig it out of her grandmother during her visits to Murcia, but María Dolores's demeanor changed at the slightest mention of the subject; her countenance became somber before giving way to tear-filled eyes and her chin and lips trembled, although she kept her tears in check, never allowing them to spill over.

María José knew that the reason her parents had left enveloped a painful secret, so she stopped questioning her grandmother and continued mulling this secret in her heart. Her grandfather José Andrés was loving, but his eyes carried a vague sadness that she always wished she could erase by running her hands over it—as if when she removed it, joy would shine through.

CHAPTER 6
MARI'S DISCOVERIES

After saying goodbye to her parents, María José turned toward the building. Kurt met her just outside the door and handed her a yellow folder with the details of the week ahead, including her dorm and room number, and said, his gaze never leaving the parking lot, "I see you're close."

"Very," was her short reply, looking down to open the folder. Again, her hair cascaded softly on her face; again, she used her fingers to push it back. Again, Kurt was captivated and self-conscious.

But he did manage to say, "See you at the get-acquainted cocktail party at eight." She nodded in acknowledgment and did not miss the intensity of the blue eyes that reached right down to her toes.

Off with her jeans and cropped sweater, on with the white, thin-strapped, cropped top, denim miniskirt, and sports shoes. She went to sit on one of the benches bordering the paths leading to the various campus buildings. They seemed to beckon her to come and sit and draw from the moment she arrived.

Time stood still when she drew; this time was no different. She'd be late for the get-acquainted gathering, and although Mari did not want to be rude, she knew she would be content for the rest of the evening doing what she was doing at that moment. But courtesy won out; she reluctantly stopped what she was doing and decided to get ready and attend the event.

She wore a maxi-length strapless dress. The flowy, tiered skirt displayed small, vintage floral prints in yellow, green, teal, and bronze tones. The shirred, stretchy bodice, teal like the skirt, accentuated her bustline. As was the case with most of her wardrobe, she had designed it herself, and her mom had sewn it.

Teardrop larimar earrings, a larimar thumb ring, and teal high-heeled sandals with wide straps across the top of her foot, buckled on the side, completed her look. Mari quickly penciled a flawless, elongated line on her eyelids, grabbed lip gloss and her dorm keys, slipped them in one of her dress's hidden side pockets, and unenthusiastically left for the evening.

Since she was late and there weren't that many people—between twenty and twenty-five, including faculty members—when she walked in, all eyes turned toward her. Guilt and self-consciousness tried their best to make her lose her composure, but she kept them at bay, holding her shoulders back and moving with confidence and ease.

Mari did not notice that her discomfort went totally undetected by the other guests, who were taken aback by her simple beauty but especially by her poise. It was an innate characteristic of which Mari was unaware but that made her infinitely more appealing.

There were five round tables, each with a famous architectural design as a centerpiece and place cards by each setting. She was glad she came. The centerpiece at her table was a replica of Central Park, and on each oversized place card was a name written in calligraphy along with a drawing of a famous site. An impeccable sketch of the Cathédrale Notre Dame de Paris graced the cards at her table. She had written in her application that her main interests were historical restoration and landscape architecture; Mari was touched by the thoughtfulness and the care that the organizers had put into the event.

The program called for first spending time getting acquainted with those who shared similar interests, so it made for an enthusiastic discussion at her table on a subject that they all loved. Their host, Berk Stone, remained mostly silent, enjoying the lively interaction among the very knowledgeable group and allowing them to share their expertise.

Exquisite hors d'oeuvres distinguished each table. Her eyes fell on the thin, toasted slices of baguette with small mounds of cream cheese and chives topped with pieces of smoked salmon before her. Had they read her mind, or had the universe conspired to feed her tonight? A smile crossed her lips—smoked salmon was one of her favorite foods.

The conversation was so interesting and the people so cool, fun, and well-versed on the subject that it was difficult to move on. But soon, a small basket was passed around the table, and everyone took a number that indicated the next table they would join.

María José reluctantly got up, took her place card as instructed, and moved to her next table.

The next hors d'oeuvres consisted of a half melon with an opening in the center filled with port wine. The accompaniment was thin slices of toasted baguette, this time lined with fresh mozzarella, sun-dried tomatoes, and fresh basil and sprinkled with olive oil and sea salt. She was convinced once again that the universe was on her side.

She had been so distracted by the food that she was the last to notice the centerpiece. That is, until she saw the look of awe on the faces of her peers. They were all fixed on the impressive replica of the Sagrada Familia *basílica* in Barcelona; she of course was very familiar with the famous church. The warmth she suddenly felt on her cheeks belied the outer confidence she displayed.

The expert in interior architecture explained that this branch of architecture focused on redesigning an existing interior space, attending to both structural and aesthetic elements while being mindful and respectful of its historical significance.

The imposing church, whose construction began in 1882, was still under construction, she reminded the students.

The original architect and designer was Francisco de Paula del Villar; however, its most famous designer architect was arguably Antoni Gaudi, who began work on the church in 1883 and continued until his death in 1926. The extraordinary and intricate construction had continued under various interior architects and designers.

Although Mari's knowledge of the Sagrada Familia church probably surpassed that of the group leader's, she had not ever given a thought to the particular branch of architecture that specifically addressed the complexities of redesigning an interior space. She could almost feel her mind expanding.

The first table continued to be her favorite; she felt an affinity with the group, and she felt a connection with Berk. Plus, it had her favorite hors d'oeuvres.

Mari knew that she probably would not go into architectural lighting, but that was her next table, and the centerpiece adorning the table where the lighting expert waited to welcome them was fascinating—in fact, breathtaking.

It displayed a city park with walkways, benches, trees, shrubs, ferns, flowers, ponds, birds, people, and dogs. The right color of lighting placed in the right spot at the right distance transformed a space. Mari got lost in its beauty. It was art, science, technology—all of it! She once again had a hard time pulling herself away. It seemed a drastic change, leaving so much beauty behind to go on to urban planning. But she hesitantly moved on.

It turned out to be interesting. At the center stood a miniature scale of a city. The expert said that this field called for visionaries, professionals who could think on a grand scale and see the big picture, futurists who could plan where buildings would be built and what to do with the outdoor space.

Mari acquired a new appreciation for how cities were designed. She would look at each city that she visited with new eyes from then on, she thought. She wondered where she had been all these years. She had visited many world-class cities but had never given a thought to the visionaries that had created them and continued to think ahead to plan their expansion.

Mari was feeling almost overwhelmed by all that she had learned and realized that by burying herself in her drawings, she had made her world smaller. There is so much to learn, she thought as she made her way to the last table.

It suddenly hit her that she had not tasted the food at the last two tables, but the truth was that she felt no hunger. She had asked so many questions, and all that talking had made her thirsty.

Kurt hosted her last table. The centerpiece was a green home, Kurt's own design; he had called it his dream home. It was the same model that he had presented to the doctoral examination committee of the university.

Mari looked around for water before taking her place at the table. Then her eyes fixed on a water bottle with her name on it. "María José," it read.

"It's eco-friendly." She raised her eyes to the voice and was met with a slight smile, dimples, and blue eyes that sent a current of weakness to her knees. She had to rest her hand on the back of the chair in order to veil her vulnerability.

According to the architectural model, the home looked ample but not huge. The front yard, rather than being manicured, was overflowing with beach and ornamental grasses in various tones of green, interspersed with white and yellow wildflowers. A path of white gravel edged with pillows of wild thyme and its deep pink, almost purple, flowers led from the front gate to the front porch. The path allowed for a leisurely, tranquil walk that gave visitors time to take in the colors and the scent of the grasses and wildflowers on both sides of the path.

For a moment, Mari found herself dreaming in the dream home. It was as if she could capture the feeling that Kurt had tried to convey. She had stopped to observe it before sitting down at the table. As she looked down, a mass of dark silk tresses slowly made its way to the front of her face, blocking her view while she distractedly combed it back with her hand. This now-familiar gesture once again entranced Kurt.

When they were all seated, Kurt explained that green design used materials from renewable sources or materials obtained locally, which lowered transportation costs and energy consumption. He noticed that he had her attention—at least as much as she gave to the restoration expert, he thought with a tinge of satisfaction.

He went on to explain the new technologies being used for energy-saving, like the water management systems for water conservation through catching and recycling rainwater.

Finally, he talked about the health benefits of a green home—how the nontoxic and moisture-resistant materials used in this type of construction would improve the air quality indoors and would reduce allergies and asthma and prevent mold and mildew.

Kurt asked if there were any questions, but none came, and he felt a bit of disappointment until Mari said, "You explained it so well that all our questions were answered—it's a fascinating concept."

He looked at her and thanked her. She noticed something else about his eyes: they were not just blue, but they also smiled, and they seemed to convey all that he was feeling. He'd be hard to resist, she thought out of nowhere.

On the second day of orientation, the assignment was to pair off with another person from the team and visit a place in the city that displayed the type of architecture that most interested them. While visiting, they needed to keep in mind that the day after, everyone would give a presentation in which they would try to convey the *feeling* experienced while touring their chosen site.

Mari chose 54 Pearl Street, also known as Fraunces Tavern. Her partner was Berk, the young restoration expert. Her naiveté prevented her from realizing that Berk was behind this match.

CHAPTER 7
KURT'S AHA MOMENT

The building had a fascinating history: in 1686, Mayor Nicholas Bayard, the sixteenth mayor of New York City, granted the site to Stephanus Van Cortlandt, who in turn gave it to his daughter Ann as a wedding present. Ann and Etienne De Lancey then built their three-story family residence at 54 Pearl Street.

After that, it was used as a place for dance lessons, then as an office building before being purchased by Samuel Fraunces in 1762 and opened as a tavern. It was named the Queen's Head Tavern.

Later, many important meetings and decisions were made at this site.

In 1774, the Sons of Liberty plotted the New York Tea Party at this tavern.

In 1776, the New York Provincial Congress used the tavern as a meeting place, but when the city was occupied by British troops, Samuel Fraunces fled to the neighboring state of New Jersey. He was later captured, brought back, and forced to cook for British generals.

In 1783, the tavern was used by Governor George Clinton to host a celebration in honor of the British evacuation of New York City.

On December 4 of that same year, George Washington said farewell to his officers at the tavern.

After that, the famous site assumed various roles—government offices, boarding house, grocery store. It was submitted to several renovations throughout the 1800s.

Finally, when the building was threatened with demolition in 1900, the City of New York responded by putting into effect its rights of eminent domain and designated the site a park. The owners decided to sell it to the Sons of the Revolution in the State of New York.

In 1905, the restoration architect William Mersereau was hired to return the building to its colonial roots and look. This last fact was of course the most interesting to María José and the reason she had chosen this building for her project.

The day of the presentations, when they tried to convey their impressions to their fellow students and to the faculty members and advisors, was engrossing for her.

Each presentation transported her to that wonderful world of imagination, design, and inspiration. This was her world, and she had a difficult time leaving it and coming back to reality. There was harshness, austerity, and even cruelty in the latter, while in her imagination, she could create a world of beauty. And when beauty faded, she could restore it—like Mersereau had done with Fraunces Tavern.

When their turn came, Mari gave all the historical details of Fraunces Tavern while Berk spoke about the process of restoration of the building; they balanced each other well. There was no doubt that they enjoyed each other's presentation, with both providing attentiveness, nods, and smiles while the other was on stage.

To transmit the feeling experienced at the site, Berk expressed the exhilaration that raised within him when he envisioned William Mersereau peeling back layer after layer of paint, wood, plaster, soot, and dirt left behind by countless renovations, additions, and redecorations over hundreds of years—until the tips of the famous restorer's fingers felt the original brick and his eyes spotted the first glimpse of red.

One could hear a pin drop when Berk spoke, and when he finished, the silence continued. Mari sensed that the audience needed the time to process the feeling that Berk had so beautifully conveyed to them and stood in silence for a long moment before speaking.

Then it was Mari's turn to attempt to transfer to the listeners her feelings while consciously strolling through 54 Pearl Street. She had the lights dimmed and asked everyone to close their eyes as she began her slow, deliberate narrative.

"Imagine being a young, well-to-do bride in colonial times… your father gifts you land to build a home and you begin to dream. In your mind's eye, you see a red brick home where the sound of little feet can be heard running up and down the stairs; laughter and squeals can be heard from every room, followed by the gentle admonitions and deeper laughter of various slave nannies running close behind them.

"These beautiful rosy-cheeked, blue-eyed, blond children were conceived in the ample upstairs bedroom with large sash windows, adorned with ceiling-to-floor silk curtains that come to rest on the wooden floor as if in a puddle.

"The ornately carved wooden bed is covered with a silk brocade bedspread interlaced with gold and silver threads. Opposite the bed stands an equally ornate wood vanity, with three mirror panels encased in elaborately carved wood frames that arch at the tops. The two side panels attach to the taller middle one with gold hinges, allowing them to open and close.

"Whenever Ann sits on the vanity chair, upholstered to match the bedspread, and brushes her long, silky, fair hair with the silver brush, engraved with her initials, A. V. C. D. L., she can observe and be observed by her adoring husband, sitting quietly on their bed, leaning against the overstuffed pillows that line its ornate headboard.

"In the kitchen, a group of jolly-looking slave women labor over the roast beef set on a bed of vegetables: carrots, celery, onions covered with rosemary and thyme, gently bubbling over a wood stove. The wonderful aroma causes your mouth to water and your tongue to slowly move over your lips as if you are already enjoying the taste."

The stillness continued for several minutes after the presentation was finished. The lights were slowly returned to their normal daylight brightness; several comments came from the audience.

"I felt like I was in a past life."

"I could hear the children's laughter and footsteps."

"I could smell the roast—I actually salivated," said another student, which caused chuckles throughout the small audience.

When the giggles subsided, with everyone still in a good mood, a hand went up. It belonged to Santos, a fresh-faced student from the urban planning group.

"Was it necessary to bring up slave nannies and cooks? You used a lot of stereotypes." Suddenly the mood turned somber.

Mari took her time but looked at the expectant audience and answered with self-assurance and ease.

"These were pre–Revolutionary War times. As mentioned during the presentation, the original owner of the site, Mayor Nicholas Bayard, was a big slave owner. This was the case with most politicians, including George Washington, who became a slave owner at eleven years old. The purpose was to give an unbiased account of the times, without judgment, even though it might elicit feelings of discomfort."

"I will go into urban design in order to create spaces that are environmentally friendly while achieving social equity," answered Santos, matching the display of self-assurance Mari had put on a few moments before.

"Fair enough," was Mari's response. "The hope is that our generation will learn from history, and we will do our part in helping to create a better, more equitable world and that we will pass on the baton of equality to the next generation, and they to the next, and so on."

The room broke into applause at the amazing exchange; every heart present was filled with hope and anticipation.

Berk and Mari exchanged admiring looks, which did not escape Kurt. He had not missed even a breath of María José's from the first day he saw her. What he had missed was that Maria José had her *mind* on Berk; she admired his expertise on a subject that completely fascinated her. He did not have her *heart*; it had not yet found a home, no one had a claim to it, and Kurt's lack of awareness blinded him to the opportunity to become its home.

He had two days left to discover that Mari's heart was still free to choose an owner, and even though the heart seems to choose without a reason, the potential owners need to make themselves known.

He was suddenly hit by this insight; it came as a lightning bolt and awareness inundated his mind. Right then and there, Kurt decided to recover his old self-confident, smart, eloquent, gregarious, fun, free-spirited self.

He had allowed confusion to invade his thoughts, and somehow, they became so entangled that they were unable to reach his tongue and express themselves freely.

This was an unnatural state for him. It was arduous not to be himself, and he made up his mind to return to his essence. In just a few days, he had lost his bearings, and he knew this imbalance had been the result of, for the first time in his life, experiencing insecurity. He knew what he had to do in order to regain his essence.

Up to that point, his passion had been green design. His tongue never lost its way when the topic of conversation was green concepts. That's where he'd begin his journey back to recovering his true self, he thought—where his passion lay.

On the fourth day of orientation, the potential architects had an important assignment: the students, as well as leaders, each had to bring models of architectural objects that embodied their passion and make a presentation to their peers and some of the faculty members.

Mari enjoyed preparing for this project. Her confidence peaked as she looked through the precious drawings of the fashions that she hoped to see displayed someday on the runways of major fashion cities and in the windows of her very own boutiques.

But the other presentations fascinated her; they were brilliant. She felt captivated by them but also humbled and was filled with admiration for the remarkable and diverse talents of her fellow students.

When her turn came, Mari walked onstage with elegance and poise, displaying a light, sky-blue, scoop-neck, sleeveless linen dress. Two wide box pleats in front fell unevenly in two peaks just above the knees. She wore off-white, high-heeled sandals with a blue-jeweled ankle strap. A single-strand pearl necklace and teardrop pearl earrings adorned her neck and ears. A wide-band silver ring with a larimar stone pressed into its top curve adorned her right index finger, its color harmonizing beautifully with the soft, pearly white on her nails.

Mari was the personification of her drawings. It was as if one of them had come to life as she walked on stage and started the PowerPoint, featuring her most beloved designs, the ones that embodied her spirit. Yet the presentation was unnecessary—she would have been enough.

Kurt never took his eyes off Mari; he knew then and there that he would never again look at another woman. He also knew that in order to get her to never again look at another man, he needed to show her who he was.

He came to life when his turn came and he spoke to the students and faculty members about his dream home, where he had applied his green concept throughout.

Rather than being a single home, as the display on his table the night of the cocktail reception had shown, it was a compound of various buildings. The main house was flanked by two other smaller homes, and two additional buildings, hidden away by trees, were located at the back edge of the property. One served as storage for all the organic materials that would make the compost that would nourish the organic garden; the other would house the natural treatment system for the gray water from the homes.

The purpose of the two smaller homes was to have his parents and his future in-laws close, if they so desired, Kurt explained with enthusiasm.

Mari remembered his words to her when she had said goodbye to her parents: "I see you're close." She returned from her reverie to once again look up at Kurt. This time, she did not miss the light in his eyes, the wide smile, or the dimples it triggered.

She felt, though no words were said on the matter, his longing to fill his dream home. This realization brought tears to her eyes without her knowing why. Her next thought was that whoever accompanied Kurt in that dream needed to share that same vision. Kurt had accomplished his goal; Mari saw the real him for the first time, down deep, beyond the blueness of the eyes, the smile, and the dimples.

The next day was the last of the orientation. They would announce their decision as to whether or not they would enroll at Columbia University in the fall and then close the week with a visit to a local pub. It was an open event, and they could invite a guest—or not.

About half of the prospective students, including Mari, were undecided about their choice of school. The night that the students spoke about their passion, Kurt understood that architecture, and therefore this school, would not be her choice. It was obvious that Mari was the embodiment of fashion design.

Mari sat at the bar, head back, silky mane lightly touching the stool, lemonade in hand, laughing wholeheartedly. That was the image that greeted Kurt when he entered the pub, and the enthusiastic laughter drew his gaze toward the bar. His feet followed the lovely and, up until that point, uncommon sound.

His smiley, deep-blue eyes caught her lively, authentic, dark ones. "This, I've got to hear," were his first words.

Sandra looked up at him, and between bouts of laughter, was the first to respond. "Mari is the only one in this group who can't drink alcohol; she's not even eighteen yet."

Kurt looked at Mari with eyes wide open. He almost felt guilty about his feelings toward her, not because of the drinking age, but because she was under eighteen. Mari felt his confusion and quickly said, holding two fingers up, "Two weeks, June seventeenth—that's when I can legally drink—in Spain, that is. That's where my family is from. At home, we always have wine with our meals." She continued to laugh. Now the silky mane covered her face as she brought her head down in uncontrolled laughter brought about by everyone's questioning looks about her age.

Sandra looked at the group on the dance floor, laughing and talking with their drinks in their hands. She went to join the fun and left her laughing underage friend and Kurt on their own. They didn't seem to notice she had left and continued their dialogue, which would last for hours.

"I'm with my teacher," she had told her parents. "He'll take me home."

There wasn't one topic that they did not cover: school, family, culture, dreams, passions, hobbies, likes, dislikes, humor, fears, hopes, faith. The night was just not long enough.

Without realizing it, they had ended up facing each other on the barstools, her knees slightly inside Kurt's, her small, delicate, impeccably manicured hands resting on his open, large ones. Their talk was animated and easy. They comfortably looked into each other's eyes as they shared, laughed, questioned, answered, discovered, revealed, and noticed.

"I think I've met the love of my life; I hope you have too," he whispered when he walked her to her door. His lips were so close to hers that she held her breath, anticipating their touch. They stayed that close for what seemed like an eternity, neither one knowing if they would be strong enough to resist. They weren't, but it was as light as the touch of butterfly wings.

CHAPTER 8
BASKETS OF SURPRISES

Mari chose the Institute of Fashion Design, but she was convinced that the reason she had considered architecture and gone to orientation week at Columbia University was to meet Kurt.

She believed that their meeting had been ordered by God himself. Anger rose within her unexpectedly—then why would God snatch him away so cruelly and mercilessly? This puzzle haunted her almost relentlessly. It weakened her.

She reminisced.

After that night at the pub, they spoke on the phone every day for the next two weeks but did not meet until June 17. All he had told her about that upcoming date was to be ready at 8:00 p.m.

When they talked on the phone, she could picture the blue eyes looking down at her joined by that big, playful smile that formed the dimples that made her world turn.

Mari woke up on her birthday to the smell of a single long-stemmed rose lying beside her face. The rest of the bed was spread with daisies interspersed with red rose petals. She quickly sat up, holding in her hand the single stem rose. She cupped it with her free hand, as if to protect it, and slowly glided the rose down her cheek until it barely touched her lips, which she pursed intuitively to tenderly and softly place a kiss on the fragranced petals. Her heart was sealed forever from anyone else; its only key belonged to Kurt.

A soft knock brought her out of her reverie. "Yes," she answered, expecting to see her parents and not being disappointed. They did the same thing every year, coming in with a bouquet of balloons, singing "Happy Birthday," and handing her a special gift.

This year, the small box contained an engagement ring; inside it bore the inscription "María José 1994–1998." She looked up at her parents in awe of the beautiful, delicate diamond and in bewilderment as to its meaning.

Her father, José Felipe, was the first to speak: "You are engaged to us until you finish your university studies, so you will neither become engaged nor marry before then."

Although she vaguely saw a sea of blue in her mind, she quickly pulled the ring out of the box and placed it on the ring finger of her right hand. Her father sat on the edge of the bed, took her hand gently, removed the ring, and placed it on the ring finger of her left hand. "There," he said. "Now it's closer to your heart."

Mari stretched her hand to admire her finger. She smiled and hugged both parents, saying, "Gracias, gracias, gracias," pronouncing each word with the Castilian accent of her native Spain so the letter *c* sounded like the *th* in the word "thanks."

"What's for breakfast?" Mari asked cheerfully.

"Let's go down and see," answered María Victoria, who had sat quietly observing her daughter and wondering where the past eighteen years had gone. Her eyes watered, and the familiar ache had once again resurfaced in the depths of her heart. José Felipe knowingly and reassuringly squeezed his wife's hand. Mari attributed the gentle emotional moment between her parents to her becoming an adult.

After she showered and dressed, Mari made it downstairs as she always had since as far back as she could walk, according to her parents: two, sometimes three, wooden steps at a time. Her bedroom occupied the entire upstairs space of the midcentury town house. This space created the perfect surroundings for her creative personality.

The table was set with a single long-stemmed rose by her place setting with daisies and rose petals sprinkled around the other two plates, a replica of the delicate scene she had woken up to.

Just as she noticed that there was no food on the table, she heard a knock. She blissfully skipped to the door with anticipation and was surprised to see Sandra Miraflores holding a large basket.

Before Mari could say anything, Sandra made her way into the house and directly into the kitchen, almost singing, "I've brought breakfaaaaast." Out came grapes, Manchego cheese, baguettes, jams, olives, olive oil, sun-dried tomatoes, basil, minced red onions, smoked salmon, capers, oranges, and a bottle of cava.

She piled all the food on the kitchen counter, then pulled out a breadbasket, a bamboo cutting board, a manual orange-squeezer, crystal platters, an assortment of small crystal bowls, crystal stem glasses, cocktail forks, silver forks, knives, and spoons, and finally, a white chef's apron, which she slipped over her head and effortlessly tied behind her back.

"Birthday girl, you go sit in the living room and visit with your parents. Breakfast will be served in a few minutes." Mari happily followed instructions.

Her birthday chef adeptly cut the bread and placed it in the basket, arranged the sun-dried tomatoes and basil on a round crystal dish, washed and dried the grapes and set them alongside the cubed cheese on the bamboo board, spooned the jams and olives into some of the small crystal bowls, and assembled the smoked salmon, minced red onions, capers, and olive oil on the crystal platter. Lastly, she filled the stem glasses halfway with freshly squeezed orange juice and finished filling them three-quarters of the way with the cava.

Sandra placed the abundant, mouthwatering breakfast on the table and called Mari and her parents to enjoy. When they were sitting down, Sandra placed a card on Mari's plate. Mari sat down, picked up the card, and slowly opened it, her heart pounding. She read:

My dear, lovely, beautiful Mari,

I have done nothing but think of you since that last night at the pub.

Thinking of you has helped me to survive these two weeks without seeing you, touching you, or kissing you. But I know there is more than enough time to satisfy this longing.

Not seeing you has helped me to realize that:

I want to spend my time with you.

I want to dream with you.

I want to laugh with you.

I want to cry with you.

I want to dance with you.

I want to sing with you.

I want to greet the morning with you.

I want to welcome the stars with you.

I want to share my dream home with you.

Teardrops fell onto the card; Mari did not bother to wipe them away. When she finished reading, she dried her cheeks with the cloth napkin and, looking up at her parents through bleary eyes and with a radiant smile, said, "I couldn't ask for anything else. I will never forget this day."

She reached for her glass and began to drink her mimosa. Her mom and dad followed suit. Sandra stood nearby like a true chef, refilling their glasses, cutting more bread, slicing more tomatoes, and serving more grapes.

When breakfast was done, Sandra picked up, cleaned up, packed up, and left.

Mari asked permission to go up to her room, where she memorized the writing on the card and admired her ring. She sensed incongruence between the card and her parents' gift but ignored the still-small voice.

At about two o'clock, another basket arrived. "Señorita María José García Cortés." This one was from a restaurant called Murcia Near You. The uniformed chef that delivered the basket politely declined the tip, and Mari could not wait to discover what secrets the basket concealed.

She promptly took the basket into the kitchen; when she turned back the covering, she was transported to her grandmother's house. The aromas emanating from the basket made her mouth water, her eyes tear up, and her heart yearn.

She took out each dish slowly, closed her eyes, and took in its aroma. *Pisto Murciano*, the blend of all her favorite vegetables and herbs: tomato, eggplant, zucchini, red and green pepper, garlic, onion, basil, and bay leaf. At her grandmother's house, she ate this dish with fresh bread from the local bakery. Her grandmother sometimes served it with a fried egg on top, which Mari usually spooned out and left on a saucer on the side for whoever wanted it.

The next delicacy she pulled out of the basket was the *albóndigas de bacalao*. These were fried balls of cod fish served on a tomato-and-onion *guiso*.

There was a sealed glass container with a mixture of fresh tomatoes. When she saw the thin slices of toasted baguette, she understood that the tomato mixture—made with garlic and olive oil—was to be spread on the bread for one of her favorite tapas (savory appetizers), *pan con tomate*.

Finally, she brought out the slices of *pan de Calatrava*. It reminded one of flan, but Mari liked it much better. It was made from stale bread and covered with caramel sauce. She remembered the container in her grandmother's pantry where leftover bread was stored. Magically, on weekends, it became a delicious *pan de Calatrava*.

Mari had left the white envelope for last. She knew who the sender was, but she was eager to find out what the message revealed.

> Murcia was just a random place on the planet.
> María José was just another name in the baby book of names.
> Today, I am indebted to the place from which such beauty originated
> and to the name that now has become poetry in my lips,
> because it gives form to the essence that is you.

It was signed simply, "Kurt."

Mari looked up through bleary eyes for the second time that day and looking at her parents said, "I really could not ask for anything else; I just don't want this day to end."

Mari did not comment to her parents about what was written in the card. She simply but elegantly set the table and displayed on it everything that she had brought out of the basket. They indulged happily and leisurely.

A visit to the spa, followed by the hair and nail salon, took up the rest of the afternoon and part of the evening. She got home in time for a short nap before she began to get ready for the night ahead, the culmination of this unforgettable eighteenth birthday.

CHAPTER 9
UNFORGETTABLE DAY

Mari slowly walked down the steps in a white, slightly shimmery, sleeveless dress. The bodice was graced by a standing collar that flowed seamlessly down to an open front, unencumbered by any type of fastener until it slightly crossed over at the waist. The full, uneven skirt touched her heels at the back and gradually became shorter until its soft folds ended at her midthighs in front. White lace stockings and delicate white sandals completed the flawless look. The promise ring from her parents and teardrop pearl earrings were her only jewelry.

Kurt looked up from his seat in the living room and, captivated by the stunning sight, began to make his way to the bottom of the stairs, his eyes fixed on hers every step of the way. When Mari was standing inches from him, he whispered, barely breathing, "You're like a dream…"

María Victoria—Mavi—and José Felipe—Josefe—broke the intimate, though slightly awkward, moment.

"You look astonishing, sweetheart," were her father's first words.

Mari looked at him, her eyes full of love, and mouthed simply, "Gracias." She looked at her mom, down at her dress, and back at her mom, then said, "You did a beautiful job."

"I simply brought to life your amazing creation, *mi hija* {my daughter}."

"Thank you, Mom." Mari's words softly rolled out as she leaned over to give her a kiss. "And you too, Dad," she added, turning to her father and placing a soft kiss on his cheek also.

"*¿Por qué?* [For what?] For watching my favorite program while your mom labored at night?" her father responded with a touch of mischief in his voice.

"For staying up with her until she got tired, for bringing her endless cups of tea, for looking at her lovingly and proudly while she labored into the night," responded Mari.

He reached over and embraced his daughter, tears trickling down his cheeks.

"I can't believe you're eighteen, *mi hija hermosa* [my beautiful daughter]."

Josefe looked at Kurt and said, "My Mari is in your hands, young man. Bring her back as perfect as you found her."

Kurt nodded, as no words made it past his lips. He walked Mari to the street and stood in front of an exquisite, white, vintage limousine. She brought both hands to her mouth and let out a soft, "Oh my gosh."

"It's your night," whispered Kurt in her ear as he opened the rear car door to let her in.

He leaned in to reach for her seat belt and fasten it. When he heard it click, he slowly began to move back, taking in the delicate aroma released from her soft skin or hair—he didn't know which, but it pulled him in—and he turned his face to hers, their lips so close that they could feel each other's breath again. He paused, his intense look moving leisurely from her lips to her eyes. Time stood still.

"Your dad said to bring you back perfect," were the faltering, whispered words that interrupted the magic moment. "But that's easier said than done."

She smiled.

Kurt closed the door and walked around the back to get in on the other side behind the driver. The evening had started; from that day forward, Mari would refer to her life as BK (before Kurt) and AK (after Kurt).

Two blocks ahead, at the first traffic light, a young boy stood by the curb; the driver moved closer and lowered the window, and the boy looked at Kurt with a big smile and handed Mari two roses—one pink, one cream. Mari took them and gave Kurt a surprised look and a disarming smile. He felt defenseless under her powerful spell and wondered if she realized her power.

The scene repeated itself at the next three traffic lights until she had accumulated eight roses, four pink and four in various tones of cream. Mari greeted each stop with the same excitement as she had the first one. She held her bouquet close to her face, her hair falling forward to cover both her face and the bouquet. She brushed her hair back with her hand and, looking over at Kurt, whispered, "Thank you."

He leaned close and whispered back, "The night's just beginning." His dimples weakened her.

Their first stop was Fraunces Tavern. Mari's first thought was how quickly they had arrived. Kurt got out of the car and went around to open her door. He extended his left hand, and she rested her right in his. "Bring your roses," he whispered without taking his eyes away from hers. Mari looked like royalty getting out of the car. New York pedestrians, who are rarely rendered speechless, stood wordlessly to stare and cleared the sidewalk to allow Mari easy passage.

Two corner stools at the bar had been reserved for Kurt and Mari. Hers was next to the wall; Kurt wanted no one around her. He sat facing her, his back to the other guests. The bartender set a crystal vase in front of Mari. Beautifully inscribed on an oval-shaped, gold plate was the phrase: "Happy 18th birthday, Mari." She lovingly ran her index finger over the message and closed her eyes to inhale the flowers' scent before placing them inside the vase; the butterflies in her stomach continued their dance.

Next, the bartender handed Kurt a small, delicate, crystal hexagon-shaped box edged in gold. Inside, it displayed a lovely, cream-colored rose corsage. On one of the small crystal panels, the words, "Happy 18th birthday, Mari," had been etched. Kurt set it just in front of her. She slowly reached for the box, brought it to eye level, and delicately turned it until she came to the inscription.

"It'll be with me forever," she whispered, raising her eyes to him and captivating him.

Kurt carefully took the box, unfastened the tiny, gold clasp, and drew out the delicate flower. He just as carefully took her right hand and slipped on the corsage, then he slowly brought her hand to his lips, his eyes never turning from hers.

Mari was unable to withstand the intense look. She trembled, and her eyes fell on the crystal box and then on the crystal vase containing the eight roses.

"It's not finished yet," Kurt said softly, continuing to look at her intensely and lovingly.

He signaled the bartender, who came around to where they sat, a white cloth napkin draped over his left forearm. He stood in front of Mari and extended his right hand toward her, palm up. "*Por favor, Señorita.*" He stepped back to allow her to step down. He guided the couple to a quaint room in the back.

A deep-burgundy, velvet sofa and a glass-topped, oval coffee table with an inlaid carved base were the only furnishings. They seemed so at home in the space, as if they had adorned it for centuries.

Mari looked at the low, curved back, large, rolled arms, and deep tufting on the sofa and pronounced it a "Chesterfield."

"A what?" said Kurt, puzzled.

"The sofa—it's a Chesterfield design."

"And you are a box of surprises," he said playfully, bringing her hand firmly held in his to his lips and gently using his fingers to brush back a runaway strand of her hair. She looked at him and caressed his cheek, her thumb lightly touching the corner of his lips.

They had been so entranced with each other that they did not notice that the attentive waiter had placed the crystal vase with the roses and a gold container full of ice with a bottle of red wine and two crystal wine glasses on the centuries-old coffee table. They proceeded to make their way to the sofa. Both the gold container and the crystal glasses had the same inscription: "Happy 18th birthday, Mari."

"I wanted to be the first one with whom you had your first drink—in a formal way, I mean." He looked around the space and added, "And this private room is the best option I found to get around the underage drinking issue."

Mari rolled her eyes. "Don't get me started; I'll never understand how at eighteen years old, you can join the army of the most powerful nation in the world, vote for its president, and have an abortion but not be allowed to drink a glass of wine!" The intrepid tone of her voice surprised him.

"Strong views," he remarked.

"Yes," she said, bringing her thumb and index finger together and running them across her tight lips in tacit agreement. "But I will not waste another single breath on them; this night I only want to talk about us."

"Us, what a beautiful word when spoken by those irresistible lips." Kurt's eyes remained fixed on her lips for a long time, then looked at her intensely.

Her eyes settled in the depths of his. Mari reached to cup his cheek caressingly, her thumb gently stroking the slight indentation on his cheek. She then took in their surroundings and finally said, "Kurt, this is lovely and thoughtful, and just over the top!" she blurted out.

"Yeah, Chesterfield couch and all."

Mari laughed. "I know you're making fun of me."

"It was worth it just to hear you laugh." Kurt loosely held a strand of her hair and ran his hand down its entire length.

The wine was a Monastrell from Jumilla, in Murcia, Spain. The bartender poured the *tinto* (red wine) into the glasses and, after getting a subtle nod from Kurt, left unperceived.

She opened her eyes wide as she swallowed the delicious *tinto*.

"Too strong? It comes from Murcia, and I know you prefer red…"

She interrupted him, bringing her index finger to his lips.

"It's delicious. I am overwhelmed by your details, Kurt," she whispered, once again fixing her intensely dark look on his intensely blue one and getting her face as close to him as she could without touching. It was too much for him.

Kurt lightly placed the crook of his right index finger under her chin and brushed back a silky strand of her hair with his free hand. They kissed soft and long, the taste of wine intermingling on each other's lips. Their worlds meshed and became one—no longer you and me but bringing life to the 'us' that she had pronounced moments before.

They left the tavern hand-in-hand. A large box with engraved images of the different periods of Fraunce's Tavern, which she guessed contained the flowers and crystal ware she had received, lay on the front seat. Kurt helped her into the car and secured her seat belt, this time placing a soft kiss on her lips as he pulled back, which she gladly received and returned. He went around, squeezed in close, clasped his hand in hers, and off they went to their next adventure.

It was a live flamenco show in Midtown Manhattan; their table was up front. She was not surprised, because so far, the night had shown her that Kurt did all things perfectly. To Mari's delight, two tall, slim glasses filled with white sangria over ice were set in front of them. It contained her favorite fruits and berries: mangoes, oranges, strawberries, and raspberries. A sprig of mint topped the presentation.

Mari took a sip of her drink, savored it, and looked at Kurt. "It's missing something," she said in a playful tone.

"It's nonalcoholic, but if I'm not looking and you sip from my glass, the alcohol police will never know." He gave her a mischievous wink. She looked around before responding, "This place is full of Spaniards; no one will care, believe me!" She chuckled and drank from his glass.

She watched the show totally enthralled, her delicate hands absentmindedly following the movements of the dancers on stage.

During summers in Murcia, she had taken flamenco lessons and could hold her own, including the attitude and the *floreo* and *braceo*, the graceful hand and arm movements that went along with the dance.

One of the male dancers had noticed Mari's *floreo* and signaled her to come up. Surprised, she pointed at herself and mouthed, "Me?" The dancer smiled wide, pointed at her, and mouthed back, "You." To the delight and applause of the audience, she walked up the three steps onto the stage.

Once she was in front of her dance partner, her head went back, dark, silky hair reaching below her waist, hands up above her forehead in a clapping pose. The *cante* flamenco began singing, and Mari began the *zapateo*, or footwork, and the clapping.

She and the male dancer interlocked eyes and moved in incredible synchronicity and grace for the entire dance, which lasted about ten minutes. Kurt watched spellbound, elbows resting on the table, hands clasped, his chin resting on both his thumbs. The surprise was his; he was simply left breathless.

When the dance was over, Mari's partner brought her hands to his lips, turned to the audience, and gently moved her a few steps forward, lightly holding her right hand with his left, extending his right hand to the audience, then toward Mari. The audience gave them a standing ovation. Kurt went to meet her at the bottom of the steps, where her partner handed her over to Kurt while slightly bowing his head to him.

Kurt kissed Mari on the cheek and murmured in her ear, "Hard to top that one."

"No need. It's been an incredible night—"

Kurt put his index finger to her lip and answered, "It's not over yet, Cinderella; we have an hour before midnight."

One of the tenured professors at the university owned an apartment with a beautiful outdoor terrace and outdoor kitchen high above the city. They rode up the elevator to the twenty-first floor. The apartment was all theirs for the night.

Kurt walked Mari out to the terrace, where a small table was set for two. A single light pink rose lay across the top of her plate, and two long, off-white candles in crystal candle holders with, "Happy 18th birthday, Mari," inscribed on them served as the centerpiece.

Mari looked up at Kurt lovingly, then took his cheeks in her hands, came close, and whispered, "I can't imagine how much time and thought and care and love—" Kurt stopped her with a soft, long kiss. "—you put into this," she finished between stalled breaths when they finally broke away.

Mari looked around to take in and admire the beautiful space: flowering plants, shrubbery, short paths, firepit, wood benches, and small fountains.

"Only a landscape architect could create something like this. I feel like I'm someplace far from the city, then I look at the lights…this is absolutely beautiful."

She looked at the benches with stuffed white cushions. "What happens to that wood in the winter?"

"It's teak wood—its natural oils make it water-repellent, so it's great for outdoor settings, especially in cold weather."

"Wow!" was all Mari could say, fascinated.

He guided her to her chair, which he pulled back so she could sit. When she was comfortable, he placed a soft kiss on her neck before making his way to the outdoor kitchen to get the food. The shivers from that kiss noticeably affected her, which brought immense satisfaction to Kurt.

On the counter were some small, covered dishes. He brought them to their table along with two glasses of white sangría that he had prepared ahead of time and left in the fridge to chill for the evening.

Instead of mangoes, Kurt's version contained fresh peaches, but the berries were the same as she had had during the flamenco show—strawberries and raspberries.

"We can enjoy the sangría the way it was meant to meant to be enjoyed, with wine in it!"

She laughed. She couldn't believe that such a big deal was made out of drinking wine, but did not comment; instead, thoroughly enjoyed her drink, taking time to savor every morsel of peach and to swirl every berry that entered her mouth. Her deliberate sounds of enjoyment were music to Kurt's ears.

"You know that those sounds bring out the sexy in you and drive me crazy, don't you?"

"Maybe," was her only reply as she exaggerated the sounds of delight even more.

Next, Kurt brought out a bottle of exquisite and refreshing white to accompany the tapas: garlic shrimp, marinated olives, garlic mushrooms, goat cheese, fennel and roasted pepper tarts, and sliced baguette. They enjoyed the view of the entire city while savoring each dish. Mari enjoyed dipping the bread in the garlic mushrooms. When the sauce got on her chin, Kurt tenderly wiped it with his thumb and licked it off.

She took a sip of her wine and, still holding the glass, leaned toward him, kissed him tenderly, and said, "Everything is perfect, Kurt—the tapas, the wine, the gifts…you." She took another sip before setting the glass on the table; she then reached for his face, pulled him close, and kissed him deep.

They talked, whispered, laughed, touched hands, touched cheeks. Then a small box appeared in Kurt's hand. "For you," he whispered. "Open it."

She did. Her hand came up to her mouth, her eyes opened wide, and she looked at Kurt through the blur caused by the moisture in her eyes, then looked down again at the delicate, gold infinity name necklace. The name "Mari" completed the first circle on top; "Kurt" completed the second circle at the bottom.

After a few moments of silence, Kurt slowly got up from his chair, went around behind Mari, took the necklace from the box, gathered her hair to one side, and clasped it behind her neck. When he was finished, he gave her a tender kiss on her neck and another on her shoulder, went back to his chair, took both of her hands, and sealed this last gift with the most beautiful of admonitions: "The necklace has found its home; it'll never leave it…we'll talk about the ring on your finger another time."

Mari could hardly contain herself under such closeness, and she didn't. She cupped his face in both of her hands, brought his lips close to hers, and took them, slowly, tenderly, sensuously.

One of the beautiful discoveries that Kurt had made about Mari was that while she possessed self-confidence and boldness, it was balanced with freshness and innocence; it drove him crazy.

At 1:30 a.m., they were both standing before Josefe, Mari holding the vase with the bouquet of roses, Kurt holding the box that contained the other gifts. Josefe's eyes fell on the necklace that Mari was wearing, then his gaze continued downward and over to her left hand. Her promise ring was still in place, and he felt a sense of serenity.

Kurt broke the brief moment of uncomfortable silence. "Sir, I've brought your daughter back to you as perfect as you handed her to me. Thank you for your trust."

The wide, cocky smile slowly disappeared when Josefe answered, "Well done, young man. Just don't get used to these hours—this was an exception for Mari's birthday."

"I understand, sir." Kurt shook hands with Josefe and turned to Mari, carefully took her hand, kissed it, and whispered a soft "Thanks." That was the beginning of an unbreakable bond between them.

CHAPTER 10
AVOCADO, TOMATO, OREGANO, AND HAM & CHEESE

In the fall, Mari entered the Institute of Fashion Design, and Kurt continued to work on his thesis.

She designed by his side when not in class while he wrote about green design in his small office at the university. They drew strength and comfort from each other's presence; being together not only quenched their longing for one another, but it gave them a sense of completeness. Thus, it was unusual to see one without the other.

Green outdoor spaces became their best-loved places to create, dream, or just be. They would lie on the grass, feet in opposite directions, cheeks close and sometimes touching. There they read, Mari created new designs, they made plans, and they fed each other sandwiches and ice-cream cones.

"We'll have four kids," Kurt said one day, looking up at the clouds. "Two girls and two boys."

Mari pulled his face toward hers and added, "Or three girls and a boy, or three boys and a girl, or four girls, or—"

Kurt interrupted her discourse with a long, deep kiss. She was left weak, he breathless. "Let's get up and take you home, or those kids are going to start coming," he said.

"They better not. We're not ready," Mari replied with a nervous laugh, astonished at Kurt's comments but feeling all over her body that he was right.

They spent their nights together via phone calls, either talking or silently listening to each other's breaths. Just knowing that the other was only a breath away was enough—for now.

It was during one of those nightly conversations that Kurt unleashed the question that had been striving to come out of his lips for some weeks: "Can you tell me the meaning of the ring you're wearing?"

"I wondered how long it would take you to ask." She took a deep breath. "It's an engagement ring," Mari began. "I am engaged to my parents for four years. Until I finish my degree, I cannot marry nor leave the house."

A long, uncomfortable silence followed, and the subject was not discussed any further. In fact, Kurt's next words were totally off-topic, but straight from the heart: "Tell me all the things that one needs in order to live."

"Let's see…air, water, food, medicine, love…"

"That's what you are for me, all those things—the air that I breathe, the water that quenches my thirst, the food that nourishes me, the medicine that cures all that ails me, the love that I can't live without."

How long they remained in silence after that, neither could say, but the only words spoken for the rest of the night were two soft good nights.

Mari's closest friend was Sandra Miraflores, but since the last orientation night at the pub, Sandra had understood that there was little room for friendship in Mari's life. As a result, they grabbed a quick coffee occasionally when Kurt was busy writing and editing his thesis or in a meeting with one of his advisors.

The rest of the time, Kurt and Mari's world was only big enough for two inhabitants.

However, they would make room for one more. It happened on a crisp mid-October day.

Kurt had been house-sitting for his professor friend, and he had been struggling with the final details of his thesis: sources, footnotes, grammar, organization, flow. Had he conveyed his passion clearly?

He felt anxious and frustrated as he ruminated on the topic of his thesis. He ran his fingers through his blond head over and over—then the bell rang.

He reached with his left hand to turn the handle and continued to run his right hand through his hair. As he opened the door, Mari put down the basket she was holding, jumped on his neck without warning, reached back and pushed the door to close it, then wrapped her legs around his waist.

"I missed you," were her only words.

Kurt lost his footing and fell back onto the soft living-room carpet. She followed on top of him. No words were shared, only very long, desirous, passionate, questioning looks.

Mari rolled off to her side, facing Kurt, breaths intermingling, bodies joining. Kurt ran his hand slowly and tenderly from her left shoulder down the sleeve of her white cashmere cardigan, stopping at her hand. He took it in his and stroked the jewel that adorned her ring finger.

He tried to question her, but Mari covered his lips fully with hers, and unhurriedly but deliberately, they began to undress one another. Each button that Mari opened carried Kurt closer to the point of no return; Mari followed on the same journey as each button on her cardigan was unfastened.

When all the barriers had been removed, they lay in silence for what seemed like an eternity, he stroking her hair, she caressing his face and searching for his lips, he gladly and easily giving them. They continued to explore and explore, then he gently turned her on her back, mounted her, delicately picked up both of her hands and brought them above her head, where he clasped them. They both soared until, simultaneously, they reached the summit.

Neither was in a rush to come down from the heights, so they lingered wordlessly next to each other until Mari sat up suddenly, grabbed Kurt's shirt, slipped her arms into it, and crossed the two sides of it over one another without taking time to button it. She ran to the front door, opened it, and looking back at Kurt, let out a sigh of relief and a big smile. "Our lunch is still here," she said happily.

They spread a blanket on the floor and pulled out sandwiches made from baguette. Hers was avocado, tomato, salt, olive oil, and oregano. His was the classic ham and cheese with lettuce and tomato. She had brought a bottle of pinot grigio; it was not as cold as it had been when she first arrived, but that was totally unimportant now.

She sat scooching and leaning back into his chest, and he wrapped his legs around her. They ate comfortably and contentedly. She turned her head back and offered him a bite of her sandwich; he took it, olive oil and tomato juice running down the sides of his mouth. She turned her face toward his and gently pulled his head down until her lips reached the corners of his mouth to catch the wet, salty, oily, tasty liquid.

"It tastes better from your lips," she said mischievously.

"You are soooo dangerous," Kurt retorted. It was one of those moments that both wished could be frozen in time.

After they had finished their sandwiches, he hugged her tightly from behind as she rested trustingly on his shoulder. Kurt bent his head and kissed her cheek.

"I want you to always tell me what you want and what you need, like you did today when you knocked on my door. Reach to me when you are happy like now, when you're sad, when you want to share an idea, or just when you plain want me, OK?"

"And you, you'll do the same?" she asked in a whisper.

"Promise," Kurt whispered back.

They had become one and would never revert to being two.

Although they took precautions after their first lovemaking, by Christmastime, Mari was experiencing all the telltale signs of pregnancy. Kurt suspected it before she did one afternoon when she came to his office after her last class. She flung the door open and walked in, tossed backpack and drawing pad on the spare chair, closed the office door, and walked around Kurt's desk. She sat on his lap, took his face in both of her hands, and kissed him thoroughly.

"What have I done to deserve you?" Kurt murmured, leaning back on his comfortable, oversized office chair and clasping both hands behind the back of his head. Mari leaned in closer until both gave themselves totally to the sensations brought about by the prolonged kiss.

Without warning, Mari broke away from him, covering her mouth, and ran out into the hall in the direction of the bathroom. Kurt quickly got up from his chair and made it to the doorway, then turned around, closed the door, ran his hands upward on his face, and clasped them behind his head once again.

Both his mouth and eyes unexpectedly opened wide, but a smile surfaced on his face and remained fixed until Mari returned.

"So do we follow tradition and name her María-something if it's a girl?"

It was Mari's turn to be wide-eyed. "Do you think I'm pregnant?" she asked with a mixture of surprise and realization.

"It coincides with the afternoon that you came and seduced me." He was unable to hide his amusement and the sparkle in his eyes.

Mari sat on his lap, hands around his neck, looking into his eyes, and retorted, "Like you fought back…you could've resisted."

"Impossible," he said and kissed her passionately.

She was the first to slowly pull away. "What are we gonna do now?"

"If you think we have options, we don't. There's only one—we'll get married." He hugged her tightly, unable to control or hide his happiness.

For Kurt, Mari was his final destination. He had known that from the first day, when a mass of black silk locks made their way out of the car, followed by this girl, trying unsuccessfully to put them back in place.

The one most affected by their decision was Mari's father, José Felipe. But the signs had been there since the first day, during school orientation, he thought, trying to comfort himself. There was no question that their daughter had never turned her head in any other direction since that day. He wondered, however, how this situation would affect his daughter's studies—her future.

CHAPTER 11
SOUL COMPASS

The following days would pass in a blur. John and Mary Stewart flew to New York to meet Mari and her family and to make plans for a mid-January wedding. They felt less stress than Mari's parents, since Kurt, their youngest child, was almost twenty-four and within a few short months of becoming a full-fledged architect; they were proud of him.

He had always been different from their other two children, who had seemed content with being close to home. Peter, the oldest, had studied business, acquired an MBA, and worked for a large construction firm. He and his wife Ashley had a four-year-old son, Peter John.

Kurt's sister Katherine, the middle child, had gone to nursing school at a local university and worked at a local hospital in the neonatal unit. At home, she couldn't stop talking about the tiny babies and their amazing survival stories, so John and Mary knew their daughter had found her passion and felt happy and proud for her. They were a blessed family, Mary Stewart often said.

For them, life was uncomplicated: John, an architect, worked for a local firm that designed custom homes. Mary was also a nurse and worked at the same hospital as Katherine; they enjoyed a close mother-daughter relationship.

Sundays were family days. After attending church services, they visited either John's or Mary's parents. If not, they went to one of the local restaurants for dinner, where they met with friends from church or work. It made for a pleasant Sunday afternoon.

But Kurt was different. It was as if he heard a different drumbeat and marched to it, so he seemed out of step with the rest of the family.

Growing up, he always brought a drawing pad to the Sunday gatherings and preferred spending time transferring concepts from his mind to the paper rather than participating in the conversation going on around him.

While his parents and siblings seemed to be content, Kurt felt out of place, as if the needle from his soul compass pointed somewhere else and he needed to adjust it to fit his present settings, but this called for great effort on his part, and he was not quite able to keep that needle in place.

It caused an internal restlessness that gave him discomfort. However, this same restlessness triggered in him a desire to follow the direction of the needle rather than trying to adjust it to fit his circumstances.

He had figured during high school that New York City would put both physical and emotional distance from where he grew up. It was the place that he felt would be most different from his hometown; besides, it was home to Columbia University, where he knew he would attend someday.

Kurt had thrown conventional wisdom to the wind and had placed all his career dreams in one basket: he only applied to Columbia. Their undergraduate program was not ranked among the top ten, but their graduate program was, and that was what he was looking forward to.

During summers, Kurt did internships at various architectural firms near his hometown, including the one where his father worked, and on weekends, he volunteered with Habitat for Humanity.

In marked contrast to most of his peers, Kurt knew what he wanted to do early on and began walking in the direction that his heart was leading him.

Predictably, Kurt graduated with honors from high school, and he was indeed accepted at Columbia.

Whether he felt an assurance about Columbia and followed his heart or whether it was pure luck, he didn't know. But when he got his acceptance letter, he was not surprised, only calm and taken with a feeling that he was on his way "home" somehow.

Kurt knew it had not been pure coincidence; he had begun to prepare early in high school. When his peers went to parties and dances, he spent his time either drawing or investigating the university—the professors, the department chairs, the requirements, the rankings.

By the time Kurt arrived on campus, he had established a relationship with most of the professors from the faculty of Architecture and Planning. He knew the campus and the surrounding areas, including parks, coffee shops, pubs, and ethnic markets.

When he finally reached campus, all those dreams and ideas that had remained quiet inside of him all the years before began to surface. It seemed as if they had been waiting for the right time and the right place, and this was it. His ideas and dreams had finally found a very receptive, encouraging environment, one where they could take form and become reality.

Kurt immersed himself in his academic world, became friends with his professors, spent a lot of time with classmates in the libraries researching projects—it felt good to be with people who shared his enthusiasm about the different areas of architecture and who wanted to partner with him in interesting assignments and designs.

Saturdays, though, unless there was an important assignment or test to study for, Kurt spent time playing sports, usually basketball, with friends, and in the evenings, they went to one of the local pubs.

Even Kurt's parents recognized that their son had come into his own. He was happy, comfortable, self-confident, so even though they missed him at family dinners and other family activities, they knew that he was exactly where he needed to be.

Kurt graduated at the top of his class, as he had planned. He began his master's program at Columbia the following fall and continued working as a student adviser for incoming freshmen and as a teaching assistant.

He had been doing little else during the last year of his master's program besides research and work—then Mari happened.

All young and beautiful, at times outgoing, at times timid. His fate was beautifully sealed on that first day of orientation when that bundle of black silk was swept back with a hand and he felt himself wrapped in black velvet.

They chose a January wedding, with family and close friends.

CHAPTER 12
GLEE CLUB & TAP LESSONS

Mari designed her dress: a stunning, waist-hugging lace bodice with an off-the-shoulder scalloped neckline. The lace sleeves were a continuation of the neckline and just covered her elbows. The A-line, light-cream tulle skirt came below her knees, and lace-covered, high-heeled ankle boots completed her outfit.

Her accessories, as usual, were simple: a pearl choker with a matching bracelet and teardrop pearl earrings. Her hair was held up with an antique pearl comb, or *peineta*, and covered with a lace *mantilla*, both family heirlooms sent to her from Spain by her maternal grandmother, María Dolores. Mari could truly have graced the cover of a fashion magazine.

The religious ceremony was performed by the García Cortés family priest, Father Hernán Romero Castillo, in a small chapel. It was simple, but traditional communion was offered. Kurt and Mari partook, followed by Mari's parents and some of their friends.

The most touching part of the ceremony was the exchange of rings. Father Hernán called Mari's father up and gave the microphone to Kurt, who addressed his new father-in-law looking directly into his eyes.

"Sir, Mari will wear her wedding ring from this day forward" he cleared his throat, "but be assured that the engagement ring that you put on her finger will continue to occupy its place as a remembrance of a promise that she made to you… that she would finish her studies. I pledge to you before all these witnesses"—he turned to the audience, slowly sweeping his upturned left hand across the intimate crowd as he spoke— "that I will be behind Mari supporting her however and whenever I am needed to make sure that her promise to you is fulfilled."

Mari's dad, trembling with emotion, reached out to his new son-in-law for a warm, strong embrace. Everyone was wiping away tears, with some of the women fanning their faces, trying to keep their makeup in place.

After the ceremony, the guests made their way to the same space on the university campus where the cocktail reception had been held on the closing night of orientation. In the meantime, Mari and Kurt went to their favorite places in the city, where the photographer took incredible pictures.

They returned to the sites they visited on their first date, but this time in their wedding attire. One of their favorite pictures was the one at Fraunces Tavern, sitting on the same stools where they sat on their first date.

"Our kids will love these pictures," said Kurt, visibly delighted.

"I'm not sure who will love them more—you or the kids," answered Mari, taking his face in her hands and bringing it close to hers. The sharp-eyed photographer made sure not to miss this amazing moment.

The reception was small but elegant and, most of all, memorable. In addition to duplicating the same hors d'oeuvres of the night of orientation, they had a variety of Southern delicacies: deviled eggs, Cajun shrimp on small rounds of toasted bread, Cajun guacamole with white corn chips, tiny bites of fried okra… The cake was a replica of Kurt's dream house with three figurines on the front door, a bride and groom and a small child holding the hand of the male figurine.

Kurt had two surprises for Mari at the reception. The first one was a big surprise to everyone except his parents, who had heard him sing in the church choir and at his glee club performances during high school. But when he graduated, his studies absorbed his time and almost absorbed him—until Mari. At that point, what had been buried inside began to flow out, and they saw what they had seen in Kurt's early years—they saw their smart, talented, playful, expressive, and devoted little boy reemerge,

While Mari was going to the various tables interacting with guests, Kurt clipped a miniature microphone to his lapel and called her to him. As she walked toward him, the room was filled with beautiful music. Mari looked up in awe, wondering where the music was coming from, then a beautiful sound began pouring out of Kurt. As she reached him, he took both of her hands in his. The song was "María," from *West Side Story*.

María,
the most beautiful sound I ever heard:
María, María, María, María…
María!

I've just met a girl named María,
And suddenly that name
will never be the same to me.
María!

I've just kissed a girl named María,
and suddenly I've found
how wonderful a sound
can be!
María.

Say it loud, and there's music playing.
Say it soft, and it's almost like praying.
María,
I'll never stop saying María!
The most beautiful sound I ever heard:
María.

When he was finished, he took her face in his hands and wiped her tears with his thumbs then softly kissed her lips. She responded with a long embrace, the guests with applause, the parents with tears.

The rest of the evening was full of conversation, music, appetizers, and Spanish wine.

Toward eight o'clock came Kurt's second surprise: he handed Mari a large box and whispered something in her ear. She took it and left the room.

Fifteen minutes later, the sound of *paso doble* over the sound system got everyone's attention, and Mari made a grand entrance displaying a white lace flamenco dress and *mantilla* over her shoulders. The same pearl *peineta* held up her mass of black silk, and with her head back and hands up, the quick clapping movements began, and her flamenco skills were on display for her family and friends, just as they had been for her beloved on their first date.

This time, to everyone's astonishment, including hers (that was the real surprise), Kurt joined her.

He had taken off his jacket, unbuttoned his white shirt to the middle of his chest, and rolled the sleeves to the elbows. The tapping sound that he made against the floor came from the pair of flamenco shoes he had rented.

Kurt's family looked on flabbergasted, unable to explain how their Southern boy could perform such beautiful and precise movements. "I bet those tap lessons we sent him to when he was little helped," whispered his mom into her husband's ears.

His brother, one hand across his stomach, thumb and index finger of the other around his chin, stared at Kurt with eyes wide open, wearing a mischievous smile.

"I'll be damned," was all that he could let out. His sister-in-law Ashley stood with hands clasped, index fingers extended over her mouth, thumbs together holding up her chin, and watched dreamily. Her four-year-old son, Peter John, leaning back into the folds of her skirt, just observed the performance from his safe place.

Halfway through the dance, they waved everyone to the floor, and the *paso doble* continued with everyone making their own moves, adding to the fun and laughter.

The evening ended with the cutting of the cake, the traditional pictures of the bride and groom feeding each other the cake, and a festive mood all around, with lots of hugs, kisses, and best wishes.

When everyone had left—except for the parents, Kurt's sister Katherine, Peter and Ashley, and his little nephew Peter John—Mari turned to Kurt and took his face in her hands, the gesture so familiar and dear to him.

She brought it close to hers and said, "What a truly amazing day—I couldn't have imagined that a day could be so perfect, and where did you learn those flamenco moves?"

"I might have said that I was in a meeting with my professors when I was really at the dance studio."

She responded by kissing him deep and long. He indulged her.

"The room is ready," blurted Kurt's brother with that wide smile that reminded Mari of her Kurt.

"And you can be sure we'll use it and enjoy it thoroughly," retorted Kurt, matching his wide smile and mischievous look.

"Did we talk like that?" said Kurt's dad, looking at his wife and at Mari's parents.

But to Mari, this forthrightness was typical of her Kurt.

CHAPTER 13
FIRST AND SECOND RUNG

So, his loss caused Mari to experience such devastation and weakness that there were times that she felt her very soul kneeling inside. At other times, she felt that her soul would leave her, and she felt comfort in this and wanted more than anything to succumb to this feeling. But there was Mari-Car.

At the funeral, she experienced complete numbness. Her mother had set out an outfit that she put on robotically: a below-the-knee, black pencil skirt, a long-sleeve white blouse with black collar, black placket, and black cuff edges. A black blazer was placed on her shoulders to keep the chilly autumn air at bay.

However, Mari was unable to feel. She did somehow have enough presence of mind to go to her dresser drawer and pull out a black *mantilla*, which she wore to go out of the house and never took off until she returned home after the service; she wanted to be enveloped in blackness, like her soul.

She walked into the church holding onto her father's arm with one hand and Mari-Car's hand with the other. Her mother followed, along with Kurt's parents and family, Kurt's mother's head resting on her husband's shoulder.

The closed casket lay in front with pictures of their wedding and of the three of them—when she was pregnant, when Mari-Car was born, visiting the park, the petting zoo, visiting her parents and Kurt's.

This had been her mom and Kurt's mom's doing. Mari stared at the pictures the entire time, reliving each moment, with this action wanting to seal every memory in her mind, soul, and skin forever.

They had a Mass. She stood still and silent during the entire ceremony. Did not partake in communion, nor in any of the prayers. A continuous stream of tears flowed down her cheeks, chin, and neck until the front of her blouse became soaked and heavy with the weight of deep pain and desolation.

After the Mass, Mari received words of comfort from their friends as well as Kurt's work colleagues. It was obvious that he was admired, appreciated, and loved by his former professors. A whole team of them attended the service and greeted Mari with tear-filled eyes. Mari had remained seated while people came to her to express condolences. She felt physically, mentally, and emotionally weak and knew that her knees would not hold her up if she stood.

She was right. When everyone besides family had left, Mari tried to stand up to accompany the immediate family to the cemetery; she fainted. Kurt's dad, his brother, and Mari's father made the decision that they would be the ones to go to the cemetery.

Mari slowly came to in the emergency room. She saw her mom, Kurt's mom, and his sister through teary eyes. They could see reality gradually dawning as Mari searched questioningly from one pained face to the other looking down at her.

Then a prolonged wail that seemed to originate in the depths of her soul came out of her, carrying Kurt's name. Her mother brought her up to her chest; Mary and Katherine encircled both in their arms. The heart-wrenching scene remained frozen for an undetermined amount of time, for no one wanted to break the circle, knowing that doing so would mean facing unbearable pain and terrifying uncertainty, and for Mari… chilling loneliness and despair.

Peter John and Mari-Car walked quietly into the room, flanked by two nurses and clasping each other's hands while holding on to a nurse's hand with the other. The two angels disguised as nurses had taken them to the cafeteria to distract them from the immense sorrow that their family was experiencing.

As they neared the bed where his aunt now lay, head buried in her pillow, seven-year-old Peter John tightened his grip on three-year-old Mari-Car's hand, sensing a need to protect her. Peter John pulled Mari-Car to a stop, let go of her hand and the nurse's hand, and encircled her in a protective embrace.

After a moment, Mari-Car looked over at her mom, slowly released the arms that sheltered her, and as if in slow motion, walked to her mother's bed. When she reached the side of the bed, she tried to climb up; one of the nurses assisted the little one, who then went on to place her little arms around her mother's neck and lay her dark head on her chest.

After Mari left the hospital, she fell into a vacuum of existence where she lost awareness of her surroundings, but this situation allowed her to cope with the pain that otherwise would be impossible to bear.

The weight of the confusion, sadness, loneliness, and memories made Mari almost collapse. But strangely, she found comfort while in this state, because she didn't have to feel.

Then she would think of Mari-Car. Strength would slowly reappear, but only enough to allow her to take care of the basic needs of her small "piece of Kurt." It was true; Mari-Car had been gifted by her father the deep, ocean-blue eyes as well as the carefree, sunny personality.

Mari's parents and Kurt's had tried to do their part to pull her out of the abyss she had fallen into. They had reached through their own sea of pain to try to touch hers, hoping not to remove it—that was impossible even for them—but to lessen it.

They spoke loving and comforting words to her, bought her books containing lovely poems, created a memory album full of pictures of her and Kurt that captured all the meaningful moments starting from the first day they met… they had even made the space off Mari and Kurt's room, which was bursting with sunlight, into a drawing studio for Mari, and filled it with all the essential tools for fashion sketching: sketchbooks, drawing pencils, colored pencils, fine-point black pens, markers, scissors, pattern paper…

But everything remained untouched in the same spot it had been placed.

Mari recognized their effort but lacked the strength to respond. However, she knew that only she had the power to return to the land of the living. Not only that, but she also began to realize that for Mari-Car's sake, she had a *duty* to return. Could she? She lacked the will and feared that she had reached the point of being unable to come back.

The tentacles of pain were far-reaching. They had wrapped themselves so tightly around her—almost to the point of strangulation—that she had failed to see them around Kurt's parents, around Mari-Car, and yes, around her own parents.

How long had she been in this state of darkness and unconsciousness? The months had passed unnoticed. Mari had not felt the cold of winter, nor the heat of summer, but she now became aware of the vivid fall colors outside of her apartment window. They brought her comfort and pain.

She was *feeling*, and something told her that that was a good thing. Mari conscientiously began the slow, arduous climb out of the abyss.

The designs in her head were now finding their way to the paper, as if they too had been trapped in an abyss and were gradually reclaiming the place where they belonged.

She reached for the sketching tools that her parents and Kurt's parents had placed in the sunny space next to her room; she began freeing the designs that had been imprisoned.

Seeing them come alive opened the way for Mari and Mari-Car to return to school.

She had kept Mari-Car close to her, never out of her sight, for fear that she might lose her too. The little girl, sensing her mother's distress, always stayed near, close enough that whenever her mom stretched her hand, she was able to be touched.

Now Mari-Car sensed and saw that her mother had begun the difficult journey back and somehow sensed that the time had come for her also to come out of where she had been. She was too little to understand but *felt* the sadness she had been wrapped in. Her mother decided that the first step for Mari-Car's well-being was to return to school and her beloved Ms. Scott.

On her first day, Mari-Car did not run into the waiting arms of her teacher as she used to, but walked into them slowly and allowed herself to be enveloped in their warmth.

Tears spilled from the eyes of both teacher and pupil as they continued their long, unhurried, understanding embrace. Mari watched from a short distance. The moisture in her eyes overflowed, spreading down her pallid cheeks, but she felt comforted by the scene in front of her, reassured by the trust that Mari-Car displayed in Ms. Scott.

A new life awaited her, not by choice—she would give her life to return to what once was—but by fate. She wasn't sure what she believed in anymore. She wasn't even sure *if* she believed. She was sure of what she felt, though: anger or hatred, maybe the unnamed feeling in between. And of course, fear, which would become her constant companion. At twenty-two, Mari felt old, like she had lived a lifetime.

As she drove to her design class, she turned on the disk player and listened to the familiar song, "Historia de un Amor." She had grown up with that song, one of her mother's favorites. The lyrics had laid dormant in her subconscious for years, and now she listened intently. She felt the words down in the depths of her soul, as if the composer knew her pain. That seemed especially true on this day, when she had made the choice to place one foot on the first rung of the ladder out of the abyss.

That night, María Victoria and José Felipe came to visit their daughter and granddaughter—they knew this was an important day in their lives and wanted to be part of it. Mother and daughter, alone in the bedroom, could hear the soft but deep voice of the grandfather saying in his accented English, "Better to see you with, my dear," "Better to hear you, my dear," and finally, "Better to eat you with, my dear," mixed with loud chewing sounds and followed by the welcomed laughter of Mari-Car.

María José shared with her mother the impact that "Historia de un Amor" had had on her while she drove to school that morning.

"Do you know why?" her mother asked. Mari shook her head lightly. "Then, I'll tell you the story behind the story. 'Historia de un Amor' was a song written by Carlos Eleta Almarán in 1955…"

"I know; you and *Abuela* [Grandma] sang it or hummed it all the time."

"It was composed for his brother Fernando, who lost his beloved wife Mercedez to polio. Her illness got worse just before giving birth to their daughter. On her deathbed, she asked Carlos to take care of her husband—his brother."

Mari looked at her mother in disbelief. "The song is not about a lover who abandoned his love?"

"No, it's about a man who lost his one and only love to a terrible illness, leaving him with a newborn daughter."

"That's why I felt it so deeply," Mari whispered, full of realization as she reached for the disk and played the song. They both listened, and the tears were allowed to flow freely down their cheeks:

Ya no estás más a mi lado corazón
> *You are no longer by my side, sweetheart.*

En el alma solo tengo soledad
> *I have only loneliness in my soul,*

Y si yo no puedo verte
> *and if I can no longer see you,*

Porque Dios me hizo quererte
> *why did God cause me to love you,*

Para hacerme sufrir mas.
> *to cause me more pain?*

Siempre fuiste la razón de mi existir
> *You were always my reason for living.*

Adorarte para mí fue religion
> *Loving you, for me, was a religion.*

Y en tus besos yo encontraba
> *and in your kisses I used to find*

El calor que me brindaba
> *the warmth offered me by*

El amor y la pasión
> *love and passion.*

BIR ZAMANLAR

Es la historia de un amor
> *This is the story of a love*

Como no hay otro igual
> *like no other*

Que me hizo comprender
> *that caused me to understand*

Todo el bien, todo el mal
> *good and evil,*

Que le dio luz a mi vida
> *that brought light into my life,*

Apagándola después
> *later taking it away.*

Ay que vida tan oscura
> *Oh, what a dark life.*

Sin tu amor no viviré
> *Without your love, I cannot live.*

Ya no estás más a mi lado corazón
> *You are no longer by my side, sweetheart.*

En el alma solo tengo soledad
> *I have only loneliness in my soul.*

Y si yo no puedo verte
> *And if I can no longer see you,*

Porque Dios me hizo quererte
> *why did God cause me to love you,*

Para hacerme sufrir mas.
> *to cause me more pain?*

Es la historia de un amor
> *This is the story of a love*

Como no hay otro igual
> *like no other*

Que me hizo comprender
> *that caused me to understand*

Todo el bien, todo el mal
> *good and evil,*

Que le dio luz a mi vida
> *that brought light into my life,*

Apagándola después
> *later taking it away.*

Ay que vida tan obscura
> *Oh, what a dark life.*

Sin tu amor no viviré
> *Without your love, I cannot live.*

Ya no estás más a mi lado Corazón
> *You are no longer by my side, sweetheart.*

En el alma solo tengo soledad
> *I have only loneliness in my soul.*

Y si yo no puedo verte
> *And if I can no longer see you,*

Porque Dios me hizo quererte
> *why did God cause me to love you,*

Para hacerme sufrir mas
> *to cause me more pain?*

How long mother and daughter had spent in their own world of thought, neither one knew. But they looked up with tearstained faces and met the pained look on José Felipe's face.

Father and daughter locked eyes. Words were unnecessary. His comforting look said so much: I hurt with you and for you, I wish I could take the pain away, I love you.

Mari knew she could move in with her parents, but she found comfort and solace in staying in the space where she and Kurt had lived their story of *grande amore.*

The bed felt too large, even when Kurt occupied the space next to her, their faces so close their breaths intermingled, their legs entwined, her head and arms resting on his chest. Kurt's arms had encircled her entire upper body. The bed had always been too big, but now it was lonely, empty, cold...

They made plans in bed, facing each other, whispering their dreams to each other. They'd open an architectural firm; she'd have an atelier where she'd give opportunities to young designers to create fashion, and to couturiers to bring them alive. Mari-Car (and all the little Kurts and Marías to come) would grow up in a creative environment, where their gifts would be allowed free rein. They would move Kurt's parents to New York so they would all be close; that way, when Mari and Kurt traveled to the fashion houses in Milan, Paris, Rome, and beyond, the grandparents could take care of the children and take them to the museums, Broadway plays, Central Park... They had talked about their children spending time in Murcia, where they would explore their roots and perfect their Spanish.

When they dreamed together, there was nowhere else that Mari wanted to be besides next to Kurt, her head on his heart. That was her world. From there, they moved on to spending long moments uncovering and discovering each other, realizing that they were one another's world and home, and that they were the only ones able to meet and quench the other's aspirations and desires.

The day Mari had returned Mari-Car to school was the day that with great difficulty, she placed one trembling foot on the first rung of the ladder that her loved ones had extended to her at the bottom of the black hole where she had resided for the last 365 days. What made her pick up her foot and bring it to that rung? Undoubtedly, her thoughts of Mari-Car.

She would stay on that bottom rung for a long time. But it was enough to allow Mari-Car to return to school and interact with other children and for Mari to return to her studies.

She designed and designed and designed. She conceived beautiful creations, and soon her designs were being displayed in the gallery of the institute and receiving many accolades from the faculty members.

Designing was one way for Mari to keep from drowning in her pain. The other way, of course, was to concentrate on Mari-Car. Now Mari had both feet on the first rung of the ladder, not just one.

At night, she slept on Kurt's side of the bed, curled up, knees tucked in, elbows together, her favorite of Kurt's T-shirts between her clasped hands and under her left cheek, as if she were facing him.

Many mornings she woke up to the tearstained T-shirt. She refused to wash it, afraid that it would lose his scent. She kept a bottle of his cologne on her nightstand, and when his loss threatened to overwhelm her, she slowly unscrewed the small cap, brought the bottle to her nostrils, and inhaled Kurt's scent—and his essence.

Mari felt duty-bound to nurture every ray of Mari-Car's sunny personality so their brightness would never fade. It had been a wonderful gift from Kurt, so she made him a silent vow that she would always protect his little daughter's sunniness. If need be, she'd become her shield so that darkness would never touch her.

But how could Mari keep such a vow when her soul was not reached by even a tip of one of the warm rays that bathed her daughter? she wondered. She chose during this dark period to rely on her parents and Kurt's parents to stoke Mari-Car's sunrays, because she alone could not keep that promise, and she knew it.

Mari-Car enjoyed Broadway shows for children, took ballet lessons and, at her parents' insistence, flamenco lessons. It took a village to raise Mari-Car and to help her flourish, as well as to hold the ladder steady for Mari as she tried to pull herself out of the deep void she was in.

"You know, dear," said Kurt's mother to Mari one day after she and her husband John brought Mari-Car home from ballet lessons. She took Mari's hand, and both sat on the couch. Her husband took that as a sign to take his granddaughter to her room and play.

"My son was very lucky to have experienced such love," she began. "Until I saw how you and Kurt loved each other, I had only read about such great love and heard about it in song lyrics but never actually seen it."

Mari looked at her with quivering lips and managed to ask, "Then why did I lose him? Was it wrong to love and be loved so much?"

"I don't have an answer; I wish I knew. He was my son, and I loved him the same way you love Mari-Car."

Mari had not thought about the great pain that Kurt's parents had experienced and had put aside to help her deal with hers.

Kurt's mom continued, "I have a question for you. Don't answer right away; take your time. Would you rather not have experienced that kind of love, even for a short while, and avoided the great suffering that you're going through, or would you choose to live the love that you lived with Kurt and receive the gift that he left you, knowing that doing so would cause you great pain?"

Mari looked at her mother-in-law in amazement for a few seconds, then melted into her chest and sobbed for a long time. They remained in a quiet embrace until Mari was able to raise her head and manage a soft smile, then gave her a kiss on the cheek. She felt that she was ready to raise one wobbly foot to the second rung of the ladder.

CHAPTER 14
LEGO MEMORIES

After Christmas of the second year without Kurt, Mary and John Stewart returned to North Carolina in an attempt to give some sort of continuation to their former life. Katherine had begun to call daily to remind them that they had two more children and a young grandson that also needed them.

Since Kurt's death, although they had gone home to check on Katherine and the rest of the family, it seemed that their stays in New York City had become longer and longer. Mary had requested a leave of absence from work, and John had decided to take early retirement.

Their pain was the least understood by everyone. For Mary, being home brought her close to all of Kurt's childhood memories. It was a pain that she had been trying to avoid feeling for over a year.

Every time she walked into the house, memories came rushing into her heart and mind. She heard his little voice; she saw him in all the corners where he had sat building his world with his building blocks and LEGO. He opened every new box of

LEGO with the same enthusiasm as the first and immediately began building until the new project was completed.

She had kept his books; he liked to read and be read to. Some she had taken to Mari-Car; the others she had kept for herself, unable to let go of them. She would read them silently in what had once been his room and allowed her tears to fall on the pages. John would come and sit silently next to her, at times randomly putting LEGO pieces together from the boxes that they had brought up to Kurt's room after they had been stored in the basement for so long.

They would look at each other without saying a word, just knowing and feeling pain, wondering but not daring to allow their lips to form that terrible, unanswerable question: Why? Then they would find solace in knowing that they wouldn't have done anything differently to hold their son back. They had allowed him to follow his dreams, wherever the needle in his heart's compass pointed.

Sometimes people grasp at something to make themselves feel better, to justify their actions, or to survive. Mary thought that this was exactly what she and John were doing when they talked about Kurt—they were trying to grab hold of something, a word that they had spoken to him, advice given, hugs… in order to feel that they had done all they could for their beloved son.

Like all parents, Mary knew she would never feel like she had done enough. So many ifs: if they had been there the week earlier, like they had originally planned, they would have been the ones who took Mari-Car to school, and Mari and Kurt would have gone directly to the university and missed the rain, or they would have kept Mari-Car home and taken her to the park instead, like they often did when they visited, or they would have gone all together in John's car to avoid the hassle of having Kurt take the back road.

They had postponed their trip for a week because their grandson, Peter John, had a small award ceremony. So, had they left one grandchild an orphan to make another happy? This thought had come to Mary so suddenly and unexpectedly that it made her shake uncontrollably. John encircled his wife in his arms, assuming that she was overwhelmed by grief; Mary did not dare voice the thought that had passed through her mind and drowned her in panic.

The what-ifs and unanswerable questions could drive a person insane. Mary realized that and tried to avoid these enemies of peace and harmony of the mind. But at times they had a way of creeping back in, causing havoc.

That was what she was experiencing at the moment: havoc of the mind. She allowed it for a while, because, as unreasonable as it seemed, she believed she deserved some punishment for losing her child, for leaving her granddaughter without a dad, for breaking such a beautiful bond between Kurt and Mari. So she pondered, she longed, and she mourned and lived her sorrow.

CHAPTER 15
PILLOW DREAMS

To no one's surprise and everyone's delight, Mari had become a successful designer.

After graduating, she showed her designs in the great fashion shows of Milan, Paris, Madrid, and of course, New York, where she owned a boutique.

She had created the Kurt Stewart Foundation, supervised and directed by Mary Stewart. When Mari asked her mother-in-law to head the foundation, Mary answered with a flow of tears, tremoring lips, and a long embrace.

Mary quit her nursing job to dedicate more time to the foundation. She made frequent trips to New York, but remained in North Carolina with her family.

The foundation granted scholarships to young, deserving design and architecture students from under-resourced areas. It offered opportunities such as camps where they could explore their creative talents, summer courses at renowned design schools both in the US and abroad, and opportunities for some outstandingly talented students to shadow famous designers and intern with renowned architects.

Just as both Mari and Kurt had dreamed and planned while resting their heads on their pillows, Mari had opened an atelier in one of the underprivileged areas of the city whose young residents had limited resources. It had been thriving since its inception. Her mom, María Victoria, oversaw that facility.

However, Mari remained very private as far as her personal life. She only allowed room in her life for Mari-Car, her parents, Kurt's parents, and her designs. Whenever anyone began to talk to her about even the possibility of meeting someone with whom she could develop a romantic relationship, she boldly stopped them, so the subject was never broached.

In the quietness within, she had decided long ago that her heart had only belonged to Kurt and that it would be impossible to allow anyone else in. This decision had brought her peace and had helped her live. She had learned to live with that void; it was her faithful companion, almost her friend.

CHAPTER 16
MARI-CAR, PART ONE

Mari-Car was imbued with self-confidence, the result of the encouragement that she received from her grandparents and her mom to try new things and explore new worlds. Her life was filled with Broadway plays, dance classes—ballet and flamenco—and fashion shows with her mother in the major European cities. She also assisted her grandparents in the foundation and the atelier.

They had bestowed the ideal components for self-growth on Mari-Car: love and exposure to diverse activities and people to nourish her mind and soul, thereby untapping the talents and gifts that otherwise would have remained dormant.

Kurt's parents were especially attached to her because they felt that Mari-Car was the special gift left to them by their son.

They began to bring Mari-Car to North Carolina for long and short visits when she was a little girl. In fact, it began when they decided to leave New York and move back, prompted by the call from their daughter Katherine.

Mari had also encouraged Mari-Car's relationship with her paternal grandparents because she wanted her daughter to create a strong bond with her father's side of the family. Somehow, Mari felt that that bond would keep her and Mari-Car close to Kurt, not just to his family.

It was during these times that Mari-Car and Peter John—or PJ, as she called him (she was the only one that he allowed to call him that)—grew close. They were both only children, except when they were with each other.

John and Mary Stewart doted on them. They each had a room at their home, their respective fathers' former rooms when they were growing up.

Mari-Car had asked, even as a little girl, that her father's room would remain the same as it had been when he was growing up; she felt close to him that way. Her grandparents had agreed and were pleased with her request. As she grew up, she made no changes, only added a few pictures of her drawings, hoping her father was able to see them from somewhere.

Peter John's room, however, had evolved over the years. First it was a young boy's room with bunk beds and a maritime theme. As a child, he loved everything to do with the sea, especially sailboats. So, his room was painted navy blue, and the bedspread and curtains displayed a nautical theme.

One wall was covered with pictures: Peter John and his father and grandfather fishing, Peter John holding the various good-size fish that he had caught while sailing with his grandfather, and countless pictures at swim meets. He was an avid swimmer and had won many medals and trophies. These filled a glass display case; the medals covered a sizable part of the wall.

Peter John figured that his love of the sea must have come from his grandfather, because his dad, besides attending his swimming meets and accompanying him and his grandfather fishing a few times, had little to do with the sea. He preferred construction sites and the business world.

As an adult, he spent more time at his grandparents' home than at his own. The nautical theme in his room remained, although it had been updated. The bunk beds had been replaced by a large platform bed; a large anchor carved into the headboard was painted white, which made it stand out from the blue-painted wood that surrounded it. His pictures, medals, and trophies remained in place.

He had thought about studying business like his father or architecture like his uncle Kurt, but during one of Mari-Car's visits when she had just started high school and he was about to graduate, he told her what he had in mind. She grabbed his arm and practically dragged him to his room. He stood inside looking down at her questioningly.

"Look around, PJ. What do you see?"

"I see my room. What else?" He raised both hands, confused by the question.

"OK." Mari-Car modified her question. "What do you feel?"

This time he took his time before answering. He looked around, allowing his eyes to contemplate each picture, each medal, each trophy, the curtains, the bedspread, the bed, then looked back at Mari-Car,

"I feel water; I feel the sea."

"Then how the hell are you gonna feel the sea in an office? That's how you'd spend most of your time if you went into the business world." She took his hand and led him to his bed, where they both sat leaning against the headboard, and without letting go of his hand, Mari-Car continued, "You were born to be free, to feel the wind that comes from the sea, to learn about its mysteries and its creatures."

He looked down at her, came close, and squeezed both cheeks with one hand.

"You're just a kid—how did you get so smart?" He hugged her and kissed her soundly on both cheeks. They left his room with arms around each other, laughing.

Peter John applied to two marine biology programs and got a prompt response from the University of North Carolina in Wilmington.

With the application form he had included the story of how he had chosen to study marine biology rather than business—how he had followed his heart through the words of his cousin and best friend rather than automatically following in his father's footsteps.

He didn't know whether that influenced the prompt acceptance letter from the admissions office, but he had felt great putting in writing what he had experienced during that conversation with Mari-Car.

He decided not to wait for the response from the second university. He made the immediate decision to accept the offer from NCUW. Besides being the first to send him an acceptance response, it had a world-class program, it was in a midsize city, which Peter John preferred, and it was closer to home.

He was so happy with his decision that he could hardly sit still and couldn't wait to talk to Mari-Car later that night. He was sure this time he wouldn't fall asleep during their nightly conversation.

They would have long and deep talks every night, almost without fail, during the years that followed.

CHAPTER 17
MARI-CAR, PART TWO

Mari-Car was adventurous, fun, optimistic, and an idealist, ready to save the world. She had chosen her dad's profession, architecture. At seventeen, she was in the first year of her studies and hoped to specialize in green architecture. She had always been a conservationist, only using cloth napkins, taking short showers, separating trash, and making weekly trips to the recycling center. She founded the Conservation Club at her high school, which had attracted many members.

Socially active, Mari-Car was involved in countless projects around the city's most vulnerable neighborhoods. Her undertakings included designing community vegetable gardens and appointing neighborhood leaders to tend and distribute produce, setting up accessible recycling stations, and visiting local elementary schools to train children on the various conservation methods.

For her eighteenth birthday, at the end of her first year at Columbia, Mari-Car requested a year's leave. She wanted to study at the Politecnico di Milano.

Fascinated by European architecture, she had begun to research schools and had discovered that Politecnico di Milano would be a great fit for her. Besides, the school, although huge, was world-ranked; she knew this would impress both her mother and grandparents, plus in her self-confidence, she knew that she would find her niche in the sea of people.

She was fluent in Spanish and during her research on European universities, decided to study Italian. It came easily. Her knowledge of Spanish helped—it mostly needed polishing, and she knew this came only by practicing it.

Mari-Car's eighteenth birthday was a bittersweet moment for Mari. It brought back memories of her own unforgettable eighteenth birthday. She had all the special gifts that Kurt had given her, which she took out whenever she felt that she couldn't hold on.

Fifteen years had dulled the pain and kept her head barely above water, thanks to her beloved Mari-Car and her own career. Mari had become a brilliant and successful designer partly because—save for the times she spent with her daughter and the visits to her parents—most of her waking hours she dedicated to perfecting her designs.

But her last thoughts before falling asleep from exhaustion each night were always of Kurt. For fifteen years this had been so, and one of his T-shirts still remained under her pillow. At night, she would pull it out, hug it, smell it, and wipe her tears.

Did everyone love the way she and Kurt loved? she pondered. Mary Stewart, her mother-in-law (was she still her mother in-law? she wondered) had told her years before that she had never seen a love like hers and Kurt's except in movies. Mari felt that their love story was written before eternity and that it would remain for eternity. She reflected on the intensity of their love many a night and had come to the conclusion that spending most of their waking moments, and even their sleeping ones, together was meant to be, because their time as one on earth had been predetermined to be short.

Be that as it may, Mari-Car's eighteenth birthday had revived all the memories of her first date with Kurt. She relived each moment to the minutest detail: feeling the rose on her cheek and lips when she first woke up, the joy of running down the stairs for breakfast, the delight of seeing another long-stemmed rose by her plate, and daisies spread on the table, the voice of her friend Sandra announcing breakfast, the taste of the olives, the baguettes, the jams, the smoked salmon, the mimosas. Then the arrival of the lunch basket with the delights from Murcia.

What to say about the most incredible evening of her life? The roses handed to her from the children at the street corners, Fraunces Tavern, the flamenco show, and finally, up high, out on the outdoor terrace, her infinity necklace—she caressed it reflexively.

The words that came to her mind as she relived that night were "sweet pain." She embraced this feeling. It was so sweet that she didn't want it to leave and so painful that it made her heart hurt.

The preparation for Mari-Car's year abroad took weeks. Getting all the documentation ready for Politecnico di Milano; assembling her wardrobe (most of it designed by Mari); and a trip to North Carolina to say goodbye to her grandparents, aunts, uncle, and of course, Peter John.

Their bond had strengthened, not just from the time spent together during holidays but also from their nightly texting and video calls.

His pet-name for her was "glam girl" because she wore a lot of her mother's original designs and often flew off to fashion shows in faraway places.

However, although he jokingly called her a glam girl, he also admired her for those same reasons.

"Just don't forget your Southern roots," Peter John told Mari-Car when they shared the familiar parting hug, this time a little longer and a bit tighter. Maybe they both sensed that they would be a lot farther away now and it probably would be a long while before they would be together again.

She broke away, looked up at him, finally responded with eyes filled with tears, "Just don't forget that wherever I am, you have a home," and quickly left.

She's always going somewhere, Peter John thought to himself and wondered if he should not leave also and explore the actual world a bit, to see what was beyond the small part that he had occupied up to that point.

Mari-Car had always been an inspiration for him. Despite the almost-five-year age difference, when he was near her he felt that he could conquer the world.

As Peter John watched Mari-Car walk away, he remembered what she had told him when he graduated with his degree in marine biology: "You know, now you could explore an MBA in global management."

What the hell is that? he thought then. *She's always challenging me to do something else.*

Now he wished she would stay close and continue to challenge him. He felt the void in his heart deepen with each step Mari-Car took away from him.

Until Mari-Car mentioned it, Peter John had never even heard of such a thing as global management. He was content working at the yacht club, keeping the day-to-day logistics of running the midsize operation. He particularly enjoyed giving sailing lessons to the younger members.

The perks weren't bad. Peter John had his schedule full, made good money, and his clients were mostly young, beautiful, wealthy girls —so the view was also good. He relished the attention.

So maybe I am content, Peter John thought, but now that Mari-Car was parting for Europe, the wheels had begun turning in his head, and he started researching global management.

This MBA would equip students, he learned, with the tools to legally assess the possible expansion of companies in various countries. That part sounded fascinating to him. It also taught students about global marketing, international law, diplomatic strategy, and ethnic relations, among other skills. These were the topics that stood out to him and that began to keep him awake at night.

But he loved the sea. How would all these areas of global management relate to his love for the water, ships, sailing, the sea itself?

After investigating the various universities that offered global management, enduring many sleepless nights, and exchanging countless texts with Mari-Car, Peter John followed her suggestion to try to get in the program at Columbia.

"You can stay in my room and watch over my mom—she'll be all alone when I leave," she had told him, full of hope and enthusiasm.

Did this girl ever have a down day? He wondered shaking his slightly.

"Besides, don't try to figure everything out at once; in time, the connection with your first love—the sea—will become clear," Mari-Car had told him.

"You're just a kid—who made you so smart?" came Peter John's familiar words just before he hung up.

Peter John ran both hands over his blond head and down his face. He was so excited and nervous at the same time. Could he do it? Could he step out of his comfort zone? His stomach began to make funny sounds and his head hurt.

CHAPTER 18
PETER JOHN

His parents and grandparents were apprehensive when he brought up the idea of moving to New York City.

That night they were at his grandparents' dinner table, where Peter John had gathered them after speaking with Mari-Car a few hours earlier. He thought that if he waited any longer, he might get cold feet and complacency would win over.

The reason for the elders' hesitancy was clear: they had lost Kurt when he was following a similar dream. Ashley, his mother, was downright terrified and a bit miffed at Mari-Car. She knew that Mari-Car was the one who had put such ideas in her son's head.

Ashley could not control her tears. Her hands shook, and her head began to spin scenes of horrors: what if he were mugged, or worse, in that big frightening city, what if he got into drugs—after all, he was a naïve, small-town boy, not used to the "malice" of the big-city youth.

Although his father was not fond of the idea, he told Peter John that he would not hold him back.

"Sometimes I wish I had done some traveling of my own," he had said.

"It's not like it's too late, Dad. Maybe this will be the inspiration that you need."

"Maybe, Son, maybe" came his quiet response as he squeezed Peter John's shoulder.

Peter thought of how much he loved his son and how difficult it was for him to tell him so. He was his and Ashley's miracle. After Peter John was born, they had tried to give him siblings, but a series of miscarriages and subsequent disappointments put a stop to that.

Unexpectedly, Peter got up from the table and tapped his son's shoulder.

"Get up, Son, get up." When Peter John stood in front of him, Peter reached out and hugged him tightly.

"I know that I don't say it nearly enough…well, hardly ever, but I want you to know that I love you and I'm proud of you, Son."

There was not a dry eye around the intimate family table, including the eyes of father and son. Ashley sent a silent, heartfelt thank you to her dearest Zoey.

She later called the leader of the prayer chain from her church, who immediately began to pass the word to the other members to pray for Peter John Stewart. That God would help him make the correct decision, that if he left, he would be under the Almighty's protection, and that his family would have peace.

CHAPTER 19
MARI-CAR PART THREE

Meanwhile, back in New York, preparations for the big day continued. Mari took Mari-Car to be blessed by their local parish priest and to request that her name be mentioned in prayer during Sunday's Mass.

Mari also bought Mari-Car a small stamp featuring the image of Saint Christopher, the patron saint of travelers, so she would keep it in her wallet.

"He will accompany you wherever you go, *mi hija* [my daughter]," Mari had told her daughter.

Finally, Mari handed Mari-Car a small glass bottle containing *agua bendita*.

"It's holy water. Always keep it with you. Moisten your finger with it and do the sign of the cross before making an important decision," Mari instructed her daughter. Mari-Car acquiesced and gave her mother a hug.

"*Mamá*, we've traveled a lot. I'll be all right—you're acting as if this is the first time I am going on a trip."

"It's not that. It's just that this is the first time that you are traveling as an adult; I feel like this is a defining moment, one that will forge your future."

Her mother's words left Mari-Car pondering. They hugged.

Mari-Car's outgoing personality and her community involvement had made her lots of friends, and they threw her a going-away party at a local pub near the university the night before she parted.

All these rituals flooded Mari with memories of her and Kurt. Where had all the years gone? Did she really have an eighteen-year-old daughter? She reminisced about the time when she found out she was pregnant at Kurt's office, on his lap, loving him.

On parting day, Mari-Car was accompanied to the airport by her mom, and grandparents, María Victoria and José Felipe. She had received a call from Kurt's parents earlier in the morning full of loving words and good wishes.

A few days earlier, they had deposited money in her checking account with the lovely message, "To help you in the pursuit of your dreams."

She knew she was lucky to have a loving and caring family, and a sense of gratefulness invaded her. But excitement rather than sadness was what she experienced foremost. She knew her mother would make frequent trips to Milan to visit her fashion boutiques and she'd only be a half hour away. She was looking forward to starting her new program.

In spite of that, hugs and tears were plentiful during the goodbyes. That was especially true of her grandparents, whose constant presence in her life she had almost taken for granted, but now, a lonely feeling engulfed her as the reality of not having them close dawned on her. Mari-Car looked them in the eye and hugged them tight; words were spared.

But then Mari-Car's heart began jumping with excitement at all the possibilities and wonders that awaited her, and it reflected on her bright, smiley face.

Her father's sunny personality, thought Mari as she gave her daughter a last hug before she turned happily to pass through security. They stayed until Mari-Car had gone through. She turned and waved enthusiastically at them. Then she was gone.

CHAPTER 20
CAMPUS LIFE

She had chosen to live at one of the residence halls, mostly for the social experience, and she had chosen La Presentazione Hall for its proximity to Lake Como in the city of the same name and the fact that it reflected one of her loves: Renaissance architecture.

When she arrived, Mari-Car felt like she always felt when in the Lombardy region, particularly the picturesque town of Bellagio—like she was inside a painting. She wondered once again if she'd be able to leave all this beauty behind when the time came for her to return to New York.

And as she had before, Mari-Car felt overwhelmed by the magnificent surroundings of the pre-Alp region and the mountains that encircled Lake Como. "It does really take my breath away," she whispered to herself.

Mari-Car tried to capture the exquisite scenery in pictures and immediately sent them to Peter John, with the message, "A new home (and life) awaits you. I'm anxious to take you to the Museum of Navigational Instruments here in Como."

Butterflies danced in her stomach as she imagined Peter John relishing the visit to the museum.

"The pictures don't seem real. What's that museum? I'm not much of a museum person."

"You'll love this one! It displays compasses and sundials…a sea guy like you will be fascinated!"

"Go easy on me. My family went emotional and berserk when I told them I'd be moving to New York for my master's program. Can you imagine their reaction if I told them I was going to Italy?"

Mari-Car's surprise was expressed in one word, "Really?" followed by the emoji with wide-open eyes. "But your family is so…let's see…self-composed," she wrote him a few seconds later.

"That's just for show, but I have to admit, though, my dad surprised me."

Peter John went on to relate how emotional his dad got the night he told the family about his plans to move to New York.

"Wow, I could cry right now. Did not expect that from my uncle Peter."

They continued to text back and forth throughout the day about their plans and bantered about how their respective parents had put them on the prayer lists at their churches.

Mari-Car always thought of Peter John first when she had some big news to tell, or a secret to share, because she was sure that in Peter John's care, a secret would be kept forever.

In fact, he was the only one she had told that she suspected there was a big secret behind the move of her grandparents from Murcia to America.

She had overheard conversations between her mother and her great-grandmother during their visits to Murcia. Her great-grandmother never said anything specific, but she saw her tears and her lips tremble each time the subject was broached. Neither of the adults suspected that she had been listening while pretending to draw on her pad.

The mystery, Mari-Car had told Peter John, full of hope and a tinge of fear and excitement, would be solved someday by the two of them.

Mari-Car also shared with Peter John that she often heard her mother cry at night and that she always slept hugging one of her father's shirts.

"I think my uncle Kurt was lucky," Peter John had told her during one of their serious video chats. To her questioning look, he answered, "He was loved so extremely."

"So was my mom," explained Mari-Car. "That's why she never remarried—where could she find such love again?"

"Would you have been hurt if she had found someone else?"

"Hard question to answer," Mari-Car responded slowly and thoughtfully. "I want my mom to be happy, but my dad was too special. He not only loved my mom beautifully but me also. I still miss him."

"So do you remember him?"

"Well, his pictures are there to never let me forget what he looked like, but what I really do remember is *feeling* his love."

After a long pause (that was one thing that made their conversations special—they were comfortable with silence and allowed each other time to think), Mari-Car added, "I think it'll be a long time before I marry, if I ever do…because I want nothing less than what they had."

"Tall order," responded Peter John. "Even I could see and feel the beautiful and unusual connection between your parents, and I was small!" After another long, familiar pause, he added, "You know, I still remember their wedding."

"What?" Mari-Car couldn't believe her ears. "Why didn't you ever tell me that?"

"Don't know. We've never talked about marriage before, and doing it now brought back the most beautiful wedding ceremony I've ever been to."

They continued their easy conversation, with Peter John doing most of the talking, relating the details of his uncle Kurt and aunt Mari's wedding, which he observed with fascination from inside the folds of his mother's skirt. He remembers feeling like he was inside of a fairy tale, and he told this to Mari-Car.

"Can you imagine?" said Peter John, a sudden realization hitting him like a bolt of lightning. "If it weren't for that secret that brought your grandparents to New York, your mom and dad would have never met, you would not have been born, and you and I would have never met!"

"Wow! That is really more than I can process right now. Can we change the subject? That thought scares me."

"Which part?"

"All of it! Let's talk about something else."

"Sooo, back to that fairy tale you were talking about," Mari-Car adeptly and swiftly changed the subject, "anyone anywhere close to fulfilling that fairy tale for you?"

Peter John rolled his eyes. "Would anything like that ever happen without you being the first to know?"

She laughed. "If it did, I'd never speak to you again. Plus, I'd have to approve her first. Only thing is…" She left the sentence hanging, and Peter John waited a long time since he was accustomed to their long pauses, but the sentence remained in the air.

"Only thing is what?" he finally asked, quietly and pensively.

"Only thing is that I might not approve of anyone for a long time, because I don't want to lose my best friend."

"Nor I mine," came the soft response.

"Anyway, when are you coming to Milan?" Mari-Car again suddenly changed the topic of conversation.

"Let me get to New York first, OK?" They blew kisses, and both went back to their respective routines. However, they talked long and deep at least once a week, complemented by quick messages during the day every day.

They helped each other make decisions. Mari-Car had told Peter John about the top-ranked architecture universities, and he had been the first to know that she had been thinking about going to study abroad after her first year at Columbia. She had blurted out to him the different possibilities that were floating in her head. It was as if she had a small screen on her forehead that exposed her brain and Peter John was the only one allowed to watch it unfiltered.

At first, she had considered studying in Switzerland, but he brought her back to center and helped her organize her ideas. In his view, the Politecnico di Milano was a much better fit for her.

"For one thing, you love Renaissance architecture. Also, you have been studying Italian your entire first year of college. It's like you've been preparing for this place without realizing it; maybe it's meant to be."

"I know. When I began investigating it, I liked it immediately. Everything I read about it reminded me of…well, me! Plus, Milano is very familiar to me. Its size scares me—it's huge!" Mari-Car opened her arms wide to make her point. "I like more intimate settings."

In the end, she had listened to Peter John—and to her heart. And here she was! She felt tiny butterflies inside. She kept mulling over in her mind, Peter John's words: "Maybe it's meant to be." If it was, Mari-Car reasoned, then there must be something good ahead. Her heart jumped inside her chest. She brought both hands to her chest and smiled in anticipation of what was to come.

Mari-Car did not listen to Peter John concerning the type of architecture that she'd study, however. He felt that she would be happier if she concentrated on restoration. She wanted to study green building design, like her dad.

It was true that restoration in general, and especially the restoration of buildings from the Renaissance period, fascinated her, but as his only child, she wanted her field of studies to be a continuation of her father's dream, including his dream home. It was her way of acknowledging and honoring him.

During their growing-up years, Peter John and Mari-Car had promised that they would always tell each other the truth and that they would never keep secrets from one another. So, she didn't get offended when he told her that he thought she had chosen the wrong branch of architecture, but it did confuse her a little because, intuitively, she made choices that backed his point.

For instance, she had chosen La Presentazione Hall, a restored nineteenth-century building.

She embraced the amazing feeling that enveloped her when she walked its halls, its cloister, or its interior garden, where she spent most of her free moments studying, drawing, or just drowning in the well-being that it brought her.

She also loved to sit on one of the benches around the ancient well and allow her imagination to go back in time. So yes, she was a little confused. She was undeniably attracted by a historical building that had been restored—just like Peter John had pointed out.

One of her most frequent stops was the quaint prayer chapel on the first floor. It summoned one to silent reflection and prayer. She often pulled out the white-and-gold rosary given to her by her great-grandmother for her First Communion; through it, she felt connected to her forebears.

But Mari-Car still insisted on green architecture, ignoring the inner struggle that during her quiet moments subtly made its presence known by way of a vague pang of loss when she tried to embrace her father's dream.

Mari-Car settled in a single room with a private bathroom, her only nonnegotiable.

"It sounds perfect, Mari-Car—no downside from what you're telling me. Can't wait to go!" Peter John told her from underneath his blanket-made tent on his bed.

"Well…" She had gone out to the courtyard and wrapped herself in a blanket on one of the benches around the ancient well, laptop leaning against her bent knees. This was her favorite spot to be, and he was her favorite person to be with during her downtime after studying in the evening. "The only downside, if you can call it that," she continued, "is the distance from the dorm to the Bovisa campus where I take my classes. I'll talk to my mom about using some of the money that my grandparents gave me to buy a small car. Otherwise, I get around the Como area by Vespa."

"Well, how far is the campus?"

"About forty minutes by car. Otherwise, it's either by bus or by train—that takes up a lot of time!"

"Mari-Car, my smart one, why didn't you find a residence hall closer to the campus, then?"

"I fell in love with the historical feel of the residence hall and the beauty of Como and the surrounding areas—" She stopped abruptly. "I know exactly what you're doing—you're trying to confuse me!"

"Hmmm, it sounds like the girl would feel more at home restoring buildings than concentrating on the environmental qualities of buildings…not that that's not important. I'm talking about where and how I see you, my smart one, my one and only."

Many a night, she got carried away talking about her classes, the dorm, Lake Como and its stunning scenery… and when she stopped, she realized that Peter John had fallen asleep. She'd whisper at the image on her computer, "You are the best friend anyone could ever ask for. What would I do without you?"

CHAPTER 21
OZAN, PART ONE

"Allah, Allah, we have perfectly good universities right here in Istanbul. Why do you need to go abroad for another degree? Plus, your father needs you. He's tired; he needs someone to run the company, to take over when the time comes."

Ozan stopped packing his suitcase and turned around to bend down and kiss Ceyda *Hanim*, his grandmother.

"*Babaanne canim* [my dear grandmother], aren't you putting too much pressure on your only grandson, ah? Deniz-Mare is very capable. What century do we live in? Where is it written that the son needs to take over the father's business, ah? Show me!" Ozan, hands on his waist, raised his voice as he said the last phrase.

"You know your sister will get married someday, maybe not too far away, and we wouldn't want a stranger running the family business," came the reply.

"*Babaanne* [grandmother], if it was my sister's husband, he would not be a stranger, would he? Plus, is there something I should know about my sister?"

"*Hayir, Allah korusun* [No, God forbid], but your sister is young and beautiful, accomplished…"

Deniz-Mare was their youngest grandchild. When she was born, her deep-blue eyes reminded Meryem, her mother, of the sea back home. It seemed like the name Deniz— "sea" in Turkish—was made for that baby. Mare— "sea" in Italian—was given in honor of her country of birth. Both children were born in Italy, during the three years that Mehmet, their father, studied for his MBA.

CHAPTER 22
KADER {FATE}

Meryem and Mehmet had married young. Their families had been business partners at the time, and the kids seemed to be in love, especially Meryem, who pursued Mehmet relentlessly at the university that they both attended. She was in the faculty of art history; he was pursuing his undergraduate degree in business.

Mehmet graduated two years before her, but this did not deter Meryem, who, in connivance with her mother-in-law, Ceyda *Hanim*, convinced both Mehmet and Ozan *Bey*, his father, that it was the right time for marriage.

Mehmet did not need much convincing. He was young and somewhat timid, and Meryem was beautiful, desirable, and came from a powerful, wealthy family who supported their choice. So, Mehmet and Meryem were married in a lavish wedding ceremony that united two powerful Istanbul families, the Ulusoys and the Yildirims.

Almost immediately, Meryem interrupted her studies, and the young couple moved to Italy, where Mehmet would finish his graduate studies.

Unfortunately, Italy did not turn out to be as glamorous as Meryem had imagined; Mehmet spent most of his time studying. She was young and bored and now wished she had not discontinued her studies. She was intelligent and enjoyed learning.

In retrospect, with so much time to think, she wished that she would have waited until she graduated to make such a huge commitment. And why was it that she had been the one to give up her studies to follow Mehmet? He could have waited for her to finish before leaving Istanbul, she began to reason, rancor's ugly head finding fertile ground in her mind. The more she allowed her mind free rein, the more frustrated she got, mostly with herself—*she* had made the choice to stop her studies and follow Mehmet.

Thank God that *kader* (fate) intervened. She found out they were expecting their first child; the young couple was thrilled, and now she thought of nothing but her child. She used every single moment of her nine months of pregnancy to get prepared for her baby.

Meryem created a beautiful space for her child, filled it with children's books, music, furniture, stuffed animals. She painted a mural with the breathtaking scenery of the Como Province countryside: beautiful Lake Como at the foot of the magnificent Alps with peaks blanketed with snow, cypress and palm trees, hilly vineyards with lake and mountain views, impressive mansions at the edge of the lake enfolded in flowering trees.

It was stunning. Mehmet complimented Meryem on her beautiful rendition. It was the last time that she would experienced genuine interest from her husband.

When Ozan was born, both parents and grandparents were ecstatic, especially the grandfather whose name was passed on to his first grandson. Italy had become a second home for the grandparents, who encouraged Mehmet to work hard and fast to finish his degree and get back to run the family business in Istanbul.

So Mehmet plunged into his studies, allowing no time for Meryem and Ozan. Meryem had told him that she felt lonely and that she and Ozan needed to spend more time with him.

"Your son barely knows you, Mehmet. You leave before he gets up and return when he's in for the night—seven days a week!"

Mehmet either ignored or purposely put aside her words and concerns. It was difficult for Meryem to figure out what he was thinking; she wondered if this distant father and husband situation would last the entire year and a half he had left before he finished his master's.

He ignored her pleas and, in fact, became even more distant.

However, Mehmet had miscalculated, underestimated, or deliberately disregarded Meryem's emotional state.

They spent so much time apart that Meryem, overwhelmed with the interminable tasks of—for all practical purposes—an abandoned young mother, decided to join a young group of expats from all over the world that were in Italy to either study or work.

The group was called "Home Away from Home." They got together for picnics, visits to the vineyards and museums, day trips to Milan to attend the theater or the fabulous fashion shows.

With her new friends, Meryem enjoyed everything that made Italy, and the Como region, an amazing place to live and visit. Her involvement with the expat group benefited both Mehmet and Meryem. He could concentrate fully on his studies without feeling the pressure of having to devote time to Meryem and Ozan; she could assuage the boredom and frustration of the daily home routine and caring for a small child alone.

The truth was that without any outside stimulation, Meryem had felt her mind eroding, like her essence was wasting away.

Her beauty, charisma, self-confidence, and gregarious personality allowed Meryem to make friends quickly within the group. She was especially drawn to the few young mothers whose husbands had been sent to Italy for work reasons. They shared picnics in the parks, luncheons at each other's homes, and at times, left the children at one of their homes with a shared nanny while they visited a local pub for a girls' night out.

It was during one of these outings that fate walked in disguised as Luca Grimaldi, all charming, tall, dark, blue-eyed, and handsome. Why he chose to stand next to her and not the others—*kader*, Meryem would say; coincidence, Luca would say; opportunity, the logical minds would say. But Meryem had not talked so much in about one and a half years, since Ozan was born. Everything that had been bottled up inside came pouring out: her family back in Istanbul, her decision to move to Italy, her loneliness from being away from everything familiar, her boredom being left at home caring for her young son, and even her emotionally distant husband.

"Why are you still here? Why are you putting up with such loneliness?"

Meryem took a long time to answer. The conversation had been so engaging that she had forgotten about everything else. She finally looked up, watery eyes obvious, the attraction undeniable. Luca brought her tremoring chin closer with his index finger and slowly bent down to kiss her lips. She stopped him, delicately placing two fingers on his.

"I don't know why I am still here, but I am married and have a son, as I have said; he is one and a half years old. My husband is finishing his MBA at the university."

With that, Meryem opened her bag, took out money, put it on the counter, and left. Luca's eyes followed her until she disappeared into the crowd. She took a cab, called the nanny to have the baby ready, stopped at her friend's home to pick up Ozan, and went home.

Mehmet was sound asleep when they got home. *It didn't occur to him to call me, to see where or how we were*, she thought.

The next day he was gone by the time she got up. *Not a note, not a phone call*, she thought—again. Meryem stayed in all day and waited for Mehmet to come home. She had fixed him a lovely pasta dish with fish cacciatore and hearty Italian bread. The whole apartment smelled delicious; she was excited to see his reaction.

He walked in at around eight, looked down at the beautiful table set with Vietri handcrafted dinnerware and flatware, white linen tablecloth and napkins, and hand-cut crystal wine goblets. She was just finishing lighting the second of the two slim ivory candles. Meryem had bought the special dinnerware because, besides being beautiful, its manufacturers supported the artisans in the Amalfi coast of Italy, and she was a lover of the arts. She looked radiant, was proud of the beauty she had created, and waited with anticipation for the beautiful words she was sure would come out of his mouth.

"I ate already—I am really sorry." The words came out haltingly and had a wearisome tone to them. Meryem could not pinpoint what she felt—was it despondency, desolation, dejection? But the feeling traveled down from her head, leaving lifelessness in each part it touched. It took her a few moments. She rested one hand on the back of a chair for support, but she did regain her composure—and then lost it!

"You ate already? You ate already? Did it not cross your mind to call me, Mehmet? 'Meryem, how is your day going? Meryem, how is our son doing? Meryem, can we have dinner together?' I mean, you're busy, but according to you, you did take time to eat." The barrage continued. "Did you even notice when Ozan got his first tooth, when he took his first step, when he said his first word?" She followed him to their bedroom.

He turned around wearily and said, "Meryem, what do you want from me?"

"I want a husband; I want a phone call, a note, a conversation, and at night, at least a hug." Her voice broke.

He looked at her, thought that she definitely was beautiful, but proceeded to close his hands into tight fists, then rolled his eyes, tightened his lips, and the only words that he could muster were, "Meryem, you overwhelm me."

She stood still, her eyes filled with tears because she understood that Mehmet didn't mean that he was overwhelmed by her beauty or her thoughtfulness or her cooking or her mothering skills but that what these piercing words meant was that he was tired of her. The words cut to her core. She felt alone, heartbroken, and invisible.

CHAPTER 23
TWO PINK LINES

Feeling unappreciated, undesirable, and unwanted, the next day Meryem arranged for the group's nanny to come to her home.

She bought a bottle of expensive wine, dressed to make heads turn, left the house, and knocked on Luca's door.

He answered the door in jeans, unbuttoned white linen shirt sleeves rolled up to just above the elbows, and bare feet. Beautiful operatic music was playing in the background.

She had gotten his address from a mutual friend from the expat group but had not told him she was coming. *I'll leave it to fate*, she had thought—*if it's meant to be, it's meant to be.*

She was almost hoping he would not answer the door. That would have made the problem that she was about to create so much smaller. But when Luca answered the door, she knew her problem would be huge—and costly.

The relationship continued for about three months—no promises, no commitment of any kind. By mutual choice, Luca never met Ozan or Mehmet. Theirs became a sweet, satisfying, very private, very tender, very loving—often explosive and uninhibited—mutually faithful affair.

The two pink lines on the test strip revealed the results of the rapturous intimate moments she and Luca had shared.

Meryem was reflective, her soul disquieted about the possible consequences but definitely not regretful; rather, infinitely grateful for the priceless gift that had resulted from their exquisite and unforgettable love.

She knew that she had some difficult decisions ahead of her; the most heart-wrenching of them all was whether to tell Luca.

He was still a student and his family had plans for him to go to Stanford University in Northern California and return with an MBA to run the small vineyard that they owned in the Como region.

They had spoken of their plans during one of their introspective moments after having made supremely intense love to each other: He had ruined her plan to join him in the shower when he quickly got out to answer the persistent ring from the phone in his study. He grabbed a towel, wrapped it around his waist, and dripping water all the way to his desk, picked up the phone and sank into the oversize chair. "I've been waiting to hear from you," she heard him say into the mouthpiece.

She decided to still get in the shower even though being there alone did not satisfy what her body was craving, but she knew it was only a matter of time before her fire was quenched; she schemed every move that followed.

Meryem came out of the shower wrapped in a towel without taking time to dry. She slowly walked to Luca's office hoping that he had finished his phone call; her wet body, inside and out, was screaming for his touch.

She stood at the doorway, damp, luscious hair draping her shoulders. Luca was still on the phone, but his piercing eyes, imbued with desire that turned them from sky-blue to cobalt at the sight of her, drew her in. Her large, green-speckled, hazel eyes basked in the sight of his still-damp, disheveled hair, droplets of water coursing down his forehead and temples. Meryem had not seen anything so sexy since…since…well, since the last time she was here, she thought.

She went in and leaned on the edge of the desk facing him. He reached up and held her chin between his thumb and the crook of his index finger, then began to run his thumb along her lower lip while still on the phone discussing the purchase of a vineyard with the family lawyer.

Slowly, she guided the hand that caressed her lips down to her neck, where he allowed it to linger, his thumb continuing its sensual play with her lips. She covered his hand with hers, her twisting movements causing her towel to come undone, unveiling her full breasts. Now with insistency, she guided his hand to her breasts; her nipples hardened, and her breathing became erratic. She tilted her head back and closed her eyes to savor the sensation that his hand brought her. Soft moans joined her agitated breathing.

Seeing her heightened state of pleasure, Luca pulled her to his lap, bringing his mouth where his hand had been.

"Yes, buy it!" he yelled into the phone, leaving off his mouthful only long enough to say those three words. Meryem, not ready to suspend even for a second the immense pleasure she was experiencing, brusquely brought Luca's head back down and steered her breasts one at a time to be engulfed by his mouth once again.

"Should we buy it at the asking price?" the lawyer asked, surprised; Luca never paid the asking price.

Unable to resist the increasing bulge that pulsated demandingly beneath her, Meryem finished opening the towel that partially covered it and exposed it completely. She now performed on it the same magic that Luca had performed on her breasts. He writhed in pleasure and agony.

"God, yes!" Now he was screaming the words. "You're the boss, Luca." The lawyer hung up quickly and Luca dropped the phone and left it hanging off the edge of the desk.

Unable to restrain himself any longer, he tenderly cupped her face in his hands. She looked at him and saw the plea in his eyes; she came up and straddled him, both moaning loudly as they luxuriated in pleasure. It was a melding of bodies, breaths, rhythms, sounds…both in a frenzy to quench the torturous pleasure that imprisoned them yet hoping to remain captive forever.

The university, he had told her, was less than a two-hour drive from Napa Valley. "The landscaping is awe-inspiring, the possibilities seem limitless, it makes me believe that everything is possible when I find myself amid those spectacular vineyards. I don't think Americans appreciate what they have."

The Grimaldi family was well-known in the area. They were said to be distant relatives of the royal family of Monaco but avoided the spotlight and had been successful attaining their privacy, one of their most valued accomplishments, according to Luca.

If it became known, and there was no way to avoid it, that their sole heir was having a child with a married woman, it would unquestionably disrupt the privacy that the family had achieved with so much effort.

Then there was the question of religion. Luca and his family were devout Catholics. She didn't know how, or *if*, they would accept a grandchild from a Muslim family. On the other hand, she pondered the fairness of depriving the child of either parent's family and culture.

Telling Mehmet was deeply painful. Although they both were aware that they had been living separate lives, seeing the fruit of her actions sent sharp arrows into both of their hearts. She realized that he had been having an affair at least since the night that she had waited for him with dinner on the table in their candlelit dining room.

Meryem was brought back to that night and to his cutting words: "You overwhelm me." She still visibly winced at the thought of them. He didn't like who she was, and she could never be who he liked.

The complete silence between her and Mehmet lasted for days. Neither rushed to speak about a solution, but Meryem felt at ease in Italy, less pressure to act according to cultural and family norms. In her perfect world, she and Mehmet would quietly go through a divorce, and she would make Italy home for herself and the children. After all, Mehmet spent little time with his son as it was, and he could certainly visit whenever he wished.

But there was no perfect world for either of them. Mehmet's parents called and said that they missed their grandson too much and were on their way to visit. When they said, "On our way," they meant it almost literally. They arrived the following day.

"*Oğlum* [son], when are you going to be done with those studies of yours? Ozan needs to grow up with his family." After the warm greeting and embrace from Mehmet's parents, those were the first words out of his father's mouth.

Meryem showed up at Luca's one last time. She had sent him a message saying that things were "complicated at the moment" and that she would stay away for a few weeks. Barely five months pregnant when she knocked on his door, she could still hide her growing belly, but she knew she did not have a lot of time to do so. He stood at the door in jeans, shirtless and barefoot.

"No wine?" he asked with a mischievous smile on his face.

She shook her head softly and as if in slow motion, took a few steps forward, rested her head on his bare chest, wrapped her arms around his neck, and cupping the back of his head softly in her hand, whispered, "I want you to know that I haven't regretted one single minute of the thousands that I've spent with you."

After a long moment—though to Meryem, not long enough—she gently broke the embrace, held his face in her hands, looked deeply into his eyes with tears running profusely down her cheeks, and kissed him tenderly, long, and deep. She turned around without saying a word and left.

Luca stood at the door until Meryem was out of sight, slowly turned around, and walked inside, closing the door behind him, then leaning on it for a long time. His heart ached. At that moment, he felt and knew that he was closing not only a door but also an entire important, sweet, and unforgettable chapter of his life.

This realization pierced his heart, but he understood that her life was complicated, especially given the fact that she was from a culture that, in his mind, was so unforgiving. Behind closed doors, he grabbed his heart and tears spilled, running down his cheeks. *So this is what impossible or forbidden love feels like*, he thought. It surprised him how completely he had loved her.

CHAPTER 24
THE RETURN

Meryem withdrew officially from the group of expats and secluded herself. No one pressured her to come back; most knew of her and Luca's relationship and suspected that that was the reason for her distancing herself, and that she needed some space.

A few months later, shortly after Deniz-Mare's birth and immediately after Mehmet finished his MBA, the family of four returned to Istanbul to a lavish welcome.

Mehmet and Meryem had requested that his parents wait to meet their granddaughter on their return. They acquiesced but did not understand the reason for the unusual request. Ceyda *Hanim* was especially hurt because Meryem's mother, Neriman *Hanin* was allowed to fly to Italy for the birth of her granddaughter.

"She is as much my granddaughter as she is hers," a teary-eyed Ceyda *Hanim* had complained to her husband.

Ozan *Bey*, moved by his wife's tears and maybe softened by the birth of his new grandchild, did something totally out of character. He took her in his arms and patted her back, comforting his wife until the tears and sobs subsided.

"Let's thank Allah that the child is healthy; they'll be here in a few days, *canim* [darling], and then you'll see your granddaughter every day."

His words seemed to calm Ceyda *Hanim*. She reluctantly walked out of the warm embrace of her husband and went into the bathroom to wash her face.

The glamorous welcoming took place at the Grand Hall of Ulusoy Holdings. It was reserved for important events, and the return of Ozan Ulusoy's oldest son with his perfect family merited its use.

It was attended by many members of Istanbul high society. It was a red-carpet affair, as well as a sort of fashion show. As the rich and famous arrived in limousines and other expensive cars, a slew of reporters waited to flood them with questions: "Who designed your dress?" "Are you engaged?" "Has the wedding date been set?" "How do you keep in shape?" "Is it true that the value of your company's shares has gone down—or up?" Then they spotted Mehmet and Meryem's car, and everyone else suddenly seemed unimportant. Some of the guests were left halfway through answering their questions.

The crowd of insistent reporters pressed so hard against the door of the car that security was summoned to disperse them so that the famous couple could get out and make its way through. The reporters, contained by a team of security agents, lined up on both sides of the red carpet and shouted questions and well wishes: "Welcome back to the motherland." "Congratulations on the new family addition." "In what direction will you take Ulusoy Holdings?" "Will you expand to other markets? "Will you diversify?" Etcetera, etcetera.

Meryem looked stunning in her long, sleeveless, emerald-green gown. The scooped neckline formed soft folds that rested just below the rise of her firm breasts. She displayed a diamond necklace given to her by her parents-in-law after the birth of their granddaughter Deniz-Mare. The luxurious gown emphasized the green specks in Meryem's hazel eyes.

She responded to the well-wishers with elegance, smiles, soft waves of the hands, and slight bows of the head. Mehmet walked forward with a stern look on his face without acknowledging the crowd. Once inside the hall, Mehmet met and shook hands with colleagues and acquaintances, retaining a sober look.

The truth was that after their return to Istanbul, both Meryem and, even more so, Mehmet had changed. He had always been more of an introvert, but now he had become withdrawn and even more distant. He performed his duties as CFO of Ulusoy Holdings impeccably. He provided liberally for the physical needs of his wife and children, but their emotional needs were filled by their mother and grandparents.

The relationship between Mehmet and Meryem had been left in a sort of marriage limbo. The silence that appeared on the day that Meryem divulged her second pregnancy to Mehmet never left. It created a gulf between them that neither knew how to approach; plus, the other side of that gulf seemed unreachable for both. So avoidance emerged as the easiest, less painful, less conflictive option.

How to live in such a state of suspension?

Mehmet buried himself in his work and travel while Meryem focused entirely on the children and the managing of the household alongside her mother-in-law, Ceyda *Hanim*.

CHAPTER 25
MERYEM FINDS HERSELF

About a year after their return to Istanbul, once again, Meryem began to experience that familiar feeling of what she could only describe as "erosion of the mind." She felt like a plant that had been deprived of water, sun, and love.

So, to the chagrin of her in-laws and the indifference of Mehmet, Meryem decided to finish her degree in art history. She ignored all the, "You don't need a degree, you have more than enough money," "You can get a position at the company," "You're a married woman; you have other responsibilities" comments.

To her ears, they sounded like faraway noise; she held firm to her decision and returned to the university.

Meryem plunged into her studies. For the next two years, she focused on finishing her education and taking care of her two children. She adored them both, but she looked at Deniz-Mare as the fruit of the sweetest, truest, purest love she had ever experienced and tried to find in her all the characteristics of her father, whom she had silently sworn never to forget.

No one congratulated Meryem on her accomplishment. She didn't even tell anyone about the graduation ceremony. However, when her name was called and she walked across the stage to receive her diploma, she spotted her father-in-law, Ozan Ulusoy, flanked by her two young children, now two and four years old, enthusiastically clapping.

After the ceremony, the children ran to embrace their mother. Her father-in-law took her by the shoulders and looked into her eyes.

"*Tebrik ederim, Kizim* [Congratulations, my daughter]."

She looked at the elder Ozan, wide-eyed. "How did you know?"

"The announcement came to the company. You accomplished something great, *Kizim*. I am so sorry for my lack of support, but from now on, I am behind you no matter what you decide to do. Now, let's the four of us celebrate."

At the kid-friendly restaurant, while the children enjoyed their burgers and fries along with a tall glass of *ayran*, father and daughter-in-law talked.

"Ozan *Babam* [my father Ozan], I've already signed up for master's classes. With my master's, I can obtain a position as a curator at one of our better museums. I'm fascinated by art and history…"

"*Kizim*, you know that you do not need to work, and if you feel like you would like to, you can get a position at Ulusoy Holdings." Meryem opened her mouth to reply, but he raised his right hand, palm toward her, signaling that he wasn't done speaking. "However, if you want to pursue your own career, I repeat, I am behind you."

She got up from her chair, went to him and hugged him tightly, letting out a sigh of relief along with tears that had been held in for too long.

"I feel like a heavy layer has been peeled off my shoulders; I've carried that burden alone for too long, and I have needed a shoulder to lean on. I found a strong one. Thank you, *Babam*."

"I am here, *Kizim*. I am here."

Meryem began pursuing her advanced degree in art history immediately after graduation, which she looked at merely as a slight pause between degrees.

Her complete focus on attaining her master's paid off.

She naturally skipped all the extracurricular college activities that younger students normally engaged in—sports, pubs, trips abroad, etcetera. This smart path allowed her time to take extra courses toward the completion of her advanced degree.

After a few years, the partnership between the two illustrious families went sour. The elders had very different philosophies about running a business. Ozan *Bey* was more family- and workers-oriented. Zeki Yildirim, Meryem's father, was more ambitious and believed in a clear line of separation between workers and bosses.

The news media devoted a lot of coverage to the breaking up of the partnership. Ulusoy Holdings needed to go through this hindrance as smoothly as possible without losing any of its partners. The right person to help them navigate this precarious path was right in front of them.

Meryem, who now worked at the Istanbul Archeological Museum, knew how to convert a mountain into a molehill. She did that for a living, acquiring donors for the museum, choosing exhibitions, getting prized loans from other world-renowned museums. She accomplished these amazing feats without affecting the smooth daily routine of the famous museum and without ever being in the headlines, except to announce the valued acquisitions or loans obtained by the distinguished institution.

When her father-in-law requested Meryem's assistance in helping Ulusoy Holdings navigate through the difficult breaking-up process, she didn't hesitate. He had made her career possible; now she'd step up to help where she was needed.

Meryem took advantage of the fact that she was the daughter of Zeki Yildirim, so she spoke to the news media with confidence and poise, emphasizing—and demonstrating with her presence—that the unity of the two families continued to be strong. The disbandment of the two huge holdings proceeded uneventfully.

"*Kizim*, I know that you have outstanding status with the museum, but Ulusoy Holdings will always have the doors open for you whenever you want to come and work for us." Meryem answered him with a hug.

She turned to leave, then decided to add to her answer. "*Babacim* [Daddy], I'm not just grateful to you for my career; I am even more grateful for your closeness to my children, especially to your namesake, Ozan." She hugged him again and whispered in his ear, "I pray my son is worthy of the name he bears."

The older man held her shoulders lovingly, looked at her with tear-filled eyes, and only said, "*Tesekkur ederim, Kizim* [Thank you, my daughter]."

CHAPTER 26
OZAN PART TWO

The discussion between Ceyda *Hanim* and her grandson continued.

"Your grandfather—"

"That's another thing," Ozan interrupted. "My grandfather is perfectly healthy. So is my father. Why do I have to disrupt my studies at this time?" His exasperation and frustration were obvious as he lifted both hands up and swept them back as if pushing away his grandmother's words.

He continued to pack with his grandmother following so close behind that every time he turned around, he had to walk around her to avoid a collision.

"You know that your father is not good with clients; he prefers to be left alone in his office and work the numbers. Plus, your grandfather and your father…well, you know they don't communicate well."

Ozan stopped what he was doing, looked seriously at his grandmother, and said, "And do you know anyone who communicates well with my father?"

Ceyda *Hanim* could see that she wasn't getting anywhere, so she changed strategies. She knew how to get Ozan to do what she wanted.

"Your grandfather is not perfectly healthy." The words came out slowly, softly.

Ozan froze in place. He slowly, robotically turned around, still holding bunched-up socks and underwear in his hands. If he had a weakness, it was his beloved *dede* (grandfather). He looked down at his grandmother, then looked past her to his bed and threw the clothes that he was holding. He grabbed his grandmother's shoulders and guided her slowly to the bed, sat her down, and sat facing her, his right hand on her shoulder and covering both of her hands, which were resting on her lap, with his left hand.

"Now, *Babaanne* [Grandmother], speak calmly and clearly, please. What's wrong with my grandfather? I just saw him; he seemed perfectly fine."

"It's his heart. The doctor said he has an enlarged heart. More tests will be needed to see what's causing it. Meanwhile, your grandfather has shortness of breath, heart palpitations… the doctor told him to avoid stress and gave him medication."

They sat silently on the edge of the bed for a long while. Then, Ceyda *Hanim*, having planted the seed that she knew would produce the fruit of guilt that would keep her grandson home, got up and left the room without saying a word.

Ozan remained motionless, lost in his thoughts. His whole world revolved around his *dede*. His father Mehmet was stern and distant, but Ozan never minded that because he had his *dede*. He taught him everything—to make and fly kites, to fish, to swim, to sail, to ride and care for horses.

They were friends with all the fishermen around the seashore, where since he was a child, his grandfather would take him to eat fresh fish and drink chai (tea) while *Dede* and the fishermen talked about the old days. He listened to all the stories with fascination. They always left too soon, he felt.

"Let's go, *Oğlum* [Son]." His *dede* always used the same phrase when it was time to go. "We have schoolwork waiting to be done." His grandfather had a list of excuses when it was time to leave. Sometimes it was homework, other times it was dinner, visiting the holdings, going to the local mosque—it didn't matter to him; he just knew it was his grandfather's clue that it was time to go.

When he protested, his *dede* thought he had the right answer.

"Otherwise, you'll end up being a fisherman all your life." But to Ozan, it sounded like a great idea, and he remembered the time when he was about five and he looked up at his *dede* after being threatened with being a fisherman all his life and enthusiastically asked, "Can I do that?"

His grandfather looked down and met the big, slightly-elongated blue eyes, a perfect copy of his own. "Of course, you can, *Birtanem* [my one and only]—after you grow up, finish school, go to the university, and run your company."

"What company?"

"Ulusoy Holdings."

"Is that *my* company?"

"It sure is, My Lion."

It had almost become a game. When he was growing up, they had practically the same conversation every time they left the seashore. But as he grew up, he learned two things: that someday he'd run his own company and that he'd have to wait a long time to become a full-time fisherman.

Was it time for him to run the company, really? He just didn't think so. He hoped not; he had so much that wanted to do before then…he continued sitting on the side of his bed lost in his thoughts.

Ozan just could not imagine life without his *dede*. If his grandfather was sick, he'd stay by his side. As this thought entered his mind, he got up and slowly began to empty the suitcases and put everything back in drawers and in the closet.

Two soft knocks got him out of his reverie. The bedroom door opened, and the strong, imposing figure of his grandfather walked in.

"What are you doing, *Oğlum*?"

"I decided to stay a little longer, *Dede*. Italy is not going anywhere, and when the time is right, I'll go and do that master's in green architecture…in fact, they'll probably have discovered new technology in a year or so."

But his *dede* knew him too well: underneath the overenthusiastic speech, there was a subtle note of disappointment.

"*Oğlum*, you know that your *dede* knows you better than anyone else and that you can't hide anything from him."

Suddenly, Ozan broke into sobs and threw himself into his *dede*'s arms, hugging him tightly. His grandfather was surprised, and his eyes also flooded with tears as he patted his grandson on the back and tried to speak words of comfort into his ears, although he didn't know what to comfort him about.

After a while, Ozan broke the embrace and led his grandpa to sit on the bed, then sat very close to him.

"Listen, *Dede*, everything is going to be fine. I'll be close to you the whole time, and we'll go together to see the best doctors in Turkey and beyond." He put both arms up and made a wide circle when he said the word "beyond."

His grandfather took him by the shoulders and asked, "What is this all about, *Oğlum*? What's wrong?"

"Your heart condition—I know about your heart condition."

A dark, serious look came over his grandfather. He knew his wife had used his condition to keep her grandson close, to prevent him from his dream of going to study abroad.

He got up from the bed, went to the doorway, and began shouting his wife's name, "Ceyda! Ceyda! Ceyda *Hanım*!"

"Ozan! Stop your shouting."

Both grandfather and grandson lifted their eyes toward the familiar, commanding voice. The imposing, erect figure stood at the top of the stairs wearing a *hijab* whose soft, rich fabric draped loosely around her neck and shoulders. A beautiful brooch with small emeralds and citrine gemstones adorned the hijab where its soft folds met at the right shoulder.

Meryem also came rushing out of her bedroom and stood at the top of the stairs, wearing a concerned look.

"What's wrong, *Baba*?" she asked, rushing down the stairs past Ceyda *Hanım*, concerned that her father-in-law had suffered a heart attack.

But he hadn't. What she met was an angry look directed at his wife, who had slowly begun to descend down the long stairway. When she finally stood in front of him, without a trace of fear or concern on her face but rather a subtle look of superiority, he finally said, "How dare you use me and my health to prevent my grandson from achieving his dreams?"

Ceyda *Hanım*'s piercing hazel eyes could cut right through to one's soul. She fixed her look on her husband and met an equally piercing mien. Her words were firm and as cutting as her look.

"My grandson is not going anywhere! All the men in this family have studied in Istanbul or Ankara or Izmir, and they are great, strong, well-educated men. There are plenty of places to study right here in our own country—no need to go anywhere else. Look what happened to your younger son, to Osman: he went abroad, found a foreign bride, and ended up divorced, alone, and lonely. He even abandoned the family and the family business."

"Ceyda, woman, do not test me! Do not go there! If you hadn't interfered so much in our son's marriage, today Osman would be a happily married man and close to his family. I made a grave error, staying back while I watched you destroy our son's life and marriage, but I will not let you do the same thing to my grandson. I will not let you hold him back from his dreams… and this time…" His look cut into hers, so sharp and deep that if indeed a look could kill, they'd be carrying her to the funeral home then and there. "This time," Ozan *Bey* continued, "I will not stand back!" He shouted so hard that his face turned the color of pomegranate, and the veins on his neck swelled to the point that those present feared they would burst.

Meryem and Ozan were flabbergasted during the exchange but remained silent. Meryem had run to the kitchen to get a pitcher of water and some glasses for whoever needed them. Deniz-Mare had left early for the university. And Mehmet, as always, had left for work before breakfast.

This was the first time that the couple had spoken out loud about Osman. He was the younger of their two sons. Ozan had never met him, although he had seen pictures of him once.

One night, when he was about seven years old, he was afraid. As he often did when he felt afraid or lonely at night, he made his way to his *dede*'s bedroom.

The huge bed had more than enough room for him. As a child, he believed that the size of his grandfather's bed was so they could both fit. Ozan climbed up and snuggled tightly against his grandfather. Ozan *Bey*, familiar with this routine, encircled him with his long, strong arms and continued sleeping.

The next day, little Ozan was allowed to sleep late.

Ozan *Bey* had gone to the office, and as she did every day, his grandmother was busy in her home office, which connected to her own bedroom. Ozan never knew exactly what his *babaanne* did there, but she spent a lot of time talking on the phone and running things from her workplace.

On that day so many years before, Ozan got out of bed and began to explore the familiar, spacious, ornate bedroom. Inside one of his grandpa's dresser drawers, he found a beautifully carved, small, wooden box. He took it out, carried it to the bed, and opened it.

There were some old pictures of people that he did not recognize, but he came across one that, even as a youngster, he could identify. His grandfather had his arms around two younger men—one was clearly Mehmet, his father. He figured the other one was his uncle, about whom he had only heard whispers.

He had dark hair and elongated blue eyes—an unmistakable Ulusoy characteristic. Ozan stared long and hard at that picture, wondering what had happened to his uncle but somehow knowing that he shouldn't ask. He got out of bed and went to put the box back where he found it, never mentioning to anyone his moment of discovery nor hearing about his uncle out loud until just now, when his grandfather brought him up in a fit of anger.

Ozan was unable to hide his astonishment as he looked at his grandfather, who suddenly brought his hand to his chest and gasped. In a matter of seconds, Ozan was at his side, walking his grandfather to the broad, soft couch while screaming for an ambulance.

"*Yavaş, Oğlum, yavaş* [easy, Son, easy], I'm fine."

Ozan would have none of it. He looked around and commanded an ambulance. "*Hemen!*" he shouted. "Now!"

The almost imperceptible smirk on Ceyda *Hanim*'s face went unnoticed by everyone except her husband, who through squinting eyes, due to the pain on his chest, slowly did a panoramic sweep with his eyes of everyone standing around him. He was thinking clearly as he lay back on the couch, unable to move.

If this is the end, he thought, *I want to carry with me one last image of my loved ones.* How could he have agreed to marry such a heartless woman was his painful thought when he came across the smirk on his wife's face, but the scanning continued.

His eyes came to rest on Ozan, who was kneeling next to him, running his hands down his cheeks and through his hair. He felt Ozan's warm tears on his face and could hear his words of comfort and despair: "You'll be alright, *Dede*; help is almost here. Don't leave me, *Dede*. Please don't leave me."

I did something right, Ozan *Bey* thought with satisfaction.

The doors of the operating room opened to allow in the gurney carrying Ozan *Bey*; they almost trapped Ozan as they closed. Images of his childhood with his grandfather came flooding into his head: waiting at the door and running into his *dede*'s open arms every day when he returned home after work, sitting on his lap to eat at dinnertime, his endless trips to the seashore to fish, eat, or just to sit and listen to the stories between his *dede* and his friends, the times his *dede* would surprise him and be waiting for him outside school. He couldn't bear to lose *Dede*.

CHAPTER 27
SHOCK

Suddenly, the automatic doors that had granted entrance to Ozan *Bey* earlier opened. Everyone got up and froze in their spot, gripped by a look of astonishment.

A tall, younger, but severe-looking doctor fixed his eyes on Ozan, who ran to meet him at the door, almost blocking his way.

"Your grandfather will be fine," were the first words out of the doctor's mouth, and they were directed expressly at Ozan. "He experienced noncardiac chest pain, probably related to a problem with the esophagus. We'll keep him here overnight for observation and will conduct more tests in the morning." The doctor saw the look of despair in the young man's eyes, and placing a hand on his shoulder, added softly, "Your grandfather will be fine."

No further words were spoken by the doctor, nor did he look in the direction of the rest of the family members, left standing frozen in place.

Everyone began to move around awkwardly, hugging each other briefly and patting each other on the back or shoulder, displaying uncomfortable smiles on their faces.

Ozan had barely been aware of what had gone on around him. He did not look back at the others to see their reactions to the doctor's words. Instead, finding it difficult to breathe, he brought his hand to his throat and quickly walked out of the building. He spotted a picnic area and began to walk in that direction. He grabbed the first bench he reached and, burying his face in his hands, began to sob uncontrollably.

Ceyda *Hanim*, who had stood up when the doctor walked out of the operating room, could not remain standing when she saw him. Her knees weakened, and with the aid of Mehmet, who had just arrived, and Meryem, she sat back in her seat, unable to stop the tremors that had overtaken her entire body. She was given water, had cologne rubbed on her palms and brought to her nose so she could inhale it, and was covered with a blanket.

"I think it's better if you go home, *Anne* [Mother]. I'll stay with *Baba*, and I know Ozan will not leave his grandfather's side." Mehmet hoped his mother would heed his words.

His wife, sensing that he needed help convincing his mother, came to his rescue.

"Come, *Anne*." Meryem reached down to help her mother-in-law get on her feet. Their driver Mete was already there to assist them.

"Ceyda *Hanim*, allow me," he told her kindly as he put one arm around the elder woman's waist and took her hand with the other to slowly walk her out of the hospital.

Ceyda *Hanim* looked up at Mete—he had grown up in their household—and gratefully said, "*Teşekkur ederim, Oğlum* [Thank you, son]."

"What thanks, Ceyda *Hanim*? My pleasure," responded Mete kindly.

No words were spoken as the two ladies rode home; no words were spoken as Mete assisted them to the front door. The door closed behind them, and Meryem opened her mouth to say something. Ceyda *Hanim* quickly put her hand up, signaling her to stop. They both walked upstairs slowly to their respective rooms.

Meryem was restless; a bombardment of thoughts attacked her mind. The four walls suffocated her. She needed some fresh air.

In the taxi, she felt more relaxed and tried to organize her thoughts. Meryem wanted her words to come out right and express what was pent-up inside, because she knew that this would probably be the only opportunity that she'd have to say what she knew she should have said years ago.

Ceyda *Hanim* slowly removed her shoes, unfastened the brooch that held her hijab in place, and put it in her jewelry box. She draped the hijab over the ornate chair facing her vanity. She lay on her bed, looking up at the ceiling, feet crossed at the ankles.

A few minutes later, after a couple of knocks, Fatma walked in with a tray of hot soup. She placed it on a small table near the foot of the bed, flanked by two comfortable chairs. Ceyda *Hanim* used it for writing, reading, and at times, to discuss family matters with Ozan *Bey*.

Fatma had been part of the family for many years and knew when to speak and when to keep silent. After leaving the soup, she left quietly.

After Fatma left, Ceyda *Hanim* waited a while, then slowly got up and made her way to where the soup was. She felt a soothing comfort eating it, like a warm hug. Fatma returned and took away the tray with the empty bowl. Ceyda *Hanim* opened the small front drawer of the table, took out a hardcover diary, opened it to a blank page, and began to write.

Each page was a letter to her son Osman. She had begun writing on these blank pages over twenty years before, the day she saw him for the last time.

Her Osman had always been different, hard to fit in a box. He admired the beauty of crystal, but he was not interested in the design and production of crystal ware. So his parents' dream that he would open stores abroad and expand the family business was not likely to come true.

Desirous to get away from the family pressure, he had gone to America to study. After almost ten years abroad, he returned with both an unwanted profession and an unwanted bride. How medicine could be an unwanted profession was hard to fathom, but it meant that Osman definitively would not be working for Ulusoy Holdings.

That was a big disappointment for Ceyda *Hanim*, whose father had started a small crystal shop in a not-very-desirable section of Istanbul. It was her husband Ozan who had expanded the business, creating many Ulusoy Crystal shops in the city and abroad.

But what was nonnegotiable for Ceyda *Hanim* was the American bride that Osman had brought. She remembered well; there wasn't one day that she did not go back to that time when her younger son came home with a foreign bride. *I will never forgive that woman for taking my son away*, she thought with clenched teeth and began to write.

CHAPTER 28
BROWN-EYED BEAUTY

Zoey extended her hand to greet her mother-in-law, who ignored the gesture and turned to her son and said right then and there, "Among the millions of women in Turkey, you couldn't find one to suit you, Osman?"

Although Zoey had practiced many phrases in Turkish, hoping to impress her new family, at the reaction of Ceyda *Hanim*, Zoey's eyes filled with tears, and her mind went blank.

Ozan *Bey*, her father-in-law, *did* extend his hand.

"*Hoşgeldin, Kizim* [Welcome, daughter]." His words were courteous.

Mehmet gave a polite, formal, "*hoş geldiniz*," and quickly left. Both he and his wife Meryem would soon depart for Italy, and the last thing he wanted, or needed, was to get involved in family issues. That was the beginning of a hellish existence in Istanbul for Zoey, one for which she was not prepared.

Zoey dreamed of a place of her own where she could paint the walls the color she wanted, get up when she wanted, eat what she wanted when she wanted. But this house was definitely Ceyda *Hanım*'s, and she had rules for everything, including how to dress for breakfast and dinner. She even controlled the hours that Osman could work so he could be at the dinner table at her appointed time.

"I'll be at your house in ten minutes, Zeynep *Hanım*." Osman's words were accompanied by great care and concern.

"You're not going anywhere!" Everyone at the table froze. Zoey was flabbergasted but was the first to speak. "Ceyda *Hanım*, that's his job. Osman is a geriatrician—his patients are elderly, they trust him, and they need him." Zoey had a pleading look on her face.

"And who are you to question my rules?!" Her words were sharp, and her disdainful look cut right through to Zoey's gentle soul. The sharp matriarch's English was quite good when she wanted to make a point.

Zoey was stunned and devastated at the harshness of Ceyda *Hanım*'s words but even more so at the hatred in her eyes when she pronounced them. Zoey looked around the table—no one said a word, no one came to her defense, not even Osman. This hurt her more than the harshness of her mother-in-law's words. Everyone just kept their heads down. She hadn't expected Ozan *Bey*, Mehmet, or Meryem to intervene on her behalf, but her Osman? She was devastated.

Osman adored his wife, and he had promised to find them a house of their own once his job at the hospital allowed it.

"Can you stand it for just a few months, my beautiful Zoey?" he had asked while lovingly caressing her face after returning from a house call. He brought her lips up and bent down to meet them with an unhurried kiss. She was left weak-kneed and nodded her head while looking into his eyes, melting him with her captivating smile. At that moment, she could endure anything for the love of her life. She had no idea what she had just committed to.

Zoey was a classic, brown-eyed, blond beauty. They had met at the university while both were studying medicine. She specialized in pediatrics, he in geriatric medicine. Their dream was to go to Istanbul and open a family practice where the old and the young would interact and be each other's therapy.

They were inseparable at the university: studied together, ate together, and shared tutoring of first-year residents. In no time, they moved in together and lived an idyllic life in their own minds and within the minds of their small circle of friends.

Osman spoke little of his family, except to mention that his mother was controlling and his father loving but incapable of or unwilling to contradict her. He had spoken of his brother Mehmet as the reserved, unsupportive type whose opinions, if he had any, no one knew. That was it.

Zoey told him about her traditional Southern upbringing. She was the youngest of the three children of Martin and Zoyla Clark. They had lost their mother when they were young. She was eight, her twin brothers ten. Zoyla had gone with grace and dignity.

Zoey was too young to realize what was happening, but in retrospect, she remembered her mom complaining of abdominal pain and nausea. Naively, Zoey had been waiting to be told that a new sibling was on its way: her brothers had been talking about wanting a new brother or sister, and she'd overheard. Unfortunately, the news was not that happy.

Zoyla had discovered her pancreatic cancer too late and had refused treatment. "I wanted to spare you all the pain of seeing me suffer," she had written in her letter left to her three children. She had left a separate letter to her husband, but only he knew what had been written on those long pages.

Zoey's dad had made sure that she attended Sunday School and took ballet and theater lessons. In high school, she had distinguished herself on the swim team. However, there was not one single day that Zoey didn't miss or think of her mom.

She cried often and felt wrapped in loneliness. Her brothers had each other; her dad, although caring and loving, kept everything to himself. Zoey did the same thing and lived with the void in her life, but she was the little princess in her home—until she finished high school.

That's when her stepmother entered their lives, and a few months later, a new princess was born. Zoey felt a deep hurt without knowing why. She had had a good, happy life, she was eighteen, and her dad deserved to be happy, she told herself as she hugged him and her brothers before leaving for college.

The night before, she had gone into the baby's nursery, caressed her rosy cheeks, and said, "Goodbye, Sue-Ellen, sweet little princess, have a happy life."

Zoey knew that she would never return to her childhood home. Her brothers had already moved out and were busy working and attending college. She entered the premed program at the University of South Carolina.

Ashley Brown was her roommate, and they were an excellent fit. They had had similar upbringings, were both interested in health care, and neither had had much interest in dating in high school.

Their friendship grew slowly, quietly, and strong during college. They both enjoyed their studies and concentrated on their careers until their fourth year, when Ashley met Peter Stewart, a handsome business major. They were from opposite sides of campus but had chosen to visit the same popular pub one Friday evening.

CHAPTER 29
THE BEGINNING AND THE END

It took Ashley all day to convince Zoey to go, but when her friend called her "sad and boring," Zoey listened; she kind of was both those things, she thought. But now she was experiencing an awkward moment, alone in a corner holding a bottle of light beer. Her friend Ashley had ditched her for the handsome, less boring Peter Stewart.

And that's when Osman stood before her, also holding a beer in his hand. His elongated blue eyes and dark hair gave him a sexy, sort of exotic look that made her legs wobble. His English had a slight accent that she couldn't place but that, to her, made him even sexier.

"I'm Osman— Osman Ulusoy," he said.

She extended her hand. "Hello, I'm Zoey Clark." The words came haltingly out of her mouth. Zoey could not take her eyes off his. She noticed he was smiling down at her—what to do next to seem confident and self-assured? She didn't know, so she turned around to leave, and Osman gently reached for her arm and turned her toward him.

"Where are you going? How do you Americans say? You had me at 'hello'?"

That's how they became inseparable.

They finished premed and started medical school at the same university. That they were both accepted seemed like *kader* to Osman and a happy coincidence to Zoey. Their dream had begun, and they spent the next five years working toward that dream.

"Why did you not answer your mother when she told you not to go on your house call?" Zoey asked Osman that night as they faced each other, heads on their pillows.

He continued to caress her hair, her cheeks, her neck, her bare shoulders, her arm, her hand, each finger. Then he spoke. "It's not easy or appropriate to go against Ceyda *Hanım*."

"This is something that I could never do, Osman, no matter how much I love you. And you know that I left everything behind to follow you, love of my life."

"I know," he answered and made intense love to her that night.

Things continued to deteriorate for Zoey, however. Although she had begun to take Turkish lessons after she met Osman, the language did not come easily for her. She had taken Spanish in high school, like everyone else, and had taken courses in French and additional Spanish in college, but they were not doing her any good now. Turkish was just entirely different; she did not even know what to relate it to.

Once they started med school, there was little time for anything else besides studying, making rounds, and assisting.

Her Turkish was far from efficient enough to set up a practice in Istanbul. So while Osman spent his days at the hospital, doing what he loved, Zoey stayed home, where she couldn't seem to do anything right in Ceyda *Hanim*'s eyes.

She had even tried to prepare some of the dishes that she and Osman enjoyed back in South Carolina but was told that as the wife of one of the heirs of Ulusoy Holdings, she was not allowed in the kitchen. So this highly professional, independent woman had been relegated to a corner of the Ulusoy mansion, where she sat all day and waited for her husband to come home at night. The following day, she'd do it all over again.

Then luck seemed to smile on her: one of her friends called from South Carolina and told her that a mutual friend was spending a year in Istanbul working as a pediatrician for the children of tourists at one of the major hotel chains. She encouraged Zoey to call her, because according to her friend, they were swamped and needed English-speaking doctors. Zoey was thrilled and couldn't wait to tell Osman about this possible opportunity.

She waited excitedly for her Osman to arrive. When she saw his car from their upstairs bedroom window, she ran downstairs and beat Fatma, the housekeeper, to the door. She opened the door, jumped on his neck, wrapped her legs around his waist, and showered him with kisses. He almost fell backward, but having kicked the door closed, leaned against it and took the time to enjoy the great welcome.

"Honey, I think I found a job!" Osman looked at her, happily anticipating her next words. "I'll be working for an international hotel chain taking care of children of tourists who might need a doctor while visiting Istanbul…I know what it's like to be in a strange place feeling sick and not being able to communicate."

"What a shame and disgrace, and in front of the help. And no! No Ulusoy woman will work outside the home or Ulusoy Holdings!" Ceyda *Hanim*'s words came out one by one as her disdainful look swept over the loving scene before her eyes. With each word, the tone of bitterness increased.

"So you *do* understand English, Ceyda *Hanim*," Zoey responded defiantly. "And I am not an 'Ulusoy woman.' I'm a Clark woman—Zoey Clark."

When she looked around, everyone was in the living room, mouths and eyes wide open, looking at her. They all stopped what they were doing, but again, no one said a word, including Osman, who stood silent before her, and his father, who had welcomed her with such kind words when she first arrived at the Ulusoy mansion. Meryem and Mehmet remained frozen in their seats with their heads down.

The housekeepers, who had been busy getting the table ready for the always-splendid evening meal, froze in place, waiting for instructions as to what to do next—continue setting the table, begin bringing dishes from the kitchen, go to the kitchen and remain there until the household solved the new daughter-in-law's problems…they opted to remain silently in place until further notice.

This time, Zoey would not forgive Osman for keeping silent while she endured verbal blows from Ceyda *Hanim*. She walked silently up the stairs and into her bedroom. Osman looked at his mother in anger but was unable to muster the courage to express his feelings. He followed his wife but remained speechless until the early hours of the morning, when exhaustion won out and he fell into a deep sleep.

Osman woke up in the early morning hours, and Zoey was gone. Not to her new job with the large hotel chain in Istanbul, but just gone. She had left a letter for him.

You are, and always will be, the love of my life. Leaving the place that I considered home to follow you was a very small price to pay to be with you. The only true love that I have ever known—and somehow, I also know that you are the only love that I will ever know.

But, My Love, I could never compromise the person that I am, even for a love as big and intense as ours. If I did, I would lose respect for myself, and that, I could never do. It would mean that I would be no more.

Please do not follow or look for me. I understand that our cultures are worlds apart, and in our case, those worlds will never meet. But please know that all these years, I have not seen any other world because you have been my only world.

All my love,
Zoey

Osman finished reading the letter, and he dropped to his knees in sobs. How long was he on the floor? The warmth of the sun's rays coming through his bedroom window hinted that it had been a long time. After his tears dried up, he felt anger rise within him. He got to his feet, packed a small suitcase, and lifelessly began his descent to the main floor. Everyone was gathered at the breakfast table, seemingly enjoying the abundant, elaborate breakfast, although the only sound came from the eating utensils making contact with the porcelain dinnerware.

Ceyda *Hanim* looked up at him and gave an overenthusiastic, "*Gunaydin, Oğlum* [Good morning, son]."

She had seen her "ex-daughter-in-law" leave that same morning, when it was still dark, and counted it a victory. What she didn't count on was the high cost that came with it.

Osman walked to the table and stood in front of his mother. He looked down at her, directly in the eye. The disdain surpassed the look his mother had directed at his Zoey the night before.

CHAPTER 30
THE PRICE OF VICTORY

"I know you think that by chasing my wife away, you have won a great victory, Ceyda *Hanim*, but let me make it clear that she is not the only one that you chased away. This is the last time that you and everyone else around this table…" Osman swept a loathsome look around the table, taking time to look at each person individually until his eyes finally rested on his father; disdain turned into pain on both of their faces. Osman finished his discourse, "…will ever see me again." He turned and decisively walked toward the door.

Ceyda *Hanim*'s face became pale, then worried, then desperate. "*Bekle, Oğlum* [Wait, son]." She got up and ran after him. When she made it to the threshold, she found herself with her nose almost touching the door that Osman had just slammed.

A look of pain and disbelief settled on Ozan *Bey* as he observed the heart-wrenching scene unfolding before him. He remained pinned to his chair, unable to move, without knowing why.

Whatever love he had felt toward his wife up until that time instantly fled, and the void that remained was filled by a complete dislike of her and anything associated with her. Ozan *Bey* did not dare call what he was suddenly feeling hatred, because she was, after all, the mother of his two sons. But right then and there, still pinned to his chair, he knew that he did not want to even breathe the same air as that woman.

From that day forward, he decreed that they would be in separate rooms. For the first time, no words came out of Ceyda *Hanim*'s mouth to question her husband's decision. However, she kept her look defiant, her forehead high, her jaw locked in place by clenched teeth.

Ozan *Bey*'s pain reflected in his eyes and would remain there for years to come until the birth of his grandson Ozan, when joy made its way into the elder Ozan's heart again, and all his energy and time went into his namesake and his work.

More than twenty years had passed since the day Osman left his family home on the day his father was taken to the hospital with chest pain.

CHAPTER 31
ZOEY'S LEGACY

Zoey found herself in the pediatrics unit of a large hospital in the neighboring state of North Carolina. She loved it so much, she considered a second specialty, obstetrics and gynecology. That way, she could bring into the world the children she loved to take care of.

She had even rekindled her friendship with Ashley Brown, now Stewart, who had told her of the vacancy at the hospital where she was now head nurse of pediatrics.

When Zoey arrived, they both realized that their bond as close friends and confidants remained whole. Ashley was stunned at what Zoey had been put through in Istanbul, but she could also feel the pain in Zoey's heart at losing Osman. So they cried, they hugged, they talked, they became even closer—until they eventually ended up calling each other soul sisters.

So when Zoey confirmed what she had already suspected—that she was pregnant—she found herself in the middle of a hallway, sobbing on the shoulder of her friend.

"Zoey, you are not the first nor will you be the last single mother. In fact, you're one of the lucky ones—you're a professional, your child will be more than well provided for, better off than most!" Ashley wanted not just to console her friend but to encourage her.

"Ashley, you know me," began Zoey, looking deeply into her friend's eyes, trying to control her sobs so she could let out what pressed so heavily in her heart. "Do you think that I"—she pointed the four fingers of her right hand at her chest— "would be afraid of being a single mom?"

"Then what is it, Zoey? What are you afraid of?"

"Not being there for my child."

"Astonishment" would have fallen short in describing the look on Ashley's face.

When she could muster normalizing her breathing, she hugged her friend and guided her into her office. Ashley told her staff that she would be in a meeting and could not be disturbed. They sat in two chairs facing each other, holding hands.

They talked for hours about themselves, their families, and most importantly, their loves. Zoey poured her heart out to Ashley.

"I'm glad that I had the opportunity of a lifetime: to love and be loved by Osman Ulusoy was one of the most beautiful experiences…no, *the* most beautiful experience I ever had."

"Zoey, someday someone will show up who won't just love you and your baby but who will also fight for you two tooth and nail, not sit there while you are being insulted by his family."

Ashley knew that her words were incongruent with what her friend had shared, but she lacked the skills to come up with the right words—plus, she hoped she had somehow misunderstood what Zoey had said.

"Ashley, I need you to hear me out without saying a word until I'm done talking." Ashley didn't answer; she sat silently across from her friend, expectantly, her heart pounding inside her chest. "I found out very recently that I have the same type of cancer that my mother had…and died from." Tears began flowing profusely down Ashley's cheeks, but she remained silent. "In order to undergo treatment, I would need to interrupt the pregnancy—I'm in my fifth month. Even if I did, it wouldn't cure me; it would just buy me some time. But either way, my baby's life is nonnegotiable."

Ashley could hardly breathe from holding back the sobs that now had turned into a huge knot in her throat, but she continued to remain silent. No words came to her head anyhow.

When Zoey finished talking about her illness and the fact that her family was, for all practical purposes, nonexistent, both friends remained silent for a long time. Ashley finally broke the silence.

"The most frustrating part about this nightmarish, heartbreaking situation you're experiencing is that I can't do anything to change it or at least make it better; I feel so helpless!" Ashley felt angry and wanted to lash out at somebody but didn't know who. She wanted to blame God, but her Southern Baptist upbringing prevented her from doing so. Instead, she got up from her seat, leaned down, and pulled Zoey up by the hand.

When Zoey stood before her, she hugged her tightly, as if she wanted to make up for the time that she now knew she would never have to hug her friend.

"You can help—you can make this situation a lot better for me." Ashley broke away from her embrace and looked Zoey in the eye with a questioning look. They both sat back down. "I want you to adopt my baby. It's a boy. I have already drawn up all the legal documents; you and Peter only need to sign them."

"But what about Osman?" Ashley asked, unable to hide her shock.

"I would never allow my child to be raised in a family that treats women like objects, like possessions!" Her anger was obvious.

"Zoey, in all the years that I knew Osman through med school, I never saw that side of him. He always treated you so lovingly, with so much respect and care."

"Well, when we moved to Istanbul, a totally new side of Osman came out, and believe me, he has the family from hell. My child will never grow up in that family! I wanted to be the one to choose who would raise him, and I can't think of a better choice of mom than you for my child…besides me." They both broke into sobs again.

Peter John Osman Stewart was born prematurely, at thirty-five weeks. Zoey had chosen her son's name, adding Osman in honor of her one and only true love.

Ashley assisted with the delivery. She immediately cleaned and wrapped the beautiful baby boy and placed him alongside Zoey, who didn't have the strength to speak. She only looked deeply, lovingly, and longingly into the perfectly beautiful little face with elongated blue eyes looking right back at her. Ashley took a photo of the tender scene just before Zoey drew her last breath.

Only Ashley, Peter, and Peter's parents John and Mary Stewart knew of the arrangement. However, the details of the adoption (birth parents and background) remained a secret to all besides Ashley and Peter.

During the months prior to Peter John's birth, under the pretext of taking continuing education courses, both Ashley and Zoey took a leave of absence from their work at the hospital and moved to South Carolina.

They rented an apartment where Ashley could monitor Zoey's pregnancy as well as her cancer. Peter drove to South Carolina on weekends. During those months together, nothing was left unsaid.

Zoey wrote letters for both her baby and Osman.

"In case the opportunity ever arises, you will give the letters to them, but you are not obligated to ever do so."

The three of them were seated on the balcony; Ashley had made coffee for herself and Peter and prepared tea for Zoey. She served it in a beautiful porcelain teapot with a matching cup. Ashley wanted to make everything beautiful for Zoey, and this was one of her ways of doing so.

"I will not leave a letter for you two." Zoey struggled to try to bring trembling hands up and hold theirs. Both Ashley and Peter immediately reached down, and each took one of Zoey's hands and gently covered it with their other free hand. Zoey struggled but continued, "because we have said everything in person. You know that I love you both and that I think my son is privileged to have you as parents; I am eternally grateful to you."

Peter's trembling lips and free flow of copious tears running down his cheeks finally landed on the back of the hand shielding Zoey's, belying his usually subdued personality.

That was the last serious talk they had.

From then on, Zoey and Ashley made life as natural and pleasant as possible: they went for walks, talked about their college days, made new recipes, watched romantic movies, discussed new findings in the fields of pediatrics.

Peter and Ashley returned to North Carolina with a blue-eyed, rosy-cheeked bundle of joy wrapped tightly in a blue blanket. Visits from friends followed, and an all-out baby shower was thrown by both grandmothers.

Zoey had been right, thought Ashley: Peter John Osman Stewart was in the perfect family—hers. She felt blessed to be the one chosen to be his mom. The adoption procedure was never again discussed by Peter and Ashley nor Mary and John Stewart. Even the reason they had kept it a secret from their son was never discussed. The time just never seemed right; they were happy and fulfilled, and it was left at that.

Peter John grew up in a loving, traditional Southern family. John and Mary Stewart were the perfect grandparents. Besides attending all their grandson's activities, his grandfather taught him all the water sports. They went fishing and sailing, and of course, his grandfather attended all his swim meets. Peter John learned to swim way before he learned to walk.

CHAPTER 32
THE SEARCH

The same day that Osman slammed the door behind him and left his house in Istanbul, he flew to South Carolina to the hospital where his wife had worked before their move to Istanbul.

He began an intense search to find his wife. *God, I miss her*, he thought. Her former colleagues informed him that they had not heard from Zoey since she had resigned to follow her husband to Istanbul.

He went to their former apartment; neither the landlord nor their former neighbors knew anything about Zoey's whereabouts. Just when Osman had his hand on his SUV's door handle, a voice called him from the front door of the building. He turned to see Amy, a young neighbor who had been a good acquaintance of Zoey's.

"Amy, hello—I'm looking for Zoey."

"Zoey? Didn't you guys get married and go to Israel?"

"Istanbul."

"Whatever." Amy waved her hand in the air. "I heard she found a job at a hospital in North Carolina."

"What hospital?" asked Osman, full of hope.

"Don't know. The pediatrics unit somewhere."

"Thanks, Amy."

Osman got in his car and burned tires as he took off. He practiced in his head hundreds of ways to ask for forgiveness, including his new plan to move back to the US and begin a new life together with her.

Osman was sure he had called or visited every hospital in North Carolina, starting with the major hospitals near Raleigh, Charlotte, and the other larger cities. It seemed she had disappeared off the face of the earth, but he left his contact number and the same message at each and every hospital and clinic he visited or called: "Zoey, I'm desperately looking for you. I love you, and I'm here to stay."

And what has become of Ashley, Zoey's best friend? Osman thought all of a sudden. He had called her hundreds of times and gotten only her voicemail, so he had left hundreds of messages. It'd been months; fatigue, frustration, and disappointment had taken over Osman, but he would never give up until he once again found the love of his life, the best thing that had ever happened to him. He would explain everything. *What a fool I've been, what a damned fool, a coward!* he thought, full of anger—and guilt. Then the call came.

Dr. Solomon had news about Zoey. She was the head of pediatrics at one of the larger hospitals just outside Raleigh. She called Osman and asked him to meet her in person.

CHAPTER 33
THE HEARTBREAK

"Zoey *did* return here. In fact, she was head of pediatrics… what hospital would be stupid enough not to grab such talent?" She asked rhetorically.

"OK," Osman interrupted, not caring about courteousness. "Where is she? I thought you said *you* were head of pediatrics?" he said impatiently.

"Dr. Ulusoy—"

"Osman, please."

"OK, Osman, I am Laura Solomon. Please call me Laura—after all, we are colleagues who share a deep sorrow. Please take a seat."

The last two sentences uttered by Dr. Solomon caused Osman's color to drain from his face; he never took his eyes off hers as he began to sit down almost in slow motion. Osman braced himself for the bad news that he sensed was coming.

The impact of the news of Zoey's illness, followed by her death, was too much for him. He was unable to get up from that office chair for hours. When Dr. Solomon returned to her office in the late afternoon, he was still there in the same chair, in the same position. It was as if she had left a statue sitting in her office.

Osman got up when Dr. Solomon entered the office. "I have one last question before I go. I came to this hospital months ago and asked about Zoey; they told me they did not know her, and she actually worked here!" This last phrase Osman shouted at the top of his lungs.

"Osman, Zoey did not want to be found, especially by you. She was the boss, the head of pediatrics. All we did was follow her wishes."

He left the hospital and checked directly into a hotel room, where he stayed for weeks trying to make sense of what had happened. After he left Istanbul, he looked for his wife everywhere, and he never got the chance to tell her that he loved her and that he had left his entire family behind to be with her. If only he had had the chance to tell her that.

A broken, angry, vindictive Osman left the hotel that night, four weeks later. He had applied to various medical schools about a year before when he and Zoey still lived in Istanbul. It hadn't taken long to figure out that life in Istanbul with his family was never going to work for Zoey. Now he regretted not telling her of his plans. He wanted to keep her from disappointment if the plans didn't pan out, and to surprise her if they did.

Now Osman was reading an email of acceptance from the University of Michigan Medical School. He pursued cardiology as his second specialty, and since he had all the time in the world, he plunged himself into his career, doing research and situating himself at the cutting edge of all the new cardiological technology.

Osman made sure he trained with the best cardiologists. He wanted to find out what filled the brains of those world-class scientists, and most of all, how they put into practice all that brain knowledge. His all-out effort had the expected results: Osman became among the best in the field. When he wasn't doing cutting-edge heart surgery, he traveled all over the world conducting seminars on some groundbreaking, lifesaving procedure.

Most importantly, there was no space left in his mind to feel the pain that had been his constant companion since Zoey had left him. He was sure that if he gave into the pain, he would not survive.

CHAPTER 34
FORGIVENESS BEGINS

The day that Ozan *Bey*, his father, had been rushed to the hospital, Osman had just finished conducting a seminar at the same hospital, which housed one of Istanbul's best cardiology clinics.

He was paged urgently for two reasons: the influential Ulusoy family had demanded that the best cardiovascular surgeon took care of the elder Ulusoy, and they suspected that their expert speaker that shared a last name with the patient might be a family connection.

Osman rushed to attend the emergency call. He looked at the file and immediately knew the patient in question was his father. Either his heart had turned to stone, or he was the consummate professional, but he didn't miss a beat.

In minutes he organized the team and prepared his patient for the operating room to do exploratory surgery in case the results of the EKG and MRI required it. To the casual observer, Osman could have been treating a total stranger. He made instant decisions and called orders to his team without a hint of hesitation or emotion.

After thoroughly examining his father and looking at the results of the studies, Osman knew that his father's condition was not serious. But he had observed the devastation on his nephew's face. It moved him; he could tell that the younger Ozan loved his grandfather deeply.

Osman had never met his nephew—he'd only assumed that's who the distressed young man was. Osman and his older brother were never close, and the only thing they had in common was that neither wanted to run the family business. The difference was that Osman spoke his mind and refused to compromise, while Mehmet submitted but held a grudge and felt victimized. So he blamed everyone but himself for his situation.

The disgust Osman felt toward his family, and especially his mother, surfaced when he saw them gathered outside the operating room. In fact, he felt sick to his stomach when he thought of his beloved Zoey and what they had done to her, or rather what he had allowed them to do to her, his wife.

So Osman picked the one he considered to be the most innocent member of the family and the one most obviously affected by the condition of the elder Ozan: young Ozan. Osman approached him with compassion and gave him words of comfort and reassurance. When he touched Ozan's shoulders that day, Osman felt a slight current leave his hand, and the word "connection" crossed his mind.

Therefore, when he looked down through the window of his temporary office at the clinic that day and saw a desolate Ozan in the picnic area, Osman felt compelled to go to him.

Ozan's sobs had barely subsided when he found himself facing an outstretched hand accompanied by the confident voice. "I'm Osman."

Ozan stood up and took the hand that was offered.

"Doctor, how's my grandfather?"

"Things have not changed since I talked to you when we came out of the operating room; your grandfather is and will be fine."

"Thank you, Dr. Osman," Ozan replied, now feeling calm after once again hearing the reassuring words.

"Osman. Call me Osman."

"I'm Ozan Ulusoy."

"After your grandfather, huh?"

"Yes. I'm very proud to be both his grandson and namesake." Almost as an afterthought, Ozan added, "Osman, do you have time for a cup of coffee or a sandwich, a juice?"

Osman hesitated but agreed.

At the hospital cafeteria, Ozan talked and talked and talked. Osman listened. He learned a lot about the Ulusoy family—that Ozan and his sister Deniz-Mare were born in Italy, the strictness of his grandmother, his distant, absentee father, his doting mother, and finally, the hero in his life, his grandfather.

Ozan spoke about his perfect childhood thanks to his grandfather. He reminisced out loud about their trips to the seashore to eat the catch of the day and exchange stories with the local fishermen, their sailing trips, his grandfather waiting for him after school, Ozan running into his wide-open arms, and finally, what had brought his grandfather to the hospital.

"It was all my fault!" Osman continued to listen. "He argued with my grandmother over my trip to Milan. She did not want me to go and study there; she told him that we had perfectly good schools here at home and that all the Ulusoy men had studied in Turkey and turned out just fine."

"Didn't you say that your father studied in Italy and that's why you and your sister were born there?"

"Yeah, my grandmother doesn't always make sense. But when they started arguing about my uncle, that's when my grandfather lost it and had his heart attack."

"He did not have a heart attack, Ozan; he'll be fine."

"Anyway, my grandmother told him that she did not want me to come home with a foreign wife just like my uncle Osman had done years before; they had lost him forever…"

Ozan's words brought Osman back to that fateful day, and once again, he felt all the sharp stabs in his heart caused by each hateful word that poured from his mother's mouth and was used as a powerful weapon to attack his beloved Zoey.

Ozan, completely unaware of what had taken place or of what Osman was experiencing at the moment, continued, "That's when my grandfather's pent-up anger came bursting out. He told her that if she hadn't interfered with my uncle's marriage, he would still be around and happily married. He also told her that he had made a terrible mistake back then not sticking up for his son, sitting back silently while he watched her destroy my uncle's marriage. My grandfather went on to say that this time he would not allow her to destroy my dreams. Well, you know the rest."

Osman hadn't said much; they sat in comfortable silence for a long time.

Finally, Osman got up, lightly squeezed Ozan's upper arm, and said, "Ozan, don't let anyone—I mean anyone—interfere with your dreams." He turned to go and found himself face-to-face with Meryem.

After an awkward moment during which neither one knew what to say, Ozan came to their rescue. "Anne, this is Dr. Osman; we were discussing *Dede*'s heart…" He hesitated.

"Spasm," came Osman's quick reply.

"Yes, spasm," said Ozan, relieved.

Osman extended a hand to Meryem, and in a very formal tone, said, "*Memnun oldum* [Nice to meet you]."

"*Bende, Doktor* [Likewise, Doctor]. Can we discuss my father-in-law's situation in private?"

"As I told your son, there's nothing to worry about, Meryem *Hanim*."

"*Lutfen, Doktor Bey* [Please, Doctor]," pleaded Meryem.

Ozan, sensing that his presence would be a hindrance to whatever his mom wanted to discuss, got up and said, "I'll see how *Dede* is doing."

Osman motioned for Meryem to sit in the space of the bench that Ozan had just vacated.

"Would you like anything?" asked Osman, always the consummate gentleman.

Meryem shook her head, looked up into the bluest eyes she'd ever seen (she thought), and said, "Osman, I didn't come to discuss your father; I know he'll be fine."

"Then?" was his only response. His look was stern.

"I wanted to ask your forgiveness…" Meryem lowered her eyes.

"For what?" asked Osman, still with an unyielding attitude.

"Please let me say what I came to say, then I won't take up anymore of your time."

Osman remained silent and unsympathetic.

Meryem began, "The last time I saw you was before Ozan was born, when Ceyda *Hanim* insulted Zoey." His jaw hardened at the sound of his wife's name, but he kept still. "All these years, I've often thought, with great sorrow and regret, that I should have spoken up that night. I, too, was an outsider in that family and yet allowed the verbal blows to land on your wife freely and mercilessly. I have always regretted that and swore to myself that if one day I came across you or Zoey, I'd express my regret and beg your forgiveness. I didn't want this opportunity to pass me by."

Meryem got up to leave.

"Please stay a few more minutes," responded Osman.

Meryem noticed that his voice had softened and the furrow on his brows seemed to have relaxed a bit.

"I was the guiltiest of all the people that were present the night that my Zoey was attacked by Ceyda *Hanim*, because I said nothing to defend my wife. I have lived with that regret every single day since I left. Thank you for your heartfelt words, but you were the least guilty, for the same reason you stated before—you were an outsider."

"Osman, I don't know if I can ever be of any help to you, but I will be here, always ready to assist in any way I can. Please let me help if the opportunity ever presents itself—please."

"For now, I'll ask you not to reveal to Ozan who I am. I sense that he trusts me, and I would like to be there for him when he needs me without the complications of family ties."

"Thank you for taking time with him. He's always lacked a father figure—no need to go into that now, but he needs you in his life. You'll discover that as you spend more time with him—if the opportunity comes up. I'll always be grateful to Ozan *Bey* for filling the vacuum left by his father during Ozan's growing-up years."

No more words were uttered. Meryem got up and extended her hand down to Osman, who took it and politely got up. He, too, did not say anymore. Meryem turned and walked away; Osman felt himself relaxed, as if the heavy load that he had carried all these years had become slightly lighter.

CHAPTER 35
OZAN, PART THREE

Things at the Ulusoy mansion were calm for the next few days. No one said much about what had happened to Ozan Ulusoy Sr. He made a full recovery, or seemed to, and told his grandson in no uncertain terms to pack up and go to Italy and follow his dreams.

"That's what Osman, the doctor that took care of you at the hospital, told me. 'Don't let anyone interfere with your dreams,' he said to me."

"Osman? His name was Osman?"

"Yes, why?" was his grandson's nonchalant response.

"No reason. Finish packing, say your goodbyes. I'll take you to the airport in the morning." The younger Ozan did as his grandfather told him.

Ozan was happy and talkative on the way to the airport; he had said his goodbyes to everyone at the house without a second thought. But now, at the airport, he clung to his grandfather's neck and would not let go.

"What will I do without you, *Dede*?"

"You will not be without me. I am one of those video calls of yours away, and it's less than a three-hour flight—which would probably be easier for me to manage than the video call," he joked. "But I have a feeling that you will be so busy pursuing your dreams that you won't need me as much as you think you will." They hugged tightly, and young Ozan ran to catch his flight.

CHAPTER 36
SCOOTER STRIKE

Now Ozan stood admiring the magnificent Lake Como and the mountain peaks that surrounded it.

He'd been to Como City before and the surrounding area; he felt at home, having spent practically all his vacations, including summers, here. But the region still gripped him.

He was once again in the country of his birth. But this time, it was different; he was on his own now, an adult, which changed everything.

He did a slow, 360-degree turn to take in the full view of his surroundings and felt a current run through his body. Everything felt surreal. His future would be determined here; the thought gave him chills. Ozan instinctively rubbed his arms.

He stood facing the church of Sant'Abbondio and the mountains beyond. He took his eyes off the breathtaking view for a second, took a step back to reach for his phone to immortalize the moment with a photo. In the process, got too close to the curb and lost his footing.

While he was doing a bit of an awkward dance in order not to lose total control of his body and fall on the hard pavement, a scooter came out of nowhere, bumped into him, and both ended up on the pavement, he flat on his back, the scooter on its side trapping his leg underneath.

Mari-Car struggled to remove her helmet; as she did, the mass of thick, dark, silky hair that had been piled on the top of her head fell forward, covering her face. As she shook her head to get it into place, ocean met ocean as both Ozan and Mari-Car locked eyes and remained motionless until the distant sirens of the ambulance, which were getting louder and louder, brought them both back to the present time and space.

In the emergency room, Mari-Car sat at the edge of Ozan's examining table.

"I'm so sorry again. I—"

Ozan stopped her. "It wasn't your fault—I stumbled into the middle of the street, and you couldn't stop in time."

She stretched out her hand. "I'm Mari-Car Stewart García; I study architecture at Politecnico di Milano."

"Wow. What a strong, inspiring, beautiful, name."

"A bit of a mouthful," replied Mari-Car, bringing both hands together, chin cradled between thumbs and index fingers. She had a playful look on her face and a smile to match it. "Actually, my full name is María del Carmen Stewart García." As she looked down to hide the mischievous smile, a mass of dark hair covered her face, and when she looked up, it fell back in place.

He instinctively reached out and put a stubborn strand behind her ear.

"I'm Ozan Ulusoy—a bit of a lackluster name, I'm afraid." He also had a mischievous smile as he spoke. "I also study architecture at PoliMi."

They locked eyes and were both hypnotized by the sea of blue looking back.

Mari-Car broke the spell. "From Istanbul?" she asked.

"From New York?" he asked her.

Two yeses, followed by laughter, ended any remaining awkwardness between the two new friends.

"Why did you pick Istanbul out of all the cities in Turkey? I could be from Ankara or Bodrum or Izmir or Bursa or—"

"Lucky guess. The largest city, Turkish name, so I went for it. How about you? Why did you guess New York? I could be from Detroit or San Francisco or Raleigh…"

"Actually, I recognize the New York accent quite well; I've traveled there with my family, mainly on shopping and touristy trips."

"Well, do you want me to call your family?"

"No!" Ozan answered too fast and too loudly. It surprised Mari-Car. "Sorry, Mari-Car. I prefer not to worry them. Plus, I'll be fine in a couple of weeks, according to the doctor. It was just a bad sprain of the ankle and minor lacerations."

"I'll carry your backpack to all your classes."

"I can manage, Mari-Car, don't worry. I'll be a bit slower, that's all."

"OK; I'll just walk you to your classes. I still feel a bit guilty for your landing here." Mari-Car swept the air with her palms open to point out their surroundings.

Ozan followed her hand with his eyes, and when they reached an open crack in the privacy curtain, he thought he saw someone familiar walk by.

CHAPTER 37
KADER STRIKES AGAIN

He had a surprised look on his face, but if he was right, he didn't want to miss this chance, so he called out, "Osman, Dr. Osman!"

Osman took a few steps backward and pulled the curtain to one side. The surprised look on his face matched Ozan's.

"What are you doing here, Ozan? Are you OK?" is all Osman could say. The look of surprise turned into worry.

"No, no, Doctor—I mean, Osman—I just sprained my ankle."

"How?" asked Osman.

Mari-Car's hand slowly went up as she sheepishly said, "It's my fault."

"No, it is not," said Ozan firmly.

"Yes, it is!"

They were giving Osman whiplash with the back-and-forth until he finally said, "It's *my* fault!"

Mari-Car and Ozan stopped their silly argument, and they both looked at Osman and burst into laughter.

After the laughter stopped, everyone settled down and Osman got the whole story about how Ozan ended up in the emergency room and, more generally, at Politecnico di Milano studying architecture.

"I just did not let anyone interfere with my dreams, Osman, just like you told me, and here I am! Well, I don't mean here." He pointed at a wall of the cubicle they were in. "I mean here." And he pointed at the mountains outside the window. Then he pointed at Mari-Car and said, "And here."

She was fascinated. She learned more about Ozan in a half hour than she would have otherwise learned in months. He went on to tell Dr. Osman how after his *dede* left the hospital, he went home, packed up, and with the blessing of his mother and *Dede*, left in pursuit of his dreams. Osman reached out and squeezed Ozan's shoulder, then patted his cheek lovingly and approvingly.

"I don't know if you realize this," interrupted Mari-Car, "but you guys look alike…in a father-and-son kinda way."

Ozan rolled his eyes.

"I'd be proud to have a son like you," said Osman. "I'm glad that we ran into each other again. Here's my card. I theoretically live in South Carolina, but really, I live on a plane most of the time. I come to Milan and the Lake Como region often, so please keep in touch, and if you need anything at all…use that cell phone of yours."

Osman hugged Ozan and shook Mari-Car's hand.

CHAPTER 38
THOUGHTS REFLECTED

For the next two weeks, Mari-Car and Ozan were inseparable. They rode to classes at the Bovisa campus in Mari-Car's new electric Fiat. Once they were there, she walked him to classes to help him manage his crutches. It turned into a comfortable routine for them even after these were no longer needed.

Mari-Car loved being with Ozan but would not allow herself to think beyond the word "friend." However, it was hard to get away from those piercing eyes; they were hard to forget when Ozan was not around and hard to turn away from when he was.

Her daily texts to Peter John continued, and so did the late-night video calls, with Mari-Car on her magical courtyard bench and Peter John in his warm bed. Ozan stayed in the same dorm as Mari-Car, but he had learned to give her space, especially during her video calls with Peter John.

She had said they were cousins, and he could tell they were close and had a connection that was off-limits to anyone else. Her eyes brightened and her smile widened when she got a text from Peter John. Beyond that, Ozan had heard the laughter coming from both sides of the screen during their video calls. Mari-Car did not laugh like that with anyone else, he'd realized, almost envious, but internalized his thoughts.

"So," Peter John blurted out one night, "which language should I study now that I am here completing this global management degree you got me into? Thanks to you and Aunt Mari, I have a background in Spanish…it's not even close to perfect, but it'd probably be the easiest route, right? I mean, it's familiar."

"And which would be the hardest, most unfamiliar route, according to you?" asked Mari-Car.

"Mandarin, I suppose. Don't even go there—you always get me into these mazes, and then I can't find my way out!"

She burst out laughing, picturing Peter John trapped in a huge labyrinth, sweaty, thirsty, and frustrated, thinking of killing her whenever he got out. She described for him the image that had formed in her head.

"I would be furious at you if I ended up in that labyrinth, but not for long; who would I talk to about important stuff if I stayed mad at you? Who would put me in these impossible situations? Who would challenge me?"

"Awww," answered Mari-Car sweetly. "But you're right; we make a good team. I challenge you, and you always tell me the truth. That's why I'm so confident around you…you make me strong, Peter John."

After a long, familiar silence, Peter John said, "*Buenas noches*, Sunshine."

"Turkish!" said Mari-Car before saying good night.

"What?!"

"You should study Turkish, not Mandarin," she clarified. "I have a Turkish friend; when I hear the language, it sounds cool."

"I'm not even going to reply to that!" Peter John rolled his eyes, and to keep up with the humor, he asked, "Is she cute?"

"Who?" asked Mari-Car.

"Your Turkish friend; *is she cute*?" he asked again, accentuating each syllable.

"Yes, *he* is," answered Mari-Car, imitating his intonation. "Over and out."

She quickly closed her laptop; the last sound that Peter John heard was her giggles.

That's also the sound that Ozan heard as he walked out the door and into the garden for some fresh air.

"You must have been talking to your cousin," he said to Mari-Car, almost in a whisper, following the sounds of her giggles as he approached her bench.

"How did you know?" was her perky reply. She looked up at him, a smile still lighting up her face and sparkles still emanating from her eyes.

"Because no one else makes you this happy and bright even in the dark of night."

"He just gets me," was all she could say to him about Peter John. "But come, I'll share my bench with you—and my blanket."

They sat facing each other, leaning against the armrests, knees up, feet touching. They talked easily, and their silent pauses were comfortable. He told her about his family, spoke more than he meant to about his grandfather… Mari-Car could tell that he was probably the most important person in his life.

"And your sister? I mean, do you get along?"

"Deniz-Mare? Yes, we do. I feel protective of her, but we don't talk as much as we should. Definitely not as much as you and Peter John! She's still studying at university, and our schedules hardly ever coincide…but I miss her, she's strong, decisive, positive, and also very protective of me."

"What a beautiful name she has."

"She also was born here in Italy—in Milan, actually—and my mom wanted to give her a name that would remind her of her country of birth; that's the 'Mare' part. Plus, she has blue eyes, and my mom says they reminded her of the sea when my sister was born. 'Deniz' is also 'sea' in Turkish."

"What does she study?" Mari-Car asked.

"Business. She'll probably end up coming here and doing a master's in international business. Deniz-Mare is excellent at business, a natural, you could say. She solves problems with ease; clients love her. You should see her do business presentations!"

"Does she work? You said clients love her."

"Deniz-Mare often helps at the family company."

"You are her number-one admirer; does she know that?"

Ozan looked at Mari-Car wide-eyed. He opened his mouth to say something but couldn't find the right words. She was used to moments of silence and allowed him time to think. Ozan finally spoke.

"I know why you are so special to Peter John…" The words were left hanging in the air. It was hard to tell whether he was directing them at Mari-Car or thinking out loud, but he finally added, "You have a way of bringing out the good qualities in people, ones they didn't even realize they had. You're right, I admire my little sister, but I've kept it inside, never told her."

"Your dad?" Mari-Car pressed.

"Very, very distant. I essentially don't know him," said Ozan thoughtfully. "He's the CFO of our holdings, and he spends a lot of time at the office and traveling."

After a long period of more comfortable silence, Ozan looked at Mari-Car. The light of the moon gave her silk tresses luminous streaks; he fixed his eyes on her. He was grateful that she was looking down, seemingly in a pensive mood, rather than looking at him and possibly seeing his thoughts reflected in his eyes.

Her hair fell softly over her face. He fought the urge to reach out and smooth it back with his fingers to uncover her face—he was sure that if she looked up, he would see the cool light of the moon reflected in her eyes.

Finally, he said, "You made me spill out my guts tonight. When will you spill yours? I feel…defenseless."

"My night will come," answered Mari-Car.

"Well, in that case, I better get some sleep. Damn, it's late!" he said after looking at his cell phone.

Ozan got up from the bench, then tucked his side of the blanket under Mari-Car. He looked into her eyes, whispered,

"Thanks," then left. She nodded and curled up under the blanket a bit longer.

The next morning, after Mari-Car got ready for school and went downstairs by the main arched entrance, Ozan had already left. She figured he had an early class or a meeting, so she set out, but the forty-minute ride felt much longer without him.

Mari-Car went about her normal day of classes, studying, texting, talking with acquaintances, but did not hear from Ozan.

She missed their routine of meeting him at the front entrance and walking on the gravel path to where her car was. Sometimes, when their schedules were similar, they spent the entire day together. They had been almost inseparable since their collision, and she liked his company.

CHAPTER 39
PARTING OF WAYS

Mehmet had just returned from one of his business trips. He entered their room moody and in silence. By mutual unspoken agreement, he and Meryem had slept apart for years. The comfortable, large sofa in their room made their arrangement less obvious. Out of discretion, the subject was never discussed with the other family members, but everyone knew, or supposed, that they were only married on paper.

Meryem had sacrificed any personal life for her children. She was beautiful and successful, the consummate professional. But lately, she had been pondering the pointlessness of their so-called marriage. "Appearances" was the only word that came to mind when she thought about it. But appearances for whom? And why was she the only one required to keep up appearances?

Everyone knew that Mehmet had his own personal life, and no one ever dared to question him, let alone reproach him. But even the simple decision to finish her college degree brought her grief from all sides. The double standard infuriated her, and that was why she made sure that Deniz-Mare carved her own place in the world, developed her talents, and asserted herself.

All these thoughts were running through her mind when Mehmet returned from his last business trip. Seeing him moody and entitled, as if it were a chore to return home, she greeted him with divorce papers, which he quickly and uninterestedly browsed through, signed, folded, placed back in the envelope, and shoved into Meryem's hands.

"Don't worry, this is the last time you'll have to enter this room while I am here; appearances no longer matter," Meryem told him and left the room.

Ceyda *Hanim* almost had a heart attack. Both Mete and Fatma ran around the house frantically, calling the ambulance, getting the cologne, trying to get ahold of Ozan *Bey* and Mehmet, who rushed home after the phone call only to find out that the ambulance had already come and taken Ceyda *Hanim* to the hospital.

In the frenzy, neither Fatma nor Mete had thought of informing them that they, along with Meryem, had left for the hospital with Ceyda *Hanim*.

"What happened?" asked Ozan *Bey* when he finally reached the hospital.

"She found out about the divorce," said Meryem.

"What divorce?"

"Mine and Mehmet's. Plans were to tell you and Ceyda *Hanim* together in a more civilized manner—I don't know how she found out ahead of time."

Fatma stepped forward awkwardly.

"It was my fault. I found the envelope on the floor in the hallway outside of your bedroom, Meryem *Hanım*. It looked important, so I gave it to Ceyda *Hanım*. But believe me, please, if I had known…"

Meryem stopped her.

"No need to say more. I must have dropped it when I left the room; it just didn't go according to plans, not your fault. I don't think that she would have reacted any differently if she had found out the way Mehmet and I had planned, anyway."

Ceyda *Hanım* returned home the same day with a diagnosis of anxiety and stress.

"You are all going to kill me, I swear!" were her first words when she entered the house and was guided gently by Mete to her favorite chair in the living room. Then she demanded, "Ozan, I want to arrange a meeting as soon as possible with Meryem's parents to discuss the d-d-d…" Finally, she whispered, "Divorce situation."

"For God's sake, Ceyda! Is Meryem eighteen years old? And in all these years, did it ever occur to you to speak with Mehmet's parents"—he pointed at his wife and then at himself—"about why he takes so many business trips and why they have separate beds?" Ozan *Bey* looked at his daughter-in-law and mouthed "Sorry, *Kızım*," as he rushed irritably out of the house.

CHAPTER 40
MARI-CAR DENUDATES HER SOUL

Mari-Car experienced a vague feeling, difficult to name, maybe a void. What she did know was that this sensation was unfamiliar and confusing. Ozan barely spoke to her except when it was unavoidable, like when they saw each other in the hallways, the library, or the music room in their dorm. Then an impersonal hello or good morning were the only words that Ozan addressed to her. But Mari-Car found herself looking forward to hearing those words, as mundane as they were.

For the first time in her life, she kept something from Peter John. The unfiltered TV screen on her forehead that permitted him to see her thoughts was turned off. This realization made her sad. Had she lost her best friend too?

The days were uneventful, long, dull, and gloomy. How was this possible when she was surrounded by so much beauty, she wondered.

Then it dawned on her: it wasn't the days that were dull and gloomy; it was that she, Mari-Car, was experiencing these feelings inside.

If she continued to allow them free rein, would she fall into depression? She opened her eyes wide and panicked. Was she going through a depression? Was that what this feeling was? It was a very unpleasant and scary sensation.

Should she call Peter John? They hadn't video-chatted in days. She had somehow come up with feeble excuses for missing their long, heart-to-heart nightly conversations. It made her heart ache, because it was missing its twin; it felt lonely.

Or should she go talk to Ozan? She missed him, and it was a mystery to her why he had distanced himself just when they had begun to get close. He had opened his heart to her, and then…he basically disappeared.

Mari-Car tapped a few times on the door. When it opened, she was looking up at dancing blue flames, and she felt a bolt of heat travel through her body that held her pinned to the spot where she stood for what felt like eons.

The decisive young girl, who a few minutes earlier had marched confidently to Ozan's door, was now seized by self-doubt. Just as she turned to run, she felt a hand softly touch the back of her upper arm and heard the words, almost in a whisper, "Mari-Car…*gitme*." He realized that automatically the words had come out in his native tongue, shook his head slightly as if to clear his head and added, "Don't go."

Mari-Car broke the magic spell: Sentences began gushing out of her mouth without much breathing space in between.

"Ozan, I don't know what I've done to push you away. I got used to waiting for you by the front door to go to classes together, talking incessantly during our ride to campus, grabbing a coffee before class…I miss our talks, our texts. I miss *you*!" she finally said, tears flooding her eyes and spilling down her cheeks.

Ozan opened his arms, and she walked into them, still sobbing softly. She remained in the safety of his arms for a long time until her sobs subsided. When Mari-Car raised her head, a large wet spot remained on his shirt. "Sorry," she whispered, drowning in the pools of blue, he doing the same.

Ozan took her by the hand and led her to his bed, where they both sat comfortably side by side, leaning against the headboard.

"Mari-Car, I have had a lot of family issues lately. My parents called to inform me that they were getting divorced."

"I'm so sorry," she said.

"No, don't be. This was just a formality. They weren't like your parents; they had lived apart for years. Still, it means changes are coming to our household: my mom might move out, I'm not sure who Deniz-Mare will live with, I don't know exactly where 'home' is for me…anyway, I've been stressing about all that. However, that's not the only reason why I've been distant."

Since he was quiet for too long after he made his last statement, Mari-Car prompted him, "Then what is the reason?"

Ozan took his time, trying to come up with the right words. He finally said, "Mari-Car, I was vulnerable before you the night that we talked in the courtyard. I had never opened up to anyone the way I did to you; it kind of scared me. Then, days went by, weeks even, and I still didn't know any more about you than I did the first day we met.

"I don't think you trust me. I mean, we met recently; I don't expect to be another Peter John. But somehow, I feel that I need to protect myself or I will get hurt, and keeping my distance was the only way I knew how. I do this when I don't know how to handle a conflict, whether with family, personal decisions, or relationships."

Without explanation, Mari-Car began baring her soul: "I was born in New York City. My mom's side of the family is from Murcia, Spain; my dad's side is from North Carolina. I lost my dad, Kurt Stewart, in a car accident when I was three years old. I was the apple of his eye. My mom was in the car with him but survived…physically, that is, because she was never able to overcome her loss. She survived emotionally because she had me to take care of. Otherwise, I think she would have died of grief. They had a fairy-tale, *grande-amore* type of love story.

"All four of my grandparents are alive and well and are very protective of me, especially my dad's parents, because they see me as the gift that my dad left them. My dad's only brother is my uncle Peter, Peter John's dad; his mom is my aunt Ashley. I have another aunt, Katherine Stewart, who did not marry but lives with her boyfriend, Matthew. They don't have any children, but she's a nurse and works in the neonatal unit of our local hospital, so she says those are their children. My mom, María José García Cortés, is a fashion designer, well-known in the industry; she designs most of my clothes.

"Ozan, the loss of my father was so great that it left a deep wound, not to mention a void, in all of us—even me, at my young age. It's difficult for me to talk about myself because I can't do it without talking about my dad. And if my mom never remarries, and if I never marry, it's because we are both sure that we'll never find anyone like him. But I miss us." Mari-Car finished her speech, breathless, pointing her index finger back and forth at Ozan and then herself.

She let out a deep sigh, and a very long silence followed. She was exhausted and leaned her head on his shoulder, where she fell asleep soundly.

While she slept, Ozan was left to ponder this relationship. What was it? he wondered. Were they friends? Soulmates? He didn't dare think beyond that.

The next day Mari-Car was looking up into pools of infinite tones of blue. She stretched leisurely before she realized where she was, and every thought from the previous night began to cascade. She sat up suddenly.

"Ozan, I'm embarrassed. I think I fell asleep from exhaustion."

"Yes, you did, and I didn't have the heart to wake you."

As he spoke to her, he was stunned by the realization that for the first time in his life, he had met someone that he couldn't get out of his head no matter where he went or what he did. He felt that he had jumped into the deep end of the pool before learning to swim. He was drowning and didn't know how or where to get a life jacket.

Ozan was assaulted by images of Ceyda *Hanim* giving him an ultimatum if he started a relationship with a "foreign" girl. "You will either stop this relationship, or you will leave this house!" The words reverberated in his head. He didn't remember his uncle Osman, but he was there the day his grandmother said to his *dede* that they had lost Osman because he had brought home a foreign wife. Ozan was not thinking of marriage—far from it—he was just reflecting on the impossibility of Mari-Car and him ever having a relationship beyond friendship. The thought made his heart ache.

He thought of the only two possibilities to deal with the hopelessness before him: to run or distance himself. He once again chose the latter, since it was a familiar path.

CHAPTER 41
BETRAYAL

Mari-Car was left mystified by the new Ozan. She felt betrayed and mortified, because she had poured her heart out to him the night before and had even slept in his bed! When she thought about it, she instinctively covered her face as if to hide the embarrassment that enveloped her.

She was unable to shake it but put on a brave front, saying perky hellos when they were unable to avoid each other in some area of their residence hall or in the classes that they shared.

This distancing had occurred before she spilled her guts out to him. How could she have fallen into the same trap again? If she didn't open up, he stayed away; if she did, he stayed away. The embarrassment almost paralyzed her. She found herself in a no-win situation. She missed her best friend, whom she had neglected so much lately.

That night the conversation with Peter John was longer, deeper, and more teary-eyed than ever. She poured her heart out to him and had long moments of uncontrollable sobs. He was mostly silent, a sounding board. After Mari-Car had emptied her heart, she waited for his reaction. She waited a long time, but this time, it wasn't a comfortable wait; she felt uneasy.

He finally spoke.

"Do you know that this is the first time that you have kept something from me? Something important, I mean…"

"I hurt my soulmate. I am so sorry, so sad. I don't want to lose you or your trust."

"Mari-Car, you will never lose me, I promise you! But I need a little bit of time, OK? Yes, I can't hide that I feel sad…and hurt."

A week later, Mari-Car was landing at John F. Kennedy International Airport in New York. A couple of hours later, she was coming out of the Uber that had parked in front of her mother's apartment, carrying a backpack in one hand and her purse hanging from her shoulder. She rummaged through her purse for the keys and made her way upstairs to her former room.

A few hours after that, she opened her eyes to look into familiar blue eyes. For a few seconds, she thought she was looking into Ozan's.

"Mari-Car, what are you doing here? Are you OK?" She jumped out of bed, then onto his neck, clinging on as if her life depended on it.

"I came to ask you for forgiveness. I couldn't stand to make you sad and lose your trust—I just couldn't." Tears flooded her eyes, spilled over, and finally ran down her cheeks.

He unlocked her arms from the back of his neck, took her hand, and led her to the edge of the bed, then sat facing her.

"Listen, Mari-Car, you've exhausted yourself trying to show me that you're sorry, that I matter, that I'm important to you… this is just crazy—you, here!" He clasped his hands behind his head in disbelief.

Peter John moved both hands aimlessly through his hair, trying to make sense of what had just happened. Mari-Car had not hesitated to hop on a plane and fly across the big blue ocean just to regain his trust. No one had shown him that much love and care before. His heart ached, but in a good, comforting way.

Peter John and Mari-Car got ready and went into the city to spend time with one another. They went to a small pub, where they talked, laughed, and listened to music.

"Mari-Car, promise me that before you decide to be with that Ozan, or anyone else, you will call me and we'll discuss it, OK? I promise I'll do the same…it's just that I have the feeling that you will find someone before I do."

Mari-Car raised her glass and said, "I promise." A kiss on his cheek sealed the vow.

When they returned home, Mari almost died from the surprise of Mari-Car's visit. She jumped up from the chair, nearly spilling the coffee she had been enjoying while thinking introspectively at the kitchen table.

"Oh my God, *Dios mío*, what's going on?"

"*Tranquila*, *Mamá*; everything is OK. I just needed to come talk to Peter John…in person."

"In person, huh? It must be very serious for you to fly all the way here to talk to Peter John. When do you go back?"

"Tomorrow. I just flew in for the weekend."

"OK, *Hija* [daughter]. Tonight, we need to talk…alone, just you and me." Mari firmly pressed her index finger on Mari-Car's chest and then hers.

That night, Mari and her daughter talked in Mari's room.

"Mari-Car, *Hija*, what is the relationship that you and your cousin Peter John share? Is there something I don't know…and should know?"

"*Mamá, por Dios* [for God's sake]! Get your mind in the right place. You know very well that since forever, Peter John and I have been inseparable; he's the person that I trust the most in this world. But…but…I betrayed his trust, and I felt awful about it, so I came because I felt that I owed him an explanation for my behavior."

"*A ver Hija*, and what kind of behavior was that?"

"I don't want to talk about it, but suffice it to say, we have always had an understanding. We made a promise that we would never keep important information that would affect our friendship, from each other. I broke that promise, and I wanted to come and apologize in person."

Mari caressed her daughter's cheek, kissed it, and said, "*Bien Hija*, I trust you, but remember that you and Peter John are first cousins, did you hear? *First* cousins. Be careful not to cross any lines."

"With you constantly on my case, that would be hard to do." Mari-Car gave her mom a long, tight hug, followed by kisses all over her face and both hands.

Mari-Car and Peter John's bond returned to pre-Ozan days, with texting throughout the day and long video calls most nights. She had regained his trust, and this put a bounce in her step, a smile on her face, and a sparkle in her eyes.

CHAPTER 42
DR. OSMAN TO THE RESCUE

"Dr. Osman, forgive me if it looks like I'm taking advantage of our friendship, but you said that if I ever needed anything to give you a call. I didn't know who else I should talk to about a personal matter. Let me know when we could talk after you listen to this message."

Ozan heard from Osman that evening. They made plans to meet the following week, after Osman finished his commitment at a medical conference in Milan where he would be the keynote speaker.

Ozan was restless and had been so since the night that he had had that personal conversation with Mari-Car. He had not been able to concentrate on his courses and had even considered returning to Istanbul—to run. But what would he say to his family? What reason would he give for leaving everything halfway and returning home? He had stood up against the controlling, dictatorial Ceyda *Hanim* to come study in Milan and had gotten his *dede* to do so as well. There must be another solution, he thought.

He hoped that Osman would help him to make a sensible decision. After all, he had talked to the doctor at length about his family the day they met in the outdoor area of the hospital. They shared a mutual like and respect and a common culture, so Ozan couldn't think of a better-qualified person to help him think clearly. He wanted to go forward with his relationship with Mari-Car without affecting his bond with his family, especially his *dede*.

"I feel like a coward, Osman," said Ozan when he finally met with his doctor friend. "I have not even looked at Mari-Car since that day. I can hardly roll out a 'good morning' or a 'hello' without stammering. I know how inflexible my family is about having a relationship with anyone from outside our culture and religion. I was there the day that my *dede* had a heart attack."

"Heart spasm," interjected Osman.

"Right. Anyway, the day that my *dede* accused my grandmother of being the reason that my uncle Osman…" Suddenly he had a realization and got sidetracked. "I just realized that you have the same name as my uncle, and really, you are kind of like an uncle to me."

"I'd be so proud to have a nephew like you," said Osman, patting Ozan's cheek and squeezing his shoulder.

"Anyway, Uncle Osman…" Osman looked at Ozan with surprise, pride, and, yes, love at hearing his nephew call him uncle. "That was the scariest day of my life so far, and I couldn't live with myself if I made a decision that would cause anything bad to happen to my *dede*. The guilt would kill me!"

"The way you told the story, Ozan—it was the grandmother who caused the grandfather to end up in the emergency room."

"Yes; he defended my uncle Osman and told my grandmother that he should never have stepped aside and allowed her to mistreat my aunt Zoey."

Hearing Ozan call his beloved Zoey "aunt" brought tears to Osman's eyes. In a very low voice, he said, "Too late."

"For what?" said Ozan.

"I was just thinking that your grandfather realized too late that he should have supported his son, that's all."

"Uncle Osman, I don't want that to happen to me; I don't want to realize too late that I made a mistake and have Mari-Car pay the price. She doesn't deserve that. I would rather die of longing for her than have her go through the humiliation of rejection from my family."

"Ozan, *Oğlum*, it does not have to be an either-or situation—'Either I am happy and enjoy being with a girl that I like, but my happiness means her suffering, or I suffer and stay away from the girl that I like, but my suffering means her happiness.' You're getting ahead of yourself, Ozan. Build your friendship with Mari-Car, have fun, enjoy it, laugh together, and, if necessary, cry together. Why are you, at this early stage of your relationship, thinking about how your family back in Istanbul is going to react?"

It did Ozan good to talk to Osman; the answer seemed clear and simple after their conversation. Why he hadn't seen it that way from the beginning confused him. What happened the day that his *dede* was taken to the emergency room had marked him, had scared him beyond words, so much so that the fear blocked his mind, and he was unable to think lucidly. That was the only explanation he could find for his lack of clarity.

"Uncle Osman, it would have never occurred to me to call my own father when I needed advice. But I called you, and even though we're not even family, I felt as if we were. Do you have a family? Wife? Children?"

"No, Ozan, I don't. I did once have a wife, but it didn't work out…"

Osman responded contemplatively, a note of sadness unwittingly creeping into his voice. He still had the image of his beloved Zoey being berated by his mother, Ceyda *Hanım*, and him remaining silent, as if paralyzed. He'd never forgive himself for that.

"Uncle Osman?"

Osman came out of his trance. "Sorry, Ozan, I just had a flood of memories rush into my mind."

"And not very good ones, it seems," commented Ozan.

"Sad ones, I'm afraid, *Oğlum*, but I'm here for you, not me. Let's see, where were we? Family—no, I don't have anyone."

"Yes, you do, me!" replied Ozan cheerfully, arms wide open; he then enwrapped Osman in a warm embrace.

"Ozan, listen very carefully to what I'm going to say. This is the best piece of advice that I, as your uncle, could give you: If someday…"

There was a long pause until Ozan finally said, "I'm listening, *Amça* [Uncle]."

"Sorry, Ozan, I'm trying to organize my thoughts…if someday you fall in love—truly in love—don't allow anyone or anything to interfere with your relationship. Not culture, not religion…and especially not family. And another thing: always protect your girl against everyone and everything."

Ozan felt the impact of Osman's words right in his gut; he wished he had spoken to him before he had messed up his relationship with Mari-Car and distanced himself. Whatever it was that they had, Ozan felt sure of one thing: he did not want to lose her.

CHAPTER 43
OZAN'S RETURN

Fall was an especially enjoyable time of the year in the Lombardy region near Lake Como. The air was crisp and clean, the stunning view of the lake surrounded by the mountains reflected in its waters, the vivid colors of the magnificent gardens from the beautiful villas overlooking the lake…

No painting could replicate the spectacular landscape.

Wine tasting from the cellars of the small family businesses around the Como area and hikes to collect chestnuts, were some of Mari-Car's favorite autumn activities.

She enjoyed the bold local cuisine leisurely, without the summer crowds.

One of her favorites dishes was *missoltino*, attained by drying and salting the small fish from the lake; she complemented it with polenta—no other place in the world made polenta as exquisite as in the Como region.

The mood of the people of the region at that time of the year was buoyant, and Mari-Car's was no different. She felt that she belonged in Como more than in any other place in the world—

maybe because she was surrounded by everything she loved. Amazing architecture, the mountains, the lake, vineyards...

Every morning, when she walked out of the dorm into the courtyard, she lifted her hands toward the sky and gave various twirls before getting into her little car and going off to classes.

She reserved her scooter for going out into the picturesque towns around the area—Bellagio, Varenna, Gravedona, Lecco—hair flowing under her helmet.

She had recently arranged for, or rather convinced, Peter John to come visit her for the Thanksgiving holiday. She had promised him that they would go to a pub to watch the football game, which, judging by her jumps and screams after touchdowns and field goals during their trips to the football games in North Carolina, she enjoyed as much as or more than he did.

Thanks to the time spent in North Carolina with Peter John and the rest of the Stewart gang, Mari-Car had a total grasp of the rules of American football. She was looking forward to being with him enjoying a pastime so symbolic of American culture with Lake Como as the backdrop.

Whatever Mari-Car experienced, whether a quaint restaurant, a beautiful scenery, an emotive painting, a new flavor of ice cream, she'd immediately think that Peter John needed to experience it also. She knew that whatever she enjoyed, he would too and made a note to revisit that spot or that experience accompanied by him.

It was during one of those "head in the clouds" moments one morning while walking toward her parked scooter that, suddenly, someone hopped on her back seat. It kind of startled her, but when she felt Ozan's arms encircle her, lots of emotions collided: happiness, astonishment, anger, confusion.

"Almost missed my sightseeing ride this morning," was all he said.

Mari-Car said nothing but handed him a helmet and took off. Feeling his strong arms around her waist and his body acting as a strong protective wall behind her gave her a sense of security and well-being.

Her eyes unexpectedly welled up with tears. Where had her anger gone? she thought, angry at its absence.

"Eight tonight at your favorite bench? We'll talk—I owe you that."

Ozan dismounted the scooter at the first red light and handed the helmet back to Mari-Car. She hesitated, but he looked into her eyes and would not let go of the helmet. The light turned green.

"See you at my favorite bench," she replied.

She soon forgot about the conversation and immersed herself in the beauty around her, absorbing fully the spectacular gardens, the picturesque villages, and the breathtaking scenery. It was Saturday, her day for sightseeing.

She found herself daydreaming about restoring old buildings and villas. What were the intentions of their architects and designers? she wondered, knowing that this would be a required ingredient in order to bring them back to their original glory.

Mari-Car allowed her imagination unrestricted freedom to travel back in time: she envisioned the original dwellers of the Province of Como visualizing, designing, and building the magnificent structures. That so much beauty could be created with such simple instruments both fascinated and baffled her.

The rounded arches, porticoes held by graceful, slim columns, and inner courtyards of the fabulous villas overlooking the lake were definite reminders of the splendor of the Renaissance.

The unmistakably Gothic façade of Catedral de Como, with its mixture of Romanesque and Renaissance characteristics, captivated her. She had stood before it countless times engrossed in its features, and each time found a new element that she had missed before.

Mari-Car happily lost herself in thought and went back centuries to the world of building and restoring that made Como and its surroundings what it was at that point in time.

She 'heard' the sounds of the mason's voices and of the rudimentary tools against the stones; 'felt' the cobblestones under her feet; 'smelled' and 'tasted' the polenta and pasta cooking, and the dark bread baking.

Unexpectedly, she shook her head to bring herself back to reality.

A dilemma emerged in her head: How can I merge green design—and bring to life my dad's green home—and restoration? The day had gone fast.

Once again Ozan and Mari-Car were facing each other, leaning against the armrests of the bench, the toes of their sports shoes touching.

"I was scared, Mari-Car, scared of the feelings that arose within me once you opened your heart and your life to me. I thought of the differences in our families…your relationship with your mother, your grandparents, Peter John… and I felt lacking because, except for my grandfather, I don't have that closeness with my family. You heard what happened to my grandfather when he brought up my uncle Osman, who left the family years ago because my grandmother never accepted his choice of a wife."

Ozan grimaced as he spoke and twisted his hands. Mari-Car covered his hands with both of hers, and he stopped the twisting motion. He looked questioningly into her eyes, and she tried to alleviate his discomfort and make the moment easier for him.

"Ozan, we were just getting to know each other. If knowing me better scared you, why did it upset you that you knew little about me and my family? That's why I opened up to you, to please you, and you withdrew! Why did you stay away? What do you want from me?"

"I'm sorry, Mari-Car. I was just scared of my feelings because they were new for me and I didn't know what to do with them, so I allowed my mind to take wings and carry me to unknown places."

A long silence followed, and neither was in a hurry to break it. The first light of dawn broke on the horizon. Ozan was the first to open his eyes. He spent a long time looking at Mari-Car sleep. Then he got up and went over to her and pulled the blanket up to cover her well. He was mesmerized by the sleeping beauty lying before him. He looked at Mari-Car closely—her hair, the long, dark lashes, small nose, full, red lips. He stopped there, unable to take his eyes off them, unable to stay away from them. They pulled him as if they were a magnet.

Ozan touched her lips with his with the tenderness of a mother's first kiss of her newborn child. As he began to pull his lips away from hers, Mari-Car opened her eyes and found herself reflected in his. She tenderly brought her hand to the back of Ozan's neck and very gently pulled him down to her. She did not, however, use the same tenderness he had demonstrated toward her; she parted her lips to receive his with urgency.

As Mari-Car arched her back in response to the desire that Ozan had awakened in her, it caused every muscle in his body to harden. Ozan squeezed into the bench to lie next to her, but it was too narrow. He kept nudging in until he took her place on the bench, and she was lying on top of him.

Mari-Car raised her head to look into his eyes. Ozan responded by gathering her black, silky mane and pushing it to one side to give him free access to her neck, which he kissed lovingly and tenderly. His left hand ran down the length of her hair, caressing it. With his right hand, he gently took her face and pulled it down toward him until their lips came together.

Mari-Car tried to accommodate herself better by lying beside Ozan, scooching into him. Now pushed against the back of the bench, he gently yielded space to her until he lay halfway on top of her, and her head rested on his left arm. Ozan tenderly turned her face toward him so he could caress her and then kiss her thoroughly.

They both felt that they were reaching Mount Everest, and when they did, thought Ozan suddenly, they would fall, and neither would know what that would look like or feel like emotionally, or how it would affect their relationship. So he gently unmounted Mari-Car, his right leg touching the ground first, then, still bent over her, he gently lifted her head to free his left arm and transferred it lovingly into his right hand.

He knelt in front of the bench, still cupping the back of her head in his right hand and began to caress her face. He brought his lips down to engulf hers. Neither wanted the moment to end, but Ozan delicately, as if handling a porcelain doll, brought her up to a sitting position. He stood up and extended his hand to her; Mari-Car took it, and they both strolled hand-in-hand into the residence hall, she dragging the blanket behind her.

When they got in, she stopped at his door and looked up at him longingly. "No, Mari-Car, no. I'm not that strong…"

"I'm not either. Just walk me up to my room," she answered, getting on her tippy toes, taking his face in her hands and bringing it down to meet her lips once again.

"Mari-Car, even this is too much for me," Ozan said, removing both of her hands off his face with both of his. "I can't hold back, so if you're not ready…we can't get this close because even a slight touch from you—or a look, a smile, a strand of your hair falling on your face—makes me lose my resolve not to make you mine just yet.

Until…until you're ready, we're ready, the right time…I don't know, Mari-Car, that's why I stayed away. I knew what I was feeling; that's why I got carried away and began to wonder about our families, what happened to my uncle Osman, and all that."

Ozan walked Mari-Car to her room, stayed in the hallway, and closed the door, then he leaned against it while nervously running his hand through his blond hair. He didn't move for a few minutes, but just as he was about to, Mari-Car opened the door, not surprised that he was still there.

"Ozan, I was leaning on the other side of the door and could sense your presence. I've liked other guys but never enough to go beyond a kiss or a hug. I've been so daring and fresh with you that I hardly recognize myself…or rather, I'm discovering another facet of myself that I didn't know was there, but I'm glad to discover it. It makes me wonder how many more facets there are waiting to be discovered."

"I want to be the one to help you discover every one of them, Mari-Car."

"And I want you to be the one to walk me through every one of my discoveries, Ozan."

"Then I'm leaving right now. Tomorrow we'll go to our classes and will continue to get to know each other as friends until the time of discovery, OK?"

CHAPTER 44
BETRAYAL, GUILT, AND JEALOUSY

The next evening Mari-Car was back on her bench having another deep conversation with Peter John. They talked about school, their careers, their families, his upcoming trip to Como via Milan. Then, out of the blue, Mari-Car introduced a totally different topic.

"PJ," she began, stumbling over her words, "I've met someone…well, not 'met.' I mean, Ozan and I…" Feeling the cold, gripping silence from Peter John, she stopped before finishing what she was going to say. It was a long and uncomfortable silence. She waited patiently, as she had done so many times before, for Peter John to say something. She waited and waited and waited.

No response came pertaining to her disclosure. But a response did come in two words: "Good night."

His image disappeared, and Mari-Car found herself staring into a dark screen. She remained in place, her eyes flooded with tears. She allowed them to flow freely. Her lips quivered, her heart ached, her soul mourned.

The next morning she was unable to leave her bed. Her head ached, her body shivered, she felt feverish. When Ozan stopped by in the afternoon, he found Mari-Car semi-responsive, drenched in sweat, and burning up with fever.

He called a taxi, wrapped her in a blanket, picked her up in his arms, and ran out of the dorm, into the courtyard, and out into the street, where the taxi waited to rush them to the emergency room. Ozan got in the back seat, still carrying Mari-Car; he was in despair and yelled at the driver for not going fast enough.

Once they arrived at the hospital, he opened the door of the taxi even before it came to a complete stop and rushed into the emergency room with Mari-Car in his arms, shouting for help.

An orderly pushing a gurney took Mari-Car out of Ozan's arms and hurried her to an examination room. The doctor came in almost immediately, ordered an IV with painkillers and antibiotics, and took a few minutes to comfort Ozan, who seemed to be in total distress.

"Calm down, young man. She'll be fine, but it looks like she is fighting a bad case of pneumonia and will have to stay here for a few days."

While she slept, Ozan stepped out of the room to make a sort of uncomfortable but necessary call. "Peter John, I am Ozan, Mari-Car's friend—"

"I know who you are," interrupted Peter John curtly.

Ozan continued, "I'm calling because…because…Mari-Car is in the hospital—"

"What?! Why is Mari-Car in the hospital?"

"The doctors say she has pneumonia…in any case, her fever is very high and she's very weak and lethargic."

"She was fine when we talked two days ago."

"After talking with you, Mari-Car was very distraught. When I called, she told me that she did not want to talk to me or see me for a while. The next day, she did not attend classes, so I stopped by her room in the afternoon and found her burning up with fever."

The only information that Peter John had requested from Ozan before finally ending the conversation was the name of the hospital. Once Ozan complied, Peter John hung up without further comment.

It was too much for Ozan. He felt guilty, desolate, confused as to what to do, and unsure of who to entreat for help.

Frustrated and feeling helpless, he stomped his foot on the floor, took a cushion off the oversize chair in the room, and threw it against the wall. "*Allah kahretsin*! [Damn!]" was all that came out of his mouth.

He thought of his *dede*; he wished to be encircled in his strong, safe, and familiar arms. Then an image of Dr. Osman, his "uncle" Osman, formed in his mind.

"*Sakin ol, Ozan, sakin ol* [Calm down, Ozan, calm down]. I'll be in Milan in a couple of days for a symposium. I'll drive to Como, and we'll talk, My Lion, *tamam* [OK]?"

"Uncle Osman, it is so good to have you in my life. Thank you."

"Then it's good that we have each other, my Ozan. How about if you come and stay with me at the hotel in Como for a while? Actually, it's a small apartment within the hotel, which is also part of the hospital of the same name, *Famiglia Estesa* (Extended Family). Some of the patients' families stay in the apartments rather than the hotel rooms…they get more space and privacy, especially if their loved ones need to be hospitalized for long periods." Before Ozan could answer, Osman added, "I'll authorize the hotel to give you a key to the apartment."

"Thank you, Uncle Osman, but for now, I won't move from Mari-Car's side. She sleeps a lot, and during her awake times, she's so groggy that she hardly knows where she is, but I want to be here when she wakes up."

"I get it, My Lion. Then I'll see you in a few days, and please keep me informed of Mari-Car's progress."

In the evening of the second day, Mari-Car finally opened her eyes and was able to slowly piece together the events that had brought her to her current surroundings and state. She still had a cough and felt weak, and her breathing continued to be slightly labored, but she felt better.

The first person she saw was Ozan, next to her, caressing the tresses of dark hair that framed her face.

That was the scene that Peter John came upon as he stood at the door to Mari-Car's room. He said nothing for a few moments, just stood frozen at the doorway observing the tender scene before him. He had lost his courage and begun to turn back when Mari-Car called his name and, pushing Ozan away, tried to get out of bed to get to him. She stood up in front of the bed, but the whole room began to turn in her head, and she collapsed—into Peter John's arms.

He settled her back in bed. "Peter John, I'm sorry, I'm so sorry." She clung to his neck and broke into sobs. "We had made each other a promise…" Ozan grimaced, and Mari-Car detected a look of perplexity, hopelessness, and maybe sadness in him, but her priority was enfolded in her arms.

"I'll let you talk alone," were Ozan's words as he got up from the side of the bed and left the room.

Peter John helped Mari-Car to lie back down on the bed. He arranged her pillows, covered her up tenderly with the blanket, and made her comfortable. Then he sat on the side of the bed and took her hand. They remained in warm silence for a long while.

"Mari-Car, it was so easy when we first promised one another that before we fell in love or began a relationship, we'd tell each other and that we'd need to approve the relationship, because we are best friends, soulmates, and would never allow anyone to interfere with those plans. So when you told me that you had found someone and that person was Ozan, who had run off twice already and left you without any explanation…I felt let down, betrayed, and I didn't know what to say…I felt like I had lost you. But here I am."

"Our plan backfired, didn't it, PJ? I guess it was easier said than done, but please tell me that you are still my best friend, that you forgive me, that we are still soul mates. I can't bear to hurt you or to be without you."

"Do you still doubt how important you are to me? I took the first flight available to be next to you. Nothing has changed, and I'll be here not only until you are out of the hospital but also until you are feeling healthy and strong."

Mari-Car welcomed Peter John's offer to stay until she felt healthy enough to return to classes. She didn't even try to tell him that he should go back to the university in order not to miss classes, that he shouldn't be taking so much time to care of her. Instead, she willingly let him, because under his care, she felt safe, at home, happy.

"And my mom?" Mari-Car gave him a look of concern.

"I didn't want to worry her, so I told her that I had a few days off and I'd come to see you."

Ozan decided to allow Mari-Car and Peter John time to sort things out while he spent time with his uncle Osman.

The truth was that he didn't understand their relationship. If it weren't for the fact that they were first cousins, he'd be jealous—well, he *was* jealous. He knew he would never be able to compete with Peter John for Mari-Car's attention, but he wished he could at least have her trust, like Peter John.

Ozan envied Peter John. He wanted Mari-Car to see him as someone with whom she could share her dreams, her troubles, her plans. But that role belonged to Peter John, and Ozan felt sure that it would always be so.

CHAPTER 45
OZAN'S SURPRISING PROPOSAL

Osman listened intently to Ozan's concerns, definitely shared his point of view, and told him so.

"Maybe you should keep your relationship with Mari-Car strictly a friendship, if you are able…"

"Uncle Osman, you're right, I should do that, but I can't."

"That is your choice, *Oğlum*. Going beyond giving you some advice would be interfering in your private life, so I won't do that, but I will give you one last piece of advice: if you cannot keep your relationship strictly as friends, don't disappear without telling her what you're going to do and why you're doing it."

"Would you like to stop by and see Mari-Car—and meet Peter John—Uncle Osman?"

"This time you will have to excuse me with Mari-Car; I have to be at the airport early in the morning but do wish her a prompt recovery for me."

They shared a long, heartfelt embrace, and Osman promised Ozan he would be back soon and handed him a set of keys to his apartment. "Use it whenever and for as long as you want—it might come in handy if you decide to keep your distance with Mari-Car for a while."

Ozan took Osman up on the apartment offer and decided to stay there and give Mari-Car and Peter John their space.

In the meantime, he would concentrate on his own family, which he had neglected a bit lately.

He began making daily calls to his *dede* and texting his mom and sister. If he had learned one thing from Mari-Car and Peter John's relationship, it was how special it was to have a sibling, someone who stood by you on your good days and your bad ones, someone to run to with your hopes and dreams, who embraced them with the same enthusiasm they did their own.

Had he not reconnected with his family, Ozan would not have found out what went on in their daily lives. For instance, Deniz-Mare had missed quite a few days of class due to fatigue, weight loss, and catching whatever germ or infection had affected the other students at the university.

"Your defenses are down; it could be from stress," Ozan said, then added playfully, "In fact, it sounds like an acute case of 'missing your brother' syndrome."

"I *have* missed my brother—a lot! *Anne* and *Baba*'s divorce made me feel insecure…I know that they didn't have a real marriage, but there was some sort of stability—in my mind, anyhow." Deniz-Mare struggled to find the words to express what she was feeling. "Making their divorce official brought me unexplained loneliness. Plus, you left a deep void: I feel unprotected, I only have my mom to talk to, and there are things that only a brother would understand…I do miss you, *Abi* [big brother]."

"Wow, that's a lot to carry alone. No wonder you have so much stress! Come be with your brother, *Kiz Kardeşim* [Sis]. Remember, this is your country too, and we can live together." He sounded excited.

"But my studies…"

"We have universities here too, *Kiz Kardeşim*." Ozan's response came quickly and effortlessly. "Now I understand what's making you sick. Come!" he pleaded.

That evening Deniz-Mare spoke with her mom about Ozan's proposal.

For reasons that she found difficult to explain even to herself, Meryem felt a sense of rightness about her daughter going to be with her brother.

Ozan *Bey*, her grandfather, was also understanding, even encouraging.

"The house is getting emptier a lot faster than I had anticipated. Change is inevitable, but I don't have to like it, do I, *Kizim*?" He embraced his granddaughter.

"Go and live your dreams— be near your brother, but return to your home someday, *tamam*? Both you and your brother."

"*Dede*, what are you saying? Of course, we'll return—this is our home!" She hugged him, then took his aged, tired face (maybe from sadness, she thought) in her hands and rewarded him with three lovely words: "*Seni seviyorum, Dede* [I love you, Grandpa]."

"*Ben de seni seviyorum, Kizim* [I love you too, daughter]." He held her tightly for a long while, then gathered her small hands in his large, warm ones and exhorted her gently. "Now go and talk to your grandmother. Tell her that you love her; she needs to hear that too. It'll do her good, as it did me, *tamam*?"

"*Tamam, Dedecim* [OK, my grandfather]."

Ozan called Osman to ask if his sister could stay with him at the apartment while they looked at a place for the two of them.

"I'll tell you what—someone from the hotel will contact you and show you a larger apartment unit within the hotel. I just got that small unit because it was only me, but now that 'our' family is growing, let's get a larger place. Your sister will need her own space."

Ozan was now feeling really bad. "No, no, Osman *Amça* [Uncle Osman]. We can look for a place of our own, really!"

"Do you trust me, Ozan?"

"I sure do."

"Then do as I say. Someone from the hotel will contact you, OK? It'll be nice to have you at my place while I'm gone. Empty places are depressing and gloomy. I want to have people greet me when I arrive, *tamam*? But I have one request: let your sister choose the unit. Girls are better at that; they have a different perspective and notice things that we don't, like the view, the lighting, and so on."

"*Tamam*, Osman *Amça* [OK, Uncle Osman]."

It took a couple of weeks to get her college transcripts apostilled as required by the university. Deniz-Mare had applied at Politecnico di Milano, but it would be a while before she heard from them. She was sure that the best-case scenario would be to start in January, during the second semester of the school year. In the meantime, she would follow Ozan's advice and rest. She needed it desperately, she thought.

CHAPTER 46
DENIZ-MARE ARRIVES IN MILAN

Deniz-Mare arrived in mid-October on a cool, sunny day. She ran into Ozan's arms; he picked her up off the ground and gave her a twirl. Her laughter and squeals brought smiles to all the passersby.

When Ozan finally set her down, he held her back and took a closer look at his sister. "Beautiful as ever, but you have lost weight, and your eyes are tired. Let's go feed you some pasta—that will put some kilos back where they belong."

"*Abi*, can we go to your place? I'm really tired."

"Of course, *Canim*. Let's go home and have something there. But you might get very hungry before that—even the fastest train takes almost forty minutes," Ozan replied, but not without experiencing a current of apprehension pass through his gut.

"I'll be fine now that I'm with you. I'll eat at home."

Ozan encircled her waist and kissed her head. The baggage handler wheeled the cart to the waiting taxi and placed everything in the trunk. Ozan distractedly pulled money out of his jeans pocket and handed it to him.

He helped his sister to the back seat, then sat next to her, allowing her head to rest on his shoulder.

"*Milano Centrale*," were his only words to the taxi driver.

The ride was uneventful and familiar to both of them, but Deniz-Mare slept most of the way, and she felt very warm to his touch.

Once at Osman's apartment, Deniz-Mare went right to bed. Ozan kissed her on the forehead. She definitely has a fever, he thought. I'll contact Osman *Amca*.

While she slept, Ozan wrote to Osman, who called him almost immediately.

"What exactly are her symptoms, Ozan?" His voice carried concern, even though he tried to hide it by adding, "She's probably tired from the trip."

This explanation made no sense to Ozan since it was barely a three-hour flight, one both he and his sister had taken many times. They often went directly from the airport to check out the shops and restaurants in Milan, not getting into their hotel room until late at night. Something was not right—he felt it.

Osman pressed Ozan for detailed information on Deniz-Mare's symptoms.

"She feels very warm right now, and she refused to go anywhere; she said she felt tired and wanted to come home and rest."

Although Ozan was unable to tell him how long his sister had been experiencing the fatigue and the fever, Osman asked him to check one more thing.

"Listen to me, Ozan, *Oğlum*, I need you to check something for me. Go in and check Deniz-Mare's lymph nodes."

"Her what?" responded Ozan, almost in a panic.

"*Sakin ol, Oğlum, sakin ol* [calm down] and listen to me. It's just so I'll know which doctor to call on. I have excellent connections in that hospital. I don't want you to worry. I only want to find the best way to help you. Now go and do as I say. Ready? I'll walk you through it."

Ozan walked to the bedroom where Deniz-Mare was fast asleep; she still felt warm, warmer than before.

"Ready, Osman *Amça*."

"Now, raise her arms and put your fingers under her armpits, one at a time. Press in and upward toward her shoulder; does it feel normal or swollen or lumpy? Feel in the middle and along the border of the armpit."

Osman waited patiently on the phone for Ozan to report his findings.

Deniz-Mare winced but did not open her eyes.

"Osman *Amça*, I think I feel lumps. You're right…and *Amça*, Deniz-Mare's fever has gone up." Ozan's voice was shaking as he spoke.

"OK, *Oğlum*, don't panic; she'll be fine. Now, wake Deniz-Mare up. I'll send a nurse with a wheelchair. You'll follow the nurse and accompany your sister to the emergency room at the Lombardy Institute of Oncology. It's on the third floor, and you can access it without going outside. There is a connecting bridge between the apartment units and the hospital. My friend and world-renowned specialist Dr. Murat Urgancioğlu will already be there waiting for you."

"Oncology? What are you saying, *Amça*? I thought Deniz-Mare was just tired and had caught a virus on the plane!"

"Ozan! Calm down, *Oğlum*. You're the man there, the one who's in charge. Focus, OK? We're just eliminating possibilities, and this is the fastest way of doing that. Now help me here—don't fall apart."

"*Tamam, Amça, tamam.*"

"OK, *Oğlum*. I'll be there in a couple of days. In the meantime, you stay with Deniz-Mare at the hospital until they complete all the tests, *tamam*? And one more thing: don't tell your family that you're in the hospital until the test results are in. There is no need to worry everyone without cause. I'll be monitoring everything from here."

"*Amça*, I'm sorry to get you so involved in my family problems. I—"

"Who am I, Ozan? Who am I?"

"What do you mean, Osman *Amça*?"

"What did you just call me?"

"Osman *Amça*."

"See there? '*Amça*,' you called me. Is an '*amça*' family?"

"Yes, an *amça* is like a half father…"

"So I *am* family! Now, we'll get through this together, and I'll see you in a couple of days. As I told you, I'll be monitoring closely from here. Dr. Murat is a close friend and one of the best in the field."

"What field?" asked Ozan, unable to control his voice; it still quivered. His entire body shivered.

"I'll see you in a couple of days, and we'll talk at length," said Osman without answering Ozan's question.

In the emergency room, they were warmly greeted by Dr. Urgancioğlu. He looked older than his uncle Osman, and calmness emanated from him. Ozan relaxed after meeting him. He felt that everything would turn out OK and that his sister only needed to rest and get something to fight whatever virus she had picked up.

While Deniz-Mare was undergoing testing, Ozan waited in the cubicle that had been assigned to her in the emergency room.

For the first time since he'd picked up his sister, Ozan thought of Mari-Car. He was beginning to understand her and Peter John's relationship. If he had stayed close to Deniz-Mare when they were kids, they would have had a similar connection.

But as a child, Ozan only had eyes for his *dede*. Everyone else was just there as part of the background, a familiar and beloved background, one he mostly took for granted, only missing those who formed part of his life when he realized they weren't there.

That's what had happened with his sister. He'd begun to miss her and appreciate her when he'd came to Milan without her.

Ozan decided that he would not interfere in Mari-Car and Peter John's relationship or try to emulate it. This decision released him from a burden; he realized he had been tense and confused, spending too much energy trying to understand the dynamic between them. "Let the water take its course," his *dede* was fond of saying, and he now understood its meaning: things will work out the way they're supposed to.

CHAPTER 47
MISSING THE TWO OF US

Mari-Car and Peter John talked at length about Ozan. No detail was passed over about what Mari-Car felt for Ozan, including all her doubts, uncertainties and fears about their relationship. But one thing she was sure about, and she told Peter John: "If you oppose our relationship, I'll break it right now, because I trust you."

"So did you find someone who makes you happy? Am I losing my best friend?"

"Yes and no," answered Mari-Car. "Ozan makes me happy, but you are not losing your best friend—that would be impossible."

"Still, it was so nice when it was just the two of us…I feel like things will never be the same again."

"Maybe not the same, Peter John, but maybe better?" She sounded more like she was trying to convince herself, but Peter John did not want her to be sad and tried to encourage her.

"Come here," he said while pulling her to him to give her a long, tender hug. Then he pulled away and wiped the tears from her eyes.

"Hey, I was just being selfish when I asked that stupid question about losing me as a best friend. Do you think that's easy to do?"

On the last night of Peter John's visit, Mari-Car decided to invite Ozan to go out with them; she wanted the guys to feel comfortable with each other and maybe even become friends, although she knew the chances of that were minimal.

The voice that greeted her gave her the impression that her call had come at an inopportune time.

"Yes, Mari-Car."

"Ozan, are you OK? You sound stressed. Maybe I'll call back later."

He took a deep breath and ran his fingers through his hair before answering. So many thoughts ran through his mind. Should he tell her about Deniz-Mare? She might decide to come, and he wasn't in the mood to talk. On the other hand, maybe he needed to talk about what he was feeling—otherwise, his insides would explode. Now he cradled his phone between his neck and chin, and both hands went through his hair and down his face.

"Mari-Car, I'm in the hospital with my sister, Deniz-Mare. She's sick."

"Is Deniz-Mare here? I didn't know. What hospital are you in?"

CHAPTER 48
OZAN FALLS IN LOVE

"You didn't have to be here, but thanks," whispered Ozan in Mari-Car's ear as she encircled his neck in a tight embrace the minute she walked into the emergency room cubicle where he was.

Ozan looked beyond as if waiting for someone else to come in, then he looked down at Mari-Car and asked, "Wasn't Peter John with you?"

"His flight leaves in a few hours, so he stayed in my dorm room and will take a taxi to the airport, but he asked me to say goodbye to you and to wish your sister a quick recovery. Now come and tell me what is going on with Deniz-Mare. Where is she?"

"They took her away for some tests. She's in the hands of one of Uncle Osman's best doctor friends, an oncology specialist, Dr. Urgancioğlu."

"Oncologist?" asked Mari-Car, bringing her hands up to cover her wide-open mouth.

"Yes, I think Uncle Osman suspects something. I thought my sister was just tired, exhausted from her studies—I hope that he's wrong about whatever he's thinking. If he weren't such a good doctor, I'd be more confident about him being wrong in his suspicions, but that not being the case, I'm worried." He looked at Mari-Car with tear-filled eyes and an overall tired look that drained his face of both color and energy.

"When is your family coming?"

"They don't know anything yet. Uncle Osman asked me to wait until he and the oncologist looked at the results. After all, it might just be a virus…" Ozan gave Mari-Car such a hopeful look that she felt compelled to alleviate his burden right then and there. She took both of his hands, drew him close, looked into his eyes, and mixed her hope with his.

She felt him relax, but when she rested her head on his chest and sensed his anxious heart, sadness and helplessness converged inside her.

She thought of her refuge, Peter John. Mari-Car looked up at Ozan and, squeezing his hands, said, "I'll run to the bathroom and be right back, OK, *Canim*?"

Her use of the Turkish word meaning "darling" brought a smile to his face. He looked down at her and answered, "*Tamam, Birtanem* [my one and only]," and let her go.

"Peter John, it looks like Deniz-Mare is seriously ill. Ozan is not taking the news well. She's in the care of a Dr. Urgangioğlu, a good friend of Ozan's 'uncle' Osman who will be here in a few days, so until then, I'll spend a lot of time here with Ozan and his sister, OK? Don't forget to call me when you get home."

"Wow…wow! I don't know what to say. If it were you… wow, I can only imagine how Ozan is feeling…listen, I'll stay around for a few more days until his uncle, the doctor, gets here in case either you or Ozan needs anything, OK?"

"What? Are you sure?"

"Very sure. Call me to update me or just to talk, OK?"

"OK. *Un abrazo* [hugs]."

Deniz-Mare was settled in a private room, and Ozan was notified that he could now go up and see his sister. He took Mari-Car by the hand, saying, "I want you to meet my sister," and they took the elevator up to the third floor, where Deniz-Mare was.

What a beautiful girl, was Mari-Car's first thought when they entered Deniz-Mare's room. Ozan went immediately to her, sat on the side of the bed, and caressed her cheek. As he took her hand and kissed it gently, Ozan looked over at Mari-Car, who had stayed about halfway between the door and the bed, not knowing what to do.

"This is my friend Mari-Car." He motioned to Mari-Car to come closer.

"It's so nice to meet you; Ozan has told me a lot about you. I'm sorry that it's under these circumstances, but you will be better soon."

"Nice to meet you too, Mari-Car," responded Deniz-Mare weakly.

Mari-Car sprang into action and brought her some water, then checked the small fridge in the room, where there were juices, cheese, crackers, and fruit.

Without asking, Mari-Car began preparing a small platter with some cut-up fruit, sliced cheese, and crackers, then brought it to Deniz-Mare.

"Here, *Canim*." Mari-Car handed a small plate to Deniz-Mare. Ozan gave her a surprised look.

"What?" said Mari-Car with a smile on her face. "I'm good with languages—I know a few words in Turkish."

At that moment, he fell in love.

Without missing a beat, Mari-Car continued giving her full attention to Deniz-Mare. "You still feel a little bit warm; the fruit will be refreshing."

She took a washcloth, filled a small bowl with cold water, and began applying it to Deniz-Mare's forehead. Deniz-Mare gave her a grateful smile, Ozan an admiring look.

They both spent the night by Deniz-Mare's side, attentive to the comings and goings of the nurses. Ozan questioned every medication that they gave his sister and then looked up its uses and side effects.

Mari-Car had told Ozan about Peter John's decision to stay until Dr. Osman's arrival in case they needed reinforcements. The act of kindness on Peter John's part made Ozan's eyes water. He felt vulnerable, maybe a little embarrassed, but welcomed the extra support; he didn't feel so alone anymore.

So Peter John did all the running around needed. He brought changes of clothes for Mari-Car, brought food, made trips to the pharmacy—he even sat in one of Mari-Car's classes to take notes. It was art history—in English, thank God, but he had never been so bored in a college class before.

"If I hadn't been doing it for you, I'd have walked out five minutes into it," he told Mari-Car in the hospital waiting area where she had been anticipating his arrival. Peter John handed Mari-Car some notes and continued his complaint. "I hope they make sense, because I understood little of what I was writing," he added, exasperated.

"Truth is…" said Mari-Car sheepishly, getting on her tippy-toes, reaching to kiss him on the cheek; he leaned his head down slightly, feigning annoyance, to facilitate her endeavor. "Truth is…"

"Truth is what, Mari-Car?" Peter John said, finally lifting his arms up to show impatience.

"Truth is that I handed you the wrong class information; I had already dropped that class at the beginning of the semester." She ended up covering her face with both hands. "I meant to give you the information on the class on the Renaissance period," she continued. "That's what I substituted the art history class for."

"Good God!" was all Peter John could say.

Mari-Car again covered her face with her hands and spread her fingers to peek through the spaces and see Peter John's reaction.

"Come here, you!" Peter John pulled her in and kissed the top of her head; she wrapped her arms around his waist.

Ozan came into the waiting room and found them so. He once again could feel the incredible connection between them and knew that it was a bond uniquely theirs. He covered the tinge of envy that he felt with a friendly greeting,

"Are you OK, *Birtanem*?"

"She's fine and needs no vitamins or whatever it is you told her."

Ozan turned toward Peter John and shook his hand.

"I haven't thanked you for all you're doing for my sister and me. I hardly know what to say—it is a bit overwhelming."

"I'm here for whatever you need." Peter John pulled Ozan in for a genuine embrace. "Don't forget that," he added.

Mari-Car felt happy with the display before her and came and put her arms around both of them.

"The two most important men in my life," she said, looking from one to the other.

Ozan looked at her and smiled, but thought, I want to be *the* most important man in your life. He then looked at Peter John. "Would you like to meet my sister Deniz-Mare?"

"I would like to, but another time. I think now you are the one she needs and wants to be with."

CHAPTER 49
GROWING PAINS

Osman called his nephew every day at least twice. The calls mainly served to encourage Ozan and give him an update on Deniz-Mare's condition. All Osman would say was that her defenses were low, and they were giving her vitamins to raise them. Osman encouraged his nephew to continue applying cold compresses to Deniz-Mare's forehead to keep her fever down.

What Osman was really doing was keeping Ozan busy until he arrived. His friend Dr. Urgancioğlu had already spoken to him about the results of Deniz-Mare's tests. The news was not good—leukemia, chronic myelogenous leukemia (CML).

Both doctors had discussed at length the various types of treatments, including targeted chemotherapy drugs as well as the only treatment that would serve as an actual cure for the disease: a stem cell transplant.

Even after Osman was finished with all his commitments, he chose to stay home in South Carolina for a few days longer in order to "organize his thoughts," as he put it.

Besides the pressure of making the right decision on a treatment for his niece, Osman knew that he would have to reveal his identity to Ozan. And of course, the rest of his family would also find out. But he was sure of one thing, he thought, curling his hands into fists and clenching his jaw: he would never reestablish a relationship with any of them! Except for his nephew and Deniz-Mare, there would never be any communication between him and the other Ulusoys.

Dr. Urgancioğlu would be in charge of guiding the family through the entire process. As one of Osman's close friends, he was already aware of the severed ties and the family dynamics.

Toward the end of the week, Osman felt that he had worked out all the details about Deniz-Mare's condition and course of treatment both in his head and on paper.

He flew to Milan, aware that he couldn't continue to keep Ozan in the dark. His nephew was about to grow up very quickly, and he was sorry that with the news he was about to bring him, he himself was bound to become part of Ozan's growing pains.

After a long, stressful flight, Osman arrived in Milan. Murat Urgancioğlu waited for him at the airport and immediately saw his friend's tension reflected on his furrowed forehead and droopy shoulders. So after a warm hug, little was said on the almost-one-hour ride to the hospital in Como.

Osman did ask his friend to go light on the details of his niece's condition when talking to Ozan. They agreed that Ozan's level of stress when they met would determine the amount of information they would share with him.

CHAPTER 50
BRAIN OVERLOAD

Ozan had been informed of his uncle's arrival in Como and of the pending meeting with the doctors to decide on a course of action for his sister. He felt the weight of the world on his shoulders. He knew the news would not be good—he sensed it. Keeping Deniz-Mare in the hospital for so many days for a simple cold or infection just didn't make sense to him, so he prepared for the worst as he held his stomach to try to control the nausea that traveled back and forth from the back of his mouth, down his throat, and all the way down to his stomach.

Ozan and the doctors met at the hospital.

The small conference room seemed to close in on Osman. He had held in the information on Deniz-Mare's illness for too long and felt that he could not live one more night with the burden, which was why he decided to go directly from the airport to the conference room to speak with Ozan.

Uncle and nephew greeted each other with a warm hug.

When Osman saw his nephew, he decided that sharing fewer details was best at this point. Dr. Urgancioğlu also saw and sensed the extreme level of stress that Ozan was in and signaled Osman to go ahead and start the meeting. He had already established a good relationship with his nephew and knew him well enough to determine how much information to share, his friend reasoned to himself as he yielded to Osman.

Ozan listened silently, patiently, attentively… to the doctors for what seemed to him a very long time.

"Ozan, *Oğlum*," Osman began slowly and deliberately, reaching out to rest his right hand on the younger man's left upper arm, "we think that what Deniz-Mare has is chronic myeloid leukemia—CML for short. It's a type of cancer that alters the blood-forming cells in the bone marrow." Ozan did not show any reaction, so Osman continued. "Patients with CML have abnormal white blood cells that grow wildly in the bone marrow and crowd out other types of blood cells…" Still no reaction from his nephew. "Those abnormal or immature cells are called 'blasts.' This type of leukemia advances more slowly than other types."

Osman stopped for a few moments and placed both hands on the table; he waited to see if Ozan had anything to say or ask. But he still remained silent. "There are various stages or phases of CML, three to be exact: chronic, accelerated, and the blast phase. There are various good options to con…"

Ozan's brain was overloaded, and as Osman spoke, it selectively chose which words to hear— "cancer," "cells," "leukemia," "abnormal," "bone marrow." Holding his stomach was no longer enough to control his nausea, and he quickly got up and left the room, barely making it to the bathroom.

Osman, having jumped out of his chair when he saw Ozan run out, was right behind him. He held him by the waist and upper arm as Ozan emptied his stomach continuously until all that remained were dry heaves. These gave way to a massive migraine that almost blinded him.

Both men reentered the meeting room. Osman, with his left arm around Ozan's waist, the other holding his right upper arm, guided him to his seat and sat next to him. Ozan was drained of color and held his temples with both of his index fingers, thumbs cradling his jaw, his elbows resting on the table.

Osman called the nurses' station and requested a few bottles of water and washcloths. Immediately, a young nurse appeared and handed Dr. Osman the items requested.

Osman himself began pouring the water into the washcloths and applying them on Ozan's head, face, and neck. In the meantime, Dr. Urgancioğlu poured some of the water into a glass and handed it to Ozan, who drank the entire glass before setting it down.

"More?" asked Dr. Urgancioğlu gently.

"I'm OK, thanks," replied Ozan, more calmly now.

"Ozan, *Oğlum*," Osman began again, "Deniz-Mare's condition is probably more serious than we had anticipated, but please hear me out and trust me…us." He moved his hand back and forth between Dr. Urgancioğlu and himself. "It's serious, not hopeless…please tell me you heard and understood what I just said."

Ozan nodded; Osman pressed on. "As we tried to explain, we don't have a final diagnosis yet." he lied. "And as we discussed, there are various possibilities and very good options. But we'll discuss them one by one and in more detail tomorrow, *tamam*, My Lion?"

Osman moved closer to his nephew, put his hand behind Ozan's head, and brought it to his shoulder, where Ozan relaxed and then broke into sobs.

When Ozan had finally calmed down, he lifted his head; Osman took it in his hands, looked him in the eye, and said, "It's not all gloom. I have some news that I hope you'll think is good, but we'll wait until tomorrow."

"Please, Osman *Amça*, I need something good, something to get me through the night and this uncertainty. Tell me the good news now," Ozan pleaded.

Dr. Urgancıoğlu got up and quietly slipped out of the room.

Ozan looked at his uncle with hopeful anticipation. Osman hesitated for a few moments, but when he saw his nephew's expectant expression, he went on. "What did you just call me?"

"Osman *Amça*," replied Ozan, "I thought I could, since—"

"Since," interrupted Osman, "I really am your uncle."

"I know I feel like you really are…"

"No, Ozan, I really *am* your uncle. I am the same Osman who left the family years ago. Ceyda *Hanım* and Ozan Ulusoy are my parents; Mehmet, your father, is my older brother, and you are my nephew, by blood!"

Ozan was speechless. He got up from his chair and began pacing the small space while breathing heavily and running both hands through his still-damp hair. His mind went back to when they first met, and everything began to make sense:

When they took his grandfather to the hospital, Osman only conveyed his *dede*'s condition to him, never addressing the rest of the family. After arriving home, his grandmother had buried herself in her room, not speaking to anyone. His uncle's advice never to allow family to interfere in his personal relationships. Mari-Car's comment on how they looked alike— "You could be father and son," she had said.

There was also the special treatment that Osman gave him, letting him stay in his apartment unconditionally and indefinitely, the special care that he had arranged for Deniz-Mare, flying to Milan and then driving almost an hour whenever Ozan needed him…it all fell into place now.

Osman waited anxiously for Ozan's response. He couldn't read the expression on his face. Was it surprise, anger, excitement, realization? He began to doubt his decision to tell him the truth at this particular time, but then he felt arms around his neck.

"Osman *Amça*, Osman *Amça*, you are really my uncle?" Ozan was both choked up and out of breath as he spoke.

He took a deep breath, knowing that he had so much to say but that his thoughts ran faster than his ability to put them into words. He continued cautiously, making sure that everything that he wanted to say was said. "You're the father I never had, I am so happy…so excited…so surprised."

The answer to Osman's question as to the nature of Ozan's reaction after hearing the remarkable revelation came tumbling out of the young man's mouth. *Did I ask that question out loud?* Osman wondered.

Uncle and nephew spent a long time talking. Ozan told his uncle that he had once seen a picture of him in his grandfather's bedroom and after that, he never heard about him until the day they had to take his *dede* to the emergency room with chest pains, when he actually met Osman in person.

Osman spoke at length with Ozan about the day that he left the family home, never to return. About the feelings of guilt directed at himself and of hatred and revenge directed at his family.

"Because even those who did not directly and actively participate in hurling poisoned arrows of hatred and humiliation toward my Zoey are guilty of standing by and allowing it without lifting one finger to defend her…including me!" Osman added before going quiet.

The silence between uncle and nephew lasted a long time. Whatever needed to be said had been said; any additional words would be superfluous.

Osman did not elaborate on the types of insults that his wife suffered under his family, nor did he disclose that his wife had eventually died. He only said that she had left. At this point, he did not want to place such a heavy burden on his young nephew; he already had way too much to deal with at his young age.

Ozan broke the silence, changing subjects and suddenly feeling guilty for taking over his uncle's place of refuge.

"Uncle Osman, if you ever want to bring a girl to your apartment, just tell me. I still have my room at the residence hall and can stay there for as long as you need me to," Ozan blurted out. Osman was quiet, searching for the right words, but Ozan continued, "Even if you want to bring a friend—or friends. Do you have friends here?"

"My dear nephew, listen to me. I don't need to bring anyone to this apartment, you hear?"

"Well, if you do…" Ozan said.

Osman did not let him finish. "I'll let you know. For now, get that idea out of your head. And yes, I do have friends. Not many—I don't need a lot of friends. But the few that I do have are priceless and I rely a lot on them." He felt the need to elaborate. "Besides my friend Dr. Urgancioğlu, whom you've met, I have a really good friend here in Como with whom I spend a lot of quality time and in whom I trust a lot—"

Ozan interrupted and decided to press on a bit more on the matter of his uncle's personal life and marriage. He seemed to be intrigued by this aspect of his uncle's life.

"Why didn't you ever remarry after Aunt Zoey left? I mean, you're still young and good-looking."

Osman couldn't help but chuckle at his nephew's words. "Thank you, my dear, but I guess the right woman hasn't shown up, and the truth is, I am not in a hurry. In fact, I'm a little scared of ever taking that step."

"Why?" insisted Ozan.

"Because I'll never get over the fact that I failed to protect my first wife, and I lost her for that reason, so…I don't think I will ever get married again."

"Were you in love?" asked Ozan, a bit embarrassed.

"Very," replied Osman in a strong voice.

With that, Ozan felt that he had reached the limit of any right he might have had to probe into his uncle's private life and began to get up from his chair. It surprised him to hear his uncle's question.

"Do you remember when I told you to never allow anyone or anything to interfere with your relationship, especially your family?"

"I do," came the reply as Ozan slowly began to sit down again.

"That's the advice that I did not follow. I allowed my, our"— Osman pointed at Ozan and then at himself as he enunciated this last pronoun— "ultra-conservative, traditions-captive Turkish family to offend my American wife, and I did nothing to defend her. She was a strong woman and refused to be insulted, so she left."

Osman felt a need to continue, even though he knew it might be more information than his nephew could handle at this sensitive time; maybe he, too, had missed family more than he had cared to admit, and that was why he felt such an urge to share.

"So," Osman continued, "I went looking for her almost immediately. I looked for her in all the places that I thought she could possibly be, asked all the people that I thought could possibly help me with information, but when I finally was able to find her whereabouts, it was too late. My Zoey was dead."

"What?" responded Ozan, astonished. "How…why did she die?"

Osman did not answer right away; it took him a few minutes to get his composure.

"Cancer." He was finally able to speak. "But I'm sure I would have been able to help her if I had been by her side…we had so many plans—she was a doctor also. We were going to open a practice together in Istanbul."

"But maybe you wouldn't have been able to help her. Plus, you tried so hard to find her…"

"I would have liked to have been able to try, my dear Ozan. I would have liked to have had that chance."

Ozan broke the comforting and revealing silence that followed with another change of subject, to the pressing matter that they were both facing.

"Now that I know that you are our real uncle, I feel more confident about whatever decision you'll make to help Deniz-Mare, because she is your real niece; she's like your daughter too. You'll save her. I just know it!"

"We will work together on the best treatment for Deniz-Mare, *Oğlum*, but you and Dr. Urgancioğlu will be working on the front lines of the decision-making process. I will be working alongside you, but behind the scenes. I promise you, though, that I will be very present, just not very visible. For now, the family will not know that I am part of the team, *tamam*?"

"*Tamam*," was Ozan's brief reply. However, he was unable to hide the broad smile directed at his uncle, along with a look of admiration.

"Now you go and be with my niece. I will go to the apartment, rest a few hours, and be back early tomorrow morning to see you both. Deniz-Mare is not aware of my connection to the family, and it will remain so for now."

"What should I call you when she's present?"

"Just 'Doctor' for now. Time will take care of the rest, *tamam*?" Osman again pulled his nephew to him and embraced him. Ozan felt encircled in comfort and safety; only in his *dede*'s arms had he experienced this feeling.

When an exhausted Ozan entered his sister's room, he was greeted by the warmest of scenes: Deniz-Mare sleeping peacefully in her bed, Mari-Car doing the same on the oversize chair next to the bed, her hand resting gently on his sister's hand. He felt overwhelming love toward both of them. Could he live without either of them? he wondered. The answer rose instantly within him: never! He thought of his uncle and what he had gone through losing the love of his life. A tightness gripped his heart, and he felt he could hardly breathe.

A nurse entered the room and found him gripping his chest. She quickly got Ozan out of the room and into an examining room. Dr. Osman was immediately contacted. Luckily, he was still on the premises and lost no time in coming to his nephew's aid.

"What happened?" Osman questioned his nephew, who sat on the examining table, and signaled the nurse out of the room. She handed the doctor a tablet where Ozan's vitals had been recorded and left.

"*Oğlum*, tell me what happened," asked Osman, cupping Ozan's face in both of his hands and looking into his eyes.

"I don't know. I entered Deniz-Mare's room, and both she and Mari-Car were asleep. I thought of what it would be like to lose either of them the way you lost Aunt Zoey. Then fear and anxiety gripped me, and I couldn't breathe…"

"Damn, I knew I shouldn't have placed such a heavy load on you!" Osman ran his hand through his abundant dark hair and paced in the small room. He felt he should've followed his first instinct not to mention the details of his wife's illness and eventual death to Ozan—it wasn't the right time.

"Please, Osman *Amça*, don't feel bad. I'm so grateful for what you shared with me. I cherish your trust. Don't regret it, please."

Osman embraced his nephew and kissed his forehead. He stayed close to him for about a half hour, and when Ozan was calm, he walked him to Deniz-Mare's room.

Mari-Car was speaking softly into her cell phone.

"OK, PJ, get a taxi and meet me here at the hospital. We'll stay up all night, and then Ozan and I will take you to the airport in the morning. You know we never run out of stuff to talk about."

"Peter John scheduled his flight for tomorrow morning," she said after hanging up, answering Dr. Osman's and Ozan's questioning looks when they entered the room. "He had stayed a few days longer to help out until you got here, Dr. Osman, so I asked him to come to the hospital, and we'll keep Deniz-Mare company all night, if you're OK with that," she added, looking from the older man to the younger one, still amazed at the physical similarities they shared.

"I have a better idea," said Osman unexpectedly. "You two take Peter John out into the town and have fun. You could all use it…"

When Ozan was about to protest, Osman raised his hand and said, "I'll stay with Deniz-Mare. She'll sleep throughout the night anyway. Now off you go!"

Osman began escorting them out of the room. When they were about to reach the door, he added, "By the way, my treat," and handed Ozan a credit card. Again, Ozan opened his mouth to protest, this time joined by Mari-Car. Again, Osman raised his hand to silence them, gently shoved them out of the room, and closed the door behind them.

Once out in the hallway, they both looked at each other with eyes wide open, Mari-Car not quite able to figure out what had just happened. Ozan knew what his uncle was trying to do: distract him to relieve the pressure caused by the scary news he had revealed earlier.

CHAPTER 51
PETER JOHN'S REVELATION

Mari-Car felt like a princess being escorted by two handsome princes. Her beauty definitely did not escape the eyes of the uninhibited Italian men, both the young and the not-so-young. And their admiration did not escape Ozan or Peter John, who, as a Southern American boy, was not used to such bold looks and comments aimed at beautiful girls. Plus, he was the more subtle type.

At one point, in one of the clubs they visited, both guys went for drinks, and Mari-Car was approached by a young admirer.

"You know, I've been watching you for a while and dying to come talk to you. I couldn't figure out which of the brothers you were with, then I decided—hoped—that you were just three friends out for the night. My name is Giacobbe." Mari-Car shook his extended hand.

She threw her head back and laughed. "I'm Mari-Car, and you're partly right: the three of us are friends, but the two of them are not brothers."

Surprised, Giacobbe asked, "Are they at least cousins?"

She was amused and continued to laugh. "No, they are not related. Peter John and I are cousins, but the three of us are just very good friends."

"*Va bene* [OK]," replied Giacobbe. "They say everyone has a double; your friends must be each other's. What can I get you from the bar?"

"Too late," said Mari-Car as she reached for the tall glass of sangria that Peter John was offering her.

The four friends were joined by others, and it made for a pleasant night and an unexpected sort of going-away party for Peter John.

After saying goodbye to their new friends, Mari-Car directed one parting glance at Giacobbe, who waved at her with an obvious look of disappointment.

The three of them ended up on the couch at Osman's apartment, where they talked and laughed the rest of the night.

"Giacobbe thought you two were brothers. I guess I didn't realize how much you look alike until he mentioned it. I also think you and Dr. Osman look alike," Mari-Car said to Ozan.

"Giacobbe, Giacobbe—he should learn subtleness," blurted Peter John, ignoring Mari-Car's comments about their looks. "He didn't take his eyes off you the entire night!"

"I agree," came Ozan's reply. "The guy should learn sub… sub…what is it?" He looked to Peter John for help.

"Sub-tle-ness," said Peter John slowly, "but the *b* is silent."

"Anyway, that Giacobbe should learn that!" All three broke into laughter.

"Well, he thought you two were brothers," repeated Mari-Car after the laughter subsided.

Peter John and Ozan looked at each other, smiled, and Peter John joked, "Who would've thought that my double would be from Istanbul, of all places?"

"Do you have any Turkish blood?" asked Ozan, half joking, half somewhat interested.

"Nope, red-blooded, Southern American boy. Although one of my middle names is Osman…my mom, a history buff, said it was a very strong name, after the founder of the Ottoman Empire. Does that count?"

Now it was Mari-Car's turn to be surprised, or rather, shocked.

"What?!" She said, astonished. "I didn't even know Aunt Ashley was a history buff. Isn't she a nurse?"

"Of course you know that! History is just one of her side interests."

"I just never knew that…worse yet, I never knew that your name was Osman," she said, dumbfounded.

"My name isn't Osman, for God's sake; on my birth certificate it says Peter John Osman Stewart—that's all."

"Show me your passport!" demanded Mari-Car. Peter-John complied; she snatched it out of his hand. Sure enough, clear as day, the passport read, "Peter John Osman Stewart."

Mari-Car was almost mad. "Why didn't I know that? I thought we knew everything about each other!"

Ozan couldn't help but feel a bit of amusement. He scooched close into Mari-Car, put his left arm around her waist, drew her even closer, and with the index finger of his right hand, which held the bottle of beer he was drinking, turned up her chin and looking down at her, joked, "So you mean there is something that I discovered about your best friend that you didn't even know?"

For a second, her breath left her.

"Evidently," came Mari-Car's response as she faked being offended. She directed her next words at Peter John. "If you weren't leaving tomorrow, I swear I would be mad at you and wouldn't speak to you for quite a few days!"

Peter John came to her, pulled her up, and gave her a hug, "What difference does it make?"

"I don't know. It feels strange that I didn't know your full name, that's all."

"Well, now you do," retorted Peter John. He then tenderly kissed her forehead.

Early the next morning, both Ozan and Mari-Car said goodbye to Peter John at the train station.

"Maybe I should go with you to Milan and keep you company…" It was hard for Mari-Car to see him go.

"No, ma'am, it'd make things worse." He gave Mari-Car a last hug.

"Take good care of my girl," said Peter John to Ozan as he shook his hand and placed his left hand on Ozan's shoulder.

Ozan placed his left hand on Peter John's shoulder as he responded, "You mean, your best friend rather than your girl, right?

Mari-Car did not wait for an answer. She once again threw her arms around Peter John's neck and said, "I'm going to miss you. Call me when you land, when you're in the taxi, and when you get home."

"I will, my girl, I will."

Ozan did not miss the not-so-subtle jab. He immediately began scheming in his mind. If Mari-Car was ever going to be his girl, he thought, he'd have to prove himself to Peter John. How? He didn't know, but he'd do it; he refused to be intimidated! Then Ozan realized that he was being inconsistent again—hadn't he decided not to get involved in their relationship?

Peter John had intimidated him even before he met him. He would not allow that to happen again, even if he lost Mari-Car—and his heart ached at the mere thought. But it was the only way to rescue himself. Did love make a person lose who they were? he wondered. He just had not been himself since he met Mari-Car.

"Are you OK?" Mari-Car asked Ozan on the way back to the car, seeing his frown.

"OK," was all he said.

CHAPTER 52
CRASH COURSE

After dropping Peter John off at the train station, Mari-Car and Ozan returned to the hospital. Back to reality, thought Ozan, letting out a long sigh, but his uncle had been right—the time spent with friends had done him good. He felt more at ease, and he seemed to be thinking more clearly.

While they were both in Deniz-Mare's room, Dr. Urgancioğlu and Osman came in and examined Deniz-Mare. When finished, the two doctors, accompanied by Ozan, walked toward the door, then, as if in afterthought, Osman turned and asked Ozan if he had time to meet with them in private.

"I was just leaving," said Mari-Car, getting up from the seat next to the bed before Ozan could answer. "I have a class later on this morning, but I first wanted to come by and check on Deniz-Mare." She leaned down to brush Deniz-Mare's hair back and asked her, "Is there anything you need, anything I can bring you, *canim*?"

Osman leaned over and whispered in his nephew's ear, "Don't let this one get away, *Aslanim* [My Lion]."

Ozan whispered back, "If that ever happens, be sure hell froze over," pleased that his uncle liked Mari-Car. Uncle and nephew winked and shared conspiratorial smiles.

Mari-Car squinted her eyes, let out a big smile, and asked rhetorically in a flirty tone, "What are you two conniving back there?"

The usually formal Dr. Urgancioğlu looked at Osman, shook his head, and said, patting his upper arm, "We're too old for this, my friend."

"But I'm not!" replied Ozan, blowing a kiss in Mari-Car's direction.

"You've got your hands full, *Oğlum*," replied the doctor, now patting Ozan's shoulder. The three men left the room bantering. It was good for Ozan to have some lighthearted, fun moments, for he was about to experience very difficult ones.

They met in the same small conference room they were in the previous day, when Osman could not tell his nephew the entire truth about Deniz-Mare's condition. All three sat down at the small round table, but this time, Osman was right next to his nephew. The tone got serious, and Osman began.

"Ozan, *Oğlum*, as we mentioned yesterday, your sister's condition is very serious, and as we also said yesterday, there are options, good options, to beat this thing."

"Uncle Osman, what is the thing?"

"As we said yesterday, Deniz-Mare has chronic myeloid leukemia—or CML, since it is a mouthful. 'Chronic' means that it progresses slowly; 'myeloid' refers to the type of white blood cells affected by the disease. The myeloid cells fight bacterial infections and keep any tissue damage from spreading, among other things…"

"Like what other things?" asked Ozan, hanging on to every word.

"Well, *Oğlum*, these cells also defend the body against parasites."

"Wow!" Ozan became fascinated by the whole thing, which helped, because it momentarily detached him from the overwhelming emotional impact that Deniz-Mare's illness was having on the family.

"Keep going, Uncle Osman." Ozan's interest remained piqued.

"Stem cells are produced in your bone marrow…"

"I've heard the controversy about stem cell transplants," interjected Ozan.

"Exactly, *Oğlum*, and these are important and unique cells because they have the ability to grow into red blood cells, white blood cells, and platelets."

"What are those last ones, in words that I can understand, *Amça*?"

Osman chuckled before answering, "I'm getting there, *Oğlum*, I'm getting there. Platelets help clot the blood to prevent excessive bleeding. So…" continued Osman, "in leukemia, there is an overproduction of white blood cells caused by a genetic change or mutation in the stem cells that produce the white blood cells. OK so far, *Oğlum*?" Ozan nodded. "The white blood cells are released prematurely; in other words, they are released before they are healthy or mature enough to fight infection. Any questions so far, *Oğlum*?"

"No, *Amça*. I'm just trying to process all this and realizing that there is so much that I don't know…it just blows me away."

"It's a lot to digest, *Oğlum*," said Osman, covering Ozan's cheek with his strong hand and stroking it with his thumb.

Ozan looked at his uncle through tear-filled eyes; his lips tremored as he let out a quiet, "*Teşekkür ederim, Amça* [thank you, Uncle]."

"Anyway, *Oğlum*, as might have already become obvious to you, the excess of immature or unhealthy white blood cells crowds out the healthy red blood cells and platelets. Their number falls, and the symptoms of chronic leukemia appear. That's it in a nutshell, *Oğlum*." Osman reached out and disheveled Ozan's hair.

"Could you go over the symptoms again, *Amça*?"

"In the early stages, they include tiredness, weight loss, recurrent infections. In the more advanced stages, the tiredness or fatigue becomes more severe…fever, bone pain…"

"Deniz-Mare's leukemia is in the advanced stage, isn't it, *Amça*? She has severe fatigue and fever."

"That is to be determined, *Oğlum, tamam*?"

"*Tamam, Amça*…what exactly do we do now? What's the treatment?"

"We will discuss the various options in detail when we meet with your mother, but one of the main considerations is stem cell transplantation from a donor."

Ozan jumped to his feet, excited about a chance to finally contribute to his sister's recovery. "As Deniz-Mare's only sibling, I will be the first one to be tested."

"The lab here in the hospital is ready to begin testing, *Oğlum*. But first things first, we must call your mother."

Ozan regained confidence when he learned from the doctors that siblings were the best candidates for bone marrow transplant recipients.

Dr. Urgancioğlu placed a hand on Ozan's shoulder and took over. "There is drug therapy, but the only chance for an actual cure, as I think your uncle already mentioned, is a bone marrow transplant." He allowed Ozan to digest what he was saying before continuing. "After consulting with various colleagues about Deniz-Mare's case, we highly recommend that we go with that last option. The best candidates are siblings, because they share similar DNA—half from the father, half from the mother. However, the more potential donors we have, the better our chances of finding a match."

After the meeting, it wasn't his mother that Ozan called first but Mari-Car.

CHAPTER 53
THE FIRST TO KNOW

"Let's meet at your bench," was all the text message said; an hour later, that's where they were.

He was already there when Mari-Car arrived; she stopped a short way off to observe him. Ozan's knees were drawn up with his chin resting on them, and his hair was disheveled. This is not good, she thought, and hurried her pace.

When he saw her, Ozan quickly got up and met her before she made it to the bench. He gave her a worried look, then pulled her toward him and hugged her tightly. They stood still and embraced for a long moment without uttering a word.

Still in silence, Ozan took Mari-Car's hand and walked her to the bench. They sat side by side, and she looked up at him anxiously and expectantly.

"Deniz-Mare has chronic myelogenous leukemia, or CML."

Mari-Car hugged him once again, this time even more tightly. Then she held both of his hands and said, "Tell me everything in detail. I understand 'leukemia,' but not the rest."

"It's cancer of the white blood cells. These grow in the bone marrow, and there is an overproduction of them. In leukemia, the white blood cells leave the bone marrow while they're still immature, before they're able to fight infection, and crowd out the healthy white blood cells, the red blood cells, and the platelets. Platelets stop bleeding." He finished almost breathless, as if he had been rehearsing how to explain all this to Mari-Car.

She was visibly impressed by his clear and knowledgeable explanation, so her only question was, "What's the next step?"

"So far, we've only talked about a bone marrow transplant. The other options will be discussed when my mom gets here. I will be the first to be tested since I'm her only sibling and siblings have an excellent chance to be a match. I so hope to be a match, Mari-Car; with all my heart I hope." Ozan crossed his fingers in both hands.

Mari-Car also felt the same hope, as if they shared one heart.

"I will also get tested," she said without hesitation, almost enthusiastically.

Ozan responded with a long, searching kiss, as if the answer to all his questions lay in the depths of Mari-Car. He left her breathless and followed with a quick kiss on the cheek.

"I'm calling my mom now. You were the first to know. Stay by my side, please, and hold my hand—this will be a difficult conversation."

CHAPTER 54
OZAN FINDS WHAT'S BEEN MISSING

The next morning Meryem and Ozan *Bey* were sitting next to Deniz-Mare's bed. They had both met with Dr. Urgancioğlu and Ozan before seeing her.

Dr. Urgancioğlu placed a hand on Ozan's shoulder, looked at Meryem and the elder Ozan in the eye, and began.

"There is drug therapy, where medication is given to slow the advancement of the cancer. It works by blocking the protein that stimulates cancer cells. However, drug therapy is given at the early stage of the cancer, and tests show that Deniz-Mare has progressed to at least the beginning of the advanced stage of chronic myeloid leukemia."

Ozan felt as if he could recite all the information that Dr. Urgancioğlu had just given his mom and his *dede*. He had learned a lot in the last couple of days, and this somehow gave him confidence—for now, anyway.

Meryem felt a wave of weakness course through her body and lodge in her knees. She knew that if she tried to stand at that moment, her legs would not sustain her. Despair reflected on her face.

"*Kizim*." The elder Ozan looked into Meryem's eyes and held both of her hands in his as he spoke. "You must be strong. We are in this together; that's what gives us strength. Deniz-Mare is an Ulusoy. We Ulusoys are not knocked down easily."

So many thoughts went through Meryem's head: Was Allah punishing her for what she had done years earlier, the thing that still remained the big secret and lie in her life? she wondered.

Dr. Urgancioglu continued, "After careful consultation about Deniz-Mare's case with various colleagues and experts on the particular type of cancer that she has, we believe that the best option for her, and the one that could actually provide a cure, is a stem cell transplant, also known as a bone marrow transplant."

The doctor waited for any reaction from the family.

"*Anne, Anne*, I'm her sibling; I'm sure I'll be a match. My sister will be fine."

Meryem suddenly came out of her reverie but could not find her voice. Her lips trembled as she patted her son's cheeks, then kissed them.

"Indeed, the best candidates for a match are siblings because they share similar DNA—half from the father half from the mother. However, the more potential donors we have, the better chance of finding a match." Dr. Urgancioğlu repeated what he had told Ozan the day before.

Meryem heard, but her head was elsewhere, and she did not address the subject directly.

Why hadn't Mehmet returned all her calls? She had explained the seriousness of Deniz-Mare's condition.

And, Meryem continued to think, if Ozan was not a match, should she try to contact Luca? She'd go to the end of the world, if need be, to make sure her daughter lived. At this point, Meryem knew that she didn't give a damn what anyone thought; she only knew that a donor needed to be found.

After Dr. Urgancıoğlu had spoken to the family at length about Deniz-Mare's disease, he got up to leave. He knew they needed to regain composure and discuss among themselves their plan to manage this terrible and unanticipated hardship.

However, not much was said after the doctor left. Instead, all three went to wash their faces before entering Deniz-Mare's room.

She had a tired look, was pale, and had a slight fever, but somehow managed to wear a beautiful smile. Mother, brother, and grandfather surrounded her, held her hands, and spoke to Deniz-Mare clearly but reassuringly about what the doctor had said.

"Did you hear what I said, *Anne*?" asked Ozan, squeezing his mother's hand.

"What?" asked his mother, smiling up at him weakly.

Deniz-Mare looked at her brother expectantly.

"A sibling is the best option for a bone marrow match, and since I'm your only sibling…ta-daaa, I'm your first donor!"

Deniz-Mare gave her brother a broad smile and said weakly, "*Seni seviyorum, Abi* [I love you, big brother]."

"*Bende, Kardesim* [I love you too, sis]," responded Ozan, his eyes overflowing with tears.

"I know, *Oğlum*, I know," Meryem said in response to Ozan's enthusiastic comment about being his sister's best option for a bone marrow match.

"We will all be tested, *Canim*," said Meryem while lovingly caressing Deniz-Mare's cheek.

"Everybody, give me some space; I have to kiss my granddaughter," interrupted *Dede*. Meryem and Ozan stepped back and allowed Ozan *Bey* to caress his granddaughter.

"*Kizim*, listen to your old *dede*. Our family is strong, and when we're together, we're even stronger. You'll be fine because we'll make this journey with you, and we'll come out on the other side stronger than we went in, *tamam*?"

"*Tamam*," whispered Deniz-Mare.

Dede waved Meryem and Ozan in, and they all leaned down and hugged.

"*Babam, ve Babanee, nerede?*" inquired Deniz-Mare, wanting to know the whereabouts of her father and grandmother.

"They'll be here before you start treatment. They're getting tested also. But you know your *babaanne*—she likes to order everyone around—so we thought it would be better if we came ahead."

Deniz-Mare looked at her mother and then at her *dede* with an understanding look and grateful smile.

"And now your *dede* will go to Ozan's apartment and take a good shower and a good nap." He looked at his grandson and daughter-in-law and asked, "*Tamam?*"

All three responded, "*Tamam, Dede, tamam.*"

Ozan had decided to stay at his uncle's apartment permanently to avoid being so close to Mari-Car. He knew that if he stayed too close, he could not resist her; he'd have to touch her, play with her hair, run his thumb along her lips and the back of his hand along her cheeks, watch her sleep, cover her with a blanket so she wouldn't be cold, hop on the back of her scooter to protect her and to feel her hair brushing against his face...

Maybe, he reasoned, if he stayed away, Mari-Car would miss him. Even if it was half as much as he missed her, it would be enough. As all these thoughts built a world in his mind, Ozan was gripped by the realization that he was imprisoned in Mari-Car.

His uncle Osman was delighted with Ozan's decision to live in his apartment. After being without family for so many years, he welcomed the warmth that being close to family brought him.

For Ozan, who in essence had grown up without a father's love and affection, not to mention guidance, having Osman in his life filled all those voids. It was like he had found something that he'd been missing without knowing what.

CHAPTER 55
SENI SEVIYORUM

The testing process began almost immediately. Ozan was the first to be tested, and he was convinced that he'd be a match. Actually, everyone's hopes rested on him as they waited anxiously for the results, and he felt the weight of that huge responsibility.

"I'll meet you at your bench," messaged Ozan to Mari-Car.

The minute he spotted her, he ran to embrace her, then he collapsed to his knees just before reaching her. She fell on her knees before him and took his face in her hands, searching for an answer to his bewildered state.

"Mari-Car, I'm not a match for my sister. I'm not a match…"

"*Birtanem*." Ozan looked at her tenderly; he knew that using endearing terms in Turkish was Mari-Car's way of expressing to him how much he meant to her. In the midst of his overwhelming sadness, he pulled her in and took the time to kiss her thoroughly. She was like a shot of hope and energy.

Ozan pulled away slowly; he was breathless. The words came out naturally. "*Seni seviyorum*, Mari-Car [I love you, Mari-Car]."

"*Ben de seni* [And I you]," replied Mari-Car.

Ozan again brought her close, caressed her hair and her cheeks, took her lips again fully, and she gave willingly.

"There's no turning back, Mari-Car. From now on, we are together. For me, it's a forever thing."

"*Ben de* [Me too]," she said with a mischievous smile that reached her eyes. "Ozan, let me finish what I started to say before you so deliciously interrupted me."

"*Tamam*, finish, *Canim*."

"OK *Birtanem,* what I started to say is that, even though you are not a match for your sister, there are still a lot of us that will be tested. Don't lose hope at the first obstacle—we have a lot of them to cross."

"We?" asked Ozan.

"We," answered Mari-car. "I'll be with you all the way."

"I was so hoping to be the one to give my sister life. I was her best chance."

"Maybe her best, but not the only one, *Canim*. Peter John and my mom will both be flying in to get tested; I've already talked to them, and they immediately offered."

Ozan hugged her and showered her with kisses. "I can't get enough of you."

"You won't have to. You'll have me all the time…is that too forward?" she asked, somewhat surprised at her boldness.

"I'll take it exactly the way it came out." Ozan could not hide his joy at hearing how she felt.

Within the week, all family members were tested, but there were no matches. Peter John and Mari flew in that weekend to be tested. Mari-Car and Ozan met them at the airport.

CHAPTER 56
DO YOU KNOW HOW BEAUTIFUL YOU ARE?

Mari-Car jumped on Peter John's neck the minute she spotted him; he twirled her a few times before setting her down. In the meantime, Mari stood by looking at the scene before her, smiling and shaking her head. Ozan stepped forward and extended his hand,

"Welcome. I'm Ozan, Mari-Car's friend. Thank you for coming."

"Ozan, dear, nice to meet you. How is your sister?"

"She's holding on, thank you."

"I'm praying that we will be of help."

"I don't know how to thank you enough for coming."

"No need. We'll do all we can, my dear. Mari-Car has told us how special you are to her, so if you're important to her, you're important to us."

Mari looked over at Mari-Car and Peter John, then back at Ozan before speaking.

"I'm sure you know of the unique bond between those two."

As she spoke, they both turned to observe them. They walked arm in arm, laughing and talking enthusiastically, totally unaware of the world around them.

"Yes. It's taken me a while to understand their relationship. I'm still not sure that I do, but I accept it, admire it, even, and I know that it's uniquely theirs. In fact, Mari-Car and Peter John's relationship inspired me to get closer to Deniz-Mare."

"That's beautiful, my dear, and she is the reason we are all here." They got closer to Peter John and Mari-Car, who had gone ahead of them. "I'm here, too, beautiful daughter. You just saw Peter John not too long ago."

Mari-Car left Peter John and ran to her mom, kissing her loudly on the cheek and hugging her tightly.

"Don't try to make up for it. I know I take second place, maybe even third," she said, looking at Ozan.

"*Ay no, Mamá*, you are number one, I promise."

Ozan walked over to Peter John, shook hands with him, and squeezed his shoulder.

"Thank you for coming. Really, thank you."

"Are you kidding, bro? Of course we'd be here. Got you covered," answered Peter John, giving Ozan a hug.

"Now let's do this! Let's get tested and pray that one of us is a match." Peter John looked at Ozan with fingers crossed on both hands.

"I pray the same," answered Ozan, raising both hands, fingers crossed.

Mari looked at the two young men and commented to her daughter, "They say everyone has their twin somewhere. I guess those two found theirs; I can't believe how much they resemble each other. What part of Europe did you say Ozan is from?" Mari turned to her daughter for an answer, but Mari-Car had already gone to join her two guys.

She got in the middle, arm in arm with Ozan and Peter John. She could not feel happier, looking up at each of them with a broad smile. Her eyes sparkled.

They all walked to the taxi, Mari following close behind, still shaking her head.

Oh, love of my life, if only you could see the fruit of our *grande amore* now, she thought, looking up to the sky.

Her eyes filled with tears, which she tried to conceal by fast blinking and looking away.

As often happened, Mari got lost in her thoughts. The kind of love that she and Kurt had lived came once in a lifetime and could never be replaced. It was the reason, she reminded herself, that she had never looked at another man over the last fifteen years—in fact, Mari kept every man that showed any sign of romantic interest (and she had her share of suiters) at arm's length. She knew that she would measure them against Kurt, and they would all fall way short. But beyond that, how could she give herself to another? She couldn't even fathom that. But how she wished Kurt could see his daughter now. Her heart ached at the longing.

"*Mamá, por favor, vamos* [Mom, please, let's go]!"

Mari suddenly realized where she was and accelerated her pace to get in the taxi, where the others were already waiting.

"Sorry, everyone, I got distracted."

"Mom, I know where you were—or rather, where your mind was."

"I know you do, *mija*, and it'll always be that way," replied Mari, squeezing her daughter's hand with tear-filled eyes once again.

"Actually, I know too. I know where your mind went, Aunt Mari," said Peter John, squeezing her other hand. Mari was seated between him and Mari-Car.

"Well, I also know," said Ozan from the front seat. "Mari-Car has shared with me your incredible love story—I hope you don't mind."

"I'll never forget that wedding," commented Peter John pensively. "There's good news and bad news about that…the good news is, it was the most beautiful, memorable event I've ever experienced. The bad news is, it could never be replicated, nothing could even come close, and I don't want anything less for myself. So, Aunt Mari, you messed up my life!"

They all laughed.

"I wish I could've been there," replied Mari-Car with pursed lips and a frown.

"You actually *were*, *mi amor*, you really were there."

Is there an endless supply of tears? thought Mari as she carefully patted her cheeks with the back of her hand. Mari-Car and Peter John held her hands tighter.

"Let's concentrate on what we came for—Deniz-Mare! I'm anxious to meet her, and I pray that I'm a match," was Mari's heartfelt remark. It did come out as a prayer, and everyone felt it.

"Thank you," was Ozan's grateful response.

The train ride was a welcome, carefree interval between the airport and the hospital. It gave them time to relax, and Mari got to know Ozan a little more in the casual setting. She did not miss the tender looks that he and Mari-Car exchanged, nor the attentiveness that he showed toward her daughter. Once again, she noticed the physical similarities between Ozan and Peter John and wondered if Ozan's family had any English or Scottish roots—she remembered that Kurt had mentioned once that his background was British.

They went straight to the hospital, where the lab was already waiting for them to swab their cheeks.

"I expected to have my blood drawn," commented Peter John to the nurse.

"No, *signore*, we just need a sample of your DNA."

"That sounds so cool," remarked Peter John.

"What?" asked Mari-Car, curious.

"'Signore.' It sounds cooler than 'mister' or 'sir.'"

Mari-Car rolled her eyes.

After the simple procedure, Ozan and Mari-Car walked Peter John and Mari to meet Deniz-Mare. Ozan stopped at the door.

"Words are not enough to thank you for your invaluable contribution, but that's all I have: thank you. I'll go check on my grandfather and then go to class while you meet my sister."

He gave Mari-Car a brief and gentle touch on the cheek and left.

Upon entering the room, Mari walked straight to Deniz-Mare. She caressed her cheek and delicately ran her hand through her hair. She felt as if she were caressing her own daughter and radiated warmth and love into Deniz-Mare, who responded with a wide smile and a surge of energy. She was the first to speak.

"Thank you for coming, for being willing to be tested."

"My beautiful girl, of course we'd come, and I so hope that one of us will be a match…but if we're not, someone perfect will come along. I know it; I promise you." Mari couldn't believe how much love she felt for this girl, and at first sight.

"Thank you for coming. Sorry I wasn't here to welcome you." The voice came from Meryem, who had stepped out of the room for a few moments. "I'm Meryem, Deniz-Mare's mom. And Ozan's, of course. Welcome!"

Mari got up from the side of the bed, where she had been sitting next to Deniz-Mare, and went to greet Meryem, kissing both of her cheeks.

"It's so nice to meet you, Meryem. Mari-Car has told me about you—and *Dede*, of course."

"Has she told you that I am a big fan of your designs?"

Mari answered via a big grateful smile, then whispered, "Let's go out in the hallway and sit. There's something I want to talk to you about, Meryem."

Mari looked at Peter John, who had begun to walk slowly toward Deniz-Mare's bedside. She was about to tell him to keep Deniz-Mare company but realized that it was not necessary; he needed no prompting, she could see, a slight smile crossed her face.

Mari-Car, uncharacteristically, was oblivious to what was happening in the room, because she was late to an important class that she could not miss. So she just blew kisses at everyone and rushed out of the room.

Meryem and Mari made their way to the small couch just outside Deniz-Mare's room. Mari wanted to talk in private, and she was the first to speak.

"First of all, yes, Mari-Car has told me that you like my designs. Thank you!"

"No, Mari, I *love* your designs!" Meryem said, grateful to have a moment of respite from the heavy weight that pressed so hard on her chest and made it hard for her to breathe.

Mari smiled and once again thanked her. Then slowly, the smile gave way to solemnity as she addressed Meryem while holding both of her hands and looking at her straight in the eyes.

"Meryem, I want to help. Remember that I have a daughter similar in age to your Deniz-Mare; I can identify with your pain as a mom. I put myself in your place, and the truth is that I don't know how you are able to hold up."

"Mari, I do it so that Deniz-Mare will also hold on. I can't show her my desperation, but believe me, inside, that's what I am—desperate." She squeezed both of Mari's hands.

"Please, let me help."

"How?"

"For starters, I would like to put out a plea among my most influential clients…I'll ask them to get tested. The list is extensive. Someone is bound to be a match for Deniz-Mare." Meryem continued to listen attentively. Mari went on, "With your permission, I would like to circulate a picture of Deniz-Mare. No one will refuse my call for help, Meryem. I'm not one to ask for favors, and they all know that if I do, it must be of the utmost importance."

Meryem responded with an embrace, and then she placed her right hand on her heart and whispered through tremoring lips, "Thank you."

Peter John finally made it to Deniz-Mare's bedside. "I'm Peter John, Mari-Car's—"

"Mari-Car's cousin, best friend, and confidant—yes, Ozan has told me about you."

"Yes, I'm all of those things; and yes, my coz and I are pretty tight… Do you know how beautiful you are?" Peter John blurted out, surprising himself.

"You're funny," responded Deniz-Mare.

Her laugh was weak, but her look was bright, expressive, deep. Peter John could not take his eyes off hers. They were not elongated like the rest of the Ulusoys but rather almond-shaped, deep blue, encircled by long, dark lashes. When they looked at him, he felt unveiled, unprotected.

His insides were churning, melting, hurting, and he didn't know what the hell he was going to do with all that. What was this? He'd never seen such beauty, but beauty aside, he'd never experienced such feelings at first sight.

CHAPTER 57
PETER JOHN KEEPS HIS PROMISE

"Mari-Car, come quickly. I need you!"

"My God, is Deniz-Mare all right? What happened?" Mari-Car felt a lump in her stomach.

"She's fine. Me? Not so much. We'll talk when you get here."

"OK. Give me about an hour and a half. I just got out of class, and I'm walking to my car. It'll take me a half hour to get to the dorm, then I'll take a shower…or do you want me to go straight there?"

"No, I'll wait."

Peter John walked up and down the hallway, running his fingers through his hair. This girl has to live, God, please, he pleaded silently. Now his mother's prayer chain back in North Carolina made so much sense. He made himself a promise that he'd move heaven and earth to make sure Deniz-Mare was returned to health. His thoughts were illogical, scattered, and contradictory.

Was he in love? But he knew so little about her, only that she was Italian and grew up in Istanbul. She could have a boyfriend—did she experience any feelings for him upon their first meeting? He felt guilty and selfish for even thinking that. Oh God, what if she died?

Mari-Car found him in the small couch outside of the room with his elbows resting on his knees and his hands holding his chin. He was looking down but felt her presence in front of him. He got up and hugged her tightly.

"Now you're scaring me!" were her first words. She sat down next to him, holding his hands.

Peter John spilled his guts about the unfamiliar feelings that he was experiencing without leaving out any details.

Mari-Car listened silently, and this silence continued long after he had finished.

"Am I crazy? Illogical?" he finally asked.

"Illogical, yes—crazy, no! But love is illogical, Peter John. Don't try to explain it." Mari-Car's eyes filled with tears.

"What's going on?" He tenderly moved her hair back and exposed her tearstained face.

"You kept your promise better than I kept mine. I was the first one to know," Mari-Car told him. They hugged.

"What do I do now?" Peter John asked, a bit helpless.

"You act normal. We'll go in there and allow the words to come naturally if they are needed and remain silent if they're not. We'll keep Deniz-Mare company until Ozan, his mom, and *Dede* come. Ozan is in class, the rest are at Dr. Osman's apartment taking a much-needed break."

They adjusted Deniz-Mare's bed so that she'd be closer to a sitting position. Mari-Car fixed a plate with cut-up fruit and sat at the edge of the bed sharing with both Deniz-Mare and Peter John, who sat in the chair next to the bed, exchanging career talk with Deniz-Mare.

The conversation flowed easily.

Although Deniz-Mare got out of breath at times, her countenance lit up when she spoke about making presentations to the foreign investors that came to Ulusoy Holdings.

"I was lucky when I lived home in Istanbul, because I could attend classes in the morning and go to the company in the afternoon to get work experience. But I felt alone without my brother, so I came here to finish my studies…well, that was the idea; I didn't plan on this." Her eyes made a slow tour of the room.

"That's still the idea," interjected Peter John. "This is just a small detour, Deniz-Mare." He made the same slow tour of the room with his eyes.

"Thanks," answered Deniz-Mare gratefully.

"So where do you feel most at home?" Peter John wanted to know, because he couldn't figure out where exactly she was from.

Mari-Car had told him she was Italian, but Deniz-Mare spoke of Istanbul as "home." The truth was that to an American boy with Southern roots, that sounded very foreign, very exotic—maybe even too exotic?

He couldn't help thinking of his mom, who made a huge deal about his move from North Carolina to New York. Peter John chuckled as he tried to conjure up an image of her reaction were he to tell her that he'd be visiting friends in Istanbul. Better not go there, he thought, and quickly shook away those thoughts, directing his full attention to Deniz-Mare once more.

"My mom always insisted on my Italian heritage because this is my place of birth. So I've spoken Italian all my life; I've spent every summer that I can remember here. I feel most at home here. I feel more myself when I'm here."

"Well, you are very lucky, or like my mother says, blessed, because I can't think of a more beautiful place to be part of."

"But my family is Turkish," she quickly added.

"Well, it looks like both empires conspired to create exceptional beauty." The words that formed in his mind made their way to his lips and were uttered out loud.

Mari-Car's surprised look and her mouthing "What?" brought Peter John back to reality. Mortified, he got up to leave, but he heard the sweetest word he'd ever heard.

"Stay."

Peter John began to sit back down as if in slow motion, never taking his eyes off Deniz-Mare.

Mari-Car opened her mouth to announce that she was leaving but realized that something magical was happening between the two beautiful people before her and decided not to break the spell. She looked in wonderment from one to the other for a few seconds, then left without saying a word.

Mari-Car walked outside of the room and sat on the couch in the hallway. She hadn't realized that tears were running down her cheeks. It surprised her. She was experiencing bittersweetness at the realization that she might no longer be the number-one girl in Peter John's life, and she was not sure that she was ready for that but felt that it was slipping out of her hands. She allowed the tears to flow, embraced them even, grateful that no one else was there, because she did not want to share this moment with anyone. She wanted to mourn alone.

Meryem, however, walked up to Mari-Car.

"Are you OK? Is Deniz-Mare OK?" asked Meryem, suddenly worried upon seeing the redness in Mari-Car's eyes.

"No, Meryem *Hanim*, I'm OK. Just tired I guess, and a bit emotional. That's all."

"Mari-Car, you may call me Meryem, hon, and I also wanted to tell you how grateful we are to you and your family for your willingness to become part of Deniz-Mare's recovery."

"You're welcome. Ozan told me so much about Deniz-Mare that when she arrived, I felt that I already knew her. Plus, I don't have a sister," she added.

"Now you do—and a second mom!" said Meryem, embracing Mari-Car.

"And a *dede*," came the voice of the elder Ozan, all newly shaved and relaxed; he had caught the last part of their conversation.

"You, Ozan *Bey*—*Dede*—I definitely know well! I've heard so many wonderful things about you."

Meryem translated Mari-Car's words.

"*Canim*, come here." The elder man embraced Mari-Car, and she felt safe, surrounded by such strong, cottony, loving arms.

The small group entered Deniz-Mare's room together. The scene in the room warmed Meryem's and *Dede*'s heart. Peter John was seated on the side of the bed, holding Deniz-Mare's hands. They seemed to be having a lively conversation. Deniz-Mare's color was much better, and her eyes almost had their former brightness and playfulness. Peter John let go of her hands, stood up, and walked up to greet them.

"Mrs. Ulusoy, Mr. Ulusoy, how are you?"

"Take it easy, *Oğlum*." The elder Ozan was the first to speak, and Meryem translated once again. "Call me *Dede*. Your family has done so much for our girl that I don't know that we'll ever be able to repay…"

"Not at all, Mr.…*Dede*. We just hope that we'll find a donor soon. By the way, I contacted my parents—they will overnight their DNA samples before the end of the week."

"Thank you, Peter John, and you may call me Meryem. After all, if one of these DNA samples is a match, we will become a family, so let's just get ahead of the samples and be one."

"Thank you, ma'am," was his courteous response.

CHAPTER 58
WRONG CONCLUSION

For obvious reasons, Deniz-Mare unfortunately did not get a chance to choose the larger apartment as Osman had wanted, but he had gotten help from one of the hotel's administrators, who had sent him pictures.

The larger apartment, which consisted of two large bedrooms, each with a private bathroom, as well as an ample living room with a comfortable sofa bed and a guest bathroom, was ready and available on the same day that his father and Meryem arrived. They were able to spend their first night there.

This was not a nice coincidence, but Osman's doing. He had made sure that the apartment was ready for the family. Its closeness to the hospital facilitated easy movement between the hospital and "home." They could go for a shower, a sandwich, a short rest, and return in minutes.

Ozan loved the feeling of security and well-being that greeted him as he entered Deniz-Mare's room full of loved ones. His eyes fixated on Mari-Car first, but then he went directly to hug his sister and caress her hair.

"You look better—your face is bright."

"I'm OK," she said.

"And soon you'll be well. You'll see, sis."

Ozan then got up and went to kiss his mom and his *dede*, but he had a difficult time keeping his eyes off Mari-Car, which did not escape his eagle-eyed grandfather.

"*Oğlum*, take Mari-Car down to the cafeteria for something to eat. She's been here for a long time without taking a break." He winked at his grandson.

"Shall we?" Ozan said to Mari-Car, showing her the way to the door and wearing a playful smile.

Once they were outside of the room, Ozan clasped her hand and brought it to his lips.

"I so wanted to be alone with you," he said.

"And I with you," responded Mari-Car, looking up at him lovingly and pulling him toward her until she could rest her head on his upper arm as they made their way to the cafeteria.

Once they had settled across from each other, clasped hands resting on the table, Ozan brought both hands to his lips, kissed them, and looked intensely at Mari-Car.

"I can no longer be without you; I need you to breathe, Mari-Car."

She got up from her chair and went around to sit on his lap. She embraced his neck, then took his face in her hands, lightly kissed his lips, then both cheeks, then his eyes, then his nose. Finally, Ozan, unable to contain himself, brought her lips to his and kissed her slowly– and insistently.

"Ozan." Mari-Car's words came haltingly; she was a bit out of breath. "I love you in a way that scares me because it makes me vulnerable. When you love this deeply, there's one more person whom you fear to lose. It makes me think of my dad. I understand my mother's grief more than ever now."

"Mari-Car…"

"Let me finish, please, *Askim* [my love]," she said, delicately placing an open palm on his lips, then continued. "My mother's grief at the loss of my dad was so big that you could actually feel it as you walked near her or when you entered any space she had recently been in. The pain has softened with the years, but it is still there, reflected in her eyes. You saw it today when we picked her up at the airport. So I am afraid, Ozan. I am afraid to love that deeply…but at the same time, I know I am falling deeply in love with you."

"Mari-Car…"

"Wait, Ozan, *Askim*, wait." Mari-Car continued to pour her heart out. "So while I learn to manage this beautiful, wondrous, scary feeling, I want us to concentrate on Deniz-Mare's recovery. Let's not tell the families yet."

"They suspect that we like each other anyhow. Didn't you see *Dede*'s face when he asked me to bring you downstairs to the cafeteria?"

"That's because you kept looking at me, Ozan! You don't know how to hide your feelings."

"I can't, and I worry about all the obstacles that I see in front of us."

"Like what?"

"Family, culture, religion…" Ozan gently helped Mari-Car off his lap, got up from his chair, then sat her back down. He started pacing and running his hands through his hair.

Mari-Car got up, faced him, put her arms around his waist, and rested her head on his chest.

"Remember, we should not get ahead of ourselves. Of those three obstacles, only one is a bit of a concern for me."

"Which?" Ozan unwrapped her arms from around his waist, held her hands, and looked down at her anxiously.

Mari-Car made the sign of the cross and looked at him, displaying a mischievous smile.

"It's religion, isn't it?" asked Ozan uncomfortably.

"Yup, but I've got that covered for now," said Mari-Car confidently.

"How?" asked Ozan, still displaying a worried look.

"Well, I've emphasized your Italian side. I mean, I haven't lied; I've simply allowed my mom to assume that although you do have Turkish roots, you are Italian…and I think she has drawn the conclusion that you're Catholic. I didn't say that, mind you," Mari-Car added quickly. "I just didn't say that you weren't when I knew that she believed that you were." Her voice became lower and lower as she finished her complicated explanation; she ended up covering her face and barely whispering the last word.

When Ozan uncovered her face, she was smiling meekly.

"Oh my God! Mari-Car." He brought his hand to his forehead, then slid it through his hair and all the way to the back of his neck, which he rotated to remove the tension that had settled there. "I don't know the first thing about being Catholic!"

"OK, let's not worry about it for now. Let's go back up and concentrate on Deniz-Mare."

"But we haven't eaten anything yet," Ozan said.

"I'm not hungry. It was enough to be together. Maybe we can go out tonight?" Mari-Car had a hopeful look and both hands raised with fingers crossed.

"Not maybe—we will, because you are irresistible," replied Ozan, encircling her waist and bringing her close, their bodies molding to each other.

"We are in a lot of trouble," whispered Mari-Car, almost into his lips. If he licked his lips, he'd touch hers; he knew it, felt it.

"We are," is all Ozan could say before delicately kissing her lower lip, then her upper lip, then taking her by the hand and finally saying, "Let's go."

As they entered Deniz-Mare's room, Ozan *Bey* asked his grandson if they could talk in private. They walked out into the hallway, and his *dede* placed both hands on Ozan's shoulders.

"*Oğlum*, I am very grateful to your friend for his kindness in allowing us to stay at his apartment. It is a tremendous help to our family. But I insist on compensating your friend for our stay. I would feel a lot better and more comfortable.

"*Dede*, my friend does not want to accept any compensation. He wants to do something for my sister and feels that this is one way to help. Plus, he is not using it now; he's out of the country…"

"I still want to reimburse him for expenses, *Oğlum*." Ozan recognized the determination in his *dede*'s voice.

"I'll speak to him, *Dede*," he said, resigned to the fact that there was no chance of changing his *dede*'s mind. But by agreeing, he hoped to buy time until he could talk to his uncle Osman.

"Also, I want to meet him to thank him properly, *Oğlum*."

"*Tamam, tamam, Dede*." Ozan wondered how long he could keep his uncle's identity hidden.

CHAPTER 59
AT A LOSS FOR WORDS

It was exhausting for Ozan to keep up with the physical and mental stress. He felt old. Is this what "grown-up" is supposed to feel like? he wondered. He wondered whether he should take a semester off and just dedicate the time to his family. Between his studies, Deniz-Mare's illness, and keeping his uncle's secret, he was feeling overwhelmed, and he disclosed his worries to Osman during their phone conversation that same night.

"You are right *Oğlum*, I've been putting way too much pressure on you. I'll be there next week, and I'll take at least one load off. You won't have to cover for me anymore. I'll face everyone," replied Osman when Ozan tried to explain the stress he was feeling.

"Are you sure, *Amça*?"

"I'm sure. I'll have to talk to your mother about my niece, anyhow. I want to be there for them both. After that, I will talk to my father also."

Ozan breathed a sigh of relief. He did feel the load become lighter.

Everyone fell into a routine almost automatically. No one had to be assigned a role or task; each took on a responsibility and wholeheartedly dedicated himself or herself to it.

Mari was relentless in contacting her most influential clients; she spent the week personally reaching out to them. Her effort activated a chain reaction, resulting in hundreds of people getting tested. Mari had no doubt that soon a match would be found for Deniz-Mare. Beyond that, the more samples were in the registries, the better for all those who were in need of a stem cell or bone marrow transplant, not just for Deniz-Mare. The benefits would be far-reaching.

Meryem took charge of her daughter's nutrition. In preparation for the upcoming transplant, she researched the foods that would benefit Deniz-Mare and customized a menu for her daughter—broccoli, kale, cabbage, brussels sprouts to reduce inflammation, berries, including blueberries, blackberries, and pomegranate, which were strong antioxidants, and fatty fish for the fish oil that also served as an antioxidant and lowered the likelihood of developing heart problems. Snacks consisted of seeds and nuts that contained beneficial fats and anti-inflammatory ingredients.

Mari-Car and Ozan did not leave Deniz-Mare's side except for the times they attended classes—they even studied and did homework at the hospital.

Ozan *Bey* somehow knew that he was the trunk that held the tree in place. He took time to get to know his granddaughter better, rarely leaving her side. He also kept everyone at home updated on the new developments.

Although Mehmet called every few days or weekly, he was conspicuously distant. His behavior seemed odd to everyone except Meryem, who chose not to comment on it. Ozan was not so kind, lashing out whenever he couldn't hold his thoughts in.

"What kind of father does not come to see his daughter when she is gravely ill, *Anne*?" Ozan shouted at his mother while in his uncle's apartment one late morning.

"*Sakin ol, Oğlum, sakin ol* [Calm down, Son, calm down]. Everyone handles pain and difficulty differently, and your father has never been one to show his feelings."

"*Tamam, Anne*, but I'll tell you something: besides you and *Dede*, the only member of our family that I will embrace is—"

"Is who, Ozan. Who?" responded Meryem, arms up in the air, frustrated at not being able to explain Mehmet's behavior. She wasn't even sure she blamed him, although if he had wanted to, he could've become a father to Deniz-Mare. But since he hadn't even been a father to Ozan—she shook her head, trying to get rid of her thoughts.

Ozan realized that he had almost disclosed his secret relationship with his uncle Osman and suddenly said, "Deniz-Mare, that's the only family member that I will embrace…besides you and *Dede*." He had tried to clarify but realized he didn't need to; his mother's thoughts were far away, and she hadn't noticed his almost foot-in-the-mouth moment.

"*Anne, Anne, Anne!*"

"What?" said Meryem, finally coming out of her stupor. It seemed to her that she had fallen into stupors way too often since she arrived—it made coping easier, she justified.

"Nothing, *Anne*, let's just go to Deniz-Mare's room and give *Dede* a break so he can come and rest for a while."

"*Tamam, Oğlum.*"

Meryem picked up her purse, and when she was locking the door, a call came on her cell phone; it was the hospital.

She answered frantically, "Is my daughter OK?"

"Your daughter is fine, *Signora*. Her doctors require a meeting with you. Please come to the nurses' station, and someone will escort you to a conference room."

"I'll be right there!"

Ozan panicked. "Everything OK, *Anne*?"

"Fine, *Oğlum*. The doctors just want to meet with me."

"I'll go too," said Ozan quickly.

"*Oğlum*, you go relieve *Dede* from duty. I'll go to the meeting and will let you know whatever we discuss, *tamam*?"

"*Tamam*," replied Ozan, somewhat reluctantly.

Her surprise at seeing Osman in the conference room almost caused Meryem to stumble. Dr. Urgancioğlu quickly put out a hand to steady her. She couldn't take her eyes off Osman and when she finally found her voice, asked the most natural question.

"What are you doing here?"

"Meryem, I've been part of the medical team taking care of Deniz-Mare from the very beginning. Ozan called me, and I mobilized my colleagues. They are experts in the field; she is in good hands."

After settling down around a round table, the doctors went over the customized plan of action for Deniz-Mare in detail. They made it clear that the plan could be adapted as Deniz-Mare underwent more tests. Finally, they talked about the risks involved and answered all Meryem's questions.

"I don't know how to thank you, really," Meryem finally said, looking from Osman to Dr. Urgancıoğlu. She then fixed her look on Osman.

"Osman," she began, "I know I don't deserve such goodness from you. Maybe this happened to my daughter as the punishment that I deserve for not speaking out on your and Zoey's behalf when I should have. But the punishment should have been directed at me—Deniz-Mare is innocent." Meryem broke down as she said the last sentence.

"If you don't have any more questions for me, Meryem *Hanım*, I'll let you discuss family issues privately." Dr. Urgancıoğlu got up to leave.

"I have no more questions for now, *Doktor*. Only heartfelt gratefulness for all you're doing for my daughter," she spoke between sobs.

He patted her hand. "We'll get through this, Meryem *Hanım*, and I'll be there every step of the way." With those comforting words, he left the room.

Meryem once again looked at Osman and begged forgiveness.

"*Lütfen beni affet*, Osman, *beni affet* [Please forgive me, Osman, forgive me]."

It was too much for Osman. He extended her a box of tissues and responded very deliberately and slowly.

"Meryem, *seni affediyorum, tamam* [Meryem, I forgive you, OK]? I am responsible for everything that happened."

Meryem gratefully accepted the tissues, knowing that her face was a mess of tears, makeup, and probably mucus.

"*Tamam*, Osman, *teşekkür ederim*," she thanked him.

Osman's next question froze her in place; she was not prepared for what he said, or rather blurted out, next.

"Are Ozan and Deniz-Mare half siblings?"

Meryem literally lost her voice and looked at Osman in a panic due to both the unexpected question and her sudden inability to speak. She grabbed her throat. Osman thought she might be choking on something and immediately went into action, standing her up and asking her if she could breathe.

Meryem shook her head and fainted in Osman's arms. He managed to open the door while carrying her and shouted for a nurse to get an examination room ready. He placed Meryem on the table and began checking her vital signs himself.

Her heart rate was a bit fast, she was sweating, and her blood pressure was low but within the normal range.

Meryem slowly came to, but the words did not.

"I'm sorry, Meryem. I did not mean to shock you. I thought that as a doctor, I could ask you. When Ozan's DNA was tested, it did not match Deniz-Mare's as a full sibling but as a half sibling. Of course, neither sibling is aware of the results. I've instructed the lab personnel to maintain complete discretion."

Meryem signaled for pen and paper.

"Osman, I can't speak," she wrote, her face displaying total panic. "Did I have a stroke?" she wrote.

"Meryem, I think that you've just experienced shock. However, María Bianchi, a neuropsychologist and a friend of mine, is on her way. For now, just breathe in and out." She complied and was doing breathing exercises when a stunning woman with a white coat walked in.

"Hello, Meryem. I'm Dr. Bianchi, María Bianchi. Let's do some basic neurological testing, OK? Do you prefer English or Italian? One finger for English, two for Italian," said the very friendly doctor.

Meryem raised two fingers.

"Good," responded Dr. Bianchi, pleased.

She went on to instruct Meryem to follow her finger, touch her nose, stand on one foot—a whole battery of tests. Osman stood by silently.

Finally, the doctor turned to Osman, again displaying her beautiful smile.

"Your friend seems to be fine from a neurological standpoint, although, for reassurance, I'll order an MRI." Then she turned toward Meryem and added, "If you're going through some sort of stressful situation or have experienced trauma, that could be, at least in part, the reason for losing your voice."

Meryem nodded thankfully and did not miss the hesitation and the more-than-passing glance that the doctor gave Osman before leaving the room; he seemed oblivious to Dr. Bianchi's charms or maybe did not want to acknowledge them.

"*Grazie*, María," were the only words that Osman directed at the doctor before she exited.

"Now it's my turn to ask for forgiveness," said Osman. "I should have been more tactful when asking you the question."

"I would like us to talk." The words out of Meryem's mouth surprised them both.

She let out a sigh of relief and a smile. Osman seemed relieved but did not smile. When she thought about it, Meryem realized that she had never seen him smile, even years before, when he was living in Istanbul with Zoey. She of course kept her observation to herself.

CHAPTER 60
THE PUREST OF LOVES

"I'll be in a meeting." Osman's instructions were directed at the head nurse. "You may reach me on my cell if it's related to Deniz-Mare Ulusoy. If not, I am not available."

"Understood, Doctor," she responded.

Meryem and Osman took the elevator to the top floor, which could only be reached with a private key card, she noticed.

"Is that floor only accessible to doctors?" she asked, curious to know where they were going.

"No, only to me. I own the top floor; I have a private office with an apartment on the opposite side. These are my private quarters, my retreat when I am in Como."

They rode the elevator in silence the rest of the way.

When the doors opened, there was a small, circular reception desk with a friendly attendant.

"Welcome, Dr. Osman. Would you like anything brought into your office?"

Osman turned toward Meryem. "Anything for you?"

"A coffee—black, please."

"Two black coffees, please."

"Doctor, would you like two Turkish coffees?" the young receptionist asked after hearing Osman and Meryem speaking in Turkish.

Again, Osman turned to Meryem, with a questioning look this time.

"I would love one!" said Meryem, wide-eyed and pleased to have been given the choice. "Still black, please," she added.

Osman raised two fingers at the receptionist.

"Right away, Doctor," responded the attentive young man.

Osman placed his palm on the pad, and the door unlocked. He stepped aside to allow Meryem passage.

The back floor-to-ceiling glass wall let in a stunning view of the splendid, colorful villas, adorned by magnificent gardens and interspersed with cypress pines, overlooking spectacular *Lago di Como* at the foot of the majestic mountains that surround it. The vivid colors of the villas below became even more brilliant as the rays of the sun exposed their multiple tones.

Meryem stood just inside the door, unhurriedly taking in the view for what seemed to be an endless moment. Osman waited calmly at the entrance in silence. She slowly brought herself back to the space they were now in and, looking to her right, noticed a beckoning, L-shaped, white sofa against the wall facing the view. A large mirror above the couch reflected the spectacular scene, so when Osman sat at his desk, facing the door, his back toward the striking view, he saw it reflected in the mirror.

"*Dottore, Signora…*"

Meryem furrowed her forehead slightly, almost disturbed at being brought back to the mundane moment.

"Sorry to interrupt—our coffees have arrived."

"Oh gosh, Osman, I am sorry. I didn't expect…the view…" Meryem stammered, looking for words, placing her hand on her heart, then pointing at the spectacular view in front of her. "How can you work here? I would just dream, sleep, drink wine…"

"It's my retreat," said Osman, taking the tray from the young man's hands and placing it on the low, rectangular, dark-wood coffee table in front of his desk, flanked by two comfortable chairs.

Meryem's eyes were drawn to the inlaid, hand-painted tiles that made the table a true work of art. The green, blue, red, and vivid yellow tones brought in the colors from the outdoors that had mesmerized her when she first stepped in. His desk, clean-lined and triangular, was very modern and a stark contrast to the view behind it.

"So Turkish," voiced Meryem spontaneously, looking at the setup of the coffee table and chairs in front of the desk.

"My roots follow me everywhere," was Osman's only comment before he motioned Meryem to sit in one of the chairs. He settled in the other one facing her, and both began to sip their coffees wordlessly.

"He was the only man that I can say I have really loved…" said Meryem without preamble.

She went on to describe her and Mehmet's lives in Milan when they first came as two young newlyweds in pursuit of his master's degree. She explained every feeling that she experienced in their relationship and as a young mother: the distance, the loneliness, the insecurity, the fear of not knowing what to do with her young son, and later, the hurt caused by the cutting words and the perceived abandonment and disdain coming from Mehmet.

"I am not trying to justify my actions. In fact, I was quite persistent about marrying Mehmet. I'm only trying to explain the feelings that I was experiencing before going into the relationship with Deniz-Mare's father." No comment came out of Osman, so Meryem continued. "Osman, I don't know if this is right or wrong, but I regret not one second of the thousands I spent with him." Her eyes welled up with tears as she realized that she had spoken these exact words to Luca eighteen years before.

She continued, "It was forbidden love, impossible love…but the purest of loves, nevertheless."

Osman's mind suddenly filled with images as Meryem continued to speak. He saw himself in the middle of a vineyard surrounded by a valley, sipping wine, enjoying the warmth of Brianza, the hilly, green area between Milan and Como. It was one of the few places where he could spend time being himself—rare moments, but highly cherished and safeguarded by him. He continued his silence and she her narrative.

"We were mutually faithful for the thousands of minutes spent together of which I don't regret a single one." *I keep repeating myself,* she thought self-consciously.

Still no reaction or comment from Osman. But as Meryem described the relationship that resulted in the conception of

Deniz-Mare, he looked at her so intently that she, unable to stand the intensity, averted her eyes and fixed them on the far-off landscape. Not knowing what to do with her hands, she clasped them on her lap.

She shared what life was like upon their return to Istanbul with the two small children, the incredible relationship that Ozan and his grandfather had forged over the years, her studies and work, and finally, her recent divorce.

"I've gone back to my family name—Yildirim. I had been using it for a long time, since I started working at the museum…" Meryem felt that she was babbling incoherently. It might not have mattered, however, because she felt that she was talking to herself anyway.

Ceyda *Hanim* had barely come up in the conversation—or rather, monologue.

It was evident to Osman, by Meryem's omission of her former mother-in-law, that the matriarch of the Ulusoy family remained unchanged in character and attitude: judgmental, unforgiving, intolerant, inflexible, closed-minded.

Osman had remained silent, sometimes falling into his own reverie throughout the detailed account of what life had been like in the Ulusoy mansion since that fateful day when he left, slamming the door behind him and in the *grande dame*'s face.

"You're the best listener I've ever met. I don't know whether to get up from this chair and start running or sit a bit longer and wait for your reaction. But say something, for God's sake," Meryem pleaded.

Since she still got no response, even after she had stopped talking, Meryem started to get up from her chair, but she felt the touch of a strong arm on her forearm, followed by a voice.

"Stay," was the only word that Osman could muster at the moment. They remained in complete silence for another long while. It felt solemn, and neither wanted to break the almost reverential stillness.

Slowly, Osman began to speak.

"Zoey passed away years ago, and that's all I will say regarding my wife for now. Let's talk about Deniz-Mare. We surely will need to test the biological father and his family."

"I think the family owns a small vineyard here in the Como region; they used to, anyway," Meryem said.

"I think their vineyards have grown," is all that Osman said.

Meryem grabbed her throat and began to cough. Osman got up quickly and went around to the small refrigerator under his desk, grabbed a bottle of mineral water, untwisted the cap, and handed it to her.

When her coughing subsided and she had almost drunk the entire bottle of water, Meryem regained her composure and asked where the bathroom was.

"Go through those double doors."

Meryem followed Osman's look behind her to the closed doors beyond the comfortable couch that she had admired when she first entered the office. She got up and made her way through the massive doors and into a small conference room with fresh flowers on the table. The same stunning view welcomed her through the glass wall that extended into that space as well. She stood for a few moments, unable to ignore the beauty that poured through.

"Keep going." She heard Osman's instructions from his office and went through another set of doors into an impeccable and ample dressing room. She realized that the glass wall ran the length of his entire office quarters, including the conference room, his dressing room, and even the bathroom. No pictures or paintings were necessary; God had provided an enormous, matchless one.

The full bathroom, like the rest of this incredible space, was made to make one never want to leave it—double sinks, a toilet with so many buttons that she hoped she'd be able to figure it out, a walk-in shower with a rain showerhead on the ceiling and various other showerheads jutting out of the walls. The floor and walls of the bathroom were in honed beige marble.

Meryem washed her face and ran her wet hands through the luxurious strands of her hair, but the toilet intimidated her. What if she couldn't find the flush button? It'd be dreadful having to call Osman for assistance. She covered her face with both hands as the thought ran through her head. Then the absurdity of it all overtook her and laughter mixed with tears began pouring out of her. It took her a while to regain her self-control, but she felt the tension begin to release her body.

"Are you all right?" asked Osman as she reentered his office.

"Yes, I'm sorry. It's just been very emotional."

"That's understandable…" Then he quickly added, "It's important that we face everything head-on and as quickly as possible."

"I agree," Meryem answered.

"While you were gone, I received some interesting news, but I'll let the family tell you…"

Meryem felt a lump in her throat, a roller-coaster feeling in the pit of her stomach, and pounding in her heart.

"Osman, how can you tell me that and expect me to continue our conversation?"

"We'll stop now, and you'll go down and enjoy the good news, which has already been shared with the rest of the family. But we'll continue to proceed calmly and as we had originally planned with Dr. Urgancioğlu, *tamam*?"

Meryem nodded.

Osman had begun to conceive in his head what might be perceived as a far-fetched plan but could not yet share it with anyone, including his trusted friend Dr. Urgancioğlu. He first had to make sure that his suspicions were correct.

"Let's concentrate on two fronts," he said to Meryem. "Since Deniz-Mare actually has Italian roots, let's focus on the Italian National Bone Marrow Donor Registry for possible donors. Secondly, we'll test her biological family on her father's side—I'll take care of that."

"How? I didn't give you any names."

"I'll take care of that and let you know if I need further information."

Meryem understood that the conversation was over, and they both got up to leave; Osman stepped back and signaled Meryem to go ahead. She waited at the door, then moved to the side to give Osman enough room to press his palm on the keypad as he had done when they came in. He realized he'd forgotten to mention an important detail, so he turned to Meryem before she could step outside the door.

"Ozan knows who I am and that I am part of the medical team in charge of Deniz-Mare's case." Meryem brought a hand to cover her mouth, which had opened out of reflex, and her wide-open emerald eyes fixed on Osman, waiting for further details. "We've become very close. It all started at the hospital in Istanbul when Ozan *Bey*—my father—was taken to the emergency room and I happened to be on duty that day."

"I remember," murmured Meryem under her breath, almost to herself.

"Then we ran into each other here in Como," added Osman, without acknowledging Meryem's comment.

So many questions ran through Meryem's head: What exactly did Osman and Ozan talk about in Istanbul after Osman came and announced that Ozan *Bey* would be OK? How did they run into each other in Como; under what circumstances? Osman said they were "close"—what did he mean?

But Meryem was pretty spent and did not voice any of those questions. She only expressed what she was feeling at the moment.

"Osman, I am very grateful that you have become part of Ozan's life. Thank you."

CHAPTER 61
MARRIAGE SCARE

No more words were said as they went into the elevator and down to Deniz-Mare's floor. Once there, Osman went into his office space and began looking at the various patient files that had accumulated on his desk. Meryem continued to her daughter's room.

Ozan, Mari-Car, Ozan *Bey*, Peter John, and Mari were there. When they looked up, they all began to speak at once. Finally, Mari spoke.

"Let it be our elder, *Señor Ozan Bey*, that gives Meryem the good news."

Mari-Car leaned over to her mom and whispered, "*Mamá*, '*Bey*' means '*Señor*'; you don't need to say both."

Mari pinched the back of her daughter's upper arm before whispering back, "I'm trying here, *Hija*, OK? I'm trying."

Ozan *Bey* interrupted the whispering. "Let my grandson make the announcement."

"Could someone please tell me, already?!" said Meryem impatiently.

Ozan got up, cleared his throat, and with a broad smile on his face, looked at his mother and then at every other person in the room, creating an air of expectancy.

"Mari-Car and I are getting married!" he announced.

Mari turned pale; the news obviously had taken her by surprise, and she looked at Mari-Car, flabbergasted. Meryem brought her hand to her throat. Peter John seemed annoyed. Ozan *Bey* and the two young girls could hardly contain themselves—and didn't. They burst out laughing.

Mari and Meryem looked at each other and finally understood that Ozan was joking; they also began to laugh, although a bit uneasily.

When they had all settled down, Meryem could not contain herself any longer and blurted out, "Speak up already—what is the good news?" She looked at each one of them, hoping to find a clue on one of their faces about the news she was dying to hear.

Ozan stepped forward and with quivering lips, making it difficult for the words to come out, finally said, "A donor has been found, *Anne*."

Meryem broke down immediately. Ozan encircled his mother around the shoulders and gently walked her over to one of the chairs, where she continued to sob.

Mari signaled Mari-Car and Peter John to follow her out of the room to give privacy to the Ulusoy family so they could digest and enjoy the wonderful news that they had just received.

Once they were outside the room and in the hallway, Mari-Car received another pinch in the arm from her mother.

"You almost gave me a heart attack in there, talking about marriage!"

"Mom, I swear that I didn't know Ozan was going to say that. I think he said it out of nervousness."

"He could've said something else to calm his nerves!" retorted Mari.

"And how old were you when you married Dad? Huh?"

"It's not the same, Mari-Car. It's not the same…"

"I know, Mom, I know." After a comfortably long silence, she added, "And anyway, we're not talking, or even thinking, about marriage."

Peter John remained serious. "I'll go back to the dorm and rest."

"Should I go with you?" Mari-Car asked, concerned by his curtness.

"I need to be alone."

CHAPTER 62
MARI'S ADMONITION

Without having discussed their intention to go there, Mari-Car and Mari reached the hospital cafeteria. Both women got in line to order coffees and continued the conversation while they waited.

"I thought it was out of place for Ozan to joke about marriage…that's why Peter John reacted the way he did. Ozan was insensitive."

"I know. He was just nervous. That was his way of bringing lightness to a difficult situation. But I'll talk to Peter John. It seems that all I do is hurt him lately, and if there is one thing I don't ever want to do, it's hurt Peter John."

"*Lo sé mi hija, lo sé* [I know, my daughter, I know]." Mari tried to console her daughter.

Their discussion was interrupted by the barista.

"I'll bring the coffees to your table, *Signora e Signorina*," said the handsome young man, his eyes lingering on Mari-Car. She rewarded his admiring look with a smile.

"You see, you will have a lot of admirers. Don't limit yourself—you're too young, *mi amor*." Mari was pleased by the turn that their conversation had taken.

Mari-Car stopped before they reached their table and, pointing at herself, looked at her mother.

"I am too young? And yet, you told me that I attended yours and Dad's wedding. You were way ahead of me, *Mamá*."

"I was, and you did attend our wedding, and I'm glad I could give him that priceless gift. He had a chance to experience fatherhood, and you had a chance to be loved by your dad like no one else could."

They sat across from each other at the table. The thought of Kurt once again caused Mari's eyes to fill with tears, and Mari-Car reached across the table and took her mother's hands in hers.

"*Mamá*, I'm afraid I'll never find anyone to measure up to my dad. This worries me."

"That's my fault, I'm afraid; but remember, you, my dear, are not me. You'll find someone who will love you the way you want to be loved, not the way your father loved me. You have different likes and dislikes, different wants, different dreams from mine. That's what your true love will end up loving and fulfilling, so my *grande amore*"—Mari brought her right hand to her heart— "will not necessarily be your *grande amore*, Mari-Car."

"Wow, thanks, Mom." Mari-Car was visibly touched by her mother's words. She experienced a lightness, a sort of liberation of her soul.

"Now, tell me about Ozan and his family. You said they were European, but their Turkish roots seem to be pretty strong… and that's OK. It's just that…"

Mari-Car did not let her mom finish her thought, "Ozan and Deniz-Mare were born in Milan, and they are here in Milan whenever they're not in school. They spend all their vacations in Italy, they speak Italian fluently of course—"

"Of course," answered Mari before allowing her daughter to continue. "But, in their everyday lives, Mari-Car, what culture is the most prevalent? Are they practicing Muslims, for instance?"

"I don't know, *Mamá*." Frustration was evident in her voice. "I don't even know what that means."

"Does the family follow the rituals of Islam, for instance?"

Mari-Car's eyes revealed exasperation when she looked at her mom and replied, "I really do not know, *Mamá*!"

After a short pause, she continued, "I've never seen Ozan practice any rituals, nor am I even sure that I know what those rituals are. I don't think he's been to Mecca, nor have I seen him praying on a rug facing east five times a day. Those are the only ones I remember from my class on world religions." Mari-Car's annoyance seemed to increase as she spoke. She brushed her hair back with her hand and looked away from her mother.

"There's no need to be defensive—we're just talking."

"No, *Mamá*, you're lecturing and being judgmental."

Mari leaned forward and stretched her hand to caress her daughter's cheek.

"*Sí, mi amor*, maybe I am. I'm very anxious about the huge differences, especially in religious beliefs." Mari then took both her daughter's hands and went on. "It's not the beliefs in themselves; it's the actions that these beliefs may carry within them." Mari-Car looked at her mom, and her countenance softened.

Mari continued, "Depending on how ingrained those beliefs are, men can be possessive, authoritative, suspicious. They may require that their wives or girlfriends be submissive, dictate where they go, what they wear…these men may even prevent them from pursuing their careers. It all comes under the pretext of 'love.' I'm just concerned, Mari-Car." There was a long, silent pause. "I've witnessed that attitude in my field throughout the years, Mari-Car. I've seen many beautiful, talented female models who were made to give up promising careers on the prestigious runways of Paris, New York, here in Milan— to accommodate the demands of the men in their lives."

Mari's eyebrows furrowed, her jaw clenched, and one of her impeccably manicured hands rolled into a fist and firmly made contact with the table. "Let me just tell you one last thing, Mari-Car: in all these years, I have never seen one"—her right index finger went up— "one single man from that culture give up his career to support his wife or girlfriend."

"And how many men have you met from our culture, *Mamá*, that have given up their careers for their wives or girlfriends?"

Mari remained silent. She wished she could explain better what she was feeling and what she had observed during the years.

Mari-Car continued, "I don't know about the people that you've met, *Mamá*, but in Ozan's family, the women are strong and professional, and the men are not just accepting of those qualities but encouraging."

"They all are…at the beginning of the relationship, *mi hija*."

"Look at Deniz-Mare and Meryem *Hanım*, the two closest, most important women in Ozan's life. Plus," Mari-Car continued, when she got no reaction to her examples of strong, presumably Muslim women, "all those traits you listed—possessive, authoritative, suspicious—they are seen in our 'Western culture' too." Mari-Car put up the index and middle fingers of both hands to imitate quotation marks. "*Mamá*, you could be referring to Italian men!" she continued to make her point. "And if Ozan were Italian and Catholic"—she placed emphasis on both adjectives— "we wouldn't be having this conversation, right?"

"I heard 'Ozan,' 'Italian,' and 'Catholic,'" came a voice approaching their table. "Of those three words, two refer to me, I think." He looked at Mari-Car questioningly. "Or do you know another Ozan?"

"You're the one and only," Mari-Car responded, looking up at him adoringly.

Ozan cupped her chin in his hand and smiled down at her before sitting down and clasping her hand. His free hand rested on the table.

"Ms. Mari, I just wanted to personally come and thank you. I know that Deniz-Mare's donor responded to the call that you put out to all your contacts. I…my family will never be able to repay the debt that we owe to you."

"Ozan, dear"—Mari covered his hand with hers — "if it had been Mari-Car in Deniz-Mare's place, I know that you and your family would have likewise stretched out your hand to help us. That's what motivated, inspired, and compelled me to help. I put myself in your mother's place and Mari-Car in Deniz- Mare's. So there is no debt, only gratitude that the donor was found. Now the hard work begins."

Ozan's eyes watered. He looked at Mari, then at Mari-Car. "Ms. Mari, I don't know what you and Mari-Car were discussing before I came, but by the three words that I heard, I can guess that the conversation involved me. Partly at least."

"Yes, it did, Ozan," responded Mari.

Before she could say anything else, Ozan continued to speak. "Ms. Mari, I have a very strong connection to my country of birth. That is thanks to our mother, who has always felt that strong connection herself, but no, I am not Catholic. Following our Muslim tradition, I was circumcised at the age of six, just like my father and my grandfather, with whom I am very close, as you know."

Mari gave a subtle wince when she heard him say "our Muslim tradition." Oh God, would Mari-Car ever use that phrase? Mari could not avoid the thought but remained silent and allowed Ozan to continue.

"However, Turkey, as you know, is a secular country, and that's how we were brought up. I am spiritual and believe in

God, but I believe in the God that surpasses religions, even though I respect all religions."

Oh God, what's he going to say next? was her next thought. Maybe what he said in Deniz-Mare's room about him and Mari-Car getting married was no joke. But Mari, despite experiencing distress while listening to Ozan, continued her silence and listened attentively.

"I just wanted to be honest with you before asking your permission…"

Mari became visibly distraught and asked for water.

Ozan waited patiently, staring at his hand while tapping the empty coffee cup on the table. Under the table his hand continued to be entwined tightly with Mari-Car's.

Mari-Car kept silent, but there was no denying that she was surprised at the turn that the conversation had taken.

The friendly waiter brought the water in a tall, slim glass with a wedge of lemon on the rim and placed it in front of Mari-Car, who looked up at the young man, smiled, and said, "The water is for my mother."

"*Mi scuso* [Excuse me]," responded the waiter, politely and mischievously.

Ozan looked at the flirty waiter and smiled while squinting his eyes and shaking his index finger at him. The young man responded with a few pats on Ozan's back and a "*Tranquillo* [Calm down]."

The brief exchange brought smiles to everyone and softened the tension created mostly by Mari's reaction to Ozan's request for permission.

Although his sweaty palms belied his self-confidence, Ozan continued in a strong voice, as if no interruption had occurred.

"Ms. Mari, as I was saying, I would like your permission to get to know your daughter better."

Relieved, Mari brought her right hand to her heart and replied through nervous laughter, "Ozan, my goodness, how polite of you to ask. Yes, please, you should get to know each other better, I agree."

"Thanks, Ms. Mari."

Mari got up to leave, but before leaving, she went around to say goodbye. Ozan got up, and Mari-Car followed. Mari took both of Ozan's hands and looked him in the eye.

"Take time to get to know each other—there's no rush." Then she thought, How different it is when it's your child. An image of her parents when she and Kurt told them that they were going to get married came into her mind. *We were so young; I was about Mari-Car's age*, she thought. She kissed both of Ozan's cheeks.

Then Mari turned to her daughter, caressed both cheeks, kissed them, and finally embraced her.

"*Te amo, mi hija. Te amo mucho* [I love you, my daughter. I love you a lot]," she said through bleary eyes, and she turned to leave but then thought better of it and took a step toward Ozan. While lightly touching his arm, Mari directed her last admonition at him. Although it was gentle and said through watery eyes, it was nevertheless cautionary.

"One last thing, Ozan, dear..." Mari hesitated to regain her poise. "Mari-Car is all I have in this life."

The lump in his throat prevented Ozan from answering Mari. He just nodded; Mari left.

There are moments in life that are almost sacred, and to speak words at such times would be almost sinful. Both Ozan and Mari-Car seemed to recognize that they were experiencing such a moment and revered the long silence that followed.

CHAPTER 63
ALLAH'A ÜKÜR

"First of all, we are thankful that a donor could be found in order for Deniz-Mare to receive a bone marrow transplant." Stillness set in in the small conference room where Dr. Urgancioğlu had gathered the family to explain how they would proceed with Deniz-Mare's treatment now that a donor had been found.

"*Allah'a şükür* [Thanks be to God]." The words of thanksgiving flowed easily and naturally out of Ozan *Bey*'s mouth. For the first time in his life, Ozan felt self-conscious hearing the phrase that he had heard his grandfather utter so often throughout his childhood.

Ozan thought of the last conversation that he had had with Mari *Hanim* and was glad that she was not at the meeting. Then he felt embarrassed about what he was feeling and thinking; his stomach churned.

His mother's question brought him back to the present, and he made the effort to concentrate on the reason for this gathering and who really mattered at the moment.

"Dr. Urgancioğlu, I've read about targeted therapy, drugs used to target the cancerous cells. Why is that not an option again?" Meryem inquired.

"Yes, targeted therapy uses a drug that slows down," he began, emphasizing the next phrase, "the *progression* of the cancer. It does so by blocking the protein called tyrosine kinase, which, by the way, stimulates the growth of the cancer cells…"

"It sounds so much easier and simpler than the stem cell transplant," Meryem interrupted. "I mean, there's always a chance that the body will reject the donor's cells, right?" Her voice faltered as she mentioned the possibility, and her hands tremored slightly.

"Meryem *Hanim*, you are correct in that it is a simpler course of action. However, the reason our team of doctors, with your approval, of course, has suggested the stem cell transplant as the best option is that first of all, it can offer an actual cure for Deniz-Mare's disease…"

"*Allah'a şükür.*" Ozan *Bey* continued his words of thanksgiving and wiped his face with his hands.

"*Amin,*" answered both Dr. Urgancioğlu and Meryem. Ozan remained silent.

"Having said that," Dr. Urgancioğlu continued, "bone marrow transplantation is complicated and demanding, and as Meryem *Hanim* has pointed out, there is always a chance of rejection."

"We will need full cooperation from the entire family to keep Deniz-Mare in good spirits. That's important because it's tough getting ready for the procedure. She will be administered high doses of chemotherapy and probably radiotherapy, which will put a great deal of strain on the body. However, it is the most efficient way to destroy cancerous cells before the transplantation of healthy cells."

For a long time, no one said a word. Everyone was lost in their thoughts. Dr. Urgancioğlu recognized that it was an important moment for the family to reflect and meditate on the information he had just delivered.

Meryem was seated between her son and Ozan *Bey*. Both had their arms around her and leaned their heads against hers. The doctor gently pushed a box of tissues toward them, and when he sensed that the time was right, he continued, "Deniz-Mare has youth on her side, and that makes her an excellent candidate for the procedure."

"*Allah'a şükür*," once again came from Ozan *Bey*'s direction.

"*Amin*," answered Meryem.

"One last and very important thing," added the doctor. "Remember that you have a highly qualified team of doctors working on Deniz-Mare's case. I've just been selected to be the spokesperson for the team, but by no means am I the only one making the decisions."

"*Doktor Bey*." The voice belonged to Ozan *Bey*. "I would like to meet the rest of the team of doctors involved in my granddaughter's treatment."

"I'm sure you will, Ozan *Bey*. If there are no other questions to answer or clarifications needed," Dr. Urgancioğlu announced while scanning everyone's face, "I will leave you for now. We'll proceed with getting Deniz-Mare ready for the transplantation, so you'll be seeing a lot of me from now on."

Everyone began to stand when the doctor stated that he was leaving, but he signaled them to remain seated. "No need to move—you have a lot to discuss among yourselves. Good day."

However, after turning the door handle to leave, Dr. Urgancioğlu hesitated and, still with his hand on the handle, turned to Ozan with a last request. "*Oğul* [Son], when you get a chance, stop by my office; we'll chat, *tamam?*"

"*Tamam, Doktor Bey,*" was Ozan's simple response. He hoped that the sinking feeling in the pit of his stomach did not reflect on his face.

Ozan could not sit for long. After looking from his *dede* to his mother for a few seconds without saying a word and finally finding approval in their eyes, he got up and left the room.

"Dr. Urgancioğlu, Dr. Urgancioğlu!" Ozan was out of breath by the time he turned the corner after running down the long hallway.

"*Sakin ol, sakin ol, Oğul* [Calm down, calm down, son]," were the soothing words that Dr. Urgancioğlu directed at Ozan once the breathless young man reached him.

"I couldn't just continue to sit there after you told me you wanted to chat. Could we meet now?" Ozan spoke haltingly but with a determination and a sense of expectation that compelled the doctor to comply immediately with his request.

"Here, *Oğlum,*" replied Dr. Urgancioğlu, placing one hand on Ozan's shoulder and guiding him into an unoccupied examining room nearby rather than continuing the longer walk to his office.

Once inside, the doctor called the nurses' station on the same floor and, having given the room number where they were, gave specific instructions not to be disturbed.

They sat in chairs facing each other next to the examining table.

"*Oğlum*, your mother brought up targeted therapy as one of the possible treatments for Deniz-Mare's leukemia…"

"Yes, and I agree with my mother. I think it's less aggressive than either chemotherapy or radiation—or both, as you suggested that might be a possibility. I would hate to put my sister through that unnecessarily."

Ozan's lips quivered slightly as he spoke. His hands rested on his lap, entwined, then he made one hand into a fist and, covering the fist with the other hand, began to rub it gently at first, then the movements increased in intensity as he tried to continue to speak.

Dr. Urgancioğlu did not miss the obvious signs of anxiety. He called the nurses' station once again and requested two bottles of mineral water. While they waited, Ozan got up and began to pace, hands in his pockets; the doctor remained silent.

Dr. Urgancioğlu answered the knock on the door by opening it barely enough to get the water.

"*Grazie*, and I'm not available," he admonished the nurse a second time.

"*Chiaramente compreso, Dottore* [Clearly understood, Doctor]," answered the nurse.

He closed the door, twisted the cap to break the seal, handed a bottle of water to Ozan, and signaled him to sit down. Ozan took a long swig of water before sitting down. He rested his forearms on his knees and continued to hold the half-empty bottle of water by its neck, dangling it between his knees.

"I'm listening, Doc." He was self-assured as he spoke now and looked at the doctor directly in the eye.

The doctor opened the second bottle of water and took a sip before placing it on the floor next to his chair.

"Deniz-Mare's treatment needs to be more aggressive than we previously hoped…" he began slowly and waited a few seconds for any reaction from Ozan. When none came, the doctor continued, "Remember when we met with your family the first time, we spoke about abnormal white blood cells that grow in the bone marrow? These are called blasts, and when these grow uncontrollably, they push out, or crowd out, the healthy, mature cells."

Not a peep came out of Ozan's mouth. He listened intently, with an occasional clearing of the throat or scratching of the nose.

"At the chronic stage or phase of CML, patients' blood consists of up to fifteen percent blasts. Once their blood consists of fifteen to thirty percent blasts, we say it has moved from the chronic phase to the accelerated phase." Again, the doctor gave Ozan time for comments or questions; again, none came, so he pressed on. "Deniz-Mare seems to be at the beginning of the accelerated phase, with just above fifteen percent of her blood consisting of blasts. Also, her platelets, which help blood to clot, if you remember, are lower than what we would like to see."

Ozan finally spoke. "Dr. Urgancioğlu, thank you for not saying all this in front of *Anne* and *Dede*, especially *Dede*. He has had a couple of heart spasms, and they are kind of scary, even though my uncle says not to worry about them so much, but I couldn't bear to lose *Dede*…not to mention Deniz-Mare." His lips quivered; tears spilled over and ran down his cheeks.

Dr. Urgancioğlu took out a box of tissues from one of the supply drawers and gently pushed it toward Ozan.

"Ozan, you are the leader of your family. Ozan *Bey* is getting older, and I've noticed that your father has been absent during this difficult time, so of course, you've been left to bear the heavy load. *Kader, Oğlum, kader* [It's fate, Son, fate]."

"I don't know if it's *kader* or lack of responsibility from my father, Doctor. But whatever it is, it doesn't matter. Deniz-Mare is my sister, and I'm here."

"The medical team in charge of your sister's case will be meeting today to review the protocol once again and make suggestions as needed. Your uncle will head the meeting and later will meet with you. In the meantime, is there anything that you would like me to bring up at the meeting? Any concerns or questions?"

"No, Doctor, thank you; I'll wait and talk to Osman *Amça*."

Dr. Urgancioğlu smiled, got up, and patted Ozan's shoulder before walking toward the door. Ozan attempted to get up, but the doctor's open hand, making short, downward movements, urged him to remain seated, a gesture which Ozan gratefully accepted.

When he heard the door shut, Ozan burst into sobs and bawled until all energy was drained from him. Afterward, he remained there a long while. The vibration of his phone coming from the zippered inside pocket of his light jacket startled him.

His hello sounded weak and groggy.

"Ozan, *Canim*, you don't sound good. Can we meet?"

"Yes," was the only word he could muster.

"I'll be right there." Mari-Car hung up and immediately started to go. She rolled her eyes and called Ozan again.

He looked at the caller ID, and her name brought a faint smile to his face.

"I wondered where you'd be going when you said, 'I'll be right there.'"

"I got so worried at the sound of your voice that I didn't think of asking where you were."

"I'm in an examining room…" He got up from his chair, opened the door to look at the number, and said, "Three-one-one—that's the room number. Dr. Urgancıoğlu gave orders that I should not be disturbed, so we can talk in here calmly for as long as we need to, without interruption."

"I'll be right there." Mari-Car hung up and made her way to the sea of scooters parked on the grounds of her residence hall.

CHAPTER 64
MIGLIAIA DI MINUTI

"It's good that you took time for me today, old friend." Osman's words were meant as banter when he shook hands and embraced his friend.

"You made it sound so serious that you left me no choice, old friend," Luca said, imitating him.

After breaking their embrace, Osman took a deep breath and took in the spectacular view that surrounded them.

"You know, Luca, no matter how much you want to describe this beauty to someone, words fall short; you need to experience it." As he spoke, his friend poured some wine in a glass and handed it to Osman, who continued to speak while sweeping across the view with the hand holding the glass. The terraced vineyards on the hills that enclosed the wineries of the Grimaldi family gave him the feeling of being nestled in ancient times. The environs were beautiful but tranquil and unpretentious.

"This is exquisite," he finally said after taking his first sip of wine and taking time to savor it. His eyes were drawn to the bottle resting on the unassuming round, wooden table with a wine-barrel base in the middle of the green-shingled gazebo, which allowed them to take in their surroundings unencumbered by the elements. They both sat down and continued their conversation.

The label on the bottle in front of them displayed alluring emerald eyes and the words *Migliaia di Minuti*—Thousands of Minutes.

"Tell me how you came to that name on the label."

"Do you have time, Osman?"

"Maybe not thousands of minutes, but I have a lot of them—as many as you need to tell me about it."

"I have shared wine with you from my private collection before, my friend."

"I know, but not from the *Migliaia di Minuti* collection. I would've remembered that name."

"About eighteen years ago, maybe a little longer," Luca began, "I met the most incredible woman. She was beautiful, sexy, soft, deep, bold…unforgettable."

"There must be a 'but' there somewhere; otherwise, she'd be here," Osman interjected.

"There were many 'buts,' and yes, she would be…I wish," Luca responded contemplatively.

Osman could see now where Deniz-Mare got her deep-blue eyes.

"The big 'but' was that she was married. Then there were a series of smaller but complicated 'buts': she was Muslim, lived in Istanbul, had a young son…I didn't want to complicate her life. I didn't know how her family would react to her breaking up her family and running away with a foreigner; I did not want to put her in a difficult situation, so I let her go. But I'll tell you one thing: she's the only woman that I've ever shed tears over."

"And evidently continue to do so," pointed out Osman, squeezing his friend's shoulder when he saw his eyes brimming with tears.

"Anyway, I own one of the few vineyards of Nebbiolo grapes in northern Italy, in the Piemonte region, and I am approved to produce Barolo wine. It's a private collection; I don't sell it on the market—as you are aware, the process is long, expensive, and difficult due to the meticulous set of rules and regulations that must be followed. But it is a rewarding endeavor."

Luca looked over at his friend and finished by saying, "I developed various labels based on aging processes of three to five years. You are experiencing *Migliaia di Minuti*…" He sighed before continuing, "For this collection, the wine has been aged for five years, and the inspiration is the woman that I've already told you about."

Osman looked at Luca and nodded, slightly lifting his glass to him. For a long time, they continued to wordlessly sip the incredible wine and take in the placid scenery.

Osman broke the silence. "You know, Luca, we've been friends for a long time—good friends. We've called each other brother—*fratello*—and even though I've shared with you more of my personal life than I have with anyone else, you've never mentioned this amazingly great love of yours."

"And I'm not sure why I'm doing it now. It's the one thing that has remained so precious, so untainted in my life that I've thought that sharing it would break some sort of unspoken sacred vow."

Again, the moment required silence. Again, at the appropriate time, Osman broke the silence.

"Luca, I have very few friends, but I treasure them, because good friends are like rare jewels. As you know, you are one of those rare jewels in my life. You know my life story, and in my darkest moments, you were one of the few people that I could confide in and find refuge in…this valley, this vineyard, this villa, sheltered me when I had no other place to hide, and that's what I wanted to do at the time—hide. If I have the timing right, I found out about my Zoey's death soon after you lost your great love. However, you comforted me amid your great loss."

"I could feel your loss, Osman, because I, too, had experienced loss. But I knew that the comparison would be unfair… yours was unrecoverable, permanent, unthinkable, and I felt guilty bringing my experience to light and pretending that it was similar to yours."

They both continued to sip, savor, and swirl the precious liquid in their short, stemless glasses. The warmth of the autumn, midafternoon sun and the captivating, soul-gripping surroundings compelled them again into a long silence.

The man of few words had a lot to say at this time.

"My dear, selfless friend, my brother, you were there when I needed you. Thank you for putting your own loss aside to tend to mine; thank you for being there for me so unconditionally.

I, in turn, have been granted the privilege to relate to you an incredible story. You are about to receive an amazing gift."

Luca, who held his glass just in front of his lips, took one last sip before placing it back on the table.

When Osman began to speak, Luca slowly stood up; his hands brushed his dense mass of dark hair, now sprinkled with gray. As Osman continued his narrative, Luca paced nonstop inside the gazebo with his hands clasped behind his neck.

Finding it difficult to breathe, Luca clutched his throat, stepped down outside the gazebo, and continued to pace back and forth, then, accelerating his pace, he circled it over and over. Osman continued to relate the incredible tale.

Finally, Luca came back inside the gazebo. Both men stood facing each other. Luca then clung to his friend's neck and sobbed; Osman encircled him tightly with his arms. Then he spoke in a serious tone.

"DNA tests showed that you are a match for your daughter, but not a full match—parents aren't. But we'll talk about what all that means tomorrow…that's why I'm here, Luca, to bring you the wonderful news and to arrange a meeting with you as soon as possible about what I have in mind as a course of action for your daughter's treatment."

Overwhelmed by shock and desperation, Luca cupped his friend's face and looked searchingly into his eyes. Then, without saying a word, he ran into the vineyard and collapsed onto the hilly ground amid the grapevines, where he continued to sob.

Osman stayed back, seated at the edge of his chair, his elbows on the table, resting his chin between his thumbs and clasped hands.

Inexplicably, he felt engulfed in serenity, peace, and tranquility—as if he were being caressed by angels. Osman remained frozen in place, afraid to move for fear of breaking the magical feeling. Was he having an experience with God? he wondered.

He didn't know what it was, but somehow, he knew that everything would be all right.

When Osman looked out into the vineyard, he saw the silhouette of his friend slowly making his way back to the gazebo. Osman got up and began walking toward Luca, finally reaching him and opening his arms to receive him.

"I'm with you, my friend. I'm with you for the long haul."

"Osman, her name…what is my daughter's name?" he pleaded.

"Deniz-Mare." The words came out like a prayer.

Luca's knees faltered, but he allowed himself to be held up and embraced by Osman. He knew that right now, *he* was the friend in need.

"Just tell me what to do and when to do it, Osman. This is a chance that I've been given, and I don't plan to let it escape. I'm in all the way, body, soul, heart, and mind."

"I have what could be considered a mind-blowing, maybe even shocking, proposal for both you and Meryem; I'll be in touch tonight, although it could be very late."

The church bells could be heard in the distance. Luca stopped to listen, then glanced at his watch, then at Osman.

"It's almost five thirty. Mass will begin soon; I have an appointment with God." Luca squeezed his friend's arm and left.

He began walking to his car, and having walked only a short distance, turned back to Osman and said, "Do you see all this?" He used his arm to sweep a full circle around the surrounding vineyards. "This is nothing compared to the gift that you just gave me, *Fratello*. Nothing!"

"I didn't give it to you; it was always there…"

"But you brought it to me. It would have done me no good being there without my knowing about it. I am forever grateful, Osman."

He placed both hands over his heart and shouted, "You know this is your home, *Fratello*, stay as long as you want, you know where to find more wine." Then Luca turned to go to his appointment.

CHAPTER 65
KADER RESURFACES

"I couldn't sleep all night, Osman, and obviously, neither could you, seeing that it's five thirty in the morning and you are ready and waiting."

"Actually, I slept right here, Meryem. That couch is not just for looks…"

"Nor for just drinking wine," she added, to add lightness to what she anticipated would be a serious conversation. Otherwise, he would not have contacted her at eleven the previous night asking her to meet him in his private office.

It worked; her remark brought a rare smile to Osman's eyes.

"I'm sorry to be so early; I know you said six. I was just going to wait in front of the reception door, but it was unlocked, so I went in, and then I was going to wait in front of your office, but…"

"I saw you." He pointed at the screen on the wall to the left of the entrance. "I have one in the conference room and in the bathroom. That way I can see who comes to this floor."

Meryem shook her head and smiled but said nothing else.

Osman pointed her toward the couch. Meryem first removed her navy-blue boots and placed them out of the way, against the wall, before she settled comfortably on the couch, sinking back cozily into the large cushion. She wanted to bring her feet up and tuck them under her, but that would have been too much at-homeness, she thought with an underlined smile.

Osman had told her that it would be an informal meeting, so Meryem dressed in jeans and a white linen blouse that wrapped around her waist. The top button was undone, and it exposed a white-gold chain with an emerald pendant that matched her beautiful, charcoal-outlined, green eyes.

"I knew you'd be here early. So will my other guest."

Meryem was definitely intrigued and sat up straight on the couch.

"Your other guest? Someone else is coming?"

"Yes, I told him six thirty, so you'd be here a little before, but look." Osman pointed at the monitor. A tall figure in jeans, a white T-shirt, and a cream jacket, the tip of his sunglasses sticking out of his left pocket and the jacket sleeves pushed to the elbows, was pushing open the door to the reception area. He made his way confidently to Osman's office door.

When Luca walked in, Meryem was standing in front of the couch looking to her left, toward the door. She turned fully to face him, both hands suddenly went to cover her wide-open mouth, tears began to run uninterrupted down her cheeks, and her body began to shake. She had recognized him at first sight, before he entered the reception area.

Luca, eyes fixed on Meryem, began a slow walk toward her… her knees began to falter, she felt herself falling, and Luca saw it and quickened his pace. She collapsed in his arms.

Osman grabbed his laptop off his desk, stepped out of his office, and walked to the reception area, where he settled on the small couch. He opened his laptop to study with precision the proposal that he would soon be making to Meryem and Luca.

But Osman was unable to concentrate; his mind went to *kader*. He didn't know how else to label the mind-boggling events that had come together and made the improbable happen.

Even the heartbreaking experience that the family was presently faced with had a purpose, he thought—or rather, he questioned the point, because he had more questions than answers.

Osman could not wrap his mind around the fact that his closest friend had turned out to be the biological father of his niece.

CHAPTER 66
THE COSTLY VINEYARD OF LONG AGO

"I had my ideal world and my not-so-ideal world to consider, Luca. But in my ideal world, you would have suffered." Meryem let go of one of his hands and touched the left side of his chest before adding, "I wanted to avoid causing you grief."

When Meryem had finally regained her bearings and regulated her breathing, she touched and caressed Luca's face over and over but remained incredulous.

They had settled comfortably on the couch. Both were shoeless and sat cross-legged, facing each other, having joined both hands.

"Tell me more about your ideal world, Meryem."

"I would have run to your apartment on that day, holding in my hand the pregnancy stick displaying two pink lines, clung to your neck, wrapped my legs around your waist, and squealed for joy."

"And I, how would I have reacted in that perfect world of yours?"

"You would have twirled me around and around, looking into my eyes, my hair blowing in the breeze."

"I could never tire of looking into those amazing eyes of yours...not then, not now," he interjected, unable to contain himself.

"Nor I yours," she responded. "But my ideal world did not happen," continued Meryem in a whisper.

Still drowning in the green depths of her eyes, Luca wanted to know, "What happened instead, Meryem?"

"Instead...instead..." Meryem began haltingly. Luca tenderly wiped away her tears. As she spoke, they became more copious and flowed more freely. "Instead, I had to think of my almost-two-year-old son, Ozan. I feared that he would be taken away by my husband's family."

Tears continued relentlessly down her cheeks, mixing with the mucus dripping out of her nose and finally being absorbed into the collar of her linen blouse.

Luca got up from the couch, taking her by the hand; she got up and followed behind him. They walked through the small conference room and through the dressing room into Osman's bathroom.

Once they were there, Luca picked her up by the waist and sat her on the counter next to the sink. He opened the faucet and after wetting his hands thoroughly, ran them on her face and hair. She let out a big sigh followed by a barely audible, "*Grazie.*"

Luca jumped on the counter right next to her, turned her face up toward him, and bent down to place a featherlight kiss on her wet lips. Then he said, "*Prego*, would you like to continue?"

"*Si*…I wondered if your Italian, Catholic family would accept a Turkish, Muslim grandchild."

Meryem did not wait for an answer but continued to try and express what she was feeling at the time she had made the decision that caused her to sacrifice her ideal world.

She clung to the edge of the counter with both hands. He covered her right hand with his left. Her eyes fixed on the floor, and she allowed the words and tears to flow freely and easily.

"At the time, what I wanted was not as important as the well-being of my two children. They became my everything, and going back to Istanbul where they would grow up surrounded by the loving and protective care of the extended family was the best world for them." Luca continued to listen attentively, although what he was sensing felt surreal. "I did want to honor you because you were the only true love that I have ever known, and the best way that I knew was, first of all, giving our daughter an Italian name, then making sure that she loved and appreciated her father's country. So Deniz-Mare speaks fluent Italian, and we have spent all summer vacations and most holidays here in Italy."

"*Grazie*," whispered Luca in Meryem's ear; then his silence continued, unable to explain the inexplicable.

"Deniz-Mare's illness has crushed me, Luca." She now looked up into his eyes. "If I am standing here, it's thanks to a merciful God and to my amazing family, especially my son Ozan, the best son and brother anyone can have; Ozan *Bey*, the best grandfather, who has not left our side; Osman, for whom I just don't have enough words of gratitude; and some amazing new friends that have come to our aid."

Luca lifted the hand that covered hers. She felt instantly vulnerable, then felt his strong arm encircle her waist, squeezing her tightly against his body, sheltering her from all the blows she knew were coming and becoming a healing balm for the ones she had already received. He turned her face up toward him with the index finger of his free hand, wanting to make sure that he had her full attention for what he was about to say.

"I am profoundly aware of the incredible miracle that I have received finding you again, and as if one miracle were not enough, I also find out that I have a daughter. I know that I don't deserve such a monumental blessing, but I'm grateful for it and will treasure it and will protect it forever. You are no longer alone fighting for Deniz-Mare; lean on me from today on. For as long as there is breath in me, I'll be there to take the brunt of whatever grief comes our way and to share in all the joy and happiness that I know will also come our way."

Meryem's tears continued to flow freely; he wet his lips with them. Then he changed the tone of the conversation.

"Tell me about your parents, the paternal grandmother, your ex-husband…Osman told me you had divorced him."

"My parents are not aware of the extent of Deniz-Mare's illness. To tell you the truth, I'm not even sure the extent of it. All I know is that I need all my energy to go toward helping my daughter—"

"*Our* daughter." His interruption surprised her, but she felt her burden ease with those two words.

Meryem looked up at him with a grateful smile and confirmed, "*Our* daughter."

Luca held her chin between his thumb and forefinger and lifted it gently. When their eyes met, he told her, "You emphasized 'our' beautifully."

"I feel incredibly lucky and relieved to be able to say that word," she responded.

Meryem was unable to continue looking into the blue depths that so many years before had held her captive. She realized that the years had done nothing to allay their effect and that if she did not break away from the powerful gaze, she'd succumb again. She felt that truth all over her body; they both did, and both knew that the other was experiencing the same.

"Ceyda *Hanim*, my former mother-in-law, knows about the situation," Meryem continued. "How much information Ozan *Bey* has given her, I don't know. We have very little communication with each other, only when it's necessary—it's always been that way." Meryem felt that she was babbling but pressed on. "So I let Ozan *Bey* control the information passed on to her."

Luca was stronger than her, she thought, for he continued looking at her even after she avoided his intense, spellbinding, cerulean look.

Meryem cleared her throat and continued. "Mehmet and I quit talking way before Deniz-Mare was born. In fact, we had quit communicating when you and I…when you and I…"

"Loved each other over and over," he finished her sentence.

Meryem felt his words course through her entire body. "I remember you bought a vineyard that day; do you still have it?"

"Yes. I paid full price for it—a small price to pay for what I think I got in return. Deniz-Mare, right?" Meryem nodded and continued to talk about the family, hoping to divert her stubborn body from the direction it wanted to take. "He, Mehmet"—Luca smiled, knowing she was avoiding her feelings—"has been an absent father for both children, not just Deniz-Mare. Ozan felt it less thanks to his amazing relationship with his grandfather Ozan *Bey*. And then, Osman came into his life recently…"

"I hope someday to also be part of his life, although I see he is well cared for by the two wonderful men that are now present in his life. Who does she look like? My daughter, I mean." Again, Luca changed the tone of the conversation.

"You! From day one, you…wait here." Meryem jumped off the bathroom counter and ran through the dressing room, through the double doors into the conference room, and finally into Osman's office. She lifted all the cushions off the couch until she spotted her phone. She made the same trajectory back like lightning.

"Look." Meryem stood in front of Luca holding up a picture of Deniz-Mare. He gently took the phone out of her hand, took the tiny jump from the counter to the floor without breaking away from staring at the image on the phone. A girl of stunning beauty stared back.

He looked over at Meryem and said almost in a whisper, "May I?" before swiping through the images on the phone. He wanted to see more.

"Of course," Meryem whispered back and leaned against the counter to savor this extraordinary moment in which Luca was taking a first look at his daughter. Luca walked back and forth in the ample bathroom, looking at pictures of his daughter since she was a little girl. He used the back of his hand to wipe away the tears that ran unchecked down his cheeks. It was a holy moment between them; they both knew it and did not rush it.

Finally, Luca could contain himself no longer. "Her eyes—they are like my mother's."

"Do you look like your mother?"

"I guess. People say I do…she is beautiful. Thank you, Meryem. I could drown in gratitude." Luca turned his eyes to the ceiling and whispered another "Thank you," then, looking at Meryem, unclear in his mind what to ask first, he finally said, "What is she like? What does she like to do? What does she study?"

"She is a great businesswoman."

Luca turned to Meryem, eyes wide open.

"Wow." He chuckled. "I didn't expect that. I thought you'd say art history…like her mom."

"No, she studied business, like her dad; did you go to Stanford for your MBA?"

Luca nodded but was overwhelmed into silence.

"She loves it." Meryem felt the need to elaborate. "Works at her grandfather's company attracting business from all over the world. You should see her making presentations, giving her pitches. No one can resist her."

As Meryem spoke, Luca began forming ideas in his head for his daughter and his vineyard—but of course kept them to himself.

Meryem noticed his smile and faraway look.

"You're planning something, aren't you?"

Luca's only answer was a smile.

He then stood oh-so-close to Meryem, allowing their bodies to meld. Her lips parted, her breath became labored, she felt unsteady, wobbly. Her heart rate became erratic, her body remembered. Luca gently and slowly gathered her hair, his eyes drowning in hers. He, too, found it difficult to breathe as he moved the dark, silky mass away from her face, gathering any wayward strands in his fingers until he had total access to her face.

He placed his hands on her cheeks and began to caress them with his thumbs. He again looked deep and long into her emerald eyes, then at her full lips—they quivered. His eyes traveled once again to hers, but this time they questioned. The answer came wordlessly.

Meryem pulled his face the few millimeters that separated them to meet her waiting, parted lips. She succumbed completely and unreservedly. They both gave, took, and searched insistently until they found.

Luca was the first to break away. Still panting, he continued to run his thumbs the length and contour of her luscious lips until she could ease her breathing.

After a few minutes, he brought her head to his shoulder and ran his hand the length of her luxurious, dark hair. He buried his face in it and inhaled deeply.

He was taken back nineteen years, when they gave themselves over and over to each other freely, totally, completely. This is what I've been missing all these years, he thought.

"I don't want to let you go for fear that you'll disappear." His thoughts became words, and these were expressed out loud, accompanied by sentiments of fear most of all and maybe a tinge of jealousy and possessiveness, and he knew he had no right.

Luca opened his mouth to form an apology—then he heard her voice.

"I feel the same way. I do not want to let you go."

Meryem brought her forefinger to her lips. "Shhh," she said, pointing at the screen on the wall; Osman was walking into the office.

"I think it's time to go, but first, let's get ourselves put back together." Luca brushed her hair back with his hands, then allowed the cool water to run and wiped her face with it.

Her eyes were still red and a bit swollen—they had shed a lot of tears in a short time. But they also displayed brilliance and peace.

They made their way back to Osman's office, Luca walking a few steps ahead, both hands behind him, pulling Meryem by the hand.

CHAPTER 67
A SERIES OF DAMNED FINE LINES

Osman stood in front of the couch and waited for them. He seemed nervous.

"I still am unable to wrap my mind around the events of the past couple of days…but we won't dwell on them, because time is of the essence." This was how he started the conversation upon seeing them walk through the double doors. Then he added, extending his open palm toward the couch, "Please sit down."

Luca let go of Meryem's hand and grabbed Osman's shoulders. "Are you OK? is my daughter OK, *Mio Fratello*?" he asked.

"Deniz-Mare is fine, *Mio Fratello*. I'm nervous, so forgive me if I come across as somewhat insensitive or uncaring. Time is of the essence, as I've said, and I'd like to propose to you a course of treatment. I have not discussed this with any of the doctors yet because I wanted to know how you felt about what I'm going to say."

Luca took Meryem's hand, and they both settled on the edge of the couch. Meryem became pale, and Luca felt her hand sweat and begin to tremble. He let go of her hand and put his arm around her to control the tremors, which seemed to have taken over her whole body.

"*Calma, Tesoro* [my treasure]," he told her tenderly, gently turning her face toward him by placing his index finger under her chin, his signature gesture. She looked searchingly into his eyes; he used his thumbs to wipe away the tears that had once again begun to overflow.

Osman could see that his tactless introduction to what he wanted to say had affected Meryem; he went and sat on the other side of her and took her free hand.

"*Üzgünüm*[I'm sorry]." The words came naturally and softly in their native language.

Meryem's tears continued to course down her cheeks freely, but Osman's apology did calm her down.

"Speak, *Fratello*," Luca said to Osman. "We are brothers—I trust you!"

Meryem squeezed Osman's hand and looking deeply into his eyes, added, "So do I, Osman. I trust you too. Deniz-Mare is first in Allah's hands, then in yours."

All three reached for the tissues.

Osman stood up once again and began to pace slowly and pensively in the room.

"Deniz-Mare's disease has progressed from the chronic stage to the acute stage; that's why I…we…Dr. Urgancioğlu and I think the best course of action is a stem cell transplant. We've said that already, but I want to go over it once again before I tell you what I have in mind."

Meryem and Luca remained silent and attentive, their hands tightly interlocked.

"In a stem cell transplant, what we are trying to match as closely as possible are the HLA, or human leukocyte antigens. These are proteins, sometimes also called markers, on the cells of the body; they make up our tissue type. To simplify a complex system, the regulation of the immune system is encoded in the HLA. If the immune system sees the cells from the transplant as foreign and therefore as a threat, then the transplant is in danger of failure."

Osman gave them time to digest what he had just said. They remained silent, so he continued, "Again, the more closely matched the donor and patient are—in other words, the more HLA markers they have in common—the lower the risks of complications and the better the chances the donor cells have of engrafting—that is, growing—and making new blood cells in the recipient's body."

Osman walked back and forth and enunciated slowly and clearly, using his hands to drive the point across, as if he were speaking at a conference, except without the visuals.

Finally, Osman quit walking and leaned back on the edge of his desk, gripping the edge with both hands. He continued his speech, but now the doctor became the brother, the friend, the loving uncle. His words were quieter, even tender.

"Luca, *Fratello*, you are a match, but not a full or complete match; I hinted at that yesterday when we talked in the vineyard. We get half of our HLA markers from our father and half from our mother, so the match between child and parent is always only fifty percent. This is old information for Meryem—I don't want to bore you, but I want to make sure I give you a clear picture." Luca opened his mouth to say something, but Osman stopped him. "Let me say what I want to say and propose to you both."

Luca leaned back on the sofa but remained focused on what Osman was saying.

"Stem cells from a full sibling are the best possible option because there is a one-in-four chance they are a full match. Notice that I didn't say the *only* option," he added, "but the best option. It's just of utmost importance for the success of the transplant."

"Deniz-Mare does not have a full sibling…" Osman ignored the observation that Luca had just made and waited wordlessly. "Got it," said Luca when his remark went unheeded.

Meryem only nodded. Thus far, she had been unable to voice one single word. She squeezed Luca's hand tightly, and her body quivered lightly. Instinctively, she brought her free hand to her forehead and began to rub it gently.

Luca looked down at her, smiled, and gently caressed her cheek with the back of his hand. She brought his hand to her lips and lovingly kissed its palm.

Osman interpreted her gesture toward Luca as a sign that Meryem was more relaxed, so he decided that this was the time to go ahead and make his outrageous proposal. He opened his mouth to say what he had really come to say, but Luca prevented him by requesting further explanation.

"Osman, *mio caro fratello* [my dear brother], can you explain the one-in-four chance you mentioned?"

"I'm coming to that," replied Osman while working out in his head the simplest way to explain it. "There are four possible combinations of HLA markers that a child can get from the parents. Each child therefore has a twenty-five percent chance of receiving one of the possible profiles; if Deniz-Mare's full sibling could match her HLA profile, then that would be a full match."

Meryem finally spoke. She sounded a bit tired, and her impatient tone suggested frustration. "Osman, Deniz-Mare has one sibling, Ozan!" Then it dawned on her that that was one topic that she and Luca had not discussed, the possibility that Luca had another child. So she looked at him questioningly, and he once again caressed her cheek.

"Deniz-Mare is my only child," he answered her unasked question.

Meryem smiled and couldn't help letting out a sigh of relief, although she realized the unfairness of her feeling.

"Have all your questions been answered so far?" Now it was Osman whose tone conveyed a bit of frustration. He apologized immediately.

"We're all under a lot of stress, Osman. No need for apologies—we're family."

"Thank you," came the soft answer.

Neither Luca nor Meryem were prepared for what came out of Osman's mouth next.

"I propose in vitro fertilization, which will allow us to access the stem cells from the embryo."

Osman took advantage of Meryem and Luca's speechlessness to continue talking without interruption.

"The stem cells would be taken from the inner cell mass of the embryo, called blastocyst, three to five days after fertilization. But—and this is important—the stem cells are collected before implantation in the uterus, so to dispel any fears, there is no chance that the embryo would ever become a human being.

"The advantage is that my niece would have an excellent chance to have a full HLA match." Osman's eyes watered as he voiced his hopeful concept. "I'm not a very emotional guy; in fact, I think I've avoided emotions since I found out about Zoey's passing."

"You have, *Mio Fratello*," said Luca quietly.

Osman continued reflecting out loud. "It's as if I've built a protective wall around my heart, and even my body…but anyway, I've had this idea running through my head ever since I figured out that Luca was Deniz-Mare's father. I can't seem to get rid of the feeling that this will work, although I have not spoken to anyone about this, including Dr. Urgancioğlu, my friend and trusted colleague. You two have the last word on this."

Osman looked at his friends questioningly, with hope emanating from his stunning blue eyes.

"By the way, right here in Como—in fact, in this hospital—we have one of the best IVF clinics in the world. Since we will not be requesting government funds, the process could be started immediately."

Whether it was the pent-up tension, the shock of Osman's unexpected proposal, or just plain anxiety from the surreal events that had transpired since she had learned of Deniz-Mare's illness—it was unclear even to her—Meryem was overtaken by uncontrollable laughter. She brought both hands around her middle and brought her head forward, then looked at both men, who stared at her in astonishment.

An image of Osman's toilet with all the buttons formed in her mind, and this drove Meryem into further hysterical laughter.

Osman went around the desk and retrieved a small, yellow pill from the top drawer. Without saying a word, he handed it to Luca along with a bottle of mineral water.

Luca administered the medication to Meryem, who took it without even a hint of protest. Luca helped her to accommodate herself on the couch and placed a cushion under her head. He brushed her hair off her face and leaned down and kissed her forehead. Ten minutes later, she was fast asleep. Luca rested her feet on his lap and continued the conversation with Osman.

"Do you think she'll be all right? This is way off my area of expertise."

Osman pulled one of the guest chairs away from his desk and placed it in front of the couch to talk to his friend. He leaned forward to give Luca his complete attention.

"She'll be fine, Luca," Osman began while looking at Meryem in peaceful sleep. "It has just been too much on her nervous system. I'm mostly to blame. I know that we need to act quickly and therefore rushed to communicate an idea that I've had plenty of time to process."

"Osman, let's talk about the moral implications of retrieving stem cells from embryos. First of all, I am pretty sure that there are restrictions for the procedure in Italy."

"It's legal if the procedure is done from surplus embryos, if it can be proven that the stem cells will be used for treating a life-threatening illness."

"Surplus embryos?"

"Yes, the ones left unused after the IVF treatment is finished."

"Wow, what happens to those unused embryos otherwise?"

"Some couples save them in case they want to have another child later, others donate them to science or to another couple, and some just discard them."

"So, if we can use them to save the life of our daughter…"

"Yes, that is my way of thinking," Osman said, placing his hand on the left side of his chest, "but you and Meryem need to make that decision together and let me know. Also, remember that you are not just creating the embryos to retrieve the stem cells from them, although that is the motivation behind it. You and Meryem, if you agree, will be undergoing the in vitro fertilization process to also further grow your family."

"It's a fine line, *Mio Fratello*." Luca's eyes welled up with tears as he looked from his friend to his sleeping beauty.

"Life is a series of damned fine lines, especially in my profession, Luca. You just hope that you make the best possible decisions while helping the greatest number of people and hurting the fewest."

Osman got up from his chair and started to walk around the room, stopping at times to look at his friend and make a point.

"Do I perform the heart transplant on the ruthless dictator who is next on the list, knowing that upon returning home, he will continue to starve his people and make himself richer, or do I transplant the heart on the child who has little time left without it but whose place on the list is further down?" Luca looked at Osman with interest, anticipating an answer to the rhetorical question that he had just posed. "I won't burden you, my dear friend, with the decision that I made in that particular case."

He then once again leaned on the edge of his desk and looked intensely into Luca's eyes. "Do I first take care of the young critical patient who entered the emergency room after the elderly gentleman who is also in critical condition? I don't know who will suffer more from the potential loss if death were to occur as a result of my decision—the parents of the younger patient or the children of the older one…or what the aftermath of either death will be. Again, I will not burden you with my decision."

Osman then went in front of the window to take in the view; it appeased him. His tone was quieter, calmer as he continued to speak. "Recently, when I was paged to take care of my father, who had been brought to the emergency room in Istanbul, I rushed to his aid, but other patients had come in with worse heart conditions." He turned from the window and once again gave Luca a penetrating look before going on. "I was not called for any of them because I was tending to my father."

After a long pause, Osman hesitated but continued. "That night, I learned that we had lost a child that had been brought in with TGA; that's when the great arteries, the aorta and the pulmonary arteries, are connected to the ventricle opposite of the one they should be. The child belonged to an immigrant family who, afraid of being sent home, had not brought the child in earlier. It's a wonder she had lived as long as she did."

Another long pause. "The point is, Luca, that I can do that operation with my eyes closed. I could have saved that child even in the worst of circumstances…instead, I was dealing with my father, a man who never once lifted a finger on my behalf, as you well know. He had had a heart spasm—anyone could've taken care of him, but they called me instead, because we shared the same last name, and they figured he was someone close to me."

Osman walked toward the window once again and got lost in its view.

Luca delicately picked up Meryem's feet off his lap and placed them on the couch. He took the steps needed to be next to his best friend and stood in silence with his arm around him.

Osman spoke without taking his eyes off the majesty in front of him. "We do the best we can, Luca, my friend, with the choices placed before us and hope to God that we choose right."

"Speaking of choices, Osman, what if the embryos have any abnormalities? I mean, Meryem and I aren't in our twenties anymore…"

"Before freezing them, PGT, or preimplantation genetic testing, will be done on the embryos to preclude certain abnormalities and determine the HLA compatibility."

"Will that testing destroy the embryo?"

"No, Luca, but remember that the stem cell removal will."

"Will what?"

"Destroy the embryo. After the stem cell retrieval, the embryo will be discarded."

"I understand that, *Mio Fratello*, I do…" Luca's eyes got lost in the faraway hills.

After a few silent minutes, he spoke again. "I am Catholic, like most Italians, but I never considered myself religious per se. Still, I get a slight pang in my heart and in the pit of my stomach when I think of destroying a potential life to save another…"

"I face those decisions almost on a daily basis, as I've told you; it's not easy."

"*Mio Fratello*, these private concerns that I've just voiced will remain between us, OK?" He looked behind them at Meryem, who continued to sleep peacefully on the couch.

"Do you even have to mention that, *Fratello*?"

Luca's answer was an embrace.

CHAPTER 68
ONE MORE HOOP TO JUMP THROUGH

Osman mobilized two teams. He knew that if his niece's transplant was going to work out the way that he had envisioned, the timing had to be precise. He reasoned that two things were vital for the desired success: an amazing team of professionals alongside him, and help from the Universe—Kader, God.

The first was not a problem. He could control that, and began to put together a team comprised of Dr. Urgancioğlu at the head, who in turn handpicked Elisabetta Ricci, a top-notch oncology nurse, who headed the nursing and lab personnel, and Dr. Erik Nuñez, an anesthesiologist and close friend of Osman who would be determining and administering the type of sedation needed throughout Deniz-Mare's treatment.

Osman assigned his friend Dr. Vittoria Mancini, a fertility specialist, to head the team in charge of the in vitro fertilization procedure for Meryem and Luca.

Once Osman had the two experts in place to head the two teams, he knew he only had to be there as supporter, consultant if needed, and problem-solver. Otherwise, he had complete trust in them and knew that their level of discretion would be absolute.

The second needed ingredient was a bit scarier, because it involved certain crucial elements—the Universe, *Kader*, et cetera—that were outside of his control, and that was a strange, uneasy feeling for Osman; it kept him awake at night. The biggest mystery remained acquiring a perfect HLA match for Deniz-Mare. The rest would be surplus blessings.

There was one more hoop to jump through, and Osman had not brought it up for fear of overwhelming Meryem's brain. So after consulting Dr. Vittoria Mancini, the fertility expert, he followed her suggestion and arranged an informal meeting between her and Meryem.

The two women met at a quaint sidewalk café in nearby Bellagio. In the relaxed atmosphere, they immersed themselves in conversation, getting to know each other. For Meryem, it was the fresh balm that she needed. She felt totally at ease and sensed no judgment whatsoever from Vittoria.

Except for the identity of the sperm donor, no issue remained off-limits, no question about IVF unanswered. She felt knowledgeable and confident.

When Vittoria sensed that she had exhausted the subject with Meryem, she matter-of-factly brought up for discussion the matter that concerned Osman.

"Meryem, I know that Osman and Dr. Urgancıoğlu have not directly discussed with you that one of the possible side effects of chemotherapy is infertility. Osman felt that, since that it is my area of expertise, I was the right person to discuss it with you, along with some suggestions."

Whether it was Vittoria's calm demeanor and tone as she spoke or that at this point Meryem had had to face and try to solve so many complex issues she wasn't sure, but she dealt with the topic of Deniz-Mare's possible infertility calmly and confidently.

"Osman and I have had a lot of areas to cover concerning Deniz-Mare's illness. This has been a shock to our entire family, so we've had to take it slowly and have not discussed this particular topic. However, I did my research, Vittoria…"

"I know you have, and I didn't mean to imply otherwise—"

"No, it's OK. I'm glad you brought it up, and yes, I already knew that infertility would be a very real possibility due to the chemotherapy treatments." Vittoria remained silent while Meryem searched for words. "But I told myself that the most important thing was—is—Deniz-Mare's health and that nothing else mattered, so I have not given it the priority that it probably deserves." Another searching-for-words and pondering moment passed. "Vittoria, I'd like to hear your counsel and suggestions on the matter, please."

"With your permission, I would like to talk to Deniz-Mare about freezing her eggs." Vittoria's response came matter-of-factly. "It will be totally confidential. If she decides to go ahead and freeze her eggs, the only ones aware of this information, besides the doctors, will be you and Deniz-Mare. She is young, and more importantly, besides the obvious, she is healthy."

Meryem looked at her questioningly, surprised at her use of the word "healthy"; she knew that her daughter was seriously ill.

"Let me explain. I checked her chart. All her tests show that her major organs—heart, lungs, kidneys, liver—are strong."

"I'm hanging on to every positive word, and what you've just said, it fills me with hope."

"Look, Meryem, right now it might not seem important. You have started to climb Mount Everest, so to speak, and the goal is to make it to the top; it's tough to make it there, I get it. But let me do a bit of thinking for you, Meryem: Someday, Deniz-Mare will want children, and what a great blessing it will be for you all to see those children! They will be a reminder to your family that the impossible indeed became possible!"

"Say that again!"

Meryem looked at Vittoria like a bud had just blossomed in her head, like dawn had just broken into the fog that had clouded her brain ever since she learned of Deniz-Mare's leukemia.

"I said that it will be a great blessing…"

"No, before that—what did you say before that?"

"That someday Deniz-Mare will want children…" Vittoria stammered while looking at Meryem, hoping to uncover in her eyes the reason for her questions.

The answer came quickly.

"Yes, that part! You see, because you said that someday Deniz-Mare will want children, you believe that she will get through this, don't you? You believe that she will be fine and someday will have children, right?"

Vittoria took Meryem's hands, and her eyes were full of compassion as she spoke. "Meryem, I don't look at my patients thinking that the procedure I am about to perform might not work; I operate powered by hope and as if the end will always meet me bearing good news."

"Now I know why Osman wanted us to meet." Meryem's voice was soft and full of recognition and gratefulness toward the man she had come to love as a true brother. "I didn't dare think beyond the stem cell transplant. That's why I did not give importance to the possibility of infertility. I didn't dare hope…" Meryem could not finish her sentence; she brought her hand to her throat and struggled to breathe.

Vittoria came to her side, began to talk soothingly, and had Meryem sip cool water. After a few minutes, calmness returned, and her speech resumed.

"Thank you. If Deniz-Mare has a daughter someday, her name will be Mucize, 'miracle' in Turkish."

"And if Deniz-Mare does not agree?" asked Vittoria, lightening the mood.

"You have no idea how pushy—I mean assertive—we Turkish moms can be," Meryem joked.

"I bet we Italian mamas can give you a run for your money," Vittoria retorted.

The lightheartedness continued to permeate the conversation between the two new friends. Then Meryem's question brought a nuance of seriousness once again.

"So do you have any children?" She quickly apologized for what she now thought to be indiscretion. "I'm so sorry. I did not mean to pry. I got carried away...I do not have friends to share with, especially women friends, and it felt good to talk. I'm sorry."

"Meryem, it's OK. Believe it or not, I don't have many friends either—definitely none to share personal stuff with."

She felt hesitancy before answering, but realizing how much Meryem had revealed about her own personal life, Vittoria decided to open up. "The truth is that I have not found the right guy to father my children, and I do want them to have a father. But my eggs are frozen, ready, and waiting..." Vittoria finished with a mischievous smile.

Meryem's eyes became wide, and a broad smile lit up her face. "You have someone in mind, don't you?" She looked around, then whispered, "Is it Osman?"

"Well, believe me, the thought has crossed my mind, and he would be at the top of my list. I mean, what's not to like? The guy is gorgeous, intelligent, worldly, refined, responsible, wealthy...should I keep going?"

Both laughed at the rhetorical question.

"But?" inquired Meryem.

"But the guy's heart is a damned strongbox, and the code is impossible to crack. He would be a mammoth catch, though; my admiration and respects to the woman who could decipher it."

"Yes, I get the same feeling from the brilliant doctor."

"And how do you know him, Meryem? He is very involved in your daughter's case."

"He is a close friend of the family from Istanbul...but back to the subject at hand. You're not going to get out of this one, you know—who is the lucky man that those eggs are reserved for?"

"All I'll say for now is that he is Italian, and so far, has not responded to any of my subtle advances."

"Maybe," suggested Meryem, "your advances should be less subtle…"

"Believe me, I've tried; short of ripping his shirt open and literally throwing myself on top of him, I've tried everything." Both women laughed.

Vittoria enjoyed having a listening ear and unveiled more about the object of her affection. "We have attended countless charity events, even hosted a few together, but even when I have openly asked him out, he has found an excuse to politely refuse the invitation. I won't give up, I'll tire him out, you'll see; he will definitely be the father of my children!"

Meryem was surprised at the somber tone the conversation suddenly took at Vittoria's pronouncement. "You're very sure that's the one huh?" Meryem said, chuckling to lighten the mood. Her attempt failed: "As sure as my name is Vittoria Mancini!" said the doctor a bit too forcefully. Meryem couldn't identify the elusive, uncomfortable feeling deep within. She attributed it to the easiest, most visible target: stress.

After the uneasy few moments Meryem experienced—Vittoria seemed unaware—the two women continued talking and enjoying the dawning of the new and welcomed friendship.

CHAPTER 69
RARE GEMS

With his dream team in place, Osman arranged for them to meet with the family. Ozan *Bey* had expressed his desire to meet the experts that would be in charge of his granddaughter's care, and Osman knew the importance of putting family members at ease. He knew that the family, and especially Deniz-Mare, needed to see a united, self-confident team of experts.

So he organized a breakfast get-together for everyone in a large conference-room-turned reception-hall. It was surrounded by windows, so the space was bathed in the medley of golden tones created by the reflection of the sun rising behind the Alpine Mountain peaks that enveloped the waters of Lake Como.

The ambiance was light and cheery, with classical music playing softly in the background and the medical team circulating around the family members, making light conversation, answering their questions, allaying their fears.

An array of appetizer sandwiches, green juices, freshly squeezed orange juice, and fruit and vegetable trays were displayed on a large, oval table impeccably set with white linen tablecloth and napkins, beautiful hand-painted appetizer plates, silver flatware, and elegant, hand-cut crystal ware. A pink orchid graced one end of the table, and a white orchid adorned the other.

A separate, smaller, round table displayed coffee and tea sets with their respective delicate and elegant cups and saucers. The Italian porcelain displayed a Renaissance country scene hand-painted in blue; small, silver spoons were fanned alongside each set. A basket of smaller pink and white orchids was the sole decoration.

Cocktail round tables covered in white linen cloths with small white or pink centerpieces were interspersed through the space.

In the back of the room, away from the rest of the furnishings and strategically placed in front of a large picture window, two small, comfortable, cream-toned couches filled with cushions in various tones of antique pink beckoned the guests.

The perfect setting had Osman's signature all over it, although he of course was missing. To ensure complete confidentiality, Dr. Vittoria Mancini was also absent. But Elisabetta and some of her friendly nursing and lab staff were present, as well as Dr. Urgancioğlu and the affable Dr. Erik Nuñez.

Ozan kept looking at the door and at his watch. When his uncle told him that he wanted to arrange a gathering with the family and the medical team, Ozan immediately told Mari-Car that he wanted her by his side and asked her to please bring her mom, at his *dede*'s request.

He was surprised that they weren't there yet, but he'd give them a few more minutes before calling. He missed her, felt lonely and vulnerable in this crowd without her, but didn't dare voice how he felt to anyone. The only one who knew the depth of his feelings for Mari-Car was his uncle.

Osman had become his confidant and anchor during a time of uncertainty for Ozan on all fronts: his sister's illness, his relationship with Mari-Car, his choice of profession. A wave of gratefulness enveloped Ozan as he thought about the strong bond that he shared with his Osman *Amça*.

It became even stronger when his uncle took the time to share with him in more detail the extent of Deniz-Mare's condition; it made him feel grown-up, like the man of the house. However, Osman had cautioned him about sharing too much information, especially with his grandfather, who needed to avoid as much stress as possible.

"*Oğlum*, the fewer people we can cause unnecessary worry, the better," he had said to his nephew. Ozan took this advice very seriously.

The door opened, and butterflies danced in his stomach. His eyes brightened; his smile broadened.

A hospital worker had opened the door, and Mari-Car and Mari walked in carrying trays of Italian *cornetti* and Turkish coffee. Mari whispered, "*Grazie*," and the helpful assistant nodded and gently closed the door behind them.

"I'm sorry we're late—we wanted to bring a little bit of home to you all," announced Mari while carefully making her way toward the beautiful table.

"Whoever is responsible for this beautiful display," she said, looking admiringly at the table before her, "well…I'd like that number. Beautiful details, down to the colors of the orchids! White and pink orchids represent purity, innocence, beauty, elegance…" She finished her sentence dreamily.

"Wow!" said Ozan, who had walked up to greet them. "They mean all that? The flowers, I mean."

"Yes," answered Elisabette, who had heard the conversation, "all the qualities displayed by your sister."

Ozan thought of his uncle's thoughtfulness and admired him even more.

"How thoughtful," he finally said, quickly taking the tray of coffee from Mari's hands.

Mari-Car quickened her pace to catch up with Ozan and placed the tray she was carrying next to the coffee.

"Can someone really look this beautiful this early in the morning?" he whispered. He fought the urge to return a loose strand of hair behind her ear.

Happiness displayed itself all over Mari-Car's face, but she neither said anything nor looked at Ozan for fear of unveiling her feelings to everyone present.

"Mari-Car and I made Turkish coffee for the first time," Mari announced. "Please enjoy, and don't judge us too harshly—we followed the instructions off a YouTube video."

Mari's words broke any remaining ice in the otherwise restrained gathering since everyone knew the gravity of the underlying cause of the get-together and was unsure how to act.

Mari and Mari-Car spontaneously became hostesses, making sure that the conversation flowed easily and naturally, thereby turning the ambiance of the room comfortable and enjoyable.

Meryem mostly stayed by Deniz-Mare's side; the young woman looked tired and a little overwhelmed with all the attention surrounding her. Mari-Car approached her young friend and, putting on her sweetest face, asked Meryem if she could steal Deniz-Mare for a few minutes. Meryem saw the excitement on her daughter's face and pushed the wheelchair gently toward Mari-Car, requesting that she not take her too far.

"We'll just go outside the door." Without waiting for a reply, Mari-Car grabbed hold of the handles and pointed the wheelchair toward the entrance.

"Beep, beep," she said, and everyone gladly made room for driver and passenger.

Mari approached Meryem with a smile. "What's up with those two?" she asked, pointing her chin at the giggly girls.

"I don't know, but I'm glad to see a smile on Deniz-Mare's face."

Meryem looked at Mari longingly, wishing she could pour her heart out to her. The overwhelming feeling of the burden she carried bottled up inside had returned full force this morning. Maybe it was being here surrounded by doctors, or maybe it was seeing Ozan *Bey* and realizing that at some point, she'd have to reveal to him what she had held inside for so long. Imagining the disappointed look on his face brought her terrible sadness; it knotted her stomach. She didn't want to lose him.

Meryem shook the dark thoughts that had assailed her mind for a moment and looked with gratefulness and admiration at the beautiful, hand-painted, copper Turkish coffee cups and tops. She embraced Mari.

"Thank you. Thank you so much. You are so thoughtful—the Turkish cups add a beautiful touch to this already elegant event. Thank you for your friendship. I'm not one to have many friends, but I value the ones I have."

"Now you have one more. Please add me to your list." Mari's words touched Meryem deeply.

Once they were out in the hallway, Mari-Car pulled out her cell phone. "I have not listened to this video message because Peter John told me that it was especially for you and to play it at this get-together but in private. So here, you listen; I'll make sure no one bothers you." She then went by the door.

"Hi, beautiful girl with the beautiful eyes. I wish I could be there with you, but know that you are in my thoughts and prayers. My entire family is praying for you also. My beautiful girl, you are strong, and you have all of us supporting you, so lean on us and you will be OK. There are a lot of things that I want to tell you. My heart can hardly hold everything in, but it will all be here"—he placed his hands across his heart— "waiting for you, I promise. In the meantime, know that I'm always thinking of you, and feel me hugging you tightly and not letting you go."

When the message was finished, Deniz-Mare held the phone to her heart. Mari-Car looked at her from the door just a few steps away.

So this was the girl that had captured her Peter John's heart. As always happened when she thought of sharing her soulmate with someone else, Mari-Car felt a tinge of sadness behind her eyes and bittersweetness in her heart, even if she knew that it was selfish on her part.

She took the time to process the feeling that had arisen inside of her by the uninvited thoughts, then went to Deniz-Mare, who looked up at her through blurry eyes but still displayed a broad smile.

They came back into the room just as Ozan *Bey* was calling everyone to attention. He asked his grandson to stand next to him and translate into Italian and English what he was about to say. He also asked Meryem and Deniz-Mare to come and stand with him.

Meryem slowly made her way to the front of the room, pushing her daughter's wheelchair then turning it around until she stood next to her father in-law, hanging on tightly to the wheelchair's handles.

She felt weak as she looked over the assembly of goodness, kindness, and generosity looking back at her. *This is what those virtues actually look like,* Meryem thought.

She hoped she would make it through the morning without drawing attention to herself by allowing even the slightest aperture in the gates that held back the flood of tears pressing behind her eyes, threatening to overflow.

The older Ozan cleared his throat. He took time to remove his glasses and wipe the mutinous tears with the handkerchief that minutes before had beautifully adorned his suit coat pocket.

The silence was deafening. The atmosphere in the room became one of serenity and well-being. He waited, then began. "I, as the elder representative of the Ulusoy family, want to thank all of you for what you are doing for my granddaughter. The truth is that I will never be able to repay you—it's a debt that will go with me to the grave."

Even the most stoic in the group, Dr. Urgancioğlu, was fast-blinking as he listened to Ozan *Bey*. The rest, including Dr. Nuñez, who wore his heart on his sleeve, reached for the tissues or the backs of their hands.

"*Doktor* Urgancioğlu, *Doktor* Erik, Elizabetta *Hanim*, and your excellent staff: to you and to all your invaluable personnel, a heartfelt thanks. May the great Allah and the great Jesus Christ keep you, bless you, and repay you— since I can't. Mari *Hanim* and my beautiful Mari-Car, how thoughtful of you to make an old man feel at home by bringing in Turkish coffee. I have had Turkish coffee every morning since as far back as I can remember; thanks to you, the ritual has not been broken, and you made it with your own hands! *Teşekkür ederim*—thank you very much—my daughters."

They responded with big smiles, but Ozan *Bey* was not finished thanking them yet. "I'll never forget, Mari *kizim*, that it was your leadership and resourcefulness that brought us a donor in a short time. Thank you,'" he added in heavily accented English with both hands over his heart.

Both Mari and Mari-Car answered with a slight bow, mirroring him by placing both hands over their hearts.

There was a long, silent pause. Ozan *Bey* seemed unsure whether to continue speaking, but after wavering a bit, he went on.

"Allah knows that I have made many mistakes in my life and have regrets—one large one that I will not burden you with—

so I know very well that I"—he brought his right hand to his heart before continuing— "don't deserve such kindness from you all, but I'll receive it on behalf of my granddaughter." Ozan *Bey* bent down and kissed Deniz-Mare's head.

Everyone took time once again to wipe tears from their eyes, including Ozan *Bey*. "Please allow me the honor and the privilege to someday receive you in my home in Istanbul." He raised both hands toward the listeners and finished by saying, "*Tanri seni Korusun. Çok teşekkür ederim* [God bless you. Thank you very much]."

"*Amin, amin,*" could be heard by those who understood the blessing that Ozan *Bey* had just pronounced over them.

Ozan *Bey* bent down once again to embrace and kiss his granddaughter, then he turned to Meryem and his grandson and embraced and kissed them both.

The remaining time was so pleasant that no one was in a rush to go. An atmosphere of ease, friendship, trust, and love permeated the room; it overshadowed, even for a short time, the underlying heartache that had brought them together.

"*Dede*, why don't you come and sit for a bit? You haven't stopped walking around and talking to people."

Ozan *Bey* placed both hands on his grandson's shoulders, held him at arm's length, and looking at him almost sideways and mockingly scolded him. "*Oğlum*, are you trying to say that your *dede* is old? Who got tired first during our trips to the seaside, eh? And who carried whom into the house when you fell asleep on the way home?" They naturally encircled each other in an embrace.

"And who took care of two energetic kids and took them out for pizza, hamburgers, and ice cream while their mother studied and worked?" The voice came from Meryem.

"*Kizim*," said Ozan *Bey*, stretching one arm to receive his daughter-in-law and include her in their embrace. The three held each other close, then looked at each other through tearstained eyes and repeated, "*Seni seviyorum* [I love you]," several times.

Ozan's eyes met Mari-Car's from afar. Ozan *Bey* saw the longing in both young people and gave his grandson a gentle push. "Don't let Mari-Car get bored. She doesn't know too many people here; go talk to her."

Ozan nodded without taking his eyes off the one who inhabited his dreams at night and his thoughts during the day.

Meryem took advantage of these few minutes when she and Ozan *Bey* were alone.

"*Baba*," she said softly, looking deeply into her father-in-law's eyes, "no matter what might happen in the future, what you might hear, or how far apart you and I might be from one another, I want you to know that I love you and respect you like my own father. I always have."

Meryem struggled to finish and felt her breath labor to come out but ignoring the defiant tears that had finally broken loose, she managed to locate the words that she knew she needed to find and express. She knew this might be the last chance she would have to voice her gratitude and love to the man who had done so much for her and her children.

"*Baba*, I would never have made it without you, your love, your support… you have been that wall of strength behind me. Ozan and Deniz-Mare have never missed having a father present because you have lovingly and beautifully filled that gap."

Her breath became more and more labored.

"*Kizim, Kizim*, are you OK? Come and sit. I'll get some wa—"

"No, *Baba*, I'm fine, and I want to finish." Meryem took a few seconds to breathe deeply. "*Baba*, what I want to say the most is that if in the future you hear something about me or Deniz-Mare…something that brings you sadness or pain, please know that we are the same daughter and granddaughter that you've always loved, and you will always be my father and Deniz-Mare's grandfather."

Concern and fear settled on Ozan *Bey*'s eyes. Their light went dim. He reached for his no-longer-impeccable handkerchief and removed his glasses to wipe the moisture on the lenses and the tears in his eyes. He looked up and opened his mouth to speak, only to see the mass of dark hair bouncing on the back of his daughter-in-law, who had almost reached the door, then disappeared.

"Ozan *Bey*, it looks like you've been deserted." Mari looked at her daughter and Ozan, who had squatted on each side of Deniz-Mare's chair. Mari and Ozan *Bey* stopped a few seconds to listen to the girls' giggles and Ozan's cheery voice.

"Let's leave the youth to enjoy themselves. We all have some difficult days ahead," said the older Ozan before turning his full attention to Mari. "And you, *Kizim*, how are you?" He lovingly placed one arm around Mari's shoulder; the gesture reminded her of her dad. They made their way to one of the couches near the large window.

"Ozan *Bey*, it has been my pleasure and privilege to do my part in this process of finding a donor for Deniz-Mare. No thanks are necessary, really, and someday I will visit you in Istanbul, I promise." She spoke in Italian, which Ozan *Bey* managed to understand quite well, although he preferred the comfort and ease of his native Turkish. Before sitting down, he embraced Mari; she returned the embrace. "Ozan *Bey*, I will be here whenever you need me, and for whatever you need me. You'll still be seeing a lot of me…"

"*Kizim*, you are my new daughter. Of course, I'll be seeing a lot of you." Once they were both seated, he took Mari's hand and patted its back. "You have been to Istanbul more than once, I imagine. I mean, you travel around the world…" Then he thought better of the matter and added, "Or maybe you haven't been to Istanbul." Before she could answer, he elaborated further. "I can't imagine any handsome, red-blooded Turkish man letting escape a woman as beautiful and as accomplished as you!" He paused; Mari remained quiet. "Or…" He offered an explanation. "You left behind many broken Turkish hearts."

Mari's cheeks turned crimson; she felt the flow of blood through them. Instinctively, she brought her hands to feel her cheeks. She hadn't imagined it; they did feel warm.

She looked at Ozan *Bey* and saw herself reflected in the kind but penetrating eyes looking back at her. She hadn't noticed it before, but they looked and felt familiar.

"You are so kind, Ozan *Bey*, but I have loved only once, and it was so deeply and completely that when I buried him, I also buried my heart with him, and I have no more heart to share… except the piece left for Mari-Car, of course."

"So that's the sadness that lies hidden behind your beautiful eyes, *Kizim*. It's been there since the first day I met you."

Now Mari's tears spilled over. "I'm sorry, Ozan *Bey*. I'm always on the verge of tears, it seems." She blotted her eyes with the twisted tissue that she had been holding in her hand.

"How blessed that man was to have been loved so beautifully and completely by you, Mari *Kizim*—my daughter."

"Thank you," was all she could muster out of her tremoring lips.

"*Kizim*, someday another fortunate man will come and resurrect your heart. Love is a rare treasure, as you know, and blessed are the few who find it even once in their lifetime."

Mari was looking down; her teardrops fell on the strong hands that held hers. Ozan *Bey* gently lifted her chin with the crook of a slightly withered and tremoring index finger. She was forced to look into his eyes, and the older man continued his unusual speech.

"When love knocks on your door a second time, open it, and embrace the gift that *Kader* is lovingly offering you; in turn, you are a gift that *Kader* will lovingly offer to a special someone who probably has also buried his heart. Don't deny him the gift of you." His words found a place to alight on, so he continued. "You know, *Kizim*, the heart expands; you don't have to take from the part that belongs to another—that remains intact. Your heart will become bigger to make room when the time comes."

The words sounded strange indeed, but Mari recognized that she had just been given rare gems disguised as words, and she made room for them in her heart in the same space, deep within, where she kept other priceless memories and advice. She gave him a gentle hug and whispered an almost inaudible, "Thank you."

Dr. Urgancioğlu made his way to where Ozan *Bey* and Mari were. They both attempted to get up, but as always, the caring doctor stopped the attempt.

"You stay exactly where you are. We"—he pointed at the medical team— "will leave but stay as long as you want and enjoy your family. Tomorrow morning we will begin the process. Everything will be ready. Your job is to keep Deniz-Mare cheerful and positive."

They shook hands, and the medical team exited the room.

"Does anyone know where my mother went?" The inquiry came from Ozan.

"She had somewhere to go. She probably won't be long," answered Ozan *Bey*, aware of the uneasy feeling in the depths of his gut. "And if it's OK with you all, I'll make my way back to the apartment for a bit of rest."

"*Dede*, I'll go with you."

Ozan was by his grandfather's side in no time, helping him get up off the couch and taking him by the arm as they slowly made their way to the exit door.

"*Oğlum*"—the older man looked up at his namesake and patted his hand as he spoke— "when am I going to meet our benefactor? You know, the generous friend of yours who is letting us live in his apartment?" Then he shook his index finger at his grandson before adding, "And don't think I have forgotten; my memory is perfectly fine. I will pay for the use of the place."

"I know, *Dede*, it's just that he's out of the country in a different time zone and it takes us a couple of days to answer each other's message…"

"*Oğlum*," the older Ozan interrupted, "it's been more than a couple of days. You're stalling…either I will pay for the use of the apartment, or I will go find a hotel!"

"*Tamam, Dede, tamam.*"

"I want an account number where I can make a deposit by tomorrow!"

"*Emredersiniz, Dede* [Yes sir, Grandpa]."

CHAPTER 70
FIRST TOUCH

The following morning, Deniz-Mare was wheeled by Dr. Vittoria's assistant into the doctor's private office. Meryem walked alongside her daughter. The women greeted each other by kissing both cheeks, which immediately put Deniz-Mare at ease.

Deniz-Mare's maturity did not surprise Dr. Vittoria; she had seen it before in young people who had experienced serious or life-threatening illnesses. It seemed that these brave souls were able to separate the important from the trivial in life. It was good in the sense that it made them strong and mature, but on the other hand, it often robbed them of the laughter and carefreeness of youth.

After listening attentively to Dr. Vittoria's detailed explanation of the procedure, Deniz-Mare readily agreed to freeze her eggs.

"I'm not crazy about the daily injections…" She teared up. "But I would like the chance to have children someday."

Meryem felt guilty that she had given such a major issue so little importance and thanked Vittoria once again for intervening.

"It was a team effort, as you know—that's what we're here for."

"Does it hurt? Removing my eggs, I mean." Deniz-Mare suddenly felt anxious.

"Actually, my dear, egg retrieval is a minimally invasive procedure." Deniz-Mare let out a sigh of relief. "Thanks to your mother, you have received excellent dietary care since you entered the hospital; that is very helpful in terms of the number of eggs produced as well as their quality."

Deniz-Mare looked at her mom and said, "Now I know what chickens feel like."

All three of them laughed, welcoming the light moment thanks to Deniz-Mare's sense of humor.

"As explained"—Dr. Vittoria returned to the topic at hand—"we have a window of two to four days from the onset of your menstrual cycle, and you said today is day two, so we'll begin the medication right away. We've got to get those ovaries of yours producing lots of eggs, my girl!"

Vittoria was upbeat and nonchalant as she spoke. This gave Deniz-Mare the confidence that she needed and Meryem the peace of mind to bravely support her daughter.

"First, we'll perform the baseline or initial ultrasound, like we spoke about, to make sure everything is fine to start the injections. I will be with you, my dear, every step of the way, from beginning to end—and beyond, I hope."

Vittoria stretched one hand toward Meryem and grasped Deniz-Mare's hand with the other. "Everything will be just fine," she proclaimed.

For twelve days, Deniz-Mare received egg stimulation medications in the form of injections along with monitoring every couple of days in the form of transvaginal ultrasounds. These checked the uterus and ovaries to make sure that the follicles, or small sacs where the eggs were stored, were developing properly. Additionally, during monitoring, blood work was done to check the rise of hormone levels.

Unbeknownst to everyone except the medical team, Meryem began her process for IVF five days after Deniz-Mare's egg-freezing procedure. The timing of the mother-daughter procedures overlapped occasionally, and it was a delicate dance performed flawlessly by Vittoria and her team of assistants.

Meryem and Luca talked and texted many times throughout the day. She kept him abreast of every step of Deniz-Mare's egg-freezing process as well as her own preparation for IVF. However, Luca had been unable to convince Meryem to allow him in during the daily injections for the egg stimulation process.

Each night, when everyone had left Deniz-Mare's room, Meryem showered, got into beautiful silk pajamas, put on lip gloss, drew the privacy curtain around Deniz-Mare's bed, and curled up in the oversize recliner in the far side of the room to speak to Luca on video call. They'd spend the next few hours with each other until one of them gave into sleep, but not before Meryem drew back the curtain that cocooned their sleeping daughter, and turned the camera toward her, so that Luca could quietly and longingly bid her good night.

On this particular night, Luca called earlier than normal; it was a regular voice call. Meryem sounded more anxious than he was accustomed to hearing, but she was also unusually talkative, so Luca kept mostly silent and let her vent. She gave Luca the daily play-by-play of the monitoring procedure and her feelings about the whole process.

"All those people present, the discomfort of the shots, the unsexy gown…I feel guilty saying something so stupid and superficial when my daughter—"

"*Our* daughter," interrupted Luca gently. Meryem smiled and continued. "When *our* daughter is fighting a life-and-death battle." Luca continued to listen; she continued to talk. "Everyone is so nice and professional, so I feel guilty about my feelings, but you're the only one with whom I can discuss how I truly feel anyway." She continued her rant, "I've lost all my dignity; I feel helpless, ugly."

When she paused, a nervous chuckle came out of its own accord, and Luca sensed that it carried a tinge of insecurity, so he sought to reassure her.

"I'd find you sexy in a burlap bag, Meryem, but beyond that, I want to be there because this treatment involves both of us. We're in this together, *Tesoro*. Let me be with you during the treatment. I've missed too much already."

"It's all too emotional, Luca. I'm afraid that I would fall apart if you were there. I need to concentrate on the medical side of the process and on what is best for our daughter. If I think about the emotional aspect—the shock of reuniting with you, my unplanned IVF treatment, Deniz-Mare's illness, and fertility treatment—I won't be able to get through…I'm sorry,

Amore, this was a particularly stressful day, forgive my whining, I have no right."

"Yes you do, you're too hard on yourself. I will do what makes you feel more comfortable but let me remind you that *we*—there is no you and no me—we are in this together for the benefit of our daughter, Meryem. And until our daughter is cured, I will gladly go through hell, if need be, so that neither of you go through this alone."

The words triggered a flood of tears, then soft sobs. Suddenly, Meryem changed the subject.

"Are you out?" she asked between sniffles. "I hear cars and horns."

"Yes, I had to work late. I'm driving but couldn't wait to hear your voice, so I decided to call before I got home. But keep talking. I like hearing your voice, even if, like today, it carries sadness."

"Anyway, today was difficult. There was monitoring for both Deniz-Mare and me, so I had to run from her procedure to mine, without letting her know, of course. I'm tired of having things inserted in my vagina!"

"I'll keep that in mind, Tesoro."

"Oh my God, Luca! Good thing we're not on video call; I must've turned ten shades of red!"

"Ten—not fifty? Oh, I forgot, that color was gray, wasn't it? Not red."

"Luca, I am sooo glad we're not on video camera. OMG!" But Meryem couldn't help bursting into laugher.

"*Tesoro*, I know that we're experiencing incredibly stressful times, but it's nice—no, wonderful—to hear you laugh. I want to be there hugging my daughter, holding your hands, caressing your face, kissing your lips…"

"That last one sounds really good."

"I am ready, able, and very willing," was Luca's response.

The door opened. Luca walked in, still holding the phone to his ear, and without taking his eyes off her stunned face, locked the door behind him.

He approached her wordlessly, got on his knees before her, and brought her lips to meet his willing ones. "I told you I was ready, able, and willing," he said when their lips came apart.

He looked behind them toward Deniz-Mare. Her bed was enclosed inside the privacy curtain, he looked up at Meryem.

"She's lightly sedated and will sleep all night," she whispered.

Next, he made love to her with his eyes in the same way he kissed her—slow, deep, thorough—until she tremored under his intense and penetrating gaze.

Her love-glazed eyes begged him to touch her. He willingly complied, making love to her with his incredibly capable hands, tenderly caressing her cheeks, running his thumb along her lips, his hands continuing their slow trajectory down her arms, her breasts, her thighs—careful to protect the intimate area now being readied for the delicate mission of receiving and housing the precious cargo that would bring the cure to their daughter.

The realization filled Luca with awe, and an overwhelming sense of protection of Meryem overtook him. He got up, bent to take her face in his hands, delicately kissed her lips, and put the soft blanket over her. Her breathing slowed down, and she relaxed.

"Now, what I've been dreaming of doing since we met at Osman's office…" he said in the quietest, most tender, sweetest whisper Meryem had ever heard.

Luca's lips tremored; his eyes were unable to contain the tears. He turned slowly to meet his daughter for the first time.

Luca gently drew back the curtain and sat on the edge of Deniz-Mare's bed. He held her hand tenderly; it was the first time he had touched his daughter.

He stared at her in wonderment for a long time, then with both of his hands, he brought her small, delicate one to his lips without taking his eyes off her. Her hand remained encased in his two. Love expanded in his heart until he felt overwhelmed by the feeling. Tears continued to run down his cheeks to his lips and mingled with the tender kisses he placed on her forehead.

He turned to Meryem. "I still cannot believe that I have a daughter, that I found you!" he whispered incredulously.

They hadn't said much since he arrived; even the intimate moments they had experienced when he entered the room had been in silence. Meryem was still finding it difficult to form words but did finally whispered back.

"I don't think I've come out of the shock. I'm afraid to fall asleep for fear of waking up and finding out that you were just a dream."

Luca kissed Deniz-Mare on her forehead one more time, slowly encircled the curtain around the bed, and went to sit next to Meryem. She extended the cover over both of them and rested her head on his shoulder.

Luca delicately turned her head and placed a featherweight kiss on her lips. "I'll stay right here while you fall asleep, and when you wake up, I'll still be here."

She answered with a smile and closed her eyes trustingly.

A soft knock woke him up. He carefully slid out of the seat, slipped his shoes on, and went to open the door.

"I came to take Deniz-Mare's vitals," said the nurse, correctly assuming that he was her father and finding his presence in her room quite normal.

"Of course," replied Luca, and without giving any further explanation, he moved aside to allow the nurse to enter and left the room.

The notification on her phone woke her up. It was a selfie from Luca. The caption said, "I told you that I'd be there when you woke up."

Meryem brought the screen to her heart.

The surprise visit had revitalized her, which in turn also uplifted Deniz-Mare. This was helpful when the day of the egg-retrieval procedure arrived.

In order to keep the procedure private, Deniz-Mare's visits to the floor where the fertility clinic was located were masked as trips to the lab for all the blood work that was needed in preparation for the stem cell transplantation. No one questioned further.

Twelve days after the start of the stimulation medications, monitoring showed that Deniz-Mare's eggs were abundant and mature enough for retrieval. More drugs were administered to stimulate the eggs for final maturation. A day and a half later, a calm Deniz-Mare was wheeled into the waiting area, where the doctor waited for her and her mother to put them at ease before going into the operating room for the simple procedure.

Dr. Vittoria greeted Deniz-Mare as her usual, matter-of-fact, relaxed self.

"Your eggs are very healthy, my dear. Everything else looks good, so let's go get them."

Deniz-Mare couldn't help but laugh; it helped Meryem relax.

Dr. Nuñez applied light intravenous sedation, and Deniz-Mare was ready. Dr. Vittoria, guided by ultrasound, introduced a probe vaginally to locate the fluid containing the eggs. The fluid was drawn and collected in test tubes, then labeled with her name and ID number.

The fluid was immediately taken to the IVF laboratory where eggs were isolated and allowed to develop for a few hours before freezing.

After the short procedure, Deniz-Mare was taken to the recovery room and monitored by Dr. Nuñez for about fifteen minutes, which was all it took for her to come out of sedation. The doctor was mindful not to invade the family space and moved out of the way as the sedation was wearing off Deniz-Mare.

The first face she saw was her mom's, looking down at her with a big smile.

"I wish it would all be this easy," were Deniz-Mare's first words.

"One step and one day at a time, *Tesoro mio*," said Meryem, trying to calm her daughter but knowing that the hard days were yet to come.

"What you just did was monumental, *Kizim*, but you won't realize it in its totality until the day that you see tiny eyes looking up at you from your cradling arms."

"Those are beautiful and powerful words, Meryem," said Dr. Vittoria.

All three women remained silent under the power of the statement.

Meryem went to speak to Dr. Nuñez before accompanying Deniz-Mare back to her room.

"You are one of the most thoughtful people I know; I understand why you are part of Osman's inner circle. Thank you for the great kindness and care that you have shown my daughter."

"My pleasure, ma'am," was all he answered.

CHAPTER 71
IF ONLY

After the egg-retrieval process, Deniz-Mare was given a couple of days of rest and recovery from the slight vaginal soreness and abdominal cramping she was experiencing.

The discomfort was minor, and she voiced no complaints. But to avoid suspicions, her symptoms were presented as part of the illness itself to Ozan, Mari-Car, Mari, and *Dede*, who were the ones caring for Deniz-Mare while Meryem was elsewhere taking care of "administrative details," as she put it.

A central line, or intravenous catheter, was implanted into Deniz-Mare's large chest vein. It required slight sedation in order to avoid as much discomfort as possible. Again, Dr. Erik Nuñez was at Deniz-Mare's side, exercising great gentleness and kindness. She looked at him with trust and even gave him a slight smile, which in turn infused trust and ease into everyone.

All medications, including the chemotherapy required before the stem cell transplant, were infused into her body through the central line. It was easier and less painful than trying to find a vein every time medication needed to be administered. But it was one more procedure that needed sedation and preparation, and the stress on the family members was palpable, especially for Meryem, who was carrying the extra burden of IVF.

While all this was going on, Meryem was reaching the final stages of her preparation for egg retrieval.

It overwhelmed her. Seeing Deniz-Mare begin chemotherapy and anticipating its side effects, her impending IVF treatment, the need to keep her relationship with Luca totally confidential—Meryem felt that she had reached the breaking point.

So she took the chance that she had been considering for some time: she decided to confide in Mari.

Their conversation took place the day she was given the last injection that would stimulate the final maturation of her eggs; it was the last step before undergoing the retrieval of the eggs and subsequent in vitro fertilization.

The two friends removed their shoes and sank into the comfort of the familiar couch.

"What an immense weight to carry, Meryem!" The words came from Mari, who had listened to her in silence for a long while.

Osman had willingly granted his sister-in-law her request to meet with Mari in his private office. In fact, he encouraged it, knowing the tremendous amount of stress that she was under. If she had a friend, someone from outside the medical team to confide in, he would be glad—plus, although he did not know Mari, he knew that she was Mari-Car's mom and the person that had gone all out to find a donor for his niece and found him.

"Meryem," Mari continued, "I went through a period in my life so painful that the only thing I was sure of was that I was going to die; in fact, I wanted to die. But the people who loved me never left my side and helped me make it through. One thought kept me from drowning in the pain: Mari-Car needed me, and she became my reason to live. You, too, for Deniz-Mare's sake, will find strength that you didn't know you had and will come out on the other side stronger than you thought possible."

Meryem felt a current of hope course through her veins, and suddenly she embraced Mari. Words poured out of her soul that could only be expressed in her native Turkish: "*Iyi ki varsın* [I'm glad you exist]."

A surprised Mari returned the embrace and after a few minutes, continued infusing Meryem with encouraging words.

"You are doing the right thing, Meryem, by allowing into your life people who love you and appreciate you. They, we"— Mari brought her hand to her heart— "will help you make it to the other side." Both women reveled in the comfortable silence.

Mari got up from the couch and walked to the back glass wall, where she quietly took in the marvelous view beyond.

"I assume that your brother-in-law is part of the group of people who is helping you and Deniz-Mare." She finally spoke.

"Osman is a crucial part of this process. I owe him so much; I'd like to be able to express my appreciation more than what he allows me…but he's very distant and private, I think because he has been deeply hurt. But his big heart has remained intact… well, I owe him Deniz-Mare's life! Oh, by the way"—Meryem remembered something suddenly— "no one is to know that Osman is part of the team helping Deniz-Mare. In fact, no one can even know that he is around!"

"As far as I'm concerned, I haven't even heard of the mysterious man with the big heart and impeccable taste." Mari scanned her surroundings admiringly as she proclaimed the last words. "Seriously, Meryem, I feel privileged to be entrusted with such precious, personal, and confidential information, and I promise it will stay with me."

They both relaxed and remained silent, each in their own world. Mari was again the first to speak.

"You continue and finish the IVF treatment. I will not leave Deniz-Mare's side until you are strong and able. You'll know when that is…until then, I'm here."

"And your work?" Meryem asked, concerned.

"I've worked enough during the past years to last me a lifetime. It'll do me good to focus on Deniz-Mare. Plus, Mari-Car will be happy, I think, to have me close."

They both chuckled.

"Now, you relax a bit. You need to be calm and in good spirits so your IVF treatment will go smoothly, OK?" Mari helped Meryem lie down on the couch and placed cushions around her to make her comfortable. "And what a beautiful love story you and Luca have! Someday, I'll share mine with you. For now, rest; I won't go anywhere."

The words, accompanied by a rare smile from Mari, brought comfort to Meryem, and she fell asleep after uttering a barely audible, "Thank you."

Mari felt drawn once again to the window with the breathtaking view. Tears, her constant companions, made their accustomed appearance and took their familiar path down her cheeks.

"If only that were our story, my love, that we had found each other after eighteen years…" She spoke those words as a prayer into the faraway hills.

CHAPTER 72
IT'S A YES!

Luca, supported by Osman, convinced Meryem that he should be present on egg-retrieval day.

Their phone conversation was frivolous and playful.

"It'll really help me feel like I am an important part of my daughter's cure."

"*Our* daughter," said Meryem teasingly.

Luca laughed; she loved hearing it.

"Even your laugh is sexy."

"I'll laugh more if you let me be there tomorrow."

"That's a yes, and by the way, you're not just an important part, you're a crucial part; without you, there'd be no cure."

"I'll be there to present my sample…"

"And I'll be there to present my eggs…"

"I promise you, soon this process will be a lot more fun—no vials, petri dishes, or people around. Only you and I and a bottle of my best wine at a place that I've dreamed being with you all my life."

"I'm dying of anticipation, Luca."

"Me too."

"I'm feeling guilty being even a little bit happy while Deniz-Mare is suffering."

"It's when we embrace these light and precious moments that we become strong enough to face the difficult ones, *amore mio* [my love]."

Luca's words were prophetic; those difficult moments were not far away.

CHAPTER 73
SHOCKING ENCOUNTER

Vittoria's face turned pale, her stomach churned, and her breath was cut short.

"Dr. Vittoria Mancini, glad to see you. Now I know that we are in great hands."

Luca greeted the astonished doctor, kissing her on both cheeks.

"It's been a while," Vittoria replied, trying to get her bearings after the shock of seeing Luca.

"I've called," she continued. "This is a strange place to run into you…I've felt like you've been avoiding me since that elegant and memorable soiree at your vineyard. I hope I didn't scare you off."

"You know better than that, dear friend."

A serious look, quickly concealed by a strained smile, crossed Vittoria's countenance at Luca's "friend" reference. She had made it quite clear that she desired more than friendship from him, and although he had not responded in kind, she believed that all she needed was time—and the right opportunity, which she was willing to create, if only he answered one of her calls.

"Like I said, this a strange place to meet you."

Vittoria made a broad sweep of the area with the back of her hand and waited for what she hoped was a reasonable explanation.

"My girlfriend and I are going through the IVF process; today I turn in my sperm sample."

There was no pretty way to say it, and even though Vittoria was a professional, and an excellent one at that, Luca felt vulnerable and wished he were talking to a stranger. He remembered the night of the gala at his house—the beautiful doctor had been quite insistent. The thought made him uncomfortable—damn!

"We only have Meryem Yildirim with us for IVF, so I'm assuming she is your girlfriend…we're friends, and I know the story. I just didn't know that you were the other leading character. I'll take you to see her." Annoyance was definitely in the doctor's voice, but Luca, although surprised, chose to ignore it.

When he saw his beloved lying on the narrow bed, his eyes filled with love, and he tried to put aside the discomfort that he had just experienced.

One thing about Vittoria reassured him: her impeccable reputation, both as an expert in her field and as a consummate professional. *That's all that matters*, he told himself, ignoring the tinge of uneasiness that began to rise within him. He further justified his confidence by remembering that she was not only a friend of his but also Osman's, and he trusted Osman implicitly.

Luca walked confidently toward Meryem and covered her with perfect tenderness. He hugged her, kissed her forehead, brushed her hair back...

"Just think, we're here getting ready to build our family, *amore mio*."

"What a beautiful way of putting it, Luca." Her eyes shone with tears of joy.

"That's exactly what we're doing." Luca delicately lifted her head from the bed and caressed her face further.

"Now, *amore mio*, I'll go do my part, which is easy and quick. All I have to do is think of you..."

Meryem covered her face with both hands. He leaned down, kissed the back of her hands several times, and left.

Meryem looked more upbeat than usual and continued to be so during her simple procedure. Vittoria, on the other hand, was quieter and more distant than Meryem was used to.

Twelve eggs were retrieved from Meryem, an excellent number for a woman approaching her fortieth birthday.

Luca was provided with a couple of sterile sample vials for sperm collection while Meryem's eggs were being retrieved. The sperm was processed to compile the healthiest ones, and the sperm and eggs were combined.

After the procedures, in beautiful synchronicity, they met in the waiting area and walked into each other's open arms, remaining in the warm and safe embrace for a long time. Their hearts and breaths also joined in the synchronous dance.

Meryem wrapped her arms around his waist and looked up at him, uttering the first words. "When I'm with you, I feel like I'm home."

Luca pulled her head against his chest and held it there while he spoke. "Meryem, you and Deniz-Mare have become my world. In a few hours, the essence of you and the essence of me will become one in a tiny dish, and in a few days, the precious cargo in that dish will become the cure for our daughter. We are a family of three, but who knows?" Luca raised his shoulders. "Maybe we'll become a family of four, or five, or…" Meryem kissed him to stop his rambling.

She was met by the deep-blue look that reflected her soul and a disarming smile that sent currents through her entire body.

I am powerless before him, she thought. The realization scared her; she had been so independent up until now—raised her kids alone, made a name for herself in the most important museums in Europe—but now, she was experiencing total vulnerability.

Luca saw her concerned look and turned her chin up with his index finger, then bent down to kiss her.

"I'm sorry to interrupt," Vittoria Mancini cleared her throat before continuing.

"Vittoria, I'm so happy to see you. I know you already met Luca, but I wanted to invite you—"

Vittoria did not allow Meryem to finish. "We should meet soon with Dr. Urgancioğlu and Osman to compare notes and make sure that we are on track for the stem cell transplant."

Meryem felt like a vat of cold water had just been thrown at her face; the strange feeling in the pit of her stomach also told her that something was wrong. She hoped not, because she was so grateful to Dr. Vittoria that she hated the thought of having hurt her somehow.

She was mystified by the change in demeanor in Vittoria, her new friend—or so she thought. She was about to invite her, along with Luca, Osman, Dr. Urgancioğlu, and maybe Mari, to dinner.

So Meryem made a further attempt, thinking that she might have misunderstood Vittoria's brusque interruption before. Unfortunately, she hadn't.

"Yes, I would also like to meet with Dr. Urgancioğlu and Osman. Should we make it a dinner? I would love the chance to thank everyone—"

"I have busy days ahead. Let's meet in one of the conference rooms early tomorrow morning…or very soon. There is no time to waste." Dr. Vittoria turned and exited the room, leaving Meryem, but not Luca, very perplexed.

CHAPTER 74
PUZZLING BEHAVIOR

"That was so strange. We had become friends. She is the one who brought up the idea about freezing Deniz-Mare's eggs. She knows our whole story."

"*Our* whole story?" asked Luca, pointing back and forth from himself to Meryem.

"Well, she knows that I reencountered Deniz-Mare's biological father and that we fell in love again and are together and going through the IVF process."

"Did you mention me by name?" Luca was curious.

"No, I don't think so. I was so concerned about keeping everything confidential that I skipped the names, but what difference would it make?" Meryem did not wait for an answer, but still baffled, continued her account. "I told her about my relationship with Mehmet when we first got married, how I met you—I mean Deniz-Mare's dad—about my job, my family back home…oh my God, did I say too much?! We both disclosed that neither has many friends and—" "Vittoria and I know each other from before," interrupted Luca.

Now Meryem was really puzzled. "Know? How? Did you used to date?"

"Nothing like that, *amore mio*, nothing like that," Luca answered while shaking his head slowly and rubbing his neck. He was confused.

"Because you are in your right. I mean, we've been separated for many years. I don't expect you to tell me that you were at the *duomo* doing the rosary every night." She looked up at him, almost hoping to hear that he had indeed been doing that, then realized how ludicrous she was being and quickly added instead, "I know that you've had lots of women—"

He was the one to stop her ranting with a kiss this time. *Where is my willpower*, she thought.

"I don't know about lots of women," said Luca, scratching the back of his head. "I mean, I've had women, yes, of course, but to my mother's chagrin, I would never commit to any. I could not have long relationships, and now I know why: I was waiting for you."

He brought her lips close to his, and when their breaths intermingled and he was about to encircle her lower lip, she said, touching his lips with every whispered word, "Is Vittoria one of those women?"

He answered, also touching her lips, with one word. "No."

It was too much; desire overtook them, and they explored every nook and cranny of each other's mouths.

"Where were you when I had to give sperm samples? This would've made it so easy. I could've filled quite a few of those vials they gave me." Luca whispered the labored words without letting go of her lips.

"I was getting my eggs sucked out with a vacuum cleaner by a bunch of strangers."

Her words had the effect of a cold shower on both of them and they began to laugh hysterically. She went into the bathroom and came out with a wad of paper towels, which they exhausted immediately, wiping tears of laughter.

When all was said and done, Luca looked at Meryem lovingly and pulled her to him with a, "Come here, you." His strong arms surrounded her, and he kissed the top of her head over and over again.

Meryem spoke from inside the embrace. "Are you sure you and Vittoria were not a thing? She's acting very strangely, and the only difference between today and the day she and I went to Bellagio for coffee is that today she saw you and me together."

"Maybe it's because she and I made passionate love before coming here this morning, then she saw you and me together and—"

Meryem pulled away from the embrace and started beating on his chest. "You're making fun of me, I know it. Don't say that, even jokingly. I can't stand hearing about you making love, especially passionate love, to anyone but me."

Luca pulled her in once again, holding her waist tightly inside his strong arms.

"You are right, I am making fun of you. Here's the deal: I've known Vittoria for a long time. We have met at social and professional events. In fact, Osman has also attended most of those events."

Meryem remained encircled in his arms but pulled her upper body back and placed both palms on his chest. She pursed her lips and frowned.

"Hmm," she said. "What does that mean—that you've met at social events? Did you have long or interesting conversations?"

"Nooo."

"Why not?" asked Meryem, now playing with the buttons of his shirt.

"What do you mean *why not*? And should we go to a more private place so you can freely continue to play with my buttons?"

Meryem ignored his seductive question. "I mean, *why not* because she is an interesting and very attractive woman."

"Not my type," he answered quickly.

"Then who's your type?" She of course knew what he was going to say.

"You!"

"Luca, be serious, please. I am confused by Vittoria's sudden change of attitude toward me."

"First of all, I am serious! You are my type, Meryem! But—" Luca began.

"But what?" Meryem interrupted.

"I have at times sensed that Vittoria feels attraction for me and that she'd be open to starting some sort of relationship with me, but I've never thought of her as more than a friend, an acquaintance in fact. There's no way that she could've gotten the wrong impression from me…I even avoid her phone calls."

"Oh, so she calls you?" Meryem asked.

"But I don't answer," Luca said.

Meryem suddenly became solemn; she remembered the conversation at the café, when Vittoria confided in her that she had someone in mind to fertilize her frozen eggs—someone Italian!

A chill ran through her, but Meryem remained silent, because she didn't want to spoil the fun, intimate moment that she and Luca were sharing, and she still thought of Vittoria as a friend and did not want to breach any confidentiality.

"Are you OK, *Tesoro Mio*?" Luca saw the concerned look on Meryem's face and sought to reassure her. "Let's change the subject. I don't want you to be distressed over something that doesn't even exist and never has. The one thing that I can tell you is that Vittoria has an unblemished reputation, and she is an expert in her field; that's why Osman put both you and my daughter in her hands."

"That is definitely reassuring, because our future is in her hands." A hint of uneasiness began to rise in her, but just as Luca had done, she ignored it.

CHAPTER 75
SHE'S GIVING UP

Deniz-Mare began her conditioning process, which consisted of high doses of chemotherapy. The doctors had determined that ten days of arduous treatment would be necessary before infusing the embryonic stem cells.

She experienced nausea almost immediately, and on the second day, it became full-blown vomiting. It was heartbreaking to see Deniz-Mare struggle each day, and nothing seemed to calm the vomiting, not the medications, not the change in diet. When nothing remained to be expelled, which was most of the time, she was assailed by violent retching.

The light in her bright-blue eyes became dim. Her smile, which she had managed to preserve even through the prodding and poking of countless blood tests, the daily injections of medication for her egg-freezing procedure, and the insertion of the catheter into her large chest vein, had begun to wane. This became a concern to the doctors, who knew that a positive outlook could influence the outcome of the treatment.

Mari did not leave Deniz-Mare's side during the day while Meryem dealt with the IVF and solved some sort of small crisis that had developed with her fertility doctor. Meryem didn't elaborate, and Mari did not inquire further.

Mari sat next to Deniz-Mare and applied wet cloths over her face while speaking words of encouragement to her; she ran her hand softly over the length of Deniz-Mare's hair, spoke to her about traveling together to Mari's fashion shows when her treatment was finished—but Deniz-Mare remained listless, lethargic.

***

Ozan *Bey* rarely left the room except to rest and to shower. His rosary never left his hand, nor the phrase *tanri büyütür* [God is great] his lips.

He had developed a special appreciation for Mari and never missed an opportunity to thank her for her demonstrations of love, affection, and dedication to his granddaughter.

"*Kizim*," he told Mari, in his strongly accented Italian, during one of those special moments when only the two of them were present in the room caring for Deniz-Mare, "think of me as a father. I never had daughters, only sons, but Allah blessed me with Meryem and now you, *Kizim*."

"I do think of you as a father." Mari took Ozan *Bey*'s hand and buried it in both of hers. "At times, I've felt so far from God that I've doubted his existence, because he took my first and only love, the love of my life…and up until then, I had always been his faithful servant." Mari pointed up. "But I'm beginning to trust again, thanks to wonderful people like you that have unexpectedly, quietly, and lovingly entered my life. Thank you."

"You will love again, *Kizim*. I promise you," Ozan *Bey* reassured her.

"But I don't want to, Mr. Ozan *Bey*. I don't want to love again." Her eyes glistened with unshed tears.

The older man took Mari into his arms and whispered lovingly, "But you will, *Kizim*. You will."

Ozan and Mari-Car studied in the hospital. Their routine only allowed time for classes and time with Deniz-Mare. Their schedules varied, so they cherished the times when they could be in the room together. Otherwise, they mostly saw each other in passing.

Meryem no longer slept in the oversize chair in the room but in the bed holding her daughter. The nightly video calls with Luca had become a ritual that they both looked forward to.

Their days were filled with meetings, procedures, and constant decisions that needed to be made, so the only time to unwrap their hopes, dreams, and fears before each other was when everyone else was in bed.

"Luca, Deniz-Mare is not herself. I'm losing her," Meryem whispered into the screen, her eyes keeping watch over their sleeping daughter.

"We're not losing her. Chemo is harsh, Meryem. Remember that it's killing all the cancer cells to make room for the new, healthy ones that will be infused to take their place. It gets worse before it gets better, *tesoro mio*." She didn't answer and was not convinced. "I wish I could reach into the screen and hold you and her. I can't keep away much longer, *amore mio*. I can't."

Luca took the role of the strong one to protect Meryem from additional pain, but he was indeed seeing his daughter fading away, and he was concerned.

When he consulted Osman, Luca realized that there was cause for concern: Deniz-Mare's body was weakening under the chemotherapy more than they had anticipated; they were not sure if she'd be able to withstand a full ten days.

To top it off, sores had begun to form inside Deniz-Mare's mouth, so they initiated an aggressive antibiotic treatment to fight the infection. There was no question that Deniz-Mare was in trouble—had they overestimated her healthy body, mind, and emotions? The doctors relied heavily on these to help Deniz-Mare tolerate the undeniably severe side effects of the treatment, as well as to aid in the recovery process. The latest circumstances had them reconsidering their choice of treatment.

What surprised Osman and Dr. Urgancioğlu was how fast their young patient had begun to display adverse reactions. It was as if Deniz-Mare had decided to give up before the treatment had had time to work.

Although they had hoped to harvest the embryonic stem cells for transplantation immediately after Deniz-Mare's conditioning was finished and before freezing the embryos, her grave state made it impossible. They decided instead to freeze the four healthy embryos and wait to weigh the options.

Luca had become desperate. In an impromptu video call with Osman and Meryem, he requested to be an active and visible part of the decision-making team.

Osman discouraged the possibility immediately on the grounds that it would entail bringing in a complicated, unforeseen, and potentially upsetting component into an already complex situation, and all the family members were at the breaking point.

Meryem nodded in agreement; Luca finally came to the same conclusion.

"I am sorry. You are both right. Sometimes desperation makes me crazy. It was a crazy idea…and selfish."

"Luca, *Mio Fratello*, no one understands you more than I do. I also want to be an active and visible part of my niece's medical team but imagine if I showed up after having been absent for over twenty years! For starters, the attention that should be on Deniz-Mare would be on me."

"You are right, *Mio Fratello*. I am sorry."

"For now, both you and I must remain an active but invisible part of the team, *kardisim* [my brother]."

"I guess you didn't need me here. You came to a very reasonable decision all on your own." This was Meryem's only contribution to the video call.

"*Amore mio*, of course we needed you here; you are the most valuable part of this team!"

"My clue for 'over and out.'" In no time, Osman's image had disappeared.

"He looked stressed," commented Meryem to Luca once Osman went off the screen.

"He did. For him, this is not just medical but also personal. But I trust him completely, Meryem."

"Me too. That's why I feel less stressed about Vittoria."

"Oooh, Vittoria. I'd forgotten about her. *Tesoro*"—he gripped his forehead— "why did you have to bring her up?"

"Oh my God!" Meryem suddenly remembered. "Weren't we supposed to meet with Vittoria the day after the IVF? I've been so concerned about Deniz-Mare that it totally slipped my mind."

"Let's feign dementia or something and not meet, please," Luca pleaded and then laughed.

Meryem welcomed his humor at this tense, seemingly inopportune time.

"You're good for Osman…and for me too, obviously. I think Osman needs a friend like you—upbeat and with a sense of humor. You know, I've never seen Osman laugh, ever!"

"I haven't for a long time either, but whatever I can do for him, I'll do, because he gave me my life back."

"What do you mean?"

"He brought me you and Deniz-Mare—you two are my life."

CHAPTER 76
IN SEARCH OF A REASON

Deniz-Mare's puzzling downturn prompted the doctors to call a family meeting halfway through the treatment.

The Ulusoy family requested that both Mari-Car and her mom be part of the meeting since they had been such an integral part of Deniz-Mare's care. Ozan *Bey* had expressed his desire to listen to their input.

Dr. Urgancioğlu, Dr. Nuñez, and Nurse Elisabetta were the only medical personnel at the meeting.

Ozan *Bey*, Meryem, and Ozan headed the family team. No one mentioned Mehmet, but as the father of a gravely ill child, his absence continued to be very conspicuous.

The atmosphere was somber, and it was obvious that the family had hung their hopes on Dr. Urgancioğlu and his team of experts; they felt the heavy weight of the family's great expectations.

At the head of the large oval conference table sat Dr. Urgancioğlu. All eyes were on him, the brilliant mind who avoided attention. His discomfort level was reduced when the very discerning and gregarious Dr. Nuñez touched his arm slightly, leaned over, and whispered, "I've got this, Doc."

He opened with a hearty, "Good morning," followed by a very tentative, "*Gunaydin*."

"Mr. Ozan *Bey*, sir, I learned that word just for you; it sounds like 'good night' in English, but I found out that it actually means 'good morning' in Turkish."

Everyone chuckled, including Ozan *Bey*, although it was a bit delayed since he had waited for the translation. Still, it lightened the energy of the room and put everyone at ease.

Mari-Car leaned toward her mom, rolled her eyes, and whispered in her ear, "Dr. Erik did the same thing you did. He said 'mister' twice since *bey* already means 'mister,' so it's like saying 'Mr. Mr. Ozan.' Actually"—Mari-Car had a sudden realization— "he said 'mister' three times!" She put up three fingers. "Because he said 'sir' at the end: 'Mr. Ozan *Bey* Sir.' So he's worse than you!"

Mari-Car covered her mouth to contain any burst of laughter. Her mother pinched her upper arm, then her thigh, while continuing to look attentively at Dr. Nuñez.

"This meeting is to review where we are and decide where we're going concerning the treatment designed for our beautiful girl Deniz-Mare. I will speak slowly to give my man Ozan here a chance to translate for his grandfather, Mr. Ozan *Bey*."

Mari-Car did not dare look at her mother and tightened her lips to prevent laughter from escaping.

Dr. Nuñez continued. "Now, I'm from Texas—grew up in a ranch talking to horses and rounding up cattle, so speaking slowly is not in my nature."

Again, everyone chuckled. The good doctor was just what the family needed, and Dr. Urgancioğlu was relieved to be out of the spotlight.

"First of all, I am honored to be included in this remarkable team of experts." He drew their attention to Elisabetta and Dr. Urgancioğlu. "And to be surrounded by such a supportive and loving family. Our goal continues to be the same: to restore health to the brave young lady who is also a wonderful daughter, sister, granddaughter, and friend to y'all. Together we will accomplish our goal. You put in the love and care; we'll put in our expertise and compassion.

"Sometimes there are setbacks, but that's the good Lord's way of saying, 'Let me show you a different way.' It's also a reminder that we don't know everything and need to depend on him." His index finger pointed up.

"*Tanriya sükür* [Thank God]," was heard several times from Ozan *Bey*. His eyes filled with tears, which he wiped away with his ever-present, immaculate, white handkerchief.

Ozan reached over and embraced his grandfather. They held each other for a long time while Mari-Car leaned her head on her mom's shoulder and Mari reached for Meryem's hand.

The first words in response to what the doctor had just said came from Ozan *Bey*. "*Çok teşekkür ederim* [Thank you very much]."

He stood up and looked at the doctors, then went to where they were, with Ozan following closely behind him in case translation was needed. They all stood as the older man approached them. Ozan *Bey* shook hands with and embraced Dr. Urgancioğlu and Dr. Nuñez, then held Elisabetta's hand in his and lovingly patted her cheeks.

Before returning to his seat, Ozan *Bey* turned a second time to Dr. Nuñez and said, "*Çok teşekkür edirim. Tanriya sukur* [Thank you very much. God is great]."

Grandfather and grandson returned to their places, and the official meeting began with Dr. Urgancioğlu now taking over.

"We believe that we have made the correct choice in proposing a stem cell transplant for Deniz-Mare. She is young, otherwise healthy, and has a supportive family behind her, so we are at a loss as to why her health has declined even before the treatment has had a chance to act." He allowed everyone to reflect on his words before continuing.

"After consulting with my colleagues here"—he turned to look at Erik and Elisabetta—"and the rest of our great team, who are not present today, I believe that the setback is due to emotional stress rather than a result of the chemotherapy, which, as we've already mentioned, has not had a chance to impact Deniz-Mare's system fully…so we are open to any and all suggestions from you."

Ozan *Bey* kept his head down as Ozan translated quietly for him. Meryem and Mari were at a loss for words, and no one dared to speak up, so Mari-Car raised her hand.

"This isn't school, young lady—go ahead and speak. This is a very informal meeting, and we need all the input we can get."

"Thank you, Dr. Urgancioğlu," Mari-Car began shyly, then went on confidently. "I think that Deniz-Mare knows that we all love her and are here for her, but two important people are missing. The most obvious one is her father. She has felt the absence of her father and has wondered out loud why he is not here. The other person is Peter John; he has become very important to her."

She took time to think through her next words. "When we had the get-together for family and friends, I wheeled her out of the room and had her listen to a very touching but uplifting video message that Peter John had sent her. Deniz-Mare's whole demeanor and outlook changed as she listened to the message… so I think it would make a difference if both her father and her good friend Peter John were here as part of the team."

CHAPTER 77
SHOCKING APPEARANCE

Before anyone had a chance to comment, there was a knock on the door. Dr. Nuñez made his way to the door in order not to interrupt Dr. Urgancioğlu and the flow of the meeting.

Shock rather than surprise registered on the faces of Ozan *Bey*, Ozan, and Meryem. Mehmet was at the door.

Mari and Mari-Car looked at the rest of the family, hoping to find out who stood at the door. The medical team, including Dr. Nuñez, looked to the family to see whether to allow him in.

Ozan was the first to come out of shock. "*Hoş geldin*, *Baba* [Welcome, Dad]. This is our father," he announced to the expectant attendees.

"Come on in, sir," Dr. Nuñez said.

Mari-Car felt like she knew him. Ozan had spoken to her about his absent and emotionally distant father—his seemingly uncaring attitude toward him and Deniz-Mare and his indifference toward their mother. In fact, Ozan had said that he really didn't know his father and did not care to know him now. "It's too late," was all he had said on the matter.

That was the image she had of the man that had just walked in and that she had invited, she thought, telepathically, having spoken about him barely a couple of minutes before.

He was good-looking, Mari-Car noticed. There was no way that either Ozan or Deniz-Mare could turn out otherwise, she thought.

The energy of the room changed: it felt heavy and strained. Ozan *Bey* got up and opened his arms to his son. "*Hoş geldin, Oğlum* [Welcome, my son]."

After the embrace, everyone shifted to make room for Mehmet, who ended up seated between his father and Ozan. He looked at the rest of the people gathered and nodded, saying, "*Salve, buona sera* [Good evening]." His Italian was flawless.

When Mehmet was seated, Ozan *Bey* signaled Dr. Urgancioğlu to continue the meeting.

"As we were saying, Mehmet *Bey*, your daughter has developed signs of depression even before the treatment has had a chance to work. She seems lethargic and uninterested. Mari-Car is of the opinion that your presence, and that of her friend Peter John, would be of help in getting Deniz-Mare back on track."

"Mari-Car?" Mehmet questioned.

"That is me, sir. I am a friend of Deniz-Mare's and Ozan's."

"I thought this was a family meeting," Mehmet retorted, looking at Ozan *Bey*.

Then, placing his elbows on the table and resting his chin on his clasped hands, he moved his index finger back and forth between Mari and Mari-Car and fixed his eyes on Meryem. His tone became undeniably mocking. "Or are they family?" he asked his former wife.

Mari straightened up and opened her mouth to answer Mehmet in kind, but she felt her daughter's hand pressing down on her arm and held back.

Ozan *Bey* did not give Meryem time to respond.

"Both Mari-Car and her mother have been like family to Deniz-Mare since she arrived in Italy, and if your daughter—my granddaughter—today has a bone marrow donor, it's thanks to Mari *Hanim*, who worked incessantly until one was found."

"Very well…proceed, *Doktor*," Mehmet directed his words at Dr. Urgancioğlu without commenting on his father's words.

"I can only repeat what I said earlier, Mehmet *Bey*: despite our best efforts, Deniz-Mare seems to be giving up without giving the treatment a chance to work. Her close friend Mari-Car, whom you've just met, has suggested that your presence, as well as the presence of her close friend Peter John, would be of great benefit to your daughter."

"So this Mari-Car and Peter—John, whoever he is, don't have any friends of their own kind to give suggestions to?" One could hear a pin drop.

This time, Mari was unable to contain herself. She got up, grabbed Mari-Car by the hand, and politely excused herself to Ozan *Bey*.

"Mr. Ozan *Bey*, please excuse us. We'll leave you to your family. Please don't hesitate to call on either one of us; we'll help whenever and however we're needed."

"No!" In no time, Ozan was next to Mari-Car, grabbing her hand and interlocking his fingers with hers.

"If you and your mother leave, I'll leave!" He spoke loud enough for all to hear but looked directly at his father.

Mari placed a hand on Ozan's upper arm and guided him toward the door. There, Mari stopped and quietly spoke to Ozan. "Honey, thank you for thinking of us, but we'll be OK. Now we have to think about Deniz-Mare, not about our feelings… so please go back to the table, and you and your family, along with the doctors, decide what's best for Deniz-Mare, OK? We'll be here whenever you need us. You know that."

"OK," he answered, then Ozan leaned over to whisper in Mari-Car's ear, "*Seni seviyorum* [I love you]."

Mari-Car returned the sentiment, not with words but with a look so tender, so promising, that it made him weak and strong at the same time.

Ozan returned to the table and sat, not next to his father but on the other side of his grandfather, who now remained seated between son and grandson.

Dr. Urgancioğlu, knowing that time was of the essence, chose to ignore the unpleasant exchange that had just taken place and the uncomfortable feeling that it had left in its wake to continue with the critical matter at hand: bringing Deniz-Mare to a place that would allow the treatment to do its work.

"Medically, we"—Dr. Urgancioğlu looked at Dr. Nuñez and Elisabetta— "plus the rest of the team feel that we are on the right track; there is no dissension among us."

"*Doktor*, you said 'medically.' Does that mean my granddaughter's problem, the reason that it's not working, is psychological?"

"*Evet* [yes], Ozan *Bey*. We think that at this time, we need to give priority to improving your granddaughter's emotional health so the treatment will have the chance to work."

A period of silence followed, which allowed everyone time to assimilate what had just been said and to give input or ask questions.

"Does Deniz-Mare have a boyfriend or someone whose company she enjoys? Besides her family, of course?"

The question came from Dr. Nuñez, matter-of-factly. He leaned forward, pen in hand, and waited for an answer, ready to jot it down on his notepad the way that he had been doing throughout the meeting.

He knew that if the emotional condition of the patient was optimal, he'd obtain better results with less sedation. He had inserted the central line with minimal sedation and without issues, but Deniz-Mare's mood had definitely changed in the last few days, and this concerned him, because he knew it could negatively affect the outcome of the treatment.

"That's the friend that Mari-Car had talked about before she was made to leave." Ozan leaned forward and looked over at his father while he spoke. "His name is Peter John."

"Is he around?" inquired Dr. Nuñez, ignoring the tension between father and son.

"No, he's in New York," answered Ozan.

"Another Yank—that's not so bad," joked Dr. Nuñez, winking at Ozan and hoping to once again lighten the mood.

"Not bad at all, Doctor," Ozan joked back, his smile reaching his eyes.

The rest of the medical team and Meryem also smiled, and the atmosphere in the room improved some.

Ozan *Bey* leaned toward his grandson to hear the translation. He, too, smiled and patted his grandson's hand.

"There are Turks in Milan, like Dr. Urgancioğlu. Your daughter couldn't have found a Turkish boyfriend? She had to go all the way to America?" Mehmet was directing his words at Meryem; she cringed at his emphasis on the pronoun "your." Unfortunately, Mehmet was not finished being cruel. "We all know how well that turned out last time someone in our family did that."

Mehmet spilled his venom in Turkish. Besides Dr. Urgancioğlu and the other family members, the rest of the medical team did not understand what had been said, let alone the history behind the malicious words, so when Ozan *Bey* stood up and his fist came hard on the table, they jumped to their feet and instinctively ran to his side.

The elder Ozan stretched both open hands toward them and said in his heavily accented English, "Stop, stop." Then he fixed his eyes on his son and spoke. "I should have stood up to your mother when she directed her spiteful words to your brother and his wife many years ago. I've paid a heavy price for my silence—I lost my son—but I will not make the same mistake again. While I am alive, neither you nor your mother will ever offend my children's friends or partners again, no matter where they're from!"

CHAPTER 78
SURPRISING "FRIEND"

Ozan *Bey* brought his hand to his throat and slid it down to his chest.

Dr. Urgancioğlu helped him down to his chair and loosened his tie.

"I'm fine, *Doktor*, I'm fine. Take care of my granddaughter. I'm fine." Ozan *Bey* signaled his grandson to come closer. "Call the American friend, Peter…"

"Peter John," said Ozan.

"*Evet*, *Oğlum*, that one. Bring him here and pay for his plane ticket."

A gurney had already been brought into the conference room, and Ozan *Bey* was lifted onto it to be taken for tests.

"Ozan, *Oğlum*, not a word of this to my granddaughter, nor to Mari *Hanim*, Mari-Car…"

"*Dede*, relax, not a word to anyone. Now please, relax."

"*Oğlum*, call your American friend and pay for his plane ticket."

"I got it, *Dede*. I will call him right away, and I will pay for his ticket."

"*I* will pay for his ticket." Ozan *Bey* corrected him.

Ozan smiled despite his concern and reassured his grandfather. "*You* will pay for the plane ticket, I promise."

"The credit card is in my wallet—"

"*Dede*, please relax. I promise that I will find your card and pay for the ticket."

The older man smiled and patted his grandson's hand.

"I'll take it from here. You know who to inform," were Dr. Urgancioğlu's words to Ozan, and he and his team followed the gurney out of the room.

"I know. Thanks, Doc. I'm on it!"

When Ozan turned around, only his mom was left. She sat with her elbows resting on the table and her hands covering her face. Tears fell through the gaps between her fingers and onto the table.

"*Anne…*" whispered Ozan as he encircled her shoulders in his arms and kissed her neck.

After a while, Meryem looked up at her son. "*Oğlum*, take my phone, call my friend Luca, and tell him to come here—I need him."

Ozan was surprised, especially at her last phrase, but immediately complied with her request.

"I'm Ozan Ulusoy; my mom is Meryem. She wanted me to call you and say that she needs to talk to you. We are at the hospital. It's—"

"I know where it is. Thank you, Ozan. *Grazie mille* [Thanks a million]."

"*Prego, Signore.*"

"Ozan, what room are you in?"

Before he could answer, his mother said, "Tell him to meet me in your uncle's private office."

"I heard that," came Luca's response.

Ozan looked questioningly at the phone, then at his mom.

"I know, *Oğlum*. We need to talk. Just give me at least today."

"I have to go find Osman *Amça* and inform him of this whole fiasco that just took place." Ozan felt anger rise within him and left the room.

"Then I'll find Mari-Car, although I don't even know what I'll say to her. Just when things seemed to be going well…"

Ozan and his uncle were in Osman's primary office on the fourth floor of the hospital.

"Osman *Amça*, I'm tired…or angry. I don't know." Ozan wiped his face outwardly and ran his fingers through his dense mass of hair, letting out a deep sigh. "I don't even know how my father knew that we were meeting there! It was a rather impromptu meeting, but he timed it perfectly, as if he had known about it. I don't know," Ozan said, bewildered. "We were all surprised, or rather shocked, when we saw him. None of us expected it!" He paced back and forth.

"I've given specific instructions to my staff not to give any kind of information about Deniz-Mare to anyone. All outside inquiries must first be filtered through me. What we've just experienced is consequence of a protocol breach!" Osman's anger was palpable. "Heads will roll, I promise you!"

Ozan changed the topic of conversation when he suddenly remembered what had been bothering him.

"*Amça*, do you know a guy named Luca? My mom said he's a friend and asked to meet him in your 'private office.' Do you know anything about that?"

"Yes, *Oğlum*, he is more than a friend to me. My brother Luca is totally aware of all that is going on—"

"And who is he?" Ozan interrupted.

"Your mom will explain everything to you, *Oğlum*."

"That's what she said, but I feel left out." Ozan's frustration was still obvious.

"For now, suffice it to say that Luca is a good guy, and you can trust him, *tamam*?" Osman got up and stopped his nephew from pacing; he put his open hand on the back of Ozan's head and pulled it forward to rest on his shoulder.

The frustration that had built up inside due to his father's disruptive and malicious appearance at the meeting had been too much—and to top it off, his mom had suddenly come up with a "friend" that he knew nothing about. Ozan burst into sobs on his *amça*'s shoulder.

"*Tamam, Oğlum*. I'm here, *Çanim*."

Ozan felt his body relax and the level of stress slowly diminish. Until now, only his *dede* had been able to give him that much comfort.

"I have to catch Mari-Car. She got out of class about an hour ago and should be getting here soon."

Before Osman could react, Ozan was gone, and Osman was left to his thoughts. They cocooned him for a long while, until his cell phone brought him out of their comfort.

CHAPTER 79
LUCA SPEAKS TRUTH

"Osman, come up to your office—we need a plan."

"I think so too. On my way!"

Meryem sat comfortably between Luca and Osman.

"Do you guys know how wonderful it feels to be flanked by love and trust?" Meryem looked from one to the other, grabbed them both by the chin, and placed a kiss on the cheek of each man.

Osman was not accustomed to such closeness, mainly because his distant demeanor kept everyone, especially women, at bay, which suited him. However, Meryem's display of affection had a comforting effect on him—maybe because he knew it was pure, without ulterior motives.

"There's no place that I'd rather be right now than here with you two in this atmosphere of complete trust."

"Speaking of trust, how did my brother Mehmet know about the meeting with the doctors this morning?"

"No one knows, but the outward disrespect and mockery were too much even for him. I'm concerned for Ozan *Bey*, and

I'm so embarrassed for Mari-Car and Mari, her mom." Meryem shook her head and rested her forehead in her hand. "After all they've done for us!"

Luca brought her hand to his lips. "*Calmati, mio tesoro*. Mari is not the type of person that allows such behavior to get to her. She rises above it…"

"How well do you know her?" inquired Meryem.

"Pretty well. She is a very good friend of my mom's…" Luca turned toward Osman. "You know her, Osman, don't you? She's been at quite a few of my mother's charity events."

"I might have met her, but I don't remember her," said Osman, making an effort to recall.

"Well, she is rather distant—but unforgettable. And she doesn't linger much at formal affairs—does a lot of impressive work for worthy causes but has always managed to keep a low profile. Anyway, I'm sure you've both been at a few of my mom's gatherings at the same time. As I was saying before I was interrupted"—Luca turned Meryem's head toward him and softly kissed her lips— "Mari is not the type of woman that allows pettiness to affect her friendships or her work…plus, Mari-Car will probably become family someday." He winked at Meryem and reached across her back to pat Osman's shoulder. His speech carried a mischievous tone.

"With all the insulting words out of Mehmet's mouth toward non-Turks, he just made Ozan's job of convincing Mari quite a bit harder," lamented Meryem.

Osman clenched his jaw tightly, a gesture that did not escape Meryem, who quickly added, "Osman, *Çanim*, this time your father did not keep quiet. He was too late for your Zoey, yes, but not too late for your niece and nephew, *tamam*?"

Meryem got up, came around, and sat on the other side of Osman so that he was in the middle. She wrapped her arm around him, rested her head on his upper arm, and once again asked for forgiveness.

"I am so sorry, Osman. The words are not and will never be enough. I wasn't there for you then, but I am here now and until the end of my days, *tamam*?"

"I know, Meryem," he caressed her head with his free hand, "I didn't mean to bring this matter up again. What happened with Mehmet just caused me to relive that tragic day, but I'm realizing one thing: when you have loved ones supporting you during terrible moments, they become less terrible. Thank you, thank you both."

"And now back to our reason for being here: your daughter and my niece."

"Yes, let's talk about my daughter," said Luca.

"I spoke to Dr. Urgancioğlu and Dr. Nuñez, who by the way, is very insightful; he possesses a sort of sixth sense. Anyway, they both feel that we should proceed with Deniz-Mare's treatment as planned but under one condition: she should only be surrounded with loving, positive people. Dr. Nuñez feels very strongly about this."

"Osman, *Mio Fratello*, tell me when the right time is for me to be with my daughter, the appropriate time for her to learn that I am her father. I'll be good for her. I'll love her so much, she'll be cured!" Luca's longing was visible.

"Wow! I am not good at perceiving or sensing such things, *Fratello*. Plus, I'm too close to the situation and could give you wrong advice, but for the reasons that I've already mentioned, I propose that you and Meryem consult with Dr. Nuñez; see what his perspective is on that."

"One thing is for sure," said Meryem, changing topics, "I've got to meet with Mari and apologize for Mehmet's rudeness. She was so gracious about it that it made it even more embarrassing."

"And it makes that Mehmet guy—sorry, *Fratello*—sound like an even greater fool!"

They all knew that Luca had spoken the truth.

CHAPTER 80
UNEXPECTED TENDERNESS

Mehmet walked into Deniz-Mare's room; she was sleeping. He sat on the chair next to her bed and watched her sleep. It was hard to know what was going on in his mind but seeing his daughter in such a weakened state had softened his countenance since the meeting with the doctors earlier that morning.

Deniz-Mare's eyes lit up when she saw her father. She weakly began to extend her hand to him. He took it and kissed it; infinite sadness and regret engulfed him. He told his daughter that he would spend the night with her. Deniz-Mare's eyes sparkled, but she was too weak to say anything and closed her eyes again.

Ozan *Bey* was checked thoroughly. The EKG showed a normal heart rhythm, but they tried to keep him in the hospital for one night of observation, as had been recommended by Dr. Osman, unbeknownst to his father, of course. Ozan *Bey* refused.

"I'll be with my granddaughter. If anything happens to me, I'll already be in the hospital." With that, he proceeded to get dressed and was wheeled into Deniz-Mare's room, where, to his surprise, he encountered Mehmet.

Mehmet was leaning back in the large recliner next to the bed, facing his sleeping daughter and holding her frail, delicate hand in his large one. He stared somberly into the wall as if the weight of the world rested on his shoulders.

When Ozan *Bey* walked in, Mehmet did not react, but the older man was impacted by the sadness that he saw on his oldest son's face. Was this the same man who only a few hours before had insulted and mocked everyone?

Ozan *Bey* pulled a smaller chair next to his son and took advantage of the silence and what he perceived as a moment of vulnerability in Mehmet to tell him about the crucial role that Mari had played in finding a donor for Deniz-Mare and the time and dedication that she and her daughter Mari-Car had put into Deniz-Mare's recovery.

"And you, Son, why haven't you shown up until now? We have made great efforts to contact you."

After a long silence, Mehmet answered without looking at his father, "I'm here now."

No more words were exchanged, and the elder man remained in the room until late, then he got up silently, kissed his sleeping granddaughter, and left.

CHAPTER 81
A SORT OF KNOWING

Meryem and Mari met in the hospital cafeteria. It was late at night, but surprisingly, it was still open.

"We stay open, how do you say…twenty-four-seven. Dr. Osman says that many families stay here all night with their suffering loved ones, and they should have food available." The explanation had come from the night attendant upon hearing Mari and Meryem's discussion about the cafeteria's late hours.

"Dr. Osman?" asked Meryem, surprised.

"Yes, he owns this hospital; he's very kind and generous, also very private, but sometimes he comes here late at night and asks how everything is going and if we need anything."

Mari looked at Meryem, surprised. "Is that the Osman *Bey* that you told me about? Mehmet's brother?"

"Yes, I knew that he was important here in this hospital; I just didn't know that he owned it," responded Meryem, just as surprised.

"In his defense, even if I don't know who he is," said Mari, "it's hard to know how to share that kind of information. 'By the way, I own this hospital.' I don't know—I think it was probably best handling it the way he did, without comment."

"I guess you're right," said Meryem. "By the way, I guess you two do know each other: he's best friends with Luca; he said you've both been to the same charity events given by his mother."

"Hmm," said Mari, trying to remember. "Could be. I usually don't linger at those events, but maybe we've seen each other in passing." Mari dismissed the topic.

"Mari, I really wanted to meet so that I could apologize to both you and Mari-Car for Mehmet's behavior this morning…I really don't know how Mehmet found out about the meeting."

"Meryem, Mehmet is the least of our problems. Let's not waste energy trying to figure out what happened or worrying about Mari-Car's and my feelings."

Meryem placed a hand on Mari's and looking her in the eye, expressed her heartfelt thanks.

"No thanks are necessary. Please, Meryem, we're friends…"

"Maybe even family," said Meryem, looking beyond Mari. Ozan and Mari-Car were approaching their table hand in hand, smiling and looking at the moms and at each other.

Mari looked behind her and experienced a feeling of inevitability, but at the same time, she felt inner peace, because she had said what she wanted to say to both Mari-Car and Ozan regarding their relationship. Plus, Mari thought, they did make a beautiful couple.

The young couple kissed both moms and sat at the table.

"Did you two escape for coffee and leave my sister alone?" Ozan's tone was playful.

"I left a nurse with her while I took a short break to apologize to Mari and you, Mari-Car, for Mehmet's offensive behavior…"

Mari placed a hand on Meryem's and interrupted her. "I do not want to discuss what happened in the meeting with Mr. Mehmet *Bey*…" Mari-Car stepped on her foot. "I mean Mehmet *Bey*, just Mehmet *Bey*." Mari-Car rolled her eyes.

Ozan looked down to keep from bursting out laughing.

"Anyway," said Mari, giving up, "it's a waste of time and energy worrying about what happened; we are your friends, for heaven's sake. Let's put our energy into helping Deniz-Mare recover…have you all decided to continue with the transplant, or have you chosen a different course of action?"

"Thanks. You're right, Mari *Hanim*, discussing my father now would be a waste of energy, and yes, we're going forward with the transplant but decided to add another element to the new plan…"

"Peter John is coming!" Mari-Car couldn't wait any longer and interrupted Ozan.

Her excitement reflected all over her face and body.

The reaction surprised Ozan. "Will you show the same enthusiasm if I'm gone for a while and someone tells you that I'm coming to see you?" Ozan still battled his feelings of, "Maybe I will never be first in Mari-Car's heart."

Mari lovingly placed a hand on Ozan's arm. "Ozan, honey, I know that my daughter doesn't get that enthusiastic about seeing me either, even when we've been apart for a long time, but

I've learned to accept that." She raised her shoulders in a sign of resignation. "It's been like that ever since they were little; Peter John has been her older brother and the keeper of her secrets, and she his."

Ozan pulled Mari-Car close and kissed her forehead but remained pensive and silent, not sure how he felt about what Mari *Hanim* had just said.

"During our daily conversations—"

"You and Peter John have daily conversations?!" Ozan displayed mock surprise; Mari-Car rolled her eyes and continued.

"Anyway, Peter John has been anxiously waiting to come and be with Deniz-Mare but wasn't sure if his presence would be good or not—"

"You tell him that we need him!" added Meryem quickly.

"I did!" came the sheepish reply.

Ozan looked down at her, surprised to hear that she'd already told him to come, then he looked away. Mari-Car delicately turned his head toward her and forced him to look into her eyes. He did, shook his head in resignation, and kissed her forehead.

His eyes met Mari *Hanim*'s, and a sort of knowing passed between them.

CHAPTER 82
A FIGMENT OF HER IMAGINATION?

The next morning, Mari and Mari-Car were at the airport waiting for Peter John. Mari-Car, as expected, ran to cling to Peter John's neck; he picked her up and twirled her around while she squealed for joy. Mari, used to the familiar scene, stayed back and waited for her nephew to come to her and greet her.

"My favorite auntie," he said as he hugged her and kissed her.

"Yep, I'll ask Katherine about that, to see if you've told her the same thing," kidded Mari.

"She doesn't have to know that, but it is true, Aunt Mari."

"Come here, my boy." She hugged him one more time. "You know I love you, and if I had a son, I would've wanted him to be just like you."

"Great, so don't think of going out there and getting pregnant just to get a son. You already have me!"

Mari gave him a gentle push. "You insolent brat!"

They laughed and relished the moment away from the hospital, sickness, and drama; they felt good and comfortable with one another.

The three of them arrived at the hospital. They went directly to meet Meryem and Ozan at their apartment, where they would shower and change clothes before visiting Deniz-Mare.

Peter John was urged to get cleaned up and ready first, so he'd have a chance to spend time with Deniz-Mare alone.

"You go ahead, Peter John," said Meryem when he was ready. "I'm sure Deniz-Mare will be excited to see you. We'll follow later."

Mari-Car's heart sank. She still could not get used to sharing Peter John.

The area where she was having her chemotherapy session was a spacious room, but she was the only patient receiving the treatment; her recliner faced the doorway.

Deniz-Mare's eyes suddenly opened wide. Her hands automatically began to rise to cover her open mouth, then one traveled downward until it rested on her heart. But she remained unsure whether the figure at the door was real or a figment of her imagination. *Maybe it's the medication,* she thought, as he began walking slowly toward her.

Dr. Nuñez, who was always present during her chemotherapy sessions, followed Deniz-Mare's fixed look to the doorway and, realizing that this was a special visitor, moved away to observe from a distance. He had deduced that the handsome young man that had just walked in was the Yank that they had talked about at the infamous meeting.

When Peter John knelt before the recliner, tears had already overflowed.

She reached for his face with both of her hands. He placed one hand over hers and caressed her hair with the other.

"I don't think that there will be much hair left…"

Peter John placed two fingers across her lips. "So what? You are of exceptional beauty with or without hair…plus, if it goes, it'll come back sometime, so it doesn't matter if it goes away for a while."

"Thank you for being here. You are better for me than the chemo."

"Well, let's not give me so much power, but I am here, and along with the chemo, we'll get you better in no time."

"I want to get better."

"I want you to get better."

"Yes!" said Dr. Nuñez under his breath, bringing a fist above his head. *The plan is working,* he thought gleefully.

He walked forward to greet Peter John.

"Howdy, y'all," he said.

"Peter John, this is Dr. Nuñez, a countryman of yours," said Deniz-Mare, weakly but with a smile.

"I'd recognize that twang anywhere. Hiya, Doc."

"Is that English?" Deniz-Mare asked, enthralled.

"Yes, it is, but not the kind that you'd hear in this here Como region," answered Dr. Nuñez, drawing a circle in the air with his index finger pointing down.

She giggled. The doctor felt moisture in his eyes.

"Peeterrr John!"

He'd never heard so many *e*'s and *r*'s in his name. He turned toward the voice to see Ozan *Bey*. He walked quickly to greet the elderly man.

"Ozan *Bey*, sir, *merhaba. Nasilsin* [Hello. How are you]?"

Ozan *Bey* was not the only one surprised to hear Peter John's greeting in Turkish.

Deniz-Mare brought her hands to her mouth, and Dr. Nuñez let out, "Damn, the Yank speaks Turkish!"

"Don't be so impressed, Doc; that's just, 'How are you?'" Peter John shouted back at Dr. Nuñez while walking toward Ozan *Bey*.

"In my book, that's fluent, boy!" replied the doctor good-naturedly.

When Peter John reached Ozan *Bey*, he shook his hand and bowed slightly.

"No 'Ozan *Bey*,' *Oğlum. Dede*—you call me '*Dede*.'" He pointed at Peter John, then at himself to make sure he understood.

"He wants you to call him *Dede*," Deniz-Mare tried to shout from her chair; it wasn't quite a shout, but she made a great effort, and she sounded happy.

"Yeah, I got that," answered Peter John. Then, looking at Ozan *Bey*, he repeated his greeting.

"*Merhaba. Nasilsin, Dede?*"

"Damn, that's a whole sentence, boy!" Dr. Nuñez was enjoying himself.

"*Iyiyim, Oğlum, iyiyim* [I'm fine, son, I'm fine]."

The older man pulled Peter John toward him by the back of his head and hugged him. He then walked him to where Deniz-Mare was and asked his granddaughter to translate.

"Tell him that from now on he is like Ozan to me, another grandson."

Peter John responded by hugging "*Dede*" once again.

Mari, Mari-Car, and Meryem walked in at the same time; Ozan followed a bit behind.

Meryem brought her hands to cover her mouth. She hadn't seen her daughter smile and look this strong and alive in a long time.

She walked directly toward Peter John and hugged him. It surprised him.

"Had I known that I was missed so much, I would've come sooner. I just didn't want to disturb you."

"Hey, hey, you've taken my girl already. You can't take my *dede* and my mom too—and my sister!"

The two young men came together in a brotherly hug.

These two will always be in competition, thought Mari, observing from a short distance. Dr. Nuñez came and stood next to her.

"I don't think we've been formally introduced. I'm Erik." He extended his hand to Mari, who took it politely.

"Hello. Yes, I remember you from the meeting that my daughter and I left rather suddenly," she said, looking up at him with eyes he found captivating.

"Yes, that was quite a meeting, not at all what we're used to back in good, old Texas."

"Nor in good, old New York."

"Is that where you're from?"

"Yes, mostly," Mari responded, then politely excused herself and walked away to go stand next to her daughter.

Was it me? thought Erik, wanting to smell his underarms for fear that he might have forgotten to put on deodorant that morning.

Ozan, who had been only a few steps away, observing the exchange, came and stood next to Erik.

"You OK, Doc?"

"Hey, Ozan. Yeah, I'm OK, a little insecure maybe, but OK." He continued to look Mari's way as he spoke.

CHAPTER 83
THE IMPOSSIBLE DREAM

"You've heard of the impossible dream, Doc?"

"Well, I know what it is, I guess. Why?"

"Because the lady that you're looking at right now, she's just that: an impossible dream."

"Damn! Really?"

"Really!" answered Ozan, patting Dr. Nuñez's back consolingly.

The doctor let out a big sigh, put an arm around Ozan, and continued to look Mari's way.

"I guess I'll just keep on dreaming, then…"

"Well, don't say you weren't warned." Ozan's tone was a bit mischievous.

"You know, I spent four years in premed, four more in medical school, then two more as a resident, followed by another year spent studying for the board exam. That's eleven years of my life studying, taking exams, working twenty-four-hour shifts, and making daily life-and-death decisions…"

"So?" asked Ozan; he couldn't quite follow what the doctor was getting at.

"So I can't hold a dialogue of more than three to five sentences with a beautiful woman? That's crazy, man!" Erik scratched his forehead, then ran his fingers through his hair.

"I'm sure you have women coming on to you all the time, Doc—here you are tall, smart, handsome, Texan…"

"And therein lies the problem, boy. I do have women coming on to me, as you put it, but not *that* woman." Erik pointed his chin toward Mari.

"And she won't, Doc. That woman won't! But look at the cute nurse that just walked in; not all hope is lost." Ozan couldn't hold it any longer and burst into laughter.

Erik disheveled Ozan's hair teasingly.

"You guys are like two schoolkids," said Meryem, having been drawn to their side by her son's laughter, "but I'm thrilled by the uplifting and lighthearted atmosphere in the room," she quickly added.

"Yes ma'am, that it is…yes, ma'am."

"You're a good friend of Osman's, aren't you?" Meryem asked the doctor.

"Yes, ma'am, I am."

"I ask because you two are so different. I mean, you are talkative and fun, and Osman is…"

"Quiet and serious, yes, ma'am, but with a heart of gold. He is loved in my family, back at the ranch, yes, ma'am. My mom says he's like one of her kids, like one of us, so Osman is more like a brother to me. He saved my dad's life."

Ozan and Meryem looked at Erik in amazement; they had had no idea of the extent and depth of their friendship. Although, if Osman made him part of the small inner circle of specialists in charge of his niece, Dr. Erik had to be someone special.

"Yeah, my dad was pretty bad. No one could seem to figure out what was wrong with him, but he was always short of breath and had a few fainting spells…"

"Spells?" asked Meryem, not used to Erik's unique way of speaking.

"Episodes," explained Ozan.

"Osman was a guest cardiologist at the Dallas hospital where my father had been admitted and where I was doing my last year of residency as an anesthesiologist. My father's own cardiologist consulted Osman, who began the process by doing an extensive family history." Erik took a few moments to breathe deeply and collect his thoughts. "Anyways, he changed his travel plans and extended his stay to solve the mystery. By then, my father was experiencing chest pains and his fainting sp—episodes were becoming more frequent. After meticulously examining my dad and doing a lot of research, Osman diagnosed hypertrophic cardiomyopathy. I'm not going to bore you with the details, but it is a difficult-to-diagnose condition where the heart muscle thickens, making it hard for the heart to pump blood. We had visited many heart specialists before Osman; none could find the cause of my dad's heart condition, so they said what most doctors say when we don't know what to say: 'stress.'"

"Why couldn't they find the cause? I mean, it's America, where everyone, in Türkiye at least, dreams of going because that's where the best doctors are."

"The condition is hard to diagnose because at first, the symptoms are few, but Osman did something that no one else did: he took the time to ask questions and do research. My dad became important to him, not just another patient. Osman made finding the root cause of my dad's problem a priority. I learned to be a caring and dedicated doctor from my dear friend…and brother Osman." After a short, silent pause, he added, "And in the end, it was a doctor from Turkey, or *Türkiye*, as you so beautifully put it, ma'am, that saved my American dad, not the other way around. And that, ladies and gentlemen, is the story of your uncle—your brother-in-law—and me."

"Wow! Every day I'm more and more proud of my Osman *Amca*."

"He also loves you very much. I know some of the family history…" Erik put one arm around Ozan and pulled him in. "Come here, boy." They embraced.

When they separated, Ozan blurted out, "Who knows, man, maybe the impossible dream will happen."

"Maybe," said Erik, breaking into a big smile and bringing Ozan high fives with both hands.

"Is there something I don't know?" asked Meryem, looking from one man to the other.

"Yep, and it'll stay that way, Mom."

CHAPTER 84
EXCELLENT NEWS

The ten sessions of chemotherapy treatment were coming to an end. There were some OK days and some brutal ones, when Deniz-Mare experienced such weakness that she could hardly lift her head without support. The constant nausea and frequent vomiting made it almost impossible to keep anything down, which exacerbated her weakness and the fatigue that engulfed her.

On the bright side, the doctors decided that radiotherapy, which targets a specific area of the body with high radiation, would not be necessary.

"*Anne*, I don't think I will ever feel well again…will I ever get up and walk on my own?" Her voice was barely audible. It was early in the morning.

Meryem was applying washcloths dipped in cold water on Deniz-Mare's face, neck, and hair. "*Kizim, Çanim*, of course you will get well. Nothing that is happening is out of the ordinary. Just remember, it gets worse before it gets better, *tamam*?" Meryem bent down and kissed her daughter's cheeks, forehead, hair… and then took both of her hands and kissed one, then the other repeatedly.

"*Canim*," said Meryem, looking directly into her daughter's beautiful eyes, "if love alone could cure you, you'd be totally healed by now."

Deniz-Mare smiled and began to lift her hand, trying to reach Meryem, who, seeing her effort, took her daughter's delicate hand midair, brought it to her cheek, and caressed it.

Then Deniz-Mare's eyes acquired the familiar brightness as she looked beyond her mother toward the door. Meryem knew who that look was for.

"Hello, Peter John," she said without looking behind her.

"Hello, Meryem *Hanim*," he answered, but his eyes stayed on Deniz-Mare.

"I'll go get some fresh air," said Meryem, but neither of the young people acknowledged her comment. They remained fixed on each other as Meryem left the room.

She sat on the familiar small sofa outside of the room and sobbed quietly. That was how Mari found her, so she sat next to Meryem, reached for her hand, and remained silent.

"She looks so weak, so vulnerable…" Her eyes were fixed on the floor as she spoke. Then Meryem turned to Mari and added, "I don't think I can survive losing my daughter, Mari."

"I'm here for whenever you need or want to fall apart, Meryem, but losing Deniz-Mare is not in the plans, OK? This is just the dark before the dawn."

Meryem's cell phone interrupted with the familiar sound announcing an incoming message. She wiped her tears, read the screen on her phone, then looked at Mari. Before Meryem had a chance to explain anything, Mari ordered, "You go tend to whatever you need to. I'll be here."

Meryem used her special key card and took the elevator to Osman's private office.

Osman was seated behind his desk, and Luca was standing in front of the glass wall, his back to the door.

He turned when he heard the door open. Meryem gave a friendly glance at Osman and said a passing *merhaba* [(hello], then hurried into Luca's waiting arms. After a warm embrace, he held her by the shoulders and stood back to look into her red, swollen eyes.

"You've been crying, *tesoro mio*."

"She looks so frail, so weak; I'm afraid I might lose her…"

Luca pressed her against his body. "We are not going to lose our daughter, *amore mio*."

"Luca is correct—everything is going according to plan," Osman said.

"Hello, ma'am." Meryem was startled by the voice with the funny American accent coming from behind her.

"Dr. Nuñez, I'm sorry, I…"

He had been sitting on the sofa when she walked in, but her attention had been elsewhere, she realized, a bit embarrassed.

"Please, ma'am, don't worry. Osman and Luca summoned me here so we can, among other things, discuss the timing of when to reveal to Deniz-Mare the identity of her biological father—Luca, that is. I'm no psychologist, mind you, ma'am—"

"I think you can call me Meryem, I mean, seeing as you're a close friend of these two important men in my life…plus, I'm not that old!"

"No, ma'am, you're not."

"Meryem."

"Yes, ma'am."

"I am old, then."

"No, ma'am, you're not."

Osman shook his head, and a slight smile formed on his lips. Luca burst out laughing. Erik realized what was happening and turned red.

"It's my Texas upbringing, ma'am. It'll take time."

"I think you're just nervous, Erik, because you're not used to seeing such beautiful women, but this one is taken." Luca wrapped his arm around Meryem's waist and pulled her close, kissing her cheek in the process.

"Yeah, that too, Luca, my friend. There are incredibly beautiful women here, and yes, I do realize that Ms. Meryem is definitely taken. Just make sure you hang on to her real tight, hear?"

"I guess I'll just have to get used to 'miss' and 'ma'am.'" Meryem raised her shoulders and hands, resigned to the fact.

The banter gave way to the serious discussion that they had come for but were reluctant to begin.

"I learned that I have a daughter not that long ago and that the love of my life and the mother of my child was available and willing to have me. I feel so lucky, so blessed that I'm afraid that I'm going to wake up and discover that it was just a dream, because how can someone be this lucky? I know there are more deserving men than me."

Luca turned to look at Osman. He didn't say anymore, but everyone knew that he was referring to him and Zoey.

Erik cleared his throat. "I'm not that wise to know who deserves what, but you, Luca, have been blessed, and we as your true friends are very happy for you, buddy." He decided to take advantage of having everyone's attention and continued what he had begun to say. "Like I was saying, ma'am, I'm no psychologist, but part of my role here is, as I understand it, to keep close tabs on Deniz-Mare's emotional health.

"As I've shared before, a patient's emotional health affects the sedation process; at times, they require higher doses of anesthesia and a longer period of recovery when their mood is down." Erik looked at Meryem, whose hands formed tight fists as he spoke. "Dr. Urgancıoğlu has assured us that Deniz-Mare is responding well to the chemotherapy treatment; the nausea, vomiting, and even the mouth sores are unfortunate but expected side effects. We're just grateful that the mouth sores are not as severe as some cases that I've unfortunately witnessed. As difficult as I'm sure it is, my suggestion is to wait until your daughter is emotionally stronger, Luca, before you reveal the wonderful but potentially overwhelming information."

Dr. Nuñez paused and looked from Osman to Luca, unsure if he should keep talking; he did not want to overstep his bounds. Osman remained silent, elbows on his desk, chin resting on fisted hands, looking at and listening attentively to Erik.

Erik looked at Luca and Meryem and continued, "I guess I have been given the wonderful privilege of giving you the great news."

Luca and Meryem looked at each other expectantly, not daring to breathe. Luca felt Meryem tense up. "*Calmati caro mio* [Calm down, my dear]." He caressed the tresses of hair that had fallen on her face. "The doctor said 'great news.'" Meryem let out a deep sigh.

Noticing how tense Meryem was, Erik felt that it was best if Osman continued.

"If you don't mind, Osman, I'd like you to take over from here, bro."

Osman got up from behind his desk and came to stand near Meryem and Luca.

"The PGT testing shows that one of the embryos is a full HLA match with Deniz-Mare; that's the great news that my friend and colleague here wanted to give you," Osman said without missing a beat.

Meryem's reaction was unexpected, not the exuberant response that Osman was expecting. "Remind me again about PGT and HLA? Sorry, I just want to make sure I don't miss anything," she said in a faltering tone.

"HLA are proteins, also called markers, which are found in the cells of your body. They help the immune system recognize which cells belong in your body and which do not belong. So the more HLA markers in common, or matching, the donor and bone marrow recipient have, the less chance of rejection and complications for the patient later. Also, when they encounter matching cells, the donor cells will engraft, or take hold better, in their new environment. In other words, they will grow and make new blood cells, which is what we want."

Damn, that was good! I couldn't have done that good a job explaining, Erik thought but remained silent.

Luca kept his eyes on Meryem during Osman's explanation. She was exhausted and so was he. He slept little these days: after his nightly video calls with Meryem, he spent most of the remaining night hours thoroughly investigating everything about his daughter's illness.

He was well aware that the brunt of the weight of Deniz-Mare's illness fell on Meryem's shoulders, and he longed to relieve her and spend time with their daughter, but everyone agreed that the timing was not yet right.

"Sorry, Osman," Meryem finally said. "I now remember that you have already explained all that. I am so sorry…"

This time, it was Erik's words that helped relieve her stress. "You don't have to apologize Meryem, ma'am. This is complicated stuff! But rest at ease, ma'am, because you see that guy standing in front of you?" Erik pointed at Osman. "Remember how I told you he helped my family? You and Deniz-Mare and my buddy Luca here are in fantastic hands! Now, let's remember that the reason that he brought us here today is to give us all, but specially you two"—Erik moved his hand back and forth from Luca to Meryem— "not just good news but fantastic news."

Meryem gave Erik a grateful look, then rested her head on Luca's chest for a moment; she seemed to draw strength from him. Meryem then straightened up and looked at the three towers of strength before her.

"I'm sorry, I'm falling apart here. I don't know what's wrong with me. Erik and Osman, you've just given us terrific news, I get it: one of our embryos is a full HLA match with Deniz-Mare. In other words, this potential person, who I'll never meet, will become a savior for the sister that he or she will also never meet. It'll be like a savior sibling."

"That's an actual term," Osman replied.

In spite of the strength that she had just displayed a few moments before, Meryem broke into sobs. Luca embraced her even more tightly. Erik signaled Osman that he would be leaving. Osman assented and walked him the short distance to the door. Outside the door, Erik reached to embrace his friend.

"Bro, I know that everything will be fine, and please reach out to me—I'm available and would love to help in whatever way I can. Remember that I came just for you." Erik touched Osman's chest with his finger. "I don't have a specific time that I need to go back home…unless they deport me," he added playfully.

"Thank you, my brother." This time, it was Osman who initiated the embrace.

CHAPTER 85
PREPOSTEROUS PROPOSAL

When he went back into the office, Meryem was seated on the couch, her beautiful eyes still red and swollen, but she was calmer, having found refuge once again under Luca's arm. She looked up at Osman from her safe haven.

"I don't know how else to apologize, Osman—you bring me here to give me good news, and I fall apart." She couldn't stand Osman's penetrating look and lowered her eyes.

Meryem unwittingly continued to force Osman out of his comfort zone. Uncharacteristically, he went, sat next to her, and took the hand that was free from Luca's embrace.

"Meryem, this is the place, and we are the people where and with whom you should be able to fall apart without apologies or explanation. Don't be afraid to ask questions, *tamam*?"

"*Tamam*...so PGT?" She covered her face, still a bit embarrassed.

"Preimplantation genetic testing. After fertilization, the embryos are tested for abnormalities before implantation in the uterus," Osman responded calmly, almost as if talking to himself. "No abnormalities were detected," he added, anticipating the next question.

There was a long moment of welcomed silence, which Osman used to get up and get three bottles of mineral water from the fridge under his desk. He handed them each a bottle and went to stand by the window, silently partaking of the view and the water.

Meryem remained silent but calm. Luca unwrapped his arm from around her, got up slowly and walked up to the window. It seemed to be the spot for contemplating. Both men stood side by side, taking in the healing view beyond while Meryem stayed on the couch, giving the men their needed space.

Luca turned sideways so he could look from Meryem on the couch to Osman, who still faced the window and remained doing so even as Luca spoke.

"I have been spending a lot of time doing research. As you know, sleep evades me, so I use those sleepless nights to investigate new findings and cutting-edge technology related to my daughter's illness. It is what motivates me to keep going." Since he did not elicit any reaction from either Osman or Meryem, Luca continued his speech. "This potential child of ours, I already love, because it'll save my daughter; it'll give me a chance to get to know my daughter, to be a father to her. But…"

The silence was too long. Luca's "but" remained suspended in the air.

"But what?" Meryem was unable to wait any longer.

"But I would like a chance to be a father to him or her also."

"To whom?" asked Meryem, almost afraid to hear the answer.

"To the one who will save our daughter."

"How?" whispered Meryem, stunned, not knowing if she could take on another burden.

"By using fetal stem cells rather than embryonic stem cells." The answer came from Osman, who continued to stand by the glass wall, contemplating the clear waters of the lake— which mirrored the cumulus clouds above and the majestic mountains beyond— while remaining well aware of the conversation behind him.

"Don't think we didn't consider that possibility…" Osman continued. "We set it aside for multiple reasons: the chances are reduced because there is the very real possibility that the embryo will fail to implant. Once the embryo implants, the fetus needs to be allowed to develop for at least five to eight weeks. Finally, we were not sure that you and Meryem would be ready to have a child in the midst of the emotional and stressful upheaval that the family is experiencing. I mean, the effect that a new, unexpected sibling would have on Deniz-Mare and Ozan…"

Everyone lingered wordlessly on the same spot.

Osman finally turned around and faced both Luca and Meryem. "Having said all that, you two have the final word; I'll get the team ready for an immediate meeting."

Osman left the room. Luca and Meryem remained immobile.

Luca had turned toward the beautiful landscape once again, hoping to find in it something that would speak to him, a sign that would tell him that he was not out of his mind—but nothing came except desolation and heaviness. The fact did not escape him that in trying to save a potential child, he might lose two, and he knew he could not live with that experience.

He heard Meryem speaking on the phone; her voice sounded weak, strained.

"Mari, I need to talk. I'm under such stress that I can hardly stand under the weight that I'm carrying."

"Tell her to meet you at my vineyard. I'll take you and leave you two to talk."

The lines on his forehead and the corner of his eyes had deepened. His shoulders had drooped. The weight was even heavier on him. The consequences if his proposal failed would be insurmountable.

CHAPTER 86
IYI KI VARSIN

They all got there within fifteen minutes of each other. Mari was guided to the gazebo surrounded by the vineyards, where Meryem had been waiting seated in a green rattan sofa with floral-print cushions. The green tone of her cashmere sweater matched perfectly with the leaves of the surrounding grapevines. The earthy hues of her jeans and ankle-high boots picked up the color of the ground underneath. It was as if Meryem knew where she was going to end up when she got dressed that morning.

When Mari reached her, Meryem got up and embraced her. Mari could feel the tremors coming from Meryem's body. They remained entwined until these subsided, but even after they both sat down, Mari didn't let go of Meryem's hand.

Luca walked up, carrying a wood block displaying various types of cheeses, different varieties of grapes, bread, and a bottle of mineral water.

He greeted Mari warmly, kissing her on both cheeks. "Welcome. It's been a while since your last visit."

"Thank you, Luca. I've snuck in a few times to spend time with Kattia, but you have not been here."

"My mother loves you; she thinks of you like the daughter she never had," he replied. Mari rewarded him with one of her infrequent smiles. "I'll be right back with the wine, then I'll leave you two beautiful ladies alone."

"I didn't even know his mother's name," commented Meryem regretfully.

"You're hard on yourself, Meryem. With everything that has been happening in your life, you're concerned about not knowing Luca's mother's name? Don't do that…and by the way, you look amazing—I love your outfit."

"That's a huge compliment coming from you. Thank you."

"I'm here for you, Meryem. I'm listening."

Meryem began relating the details of the meeting that she had had earlier that morning with Luca and Osman and the new dilemma that they were facing after having previously agreed on a decision, or so she had thought, to perform an embryonic stem cell transplant.

"Just when we were getting close to accomplishing our goal, suddenly there is a setback created by us—well, Luca. One of the embryos is fully comparable with Deniz-Mare, so it'd seem to be the obvious path to take, but now, we're facing a new option that would cost us time, and…and…" Meryem could hardly bring herself to finish the sentence. Mari tightened her grip on Meryem's hand. "And that it could cost us Deniz-Mare's life. Mari, I just needed to say that to someone I trusted."

Mari waited, then straightened herself and reached once again for Meryem's hands.

"How would you feel if you took that new option and failed?" Mari asked, looking directly into her friend's eyes.

"Devastated!" said Meryem, surprised and distressed that Mari would ask her a question with such an obvious answer.

"Would you blame Luca?" pressed Mari.

Meryem looked at her in confusion and anguish. "Of course not! He wants this to work as much as I do. He's trying to find the best solution. He's trying to save both of our children—well, our potential child as well as Deniz-Mare. Poor guy; he's carrying the weight of the world on his shoulders."

Meryem felt a wave of sadness envelop her, almost as if she felt what Luca was feeling.

Mari lifted Meryem's chin, forcing her to look at her. "Meryem," she said gently, "I can't tell you what the right thing to do is—whether to transfer the embryo or extract the stem cells from it. That is too personal; that decision belongs to you and Luca." Mari hesitated for a few seconds before continuing. "But what I can tell you is that I think Luca needs to hear from you what you just told me: that whatever happens, he has your full support, that even if the outcome is not what you both are hoping for, you won't blame him for it."

Meryem took a few seconds to assimilate Mari's words.

"*Iyi ki varsin*," she finally said, encircling Mari in her arms.

"I know that you just said something good since you're giving me a hug," said Mari, returning the embrace.

"Yes. I said that I'm glad you exist, Mari, that I'm glad you're here, that I'm fortunate to have you."

"You said all that in those few short words?" Mari joked.

"I did. I actually did say all that."

"What a beautiful language you have."

The good mood continued between the two friends.

"Is that laughter I hear?" Luca was approaching the gazebo.

"Come, come, *Tesoro*." Meryem extended her hand, which Luca took and brought to his lips.

"Friends, you have a lot to discuss, and I have a beautiful young lady to tend to." Mari winked at both of them and got up to leave.

She leaned over and kissed Meryem.

"I'll walk you to your car," offered Luca, and without waiting for a reply, he kissed Meryem's hand once again and accompanied Mari.

"Mari, I don't know how to thank you for what you're doing for both Meryem and Deniz-Mare."

Mari placed her hand gently on Luca's arm as she spoke. "Luca, do you know the hours that your mother spent caring for me right here in this vineyard? Especially at the beginning of my career, when after countless fashion shows, I was gripped by such overwhelming sadness, loneliness, and anxiety that I literally could not stand." Her eyes welled up with tears. "Kattia held me up physically and emotionally…for me to be able to be there for her son and his beautiful family"—Mari looked over Luca's shoulder at Meryem— "is a great privilege. Allow me to do this, Luca, please, without you feeling indebted to me."

He bent down and hugged her tenderly.

"Since my mother thinks of you as a daughter, you are *mia sorella* [my sister], Mari, and our children's aunt."

The use of the plural did not escape Mari.

"Thank you, Luca. Then I'm a proud aunt who is now on her way to take care of her beautiful niece."

CHAPTER 87
REMEMBERING THE EARLY DAYS

Luca walked back slowly, hands in his pockets, head down as if in deep thought.

When he reached the gazebo, he sat wordlessly next to Meryem.

She rearranged herself until she ended up cross-legged, facing him. Wordlessly, she leaned over, held his face between her hands, and kissed his lips. Luca gently reached behind her neck, bringing her head forward to take her lips for a lingering kiss.

"*Aspetta* [Wait]," whispered Meryem.

"*¿Que cosa, Tesoro mio* [What, my treasure]?" Luca's breath was labored.

"I have something important to say regarding what we discussed in Osman's office."

"You might as well pour a glass of ice water over my head; it would've had the same effect."

"It's important that I say this, and I want to say it now. Look at me."

He did; she melted.

"You know that you disarm me when you look at me, don't you?"

"OK. Is that what you wanted to say? Thank you. Now, where were we?"

He pulled her lips to his once again. She was powerless, and he knew it, which made him crazy.

He got up and grabbed the unopened bottle of wine, a corkscrew, and one wine glass with one hand and Meryem with the other. They walked down a slight incline into a private, ample terrace with a huge, U-shaped couch.

When Meryem looked up at the vineyards that surrounded her, she felt enveloped in their beauty and warmth.

"It's like I'm being hugged, protected by the vineyards, the way I feel when I'm with you." Her words were almost whispers when she looked at Luca—then she lost herself in the view once again.

"I wondered what your first reaction would be when I brought you here. It was better than I had dreamed."

Luca placed the bottle of wine, the glass, and the opener on the giant, square coffee table with inlaid, hand-painted tiles, which displayed clusters of grapes on grapevines against the background of the vivid colors found throughout the Lombardy region. Everything here is a work of art, Meryem thought, staring at it fascinated, having finally broke away from her mesmerizing surroundings.

He gently pushed her onto the couch. He opened the bottle of wine, but his eyes barely left hers, only doing so for the second or two that it took to pour the wine into the glass.

He returned the bottle to the table, his eyes still fixed on her, and sat so close that even a breath would struggle to fit between them. Luca pushed her hair away from her face and brought the glass to her lips. Meryem took a full sip of the precious liquid without breaking away from the mesmerizing look, which exposed even her soul. He also sipped—long and slowly—from the same glass before setting it back on the table.

Luca stood up and began to unbutton his shirt, she hers, their eyes intently fixed on each part of their bodies that became exposed.

Luca then began unzipping his jeans; she mirrored his moves.

He then came down on her and possessed her lips, her neck, her breasts, her shoulders, her belly—she leaned back against one of the large, comfy cushions and arched her body.

Luca felt his entire body swell.

"Luca, *amore mio*, it's been a long time," she whispered breathlessly. "If you don't take me now, I'll burst."

"Relax, *amore mio*, *piano*, *piano* [slowly]."

He put his fingers across her lips until her breath became calmer, then he brought his lips to hers, and she became agitated again.

"Luca…"

Luca placed his hand behind her head and brought it up to give her another sip of wine. Meryem sipped, savored, sipped, then grasped Luca's chin in one hand and pulled him close. Just before meeting her lips, Luca took a long sip of wine and once again, placed the glass on the table; his eyes traveled back and forth between her beckoning, swollen lips and her entrancing eyes.

Their tongues danced, entwined, chased, searched, found.

"Luca, how much longer?"

Once again, his fingers covered her lips. She relaxed.

"We have time, *Tesoro*, don't rush."

"That's easy for you to say. You have more willpow—"

Her words froze in place when he guided her hand to his swollen, throbbing manhood.

"You still think I have more willpower?" he whispered in her ear, then looked at her through glazed, deep-blue eyes.

"So?" she questioned, looking into his eyes, "tell me what you want."

"So I want us to take our time so we can remember those moments in the early days when you came to me and we made love for hours."

Their voices were low and hoarse from desire. The words came slowly and unfinished, each interrupted by slow writhing, moans, and mouthfuls of each other.

Meryem knew that she had only seconds before his name came gushing out of her very soul, screamed by her each time she rode the peak of wave after wave of unrestrained desire.

So she rushed to thread her thoughts into a string of words that became so alive that upon hearing each one, Luca also relived each moment as if it were happening in present time.

"You have no idea, Luca, how often I have relived those moments. It seems like a lifetime ago, but when I relive them, I am transported to each time, each place, each corner where we made love…and when I do, I experience the same forbidden feelings, the same illicit thoughts, the same reckless excitement."

And he exploded, having had less seconds than he had calculated before reaching unknown heights even for him.

She soon followed, calling out his name from the depths of her being. He thrashed wildly to put out her fire and her desperation by covering her mouth with his, then covering the rest of her body with his mouth and allowing his hands to explore every inch of her body—but her fire was not easy to extinguish. Meryem continued to writhe and demand more from Luca, and he continued to give until one last, slow writhe accompanied by one last call of his name, which took her to a new height with each thrust he made, each mouthful he took, each new area his hands explored.

Stillness followed.

"Damn it, Meryem, what the hell! What did you do to me?" He was still breathless, sweaty— wet.

"I've waited for you for a long time, Luca. I guess I had it all bottled up inside."

Luca turned her entire naked body to face him and cradled her in the crook of his left elbow; with his right hand, he caressed her cheeks, her lips, and her breasts… and brushed her hair back.

Meryem turned her eyes toward the wall of sliding doors behind the couch where they had just reawakened the passion and sounds that had lain dormant for over twenty years.

"What's beyond those doors?" she asked curiously as she stretched leisurely, completely aware of how Luca's body was reacting to the deliberate, provocative, slow movements she was executing under him.

"My mother's bedroom," answered Luca, calmly.

In a flash, Meryem wiggled from under him, tried to stand up quickly, and in the process fell on the corner of the coffee table. She felt pain on her upper buttock, but her determination to get out of the embarrassing situation she felt she was in was greater, so she ignored it and, trying to get back on her feet, flailed her arms wildly and knocked the empty bottle of wine and wine glass off the table. Her desperation to stand up continued. While in the act, she stepped on a piece of glass; she winced. When she looked down, her foot was covered in blood.

"Oh, *mio Dio, amore*! *Stai bene?* [My God, my love, are you OK?]" Luca wrapped a cover around her, helped her to the couch, and began to check her foot. His hands were soon covered in blood, so he ran into the room and brought bandages. He helped her dress and quickly dressed himself.

"We need to go to the emergency room; there's one not too far. I think the cut is deep, *amore*."

Meryem's eyes filled with tears, but she couldn't help bursting into laughter. He followed suit.

"Oh my God, Luca," she whined between tears and laughter. "How are we going to explain this?"

"Let's come up with something somewhat believable, shall we?" replied Luca, tightening his lips, trying hard to keep from laughing.

He picked her up and carried her to his car, parked not far from the house.

***

Five stiches and two crutches later, they were back at Luca's place in the immense bed just beyond the sliding doors she had been so curious about earlier in the evening.

"What a beautiful space, Luca, so ample and unencumbered…and this bed, how can you leave it each morning! I could live in it."

"Come, *tesoro mio*, live in my bed." He looked deeply in her eyes and brushed her hair back with both of his hands. They lingered in bed all evening and into the night…

His phone rang.

"You and Meryem come to my private office now. It's urgent—but don't tell Meryem that!" Osman's voice sounded desperate.

CHAPTER 88
YAKAMOZ

It had been impossible to keep calm. How would he tell Meryem that Osman wanted to meet in the middle of the night and make it sound casual?

Luigi, Luca's right-hand man in the vineyard, had brought the car as close as possible to the villa. He and Luca assisted Meryem into the SUV, then laid the crutches on the back seat; all was realized in total silence by mutual, unspoken understanding.

The half-hour ride to the hospital was somber. They hoped they could reach Osman's private quarters without running into anyone.

"Osman has something important to discuss with us and he is unable to meet tomorrow, so he suggested we meet tonight," was all Luca had said, and although he knew that Meryem remained unconvinced, he was grateful for her silence.

In the elevator, the silence continued.

Osman was staring into the shimmering moonlight reflecting on the waters of the lake. *Yakamoz*, he thought, the most beautiful word in his language, used to describe the scene before him. He remained fixed on it even when he heard Luca and Meryem walk in.

Luca slowly helped Meryem to the couch and propped her injured foot on a cushion. He didn't know whether to sit or stand. As he tried to decide, he heard Osman's voice.

"One of your embryos is missing."

Osman had finally turned to face his friends, who remained speechless even after they heard his words.

Luca's first reaction was panic when he looked over at Meryem, who was struggling to speak. She looked at him wide-eyed, grabbed her throat with both hands, and labored to breathe.

Luca ran to get water from Osman's fridge and quickly returned to sit next to Meryem. He leaned her head back against the crook of his arm, poured water in his hand, and began to brush her hair back.

Her struggle to say something continued; her inability to do so filled her with panic. In desperation, Luca looked at Osman, who had just hung up the phone.

"Dr. María Bianchi is waiting for us in her office downstairs," was all he said.

Luca immediately picked up Meryem in his arms and followed Osman out the door and into the elevator. Osman opened Dr. Bianchi's office and Luca walked in and sat Meryem on the examining table. He sat next to her with one arm wrapped around her, and with his free hand caressing her face.

"*Mi scusi* [Excuse me]," Dr. Bianchi said, looking at Luca.

"*Mi scusi, Dottoressa*," responded Luca, quickly getting off the examining table and allowing the doctor to freely examine Meryem.

Dr. Bianchi dimmed the lights. "Meryem, you are OK. We've been here before, so let's lie back, take deep breaths, and try to relax, *va bene* [OK]?"

Meryem complied. Luca turned to Osman, surprised at the doctor's comment that Meryem had experienced a similar situation before. Osman remained silent, one arm across his middle, holding his chin between the index finger and thumb of the opposite hand, but he signaled his friend to remain calm.

"Now, let's do more controlled breathing. I want you to place the tip of your tongue on the back of the ridge behind your upper front teeth and let all the air out."

"Good," said Dr. Bianchi as Meryem followed her instructions.

"Now breathe in through your nose to the count of four." Dr. Bianchi counted for Meryem. "Now hold your breath in for a count of seven." She counted again. "Great. Now finally, blow the air out for the count of eight. You are doing a great job. I'll let you repeat the breathing exercise on your own three more times, OK?"

Meryem nodded. The space became still and tranquil, and so did Meryem.

The doctor looked at the men and signaled with her head to go outside the office; she followed.

"Hello, I am María Bianchi." She was addressing Luca. "Meryem has experienced a similar episode before; it's her way of coping with a stressful situation. However, for everyone's peace of mind, I suggested the first time that she should have an MRI done. Although she did not have the MRI, I don't expect to find anything wrong—tumors and such. We tested all her basic neurological functions, and she did brilliantly, so"—Dr. Bianchi moved her open hands outwardly as she spoke— "you as her friends need to help her manage her stress."

When neither man spoke, Dr. Bianchi added, "In the meantime, I'll give her some breathing exercises that she can do anytime, anywhere, just as we did inside…if needed, I will prescribe medication, but for now, let's see how she does without it."

Still no reaction from Osman or Luca.

"And now, if you'd please excuse me, I am needed elsewhere. Speaking of stress, we are short of personnel and they have me helping conduct interviews. Osman, you know where to find me."

She turned to go when she felt a hand just above her elbow.

"No, *vi prego, aspetta* María [Please wait, María]." She stopped and looked up at Osman. "*Mi scusi*, María, *per piacere* [Excuse me, María, please]. Yes…we, especially my friend Luca here and Meryem, have been under tremendous stress with a dire family situation." Osman rubbed his forehead and the back of his neck as he spoke, then he began to rotate his neck and took a deep breath before continuing. "Please forgive our poor communication, María, we just received very upsetting news that has left us…well, speechless!"

María became concerned and gave him her full attention. She placed her hand lightly on his upper arm. "Osman, tell me how I can help. You know I will if you let me."

"Luca is a very close friend—we're like brothers, really. He and Meryem have a daughter, my niece Deniz-Mare, that as you know is ready to receive a bone marrow transplant. To that end, they recently underwent IVF treatment." María furrowed her eyebrows as she listened intently; Osman cleared his throat. "Anyway, we were just notified"—he looked at his watch— "early this morning that one of their embryos is missing. Meryem has not been able to speak ever since she heard the news."

María's hand went to her open mouth as her astonished look went from one man to the other. She looked around and pulled Osman by the arm. Luca followed them into an empty office.

"*Chiuda la porta* [Close the door]." Luca complied silently.

"Osman, the head of the fertility department, Dr. Vittoria Mancini, resigned suddenly last night without leaving any information as to her whereabouts. Are these two situations connected, you think?"

Luca felt sick to his stomach and rushed out of the room.

"Is that why you're conducting interviews today?" asked Osman, his thoughts wreaking havoc on him, he trying to keep them under control.

"Yes, it was sudden. That is an active department, as you know, and she is—was—the head. Currently, we have many patients undergoing various fertility treatments…but what you just told me has left me stunned."

Neither one spoke for a long moment; then Osman's level of stress created such irrepressible anger within that it overrode his self-control. "Why was I not informed of Vittoria's resignation?!" The veins on his forehead and temples bulged.

Beads of sweat ran down his face, and his entire face took on a crimson color.

"I guess the other mind-boggling incident took precedence," María suggested cautiously.

"That the two incidents happened at the same time can't be a mere coincidence, but how they could be connected is a concept almost impossible to assimilate!" Osman's anger and confusion prevented him from acknowledging María's comments.

CHAPTER 89
MIO DIO AIUTAMI!
[MY GOD HELP ME!]

"I think I know how." Luca was pale, sweaty, his hair disheveled. "Although I cringe at the possibility." He had returned from emptying his stomach in the bathroom. His breathing was irregular and labored. He had Osman and María's full attention.

He went on to tell them about the drastic change that Vittoria had displayed toward him and Meryem after finding out about their relationship, her conversation with Meryem about having someone in mind whose sperm she hoped would fertilize her already frozen eggs, and his uneasy feeling when they had met the morning he had come for the fertilization process.

"Did you two have a relationship at any point?" Osman asked, surprised that he would not know if they had. They were close and talked about everything, including the women in their lives, something Osman did with no one else.

"Never! We met casually at a few of my mother's charity events, where she had shown some obvious interest in me, but

I never encouraged her in any way, shape, or form, *mio Dio aiutami* [my God help me]!" Luca clasped both hands behind his head and began to pace.

"*Calmati, Fratello, calmati, per favore.*" Osman realized that he was giving his friend advice that he himself was having a hard time following.

The door opened, and Luca stopped pacing and opened his arms to receive Meryem inside them. She hopped in on one foot and settled in snugly, remaining in their comfort for a long time. María and Osman kept quiet in their own world, strategizing.

Surprisingly, it was Meryem who broke the silence, her voice a bit hoarse but steady.

"I apologize for falling apart once again, *beni affet lutfen.*" She looked directly at Osman, then looked from Luca to María and added, "*Perdo'natemi.* Forgive me."

"*Tesoro mio*, it's OK. *Amore*, it's OK. I'm hardly standing myself."

"No, I mean it. I don't want all of you to have to take care of me. I fell apart…again! I think I even hit bottom for a short while this time, but Deniz-Mare needs us—that's where our focus should be, not on me!"

Meryem straightened herself up and summoned energy from her deepest self as she continued her encouraging speech. "So"—she swallowed hard— "one of our embryos is missing. Where do we begin investigating? What's our next step, the police?"

"Truth is"—Osman's words came out slowly but deliberately— "truth is, Meryem, this morning we discovered that Dr. Vittoria Mancini is also missing." He cleared his throat.

Meryem gave him an astonished look. "*Ne?* [What?]"

She bent down from the waist and began a series of fast breathing exercises. Then she straightened herself up once again and turned toward Luca, her index finger almost touching his nose.

"I knew it, damn it, I knew it. I knew it, Luca!" Then she looked at Osman and repeated, "I knew it, Osman, I knew it! That woman is a devil! I had this strange feeling that morning after our in vitro procedure, but I let it go, I ignored it. I thought it was me. I didn't want to offend her; she'd been kind to me when we met for coffee. She wanted to be my friend. I needed a friend…" Meryem was getting out of breath, hyperventilating.

They all rushed to her side.

"I'm OK. Don't worry about me—I'll be fine. But I promise you, I'll find that woman and I'll find my child if that's the last thing I do. You'll see!"

She remained standing on one foot, leaning against the examining table, staring at the floor, jaw clenched, head bobbing slowly, hands fisted.

It was a side of Meryem foreign to everyone there. Dr. María stayed back, observing the scene before her as if she was watching a play. Osman's expression, as always, was hard to read. Luca stayed glued to the spot, a confused look frozen on his face.

Meryem came out of her momentary trance, looked around, and tried to put everyone at ease but without backing down a single millimeter.

"I'm all right. Really, I am, but I swear to you, I will make that woman pay for her hideous crime, or my name isn't Meryem Yildirim!"

"Nothing has been proven yet, Meryem. We don't even know if these two incidents are related. We—"

"Of course they are related, Osman, of course they are! She told me herself that she had someone in mind for her fertilized eggs. *Allah kahretsin* [God damn it]!"

"Does stuff like this really happen…in real life, I mean, can someone go from being a brilliant doctor with stellar credentials to a criminal practically overnight?! She has no criminal record or history of strange behavior—" María felt herself losing her bearings; she grabbed hold of the examining table close by.

A long silence ensued.

"But she has a history of miscarriages and failed relationships." Everyone looked at Osman. No one said a word, just waited in suspense for his next words. None came.

CHAPTER 90
THE PLAN

"I need all of us to remain cool. No, we are not going to the police—a scandal might drive the culprit—or culprits—deeper into hiding. We'll deal with this emergency internally, and we'll act as if nothing has happened. Luca, you have connections in Interpol and the local police department, and your family has good relationships with high-ranking government officials. This is the time to benefit from all the friendships that all of us have cultivated throughout the years."

Osman paced around the room in his customary pose: left hand across his waist, right hand bent at the elbow, hand touching his chin. If there had been a screen on his forehead, one would have seen his thoughts and ideas scurrying around in his brain and him threading them together to form a plan.

"In the meantime, Meryem, you'll keep the family running smoothly. Use whatever means necessary. As you now know, I own this hospital. Take advantage of that: use the apartment units on the premises anyway you see fit. Make sure everyone is comfortable—my dad, Ozan, your friend…" He scratched his head searching for a name.

"Mari, my friend Mari. She has been taking care of Deniz-Mare while I've been…eh, well…"

"Busy, *Tesoro*, busy." Luca rescued her from the ensnarement she was heading into.

"Anyway, Meryem, you are on family duty. Under no circumstances are they allowed to even suspect what's going on."

"Dr. Bianchi and I will take care of keeping the fertility clinic running efficiently and quietly. I'll be relying on you a lot, María, as far as the new personnel that you are interviewing." Osman looked at Meryem and Luca and reassured them, "Please remember that Vittoria was not the only fertility specialist. She was the head of the clinic, not the clinic itself. She was excellent in her field, yes, but not the only one. We will go on without her."

María was subdued. "The truth is, Osman, that I'm almost afraid to hire anyone. I mean, Vittoria was the best of the best. I'm still in shock at what she possibly did, and very nervous."

"Not *possibly*, did! She did it!" Meryem interjected. "Do you know what she said? That you," she pointed at Luca, "would definitely be the father of her children or her name was not Vittoria Mancini!"

"Me?" said Luca, astounded and pointing at himself. "*Mio dio aiutami.*"

"Well, she didn't mention your name, but she did say that her name was not Vittoria Mancini if the Italian man she had in mind would not be the father of her frozen eggs!" Meryem was angry, Luca felt blamed, and Osman averted the conflict he saw coming.

"I agree with Meryem—she did it. There is no other explanation. Vittoria lost sight of her humanity; she lost control of her feelings to the point that they became extreme and sick. May Allah and Jesus Christ help us."

When Osman finished talking, he and Meryem wiped their faces with both hands. Luca and María made the sign of the cross.

"Eh…" Meryem looked from Luca to Osman, unsure as to how to proceed.

María sensed that her presence was no longer needed and saved everyone the discomfort of having to say so. "Friends, I have a lot to do, as you all know; I remain at your service. Luca, it was a pleasure to meet you. Sorry that it was under these terrible circumstances."

The door had barely shut when Meryem's fear jumped out of her mouth.

"Deniz-Mare. What are we going to do about my…" She took hold of Luca's arm and continued, "*our* daughter? She's ready for her stem cell transplant."

Osman addressed her concern immediately. "I already checked with the lab; the embryo fully compatible with Deniz-Mare was not the one taken. You and Luca decided to take a chance and have an embryo transfer performed anyway. In other words, you chose that route rather than have embryo stem cell extraction…in retrospect, that decision might work for our benefit anyway."

Luca felt well-being embed in the pit of his stomach. It gave him courage; maybe Someone was looking over them.

"So my suggestion is to go ahead and have the embryo transfer done as soon as possible. Within two weeks, we'll know if implantation has occurred."

"Not if, *Fratello Mio*, *will*. Implantation *will* occur."

"Your faith and confidence might be that element that we—I—have needed during this process. I can manage the medical team—although apparently not so well, seeing as I missed the big monster that was in front of me." Osman sighed deeply.

"Anyway, faith, God, the Universe…I'm afraid that's not my forte."

Luca squeezed his friend's arm. "*Calmati, Fratello, calmati.*"

"*Amore*, we've got work to do." Luca kissed Meryem's forehead.

"So, what's next?" Her voice was strong and determined.

"I'll have María immediately get you in touch with one of the other fertility specialists since she's working closely with that department as part of the interviewing team for Vittoria's replacement—" Osman stopped midsentence, as another idea had entered his head. "On second thought, Meryem, you're very familiar with that department; you know the doctors, nurses, and other personnel. Why don't you go and talk to them yourself? They know you and Deniz-Mare well."

"They're a wonderful and caring group of professionals," Meryem said. "Osman, you have your hands full! You're right, I know everyone there. Luca and I will take care of the embryo-transfer end of things; you go solve the Vittoria fiasco."

"Thanks. You've just peeled away one layer of stress that was weighing heavily on me."

"We've got this!" Luca reassured him by sheltering his friend with a strong arm around his shoulder.

"By the way," Meryem asked almost rhetorically, as if she were talking to herself, "isn't it strange that Vittoria left the embryo that was a full match?"

"I was thinking the same thing," commented Luca. His tone was pensive but sober.

Osman gave his input: "If she weren't so brilliant—and evil—I'd say she hadn't noticed which embryo was a full HLA match, but that not being the case, I'd say she was in a hurry and took the one she could grab immediately."

"I agree," said Meryem with disdain. "The woman is evil, and she'd want to hurt us in the worst way, so she would purposely take the one that would have prevented our daughter from getting well." Meryem visibly cringed. "Something must've happened so she couldn't." She was clearly trying to discern Vittoria's intentions.

The tension on Osman was visible. A faraway look engulfed him; he unceasingly rubbed the back of his head and neck, only pausing to rotate his head and grimace.

Meryem was glad that she had removed part of the load off his shoulders, but her head was reeling with alarming questions: What if they didn't find Vittoria on time? What if she had destroyed her embryo just for evil's sake? The thought caused her to shudder involuntarily. How long could they keep Deniz-Mare in isolation now that her immune system had been suppressed in preparation for the new cells? But she was unsure whether she wanted to know the answers, so she kept quiet.

Thank God Osman was a step ahead of her.

He immediately contacted his team of doctors in charge of Deniz-Mare's case. Dr. Urgancıoğlu wasted no time in modifying the plan for cell transplantation. Deniz-Mare would have to be kept in isolation for at least six weeks, until the fetal stem cell procedure could be realized.

A specialized nursing staff of six nurses would be working exclusively with Deniz-Mare. Three would share the duties in three eight-hour shifts; the others would be on call to replace their counterparts at any given moment.

CHAPTER 91
THE BOTTLE OF PERRIER DID IT!

Meryem called a meeting for the family in the cafeteria to discuss Deniz-Mare's progress and the next stage of the treatment.

Mari, Mari-Car, and Peter John joined Ozan *Bey* and Ozan. They all seemed animated as they bantered around the table, drinking coffee while they waited for Meryem.

"Oh my God, *Anne*, what happened? Where have you been?!" Ozan pushed his chair back and ran to Meryem's side. Peter John also ran to assist her when he saw her walk in leaning on crutches.

"*Kizim*." Ozan *Bey* stood up, alarmed by his daughter-in-law's appearance.

"*Sakin ol* [Calm down]. I'm all right."

"*Emin misin* [Are you sure]?" Ozan *Bey* asked, still concerned.

"*Eminim, Baba* [I'm sure, Dad]."

Once Meryem settled in a chair, all eyes were on her as they awaited an explanation.

"I've been in meetings with various members of the medical team most of the night. During one of the meetings, having spent practically all day on my feet walking from one place to the next, I removed my shoes under the table to allow my feet to rest." They remained attentive to every word, and Meryem hoped to God her story made sense. "Anyway, they had placed bottles of Perrier at each place setting around the conference table. I accidentally knocked mine down, got up by reflex, and stepped on the broken glass."

"Wow! I am so sorry, Meryem *Hanim*," said Mari-Car. "Good thing you were right here in the hospital already."

"My poor *anne*." Ozan came, sat next to his mom, and leaned against her. She kissed his head.

"Enough about me. I'll be walking without these things in a few days." She pointed at the crutches leaning against the table next to her. "Let's talk about the new plan for Deniz-Mare. I'm really going to need your help with it."

"Go on, *Kizim*. We're waiting." Ozan *Bey* brought everyone to order.

Under the pretense that Deniz-Mare required a longer recuperation period after the long and harsh chemotherapy treatment, Meryem went on to explain that the doctors had requested that the family would assist by also forming three shifts.

"The goal is to have at least one of us plus a nurse with Deniz-Mare round the clock." As expected, everyone was delighted to be able to participate and did not question the new plan. "There are enough of us to cover for each other in case a situation comes up where one of us can't cover our shift."

"Well, Ms. Meryem *Hanim*, everyone might get sick of me, because I plan to be here all the time. Since my schoolwork is done online, I don't have to go anywhere," Peter John spoke up cheerily.

"You know, PJ, *hanim* already means 'miss,' so you don't have to say them both," Mari-Car said with a mocking air of superiority.

"You know, Mari-Car, I wish I could get mad at you when you make fun of me, but I can't." Peter John looked at her with smiling eyes, wrinkled his nose, and made a face.

Ozan swallowed hard. Will I ever feel comfortable with these two? he thought but remained quiet.

Mari's eyes remained fixed on the table. These two will bring sorrow to Ozan's heart, she thought, feeling a pang in the pit of her stomach.

"OK, team. Now that we have worked out an amazing plan for taking care of our beautiful Deniz-Mare"—optimism poured out of Mari as she extended her invitation— "let me treat you to whatever your heart desires…as long as the cafeteria has it, of course." Everyone laughed. The mood had become cheerful once again.

"*Kizim*, I will treat!" came the strong, determined voice of Ozan *Bey*.

Mari opened her mouth to protest, but Ozan stopped her. "Mari *Hanim*, you will not win this battle."

Mari looked at Ozan *Bey* and smiled, brought both hands to her heart, bowed her head slightly, and said, "*La ringrazio*," using the polite and formal way to say thank you in Italian to show him deference.

Meryem seized on the opportunity and the lightheartedness of the others to insist (at Osman's request) that Mari, Peter John, and Mari-Car stayed in one of the apartments within the hospital complex.

"I insist that it be so, and I'll cover all the costs. I beg you to allow me." The heartfelt plea came from Ozan *Bey*—of course.

"Don't try to argue, Mari *Hanim*; you'll lose," Ozan warned once again.

"It will be our pleasure to accept your generous offer, Ozan *Bey*." Mari reached across the table, took both of his hands, and squeezed them gently. Ozan *Bey* brought her hands to his lips and kissed them.

"Thank you, *Kizim*," he said.

"I will, however," Mari said, interrupting the tender moment, "be absent, but only next week, due to a previous commitment. As a matter of fact, I'll be in Istanbul, of all places." Mari looked at Ozan, Meryem, and Ozan *Bey* and chuckled, hoping that her slight discomfort at the impromptu trip to Istanbul would pass unnoticed. "I'll be attending a fashion show." She felt the need to explain.

"Before Istanbul," Mari continued, "I'll fly to Murcia for a couple of days to visit my grandparents; my grandmother is not doing well and has asked to see me. So, I'll take next week to do those two things…but," she added quickly, "I'll be here for the rest of this week, and after next week, I'm all yours!" She finished with a big, albeit rare, smile.

"But *Kizim*, I wanted to be there when you visited my city; I wanted to give you a proper welcome," a distraught Ozan *Bey* replied after Ozan translated Mari's plans.

"Actually, Ozan *Bey*, sir—I mean, Ozan *Bey*"—she corrected herself after Mari-Car rolled her eyes— "it was an unexpected trip. I was just planning to go see my grandmother in Murcia for a couple of days, as I said, but Yağmur Gülsoy, my assistant in Istanbul, had a family matter come up and notified me at the last minute that she would be unable to attend the show."

Mari waited for Ozan to finish translating for his grandfather before continuing. "It's an important event, so I must make a quick business trip; but I promise you that when Deniz-Mare gets well, I'll visit your city just to see you."

"*Tamam, Kizim, tamam.*" He leaned over and patted Mari's cheeks. "You'll make this old man very happy."

"Mari, you go and fulfill your commitments; we'll be fine, my friend." Meryem's words reassured Mari; they stood up from the table and hugged. "I have a lot to tell you, but I'll wait until you get back," she whispered in Mari's ear during their embrace. Mari rewarded her with a gentle nod and a smile.

Ozan, Mari-Car, and Peter John exchanged looks and smiles; they would all benefit from their mothers' friendship, and they knew it.

CHAPTER 92
IF ALLAH HAD GIVEN ME A LOVE LIKE YOURS

Although Meryem visited her daughter daily, she spent a lot of time resting and protecting her "other child."

The embryo transfer had been completed without incident; Luca had held her hand, and Dr. Erik was in the adjacent room in case sedation was needed, though such cases were rare.

"You'll need a lot of rest and very little stress," the fertility specialists had lovingly admonished her.

Meryem had become their most precious, though temporary, possession. They knew the loss that she and Luca had suffered and the great hope that this new child would bring.

Now they would wait about two weeks to verify whether implantation had taken place. The entire staff protected Meryem and, hopefully, her unborn child like they were endangered birds.

She was provided with a private space within the fertility clinic where she could rest and be monitored around the clock. She was surrounded by an amazing team of experts that included fertility specialists, embryologists, and reproductive nurses.

Meryem made one of her rare appearances in Deniz-Mare's room on a day that the entire family had congregated there. They had all gathered in the anteroom, which had ample seating space, before entering Deniz-Mare's new, more comfortable room, where she would be kept in isolation for about eight weeks, although the medical team had not been that specific with the family members so they wouldn't become discouraged.

The impromptu family gathering turned out to also be a chance for everyone to say goodbye to Mari before she left on her trip the following day.

Ozan was the first to complain to Meryem about her prolonged absences lately and about the fact that the stem cell transplant seemed to be taking a lot longer than they had been led to believe.

"Yes, *Oğlum*," said Meryem, hoping to calm her son, "I spend a lot of time in meetings with Dr. Urgancioğlu and other specialists going over the minute details of the procedure before we take the next step." Ozan seemed unconvinced. "I rely on you and the rest of the family members to care for Deniz-Mare when I'm not here, which has been quite often lately. It's a delicate process, and they want to make sure that Deniz-Mare's immune system is in top shape to receive the transplant and, even more so, that she is in good emotional health."

"Emotional health?" He seemed confused. "That's what we've been doing all this time! I think she's in better emotional health than the rest of us. Me, anyhow!"

Mari-Car moved closer to Ozan, clasped his hand, turned his face toward hers, smiled, and kissed his cheek.

"*Amore, birtanem*, everything is going to be OK, I promise." She kissed his cheek once again; he brought her hand to his lips.

"Sorry; thanks," he whispered, looking into her spellbinding eyes.

"*Oğlum*," commented Ozan *Bey*, who had been observing his grandson and Mari-Car's interaction, "if Allah had given me a love like yours, my life and my family would today be a different story—beautifully different, I would say."

"Thanks, *Dede*. You're right, but then it would have been so beautiful that I would have grown closer to my dad—and you and I would not be so close, my mom and dad would still be together, Deniz-Mare and I would have stayed in Istanbul to attend the university, I would not have come to Italy and met Mari-Car, Deniz-Mare would not have met Peter John, and…"

Deniz-Mare would not exist, thought Meryem.

Ozan *Bey* raised his right hand toward his grandson and interrupted his rant. "*Tamam, tamam, Oğlum*, I understand, and you are right, Allah knows what is best. Just cherish that love between you and Mari-Car *Kizim, tamam*?"

"*Evet, Dede, tamam* [Yes, Grandfather, OK]."

"A *grande amore* comes once in a lifetime," said Mari pensively. Everyone understood; no more words were said on the subject.

It was easy for them to settle into a well-organized routine; they had been devising routines ever since Deniz-Mare was admitted into the hospital. The main difference now was that they were following a rigorous hygiene protocol; when they were away from Deniz-Mare, they had to observe safe social distancing and wear masks to avoid contracting any viruses.

To make it easier, Ozan and Mari-Car went only to essential classes, wore masks during class, and did not linger with friends afterward.

CHAPTER 93
MI NIÑA HERMOSA
[MY BEAUTIFUL CHILD]

Mari took off out of Malpensa Airport in Milan and flew into Alicante, Spain. From there, she took the one-hour train ride to Murcia. She liked trains—she felt relaxed in them—so she was able to unwind and think before arriving in Murcia. It was easy to do in the high-speed train's comfort class, which offered gourmet meals and drinks.

As she slowly sipped her wine, Mari reminisced about her summers with her adored grandparents. What innocent times those were, she thought. Pain seemed so far away, except for the times she saw her grandmother's tears when she asked why her parents had left Murcia to move to New York. Otherwise, all Mari remembered was being happy and carefree.

The hour passed quickly. She wished she had more time for contemplation, but the train slowly came to a stop, and she disembarked, purse and shoulder bag across her chest, garment bag carrying two designer dresses—her own—flung over the opposite shoulder.

The taxi ride was short.

"*Mi niña bella y querida* [My beautiful and dear child]." Her grandfather's wide-open arms welcomed her.

"*Ay, Abuelo* [Grandfather], you look at me through eyes of love, so you don't realize that I'm not a *niña* anymore. Not, even my Mari-Car is a *niña* anymore; she's a young lady."

"Nonsense! You will always remain *mi niña*."

Mari's eyes filled with tears, and she hugged him even tighter.

"The truth is, *Abuelo*, that it feels good to be somebody's *niña*, and I can only be that when I'm in yours and *Abuela*'s arms, because the rest of the time, I feel very old, like I've lived a very long time."

"Pain does that, *mi niña*, and you've lived in deep pain for too long, but I don't know how to take it away." He wiped the tears off his eyes with his handkerchief; she thought of Ozan *Bey*.

"*Ven* [come], *mi niña*. Your *abuela* [grandmother] is anxious to see you. She got out of bed today just for you. *Ven*, she's in her room sitting in her favorite chair."

"*Abuela*." Mari ran and knelt before her grandmother and hugged her. Tears were flowing from every eye.

"*Mi niña, mi niña hermosa* [my beautiful child], you came just in time. Well, you see…we're getting old, *el abuelo* and I—"

"I came as soon as I could. Carmela's call worried me. Are you and *Abuelo* OK?"

"For now, *niña hermosa*, for now, but I'm getting very forgetful. Sometimes I think I'm going to forget everything, and before that happens, I wanted to talk to you, so I asked Carmela to call you."

"OK, *Abuela*. We have time to talk, but I think before that, we should have Dr. Salcedo come and check on both you and *Abuelo*."

"What for, *mi niña*? To tell us that we're getting old? We already know that, and there's no cure for that. We've lived a long and good life, *mi niña*. Some sorrow…" She teared up; it took her a few moments to continue. "But a lot of happy moments too. This is one of them. Besides, you brought us Carmela to care for us. She's very capable, and we've known her since she was a child—that's enough."

Carmela had grown up with María Victoria, Mari's mom. She had gone to nursing school and had raised three children of her own. After she lost her husband, Mari brought her to take care of her grandparents. They felt comfortable with her and enjoyed when Carmela's children and grandchildren came for visits. "Children make a house a home," they said.

CHAPTER 94
THE WOODEN BOX

"Now, *mi niña*, close the door." Mari did as she was told. "Go open that *armoire* where I keep my clothes and things."

Mari remembered the armoire being huge when she visited the house as a little girl—now, not so much. It didn't seem as mysterious either.

"In that bottom drawer, there is a small wooden box shaped like a treasure chest," continued her grandmother. "Take it out and bring it here, *mi niña*."

"I don't see it, *Abuela*, and I've taken everything out."

"Lift the bottom of the drawer and look in there."

It took some effort, but the bottom of the drawer finally loosened; it was a false bottom, and Mari was able to remove it. Sure enough, there it was: a wooden box shaped like a treasure chest.

"I found it, *Abuela*!" Mari took it out and held it up to her abuela.

"I wanted to tell you about it before I forgot where I had put it." She chuckled.

Mari brought the box to her *abuela*, set it on her lap, and knelt in front of her. "Now, *mi niña*, you have asked me many times throughout the years the reason your parents left their homeland and hometown; even your *niña* María del Carmen has been curious."

Mari remained silent, almost afraid to breathe. She was about to discover the great family secret that had haunted her for years. She stared at the box and waited for her grandmother to open it.

"There should've been a key next to the box. Did you bring it?"

"Oh, I didn't see one. Let me look."

Mari quickly got up and went back to check in the drawer she had removed the wood box from. Sure enough, it was there, but the key was so tiny that it had wedged itself in a corner; she couldn't get it with her finger.

"Take my metal *peineta* from the top of the vanity; the fine metal teeth reach into the corners and will help dig it out."

"Sounds like you've done this before."

"I used to open that box a few times a year, but now it's been a long time. I have the feeling that this will be the last time."

"Don't scare me, *Abuela*," answered Mari as she went and got the comb. It was beautiful, very elaborate.

"Are you sure you want me to use this beautiful *peineta*? I don't want to damage it."

"Beautiful it is, but you won't damage it. Use it—it will work."

Sure enough, the teeth fit perfectly into the corner of the drawer, and the miniature key was dislodged. She held the key up and looked over at her *abuela*, who was wearing a big, knowing smile.

Mari went back, key in hand, and once again knelt before her abuela, handing her the tiny key.

She opened the box easily and handed the key back to Mari, who took it and ran to put it back in the drawer for fear of losing it.

"Now, no one, not even your mother, María Victoria, knows that I'm going to show you this, but I thought you should know, because it concerns you. Whatever you do with this information is up to you. My duty is to reveal it to you before la *Virgen María* comes to get me and take me to the *Padre Celestial*."

Mari was solemn and still. Her *abuela* pulled out an official-looking document folded in thirds; she unfolded it and handed it to Mari without uttering a single word.

Mari took it gently, hands trembling slightly. She somehow knew that she was being entrusted with something precious, but just how precious, she would have never imagined.

She sat back, knees drawn up inside her arms, chin resting on her knees, and began to read the document. Her *abuela* observed her silently. Mari brought a hand to cover her mouth, which dropped open automatically as she read. She held two birth certificates.

At the top was written the legal details about the official who registered the child's birth and the code that identified the book where all data concerning the child was recorded. Then, below, it identified a child—that's what jumped out to Mari, what caused her mouth to drop open.

Name: José María Levy Cortés
Date of birth: June 15, 1986
Place of birth: Murcia, Spain

The second birth certificate read:

Name: María Jose Levy Cortés
Date of birth: June 15, 1986
Place of birth: Murcia, Spain

The only thing that differed, besides the names of course, was the time of birth. The boy was born at 11:15 p.m., the girl at 11:45 p.m. Mari looked up at her grandmother.

She then got back on her knees, still holding the two birth certificates in one hand. She stretched her free hand and caressed the withered face; compassionate eyes looked back at her.

"Did I have a brother? Why was my name changed?" Mari spoke in a halting voice; she almost did not want to know the answer to her second question. The lump in the pit of her stomach began to make its way to her throat as she thought of the possibility that her loving dad, José Felipe García Arias, might not have been her real dad—that's what it sounded like.

She looked at her grandmother, hoping to see the truth in her eyes before the words came out. She only saw pain, but words soon followed that would begin to unravel the mystery that had enveloped her for her entire life, as she was about to discover.

"It's not that you *had* a brother, *mi niña*; as far as I know, you still have a brother, a twin brother."

Mari rose slowly to her feet, placed the documents delicately on her grandmother's lap, and kissed her gently on the cheek.

"*Abuela*, I need to think. You know where I'll be."

"May *Jesús y la Santísima Virgen María* hear your prayers, *mi niña*. I've spent many years in that same place sending prayers, but God has not answered me. Maybe he'll listen to you. Maybe your faith is greater…"

Mari turned and left quietly.

CHAPTER 95
VIRGEN DE LA FUENSANTA

La Santa Iglesia Catedral de Santa María was an important name for an important and imposing church, but for Mari, it was home. Here, she was baptized as a baby, confirmed, and received First Communion. Her grandmother took her to catechism lessons during the week and to Mass every Sunday during her summers in Murcia.

I had such faith then, she thought, but the truth was that even if her faith was not that strong, within the walls of this church, she felt secure and protected.

Mari made the sign of the cross as she knelt, tears taking their familiar path down her cheeks, before the image of *la Virgen de la Fuensanta*, patron saint of Murcia.

"*Virgen Santa*, I don't know if I still have faith," she began, "and if I do, I don't know if it's strong enough to reach you. You took the most precious thing I had, and I still don't understand the reason, but here I am, as I've been so many times before. You took my Kurt, my one and only love…and even though I know that I will never love again, I am grateful that I got to experience, to live, such an uncommon love…I'm also grateful for Mari-Car, the keepsake from that great love."

Mari's prayer was interrupted by quiet sobs. Her lips and shoulders quivered; her tears flowed. She bent over from her waist, hands across her chest, and hung her head. The mass of black hair poured over her head and shoulders like a veil carried over by a delicate breeze to rest on her.

After a long while, she regained her composure, brushed her hair back with her hands, and once again looked up at the sacred image.

"*Virgencita*, you took Kurt; soon you'll take my grandparents and Mari-Car will someday marry. I know I still have my parents, but please help me find my brother."

Mari wiped her face, made the sign of the cross, stood up, and lit a candle. She remained in silence for a few moments before bowing one more time and turning to leave. At the church entrance, she turned once again to face the sanctuary, bowed, and crossed herself before exiting the church.

CHAPTER 96
IF SHE HAD GROWN UP WITH THE ABUELOS

At home, Mari tiptoed into her grandmother's room to check on her. She lay in her bed, eyes closed, holding a rosary.

"You're back, *mi niña*." Her eyes remained closed.

"*Sí, Abuela*, I'm back."

"Are you all right, *mi niña*? Our conversation isn't over, you know."

"I am fine, *Abuela*, and yes, I know we have a lot to talk about, but not today, OK?" She bent down and kissed her.

"*Bendición, Abuela* [Your blessing, Grandmother]," Mari requested.

"*Dios te bendiga* [God bless you]," came the familiar and expected answer.

Before retiring to her room, which was what she longed to do, Mari spent time talking to her grandfather, updating him about her career, Mari-Car's studies, and her parents back in New York.

"Sometimes I see the few friends that still remain alive, and I envy the fact that their children and grandchildren are near them…for us, that was not meant to be." He pulled the handkerchief from his pants pocket and wiped his tears. "Our grandchildren live in faraway places, speak other languages…"

"Now, Grandfather!" Mari feigned feeling offended and reprimanded him gently. "Both your granddaughter and your great-granddaughter speak fluent Spanish, so don't you complain about that!" She took his face in her hands and filled it with kisses.

"Oh, *mi niña*, forgive this old man. I just miss you."

"I know, *mi abuelito*, I know."

She kissed him on both cheeks and said good night.

At the door, Mari turned around and blew her grandfather a kiss.

In her bed, she thought how different life would have been if her parents had stayed in Murcia. She would have grown up next to her loving grandparents. Then her train of thought took a different turn, at which point she came face-to-face with her great truth: *And I wouldn't've met Kurt, wouldn't've had Mari-Car.*

Exhaustion took over—it was still early, but she was emotionally spent.

CHAPTER 97
THE SOUNDS AND FLAVORS OF CHILDHOOD

She awakened to the church bells and the smell of coffee.

She ran to the kitchen like she used to long ago, expecting to find the table set and on it, *pan con tomate*, freshly squeezed orange juice, and an assortment of homemade jams. She was not disappointed.

Her grandfather was at the stove making Murcian *zarangollo*.

"I wanted to prepare breakfast, but *Don* José Andrés wouldn't hear of it; he wanted to make you breakfast himself." Carmela was almost apologetic.

"Carmela, is my granddaughter here every day? No," he answered himself. "This is an event. Let me enjoy it and make breakfast for *mi niña, vale* [OK]?"

"*Vale, Don* José Andrés," answered Carmela. "I just don't want María José to think that I don't do my job…"

"I think nothing of the kind," said Mari cheerily, pinching Carmela's cheek before embracing her. She then went and hugged her *abuelo* from behind while he prepared the *zarangollo*.

"Here, Carmela." Mari handed her the cell phone. "It's all set; take a picture of us." Her grandfather turned around, held the frying pan in one hand, and embraced his granddaughter around the waist with the other. A memory was made.

"Just the way I remember it, *Abuelo*: the onions and zucchini golden brown and the eggs blended to perfection. I can't ever get them quite right; my eggs turn hard when I mix them in."

"Don't be afraid to use plenty of olive oil, *mi niña*. It's not going to harm you. Look at me—I've lived all these years drenching everything in olive oil."

"Oh, *Abuelo*, how I've missed you and *Abuela*." Mari reached for his hand. They both looked at each other through bleary eyes.

Her *abuelo* cleared his throat and blinked away the tears. "Speaking of *Abuela*, she's anxious to see you. I know you two have a lot to talk about."

"We do…" whispered Mari, squeezing his hand tighter.

But her *abuelo* felt compelled to say, "María José, *mi niña*, those were painful times that we lived through with your mother when you and your brother were born. We did what we did—sacrificed being far from our only daughter and grandchild—because we felt that you would both be better protected. Your father, José Felipe, had always been in love with María Victoria, and she liked him also. They had grown up together, so when she was abandoned with two newborns…"

It was difficult for her grandfather to continue. He broke into sobs. She was heartbroken to see him in such a state.

"*Abuelo, abuelito querido*, whatever happened back then, you did the right thing, because love guided your decision. How could that be wrong?"

He calmed down. "I hope so, *mi niña*, I hope so…" he answered ponderingly while wiping his eyes and face with his handkerchief.

"Here you made my favorite breakfast, and now we're crying over it. *Vamos, Abuelo*, let's enjoy it!"

"*Vamos, mi niña*."

Mari was hungrier than she thought, or maybe it was the memories and the love with which her breakfast was made; whatever the case, nothing remained on the plates.

"Now, *mi niña*, you go in to see your *abuela*; she has a lot to tell you, and I don't know how much time either one of us has."

"Shhh, *tranquilo, Abuelo*, none of us knows how much time we have. Believe me, I know that better than anyone."

"Don't think we don't know about your suffering, *mi niña*. Your *abuela* spent many hours on her knees at the church…" His words lingered suspended in the air before he finally added, "Now go on, and don't make me talk so much, *mi niña*—you know that when I start, I have a hard time stopping. Go see *Abuela*."

She kissed him on the cheek and left.

Mari first went into the bathroom to shower and change before going to see her *abuela*. She applied eyedrops to try and get rid of the redness and gathered her hair in a ponytail. The ever-present designer in her made its appearance in high-waisted jeans and a crop top that accented her slim figure.

CHAPTER 98
THE NAME THAT REVIVED ABUELA'S PAIN

"*Bendición, Abuelita*," she said as she entered the room; her grandmother was seated in her chair.

"*Dios te bendiga, mi niña*. You have lost weight. You're not sick, are you?"

"*Abuela*, I thought you told me that you're having a hard time seeing."

"Well, some days I do all right."

"Yes, like today, right?" she teased, bending down to kiss her grandmother.

"Now, María José, *mi niña*, tell me about María del Carmen. How is she? What does she study? Does she have a *novio* [boyfriend]?"

"As you know, she's in Milan studying architecture—" Mari started.

"Like her father," interrupted her grandmother.

"Like her father," assented Mari.

"And does *mi niña* María del Carmen have a *novio*?" She didn't wait for an answer. "Of course she does; such a beautiful girl. An *americano* like her *papá*, I imagine."

"Actually, *Abuela*, he's *Italiano*."

"*Italiano*, from Milano, of course—a good Catholic boy." Mari opened her mouth to change the subject, but the question from her *abuela* beat her to it. "What is the name of the boy, the *novio*?"

There it was! What she had been trying to avoid—getting into details. Should she lie and make up a name? Mari fidgeted.

"Ozan," she finally blurted, fast enough to be unclear, hoping her *abuela* would give up and move on to another subject. She would help her along. "So, *Abuela*, guess what my *abuelo* made me for break—"

"Lozano, did you say?"

"What, *Abuela*?"

"The *novio*, did you say that his name was Lozano?"

Seconds ticked by. Mari hesitated, trying to decide which would be better: lying about Ozan's name and thereby avoiding giving her grandparents unnecessary worry or telling the truth, knowing that it would bring them sadness. After all, she reasoned in her mind, her *abuelos* were old; they probably would never meet Ozan. The seconds kept on ticking. On the other hand, *she* was expecting to hear the truth about why her parents left Murcia.

"Ozan, *Abuela*, Ozan." She enunciated it loudly and clearly.

"What kind of name is that *mi niña*?" her *abuela* asked suspiciously.

"Turkish, Abuela. They are a Turkish family."

María Dolores's mind went back in time thirty-seven years, when her daughter María Victoria (Mavi) had come into this very room and announced not only that she was pregnant but that she was going to marry Samuel, a "wonderful boy" that she had met at the jewelry store where she worked part-time and, according to her, she had "fallen in love" with.

María Dolores wasn't sure at the time which situation to tackle first: the pregnancy itself or the marriage to the Jewish man whose wealthy family, the Levys, was well-known in the region.

José Andres had also been present in the room when their daughter came in to reveal her intention to marry. However, true to his nature, he had sat back, listening quietly before interjecting any opinion.

Her *abuela* continued to reminisce in silence about what had taken place so many years before.

"*Mamá*, times have changed," María Victoria had said back then, trying to justify the choice that she had already made. "The world is a better place; there is more understanding about race and religion. Those barriers have been knocked down. They don't matter anymore—you and *Papá* are too old-fashioned!" she had reproached. "Plus, Samuel is not religious. He doesn't care about that. He loves me; we love each other."

"Mavi, *hija mía* [my daughter], it seems that you have already not only accused us but also judged us and found us guilty as well."

"That's because I already know what you're going to say; I know you and *Papá*." Mavi wagged her index finger at her dad while still looking at her mother.

"Well, since you already know what I'm going to say, let me at least voice it. It won't hurt." Reluctantly, Mavi gave her mother a chance to speak. "First of all, *Hija*, Samuel must be a nice young man. How can he not be? You couldn't choose otherwise, *mi hija*, but the reality is that Samuel comes from a different culture, a different mentality…"

"You're being racist. What culture? His family is just as Spanish as we are; they're from right here in Murcia, *Mamá*. It's just the religion that's different. Besides, the Sephardim have been here for hundreds of years, and it was racism like yours that caused an entire group of people to be expelled from their own land hundreds of years ago! Those are historical facts!" Her accusatory index finger ran from one parent to the other.

"María Victoria, Mavi, I'm not talking about the historical facts here…but, if it is historical facts that we're going to discuss, the Sephardim do have their own culture and language—Ladino."

"For heaven's sake, *Mamá*, that's a dead language!"

"You're the one who brought up historical facts, Mavi, so no, it's not a dead language: many of the traditional Sephardic families, like Samuel's, require their children to learn it."

"What does that have to do with anything? You're talking crazy!"

Both women were desperate to make the other understand; there was no budging on either side. María Dolores, however, was sure of one thing: she did not want to alienate her daughter by trying to prove that she was right. So she softened her tone.

"*Hija mía*, as important as these facts are—to us, your father and me—they are not as important as you. You've just told me that you are going to have a child. We will welcome that child with open arms—*de brazos abiertos*. We will help you raise it. We—"

"Samuel and I will get married as soon as our baby is born!" Mavi interrupted. Her tone became aggressive. She placed her hands on her waist and leaned forward to drive home her point.

María Dolores became concerned that Mavi's anger would affect the baby she was carrying, so she addressed her daughter with tenderness. "*Mi hija, hermosa*"—she went close to her daughter and caressed her cheeks— "if you are going to get married anyway, then why wait until the child is born? Let's plan a wedding; we'll get together with the Levy family and…"

Mavi hesitated. She calmed down a bit. "The Levy family wants to wait until the baby is born."

"And what our family wants doesn't matter to you, *mi hija*?"

"They want a Jewish wedding."

"But we are not Jewish, *hija mía*," replied her mother.

"It's obviously not what we would like," her father finally interjected, "but we can compromise. We can be in charge of the reception, and the Levys can plan the ceremony." José Andrés, not too religious himself, hoped they could reach a friendly agreement.

"The Levys want to wait until after the baby is born," answered Mavi curtly but hesitantly.

"Then your mother is right, *mi hija*, it only matters what *they* want, God help us!"

Mari, unaware of what had just taken place inside her grandmother's head, only saw her face turn very red and her breathing become irregular. Her *abuela* began to complain about blurry vision.

"I told you I had a hard time seeing. Now it's getting worse," she said.

"*Abuela*, relax," said Mari as she shouted for Carmela to bring some water and call a doctor.

"I can't breathe right," continued her *abuela*.

As Carmela hurried in holding a glass of water, Mari saw her grandmother hold her chest and she shouted a second time, "Call the doctor!"

"*Tranquila, Abuelita querida, tranquila…*" Her *abuelo* rushed in carrying a blood-pressure monitor; he immediately wrapped the cuff around his wife's upper arm.

"*Tranquila, mi viejita. ¿Qué te pasa?* [What's wrong?]"

"I'm afraid it's my fault, *Abuelo*," answered Mari, mortified.

"No, *mi niña*, *Abuela* suffers from high blood pressure. This isn't the first time it's happened…look." He pointed at the blood pressure monitor; it read 140/90. He gave his wife the medication, kissed her forehead, and leaned her recliner back.

"Would you want to lay in the bed, *viejita*?" her *abuelo* asked tenderly.

"No, no, I want to be with *mi niña* next to me, here." She pointed at the side of her recliner.

Mari brought the ottoman that was in front of the vanity; it had been there forever, she thought as she tried to move it. Its weight surprised her, but she managed it, turning it back and forth until she got it next to the recliner. She sat there quietly, holding her grandmother's hand and berating herself for being so insensitive. *What harm would it have done if I had just made up an Italian name instead of throwing a bomb at her? I could've killed her!* she thought.

"María José, *mi niña*, you look very troubled. Your *abuela* is going to be fine, I promise; we've experienced this scenario many times. After the crisis passes, she's as good as new!"

"Are you sure, *Abuelo*?"

"I am sure, *mi niña*." He bent down and kissed Mari's forehead. "Now let me go and bring you some refreshments." Mari nodded, and her *abuelo* left the room.

"Dr. Alberto Salcedo, *qué gusto*!" Mari got up to greet him; he had been her grandparents' doctor since as far back as she could remember. Seeing him after all these years, Mari wondered if he was fit to take care of them. Her *abuelo* seemed in better shape.

Carmela walked in, bringing a chair for the doctor, who settled comfortably in it.

"*Mi niña*, you're as beautiful as ever. Don't worry, we're just getting old. Look at us! Who knows which of us will go first." He raised his shoulders and opened his palms up in a sign of uncertainty and surrender.

"Speak for yourself, old man. I have a few things to see yet." Her *abuelo* walked in carrying a tray with three tall glasses of freshly squeezed orange juice. After Mari and Dr. Alberto took a glass, he settled on the edge of the bed and placed the tray next to him.

"It just doesn't taste the same anywhere else." Mari had just taken a gulp of her *zumo* [juice].

"That's because *La Huerta* of Murcia is only here; it's God's gift to us—perfect soil and climate to give us the oranges that make this liquid gold." Her *abuelo* raised his glass proudly.

"You'll stay for *almuerzo*, Alberto, won't you?"

"Of course; I have a few patients to visit, but then I'll come back for sure. I want to hear about María José, our famous fashion designer. It looks like our climate and soil were good for her, too, during those summers that she spent in the region—look how beautiful she turned out."

"You two seem to forget that I'm from New York—"

"Nonsense!" interrupted her *abuelo*. "You might've grown up there, but you saw the light of day here, in God's country. And that beauty?" He looked at his friend and pointed his hand at Mari. "It comes from our soil, our climate, just like our beautiful oranges, lemons, tomatoes, apricots—"

"What are you two *cascarabias* [old gizzards] going on and on about?" The interruption came from the recliner seat.

"*Abuela, abuelita bella*, you woke up. Are you all right?"

"I wasn't sleeping, *mi niña*. I could hear everything those two old gizzards were saying."

"I told you she'd be fine…well, it looks like I'm not needed here for now." Dr. Alberto spoke as he slowly got up and picked up the chair to carry out. "But I'll see you soon."

"You too, José Andrés. Go on, I have a private conversation pending with *mi niña*."

"*Ay, Abuela*, maybe we should continue another time; you should rest."

"What other time? I don't have that much time to spare. Now, where were we…"

Mari pushed the ottoman back to its place in front of the old vanity and sat comfortably on a cushion in front of her abuela's recliner. Her hands rested on *Abuela*'s lap as she listened, mesmerized by her recounting of how Mari's mom and dad, María Victoria and José Felipe, had been forced to run away to America. The Levy family had refused to allow her mom and Samuel, her biological father, to get married after she and her brother were born, her *abuela* told her.

She barely dared to breathe for fear of missing one single detail of the story, but the spell was broken by the voice of *Abuelo* calling her to join them for *almuerzo*.

CHAPTER 99
TEARFUL ALMUERZO

Mari felt like she had just had breakfast; she did not want to break away from the compelling story that her *abuela* was relating nor disappoint her *abuelito*, whose voice was beckoning her.

Her *abuela* sensed her inner struggle.

"Go on, *mi niña*, go eat; you need *fuerzas* [strength]. We'll continue later—I also need to rest a bit."

Mari got up, kissed her *abuela*'s forehead, and tiptoed out of the room.

Carmela and her *abuelo* had outdone themselves with the *almuerzo*, having prepared everything that Mari loved: *pisto murciano*, *albóndigas de bacalao*, *pan con tomate*, *zangollo*, and for dessert, *pan de Calatrava*.

Dr. Alberto had returned from his home visits and was seated at the table with *Abuelo* and Carmela. Mari stood quietly at the table, and her eyes rested for a moment on each dish that had been set on it.

The others remained quiet, perplexed, wondering why she remained standing, but they waited to see what her next move would be. The atmosphere was peaceful and serene—to the point of feeling sacred. No one moved.

In her mind, Mari went back to the day she turned eighteen. It was about two o'clock in the afternoon. A basket had arrived from a place called Murcia Near You. The card read, "*Señorita María José García Cortés.*" She could hardly contain her excitement as, one by one, she began taking out each delightful dish: *pisto murciano*, *albóndigas de bacalao*, *pan con tomate*, and finally, *pan de Calatrava*.

Fifteen years felt to her like a lifetime. Mari lingered, standing before the table that reawakened in her everything beautiful. Tears began running down her cheeks; she allowed them to run freely and began to softly recite those precious words that had been etched in her heart since that day:

"Murcia was just a random place on the planet. María José was just another name in the baby book of names. Today, I am indebted to the place from which such beauty originated and to the name that has now become poetry on my lips, because it gives form to the essence that is you."

CHAPTER 100
NEW TEAM MEMBER

The investigation being conducted by officials contacted by the Grimaldi family, specifically Luca, revealed that Dr. Vittoria Mancini had left the country. She had taken a Swiss Air flight to Berne the same morning that she sent in her resignation. After that, they lost track of the doctor.

Luca feared that in her macabre mind, Vittoria might have conceived a plan to have the embryo transferred herself, a possibility that Luca kept from Meryem—although he was sure she too had considered it. Neither dared to speak it for fear that voicing it would make it real. All hospitals in Berne and other major Swiss cities were contacted, but nothing turned up.

Meryem and Luca had come to the conclusion that the time had come for Luca to be part of the daily care routine of Deniz-Mare. Osman's only comment was, "It's your decision. Things have changed drastically since our last meeting, so I trust your judgement…the important element now is that Meryem is relieved from as much stress as possible."

The less fanfare and explanations, the better, they all agreed. Meryem suggested that Luca be introduced as also being a good friend of Mari's.

"Your father is very fond of Mari," Meryem told Osman as an explanation.

"*Tamam*, let's take advantage of that; let's ride on the coattails of your famous model friend."

"Designer friend," Meryem corrected. "She's a designer, not a model."

"And it's true," added Luca. "We are good friends, Mari and I."

"That reminds me." Meryem reached for a hand from both men. "Mari gave me a very important piece of advice; I just haven't found the right time to tell you, but I think this is it." Both men looked at her expectantly. "Luca, *amore mio*, Osman, my friend, my brother, I believe that everything will turn out well with Deniz-Mare, I do. But if it doesn't..." Her tears reached her tremoring lips, and she had difficulty forming words. Osman and Luca tried to reassure her. "No, let me finish, please."

Meryem took a deep breath and continued. "If the outcome is not what we expect, I want you to know that I would never blame you. You two have moved heaven and earth...Osman, I have no words." She looked at Luca. "*Amore*, thank you for loving our children, born and unborn—for fighting for them. The outcome is now in the hands of God."

Meryem hugged each man individually; Osman had not felt tears darken his eyes in years.

Words were unnecessary for a long time.

"Well, *tesoro mio*, your words have filled me with unexplained joy; it's as if I've been imprisoned by terror, and your words were the key needed to free me. *Mille volte grazie* [a thousand thanks] to you, *amore mio*, and to Mari."

"I still don't understand how I never met the woman, *Fratello*, being that she's a good friend of yours," remarked Osman.

"Well…as I've said before, she only came to my mother's charity events; that's how we met. But she never stayed to socialize…she's pretty distant and has few friends, but if you're on that list, you're a friend for life. María José García Cortés is extremely loyal."

"That's quite a mouthful," is all Osman said.

All three remained silent, in their own world of thought.

The introduction took place in Dr. Urgancıoğlu's office; Dr. Nuñez was also present.

Luca was introduced first and foremost as a good friend of both Meryem and Mari *Hanım*'s, which immediately put everyone at ease. Dr. Urgancıoğlu then went on to speak about the important role that Luca had played, along with Mari *Hanım*, in finding the matching donor for Deniz-Mare's bone marrow transplant.

That's all Ozan *Bey* needed to hear; no further explanation was necessary. The old gentleman got up from his seat and went up to the front, where Luca was seated between the two doctors. All three men stood up as they saw him approach. He took Luca's hand between both of his and thanked him wholeheartedly.

"*Çok teşekkür ederim, Oğlum.*" His eyes blurred as he squeezed Luca's hand.

"*Piacere.*" Luca brought his left hand to his heart and said, "*Ben teşekkür ederim, Signore* [I thank you, sir]." His eyes, too, were blurry.

Ozan *Bey* then slowly walked back to take his place next to his grandson. Mari-Car and Meryem sat on the other side of Ozan. They all stood and waited for him. Ozan *Bey* took his time, stopping midway to wipe the corner of his eyes with his handkerchief before continuing. Once seated, he took off his glasses, wiped them clean, blotted his eyes a second time, and replaced his glasses.

"Let's continue," he instructed.

"Luca has offered to become part of the team that will be caring for Deniz-Mare during the delicate period ahead, when she should be kept in isolation from everyone but her team of medical personnel and caregivers."

During the silence that followed, Meryem observed Luca, who averted his eyes for fear of betraying his feelings for her. Deniz-Mare looks so much like him—could they see it? Meryem wondered, her face swathed by tension.

"We"—Dr. Urgancioğlu looked at Dr. Nuñez— "along with the rest of the medical team, feel that Luca *Bey* would make an excellent addition to the team of caregivers. There are unique circumstances that link him and Deniz-Mare…" Meryem held her breath, not sure what the doctor would say next. "Those being, as we have already stated, his tireless efforts, along with Mari *Hanim*'s, to find a donor, which ended in success." Meryem relaxed. "Luca *Bey*'s upbeat personality comes as a bonus," Dr. Urgancıoğlu added. With the exception of Ozan, they all smiled at the doctor's last remark.

"Mari *Hanım*'s absence today, as you know, is due to family and work commitments abroad," Dr. Urgancıoğlu reminded everyone, and then he was finished. Meryem felt relieved.

Everyone remained quiet, but their smiles and slight nods demonstrated their consent to Luca being part of the team.

Ozan would not be fooled, however. He had heard his mother talk on the phone with this Luca guy before and suspected that they were more than friends. What he didn't understand was why they would hide it; it made him mad, and it continued to bother him after they left the meeting.

CHAPTER 101
HE'S HOT!

Ozan and Mari-Car were back in the apartment that she shared with Peter John and her mom. Since they had missed their classes to attend the meeting and both were already falling behind, they decided to study.

The couch was filled with books; her head rested on his lap, and she looked content and relaxed. But Ozan's sour mood had seized him. Mari-Car felt his muscles tense up.

She sat up to face him and leaned forward as she spoke.

"Your mom is young, beautiful, and free to date. I don't understand what the big deal is—talk to her if it bothers you that much!"

He had no willpower when she got so close, especially when her eyes seemed to drill so deeply into his.

"Mari-Car, you know what you're doing, don't you?"

"Noooo, what?" she asked innocently, getting so close that with each word, their lips lightly touched, and their breaths intermingled.

"Damn it, I forgot what we were talking about!"

"I remember." She leaned even closer but then suddenly got up and walked the short distance to the kitchen with an exaggerated sway; Mari-Car continued to talk as she walked. "About your mother's boyfriend."

"What?" he asked, confused.

"You said you forgot what you were going to say." Mari-Car turned to face Ozan, leaned against the counter, flipped her hair back, and began playing with the dark strands. "And I am reminding you that you were talking about your mother's boyfriend, and I told you to talk to her."

Ozan got up and came over to her, wrapped his arms around her waist, and pulled her toward him. He was breathless as he spoke. "You are doing this on purpose, aren't you? You are driving me crazy on purpose so that I can't think and forget my train of thought…" He encircled her lower lip with his mouth, then her upper lip.

"Hello, Ozan *Bey*!" The loud greeting came out of nowhere.

Ozan and Mari-Car immediately straightened up and began to wipe their mouths with the backs of their hands.

Peter John was laughing so hard he had to hold his stomach in. Ozan came and picked him up and twirled him around.

"Where the hell did you come from?" Ozan asked him, surprised.

"My bedroom, *tamam*?"

Ozan looked at him, surprised to hear Turkish come out of his mouth, and dropped him to the floor. Without saying a word, they began roughhousing throughout the apartment like eight-year-old boys.

After a while, Mari-Car put a stop to it.

"*Tamam, tamam*, we have a situation, so let's have a meeting. Everyone here!" She sat on the couch and patted the space next to her. They obeyed.

"The problem is that Ozan's mom has a boyfriend…" she began.

"What?" Peter John was surprised. Ozan and Mari-Car stared at him.

"No, I didn't mean it like that. I meant, why not? She's young, beautiful, free."

"That's what I said, but I was interrupted." Ozan gave Mari-Car a surprised look.

"*You* were interrupted?" He disheveled her hair playfully.

She made a face at him and continued.

"And I said that he should talk to his mother." She gave him a few fast pokes on the chest.

"And I was going to say, if I had not been distracted"—he looked at Mari-Car and she at him, innocently but knowingly— "that…that…I'll talk to my uncle Osman first. Mari-Car, could you please not look at me like that? I can't concentrate."

Peter John cleared his throat before voicing his opinion. "And I'm wondering what the problem is; your mom is old enough." He gave them both a confused look after his statement.

"No, it's not that." Ozan was frustrated because he didn't seem able to express what he was feeling. "It's that I don't understand why she's been hiding it."

"Ozan, my friend, do you realize all the things that your mom has to worry about? Deniz-Mare's treatment alone is enough to break her emotionally. I myself hardly have enough energy to concentrate. I'm sick with worry!" Peter John, too, was frustrated.

Mari-Car put her arms around their necks and pulled them close.

"I can't imagine life without you two." She kissed them both on the cheek. "Conclusion: your mom is young and beautiful—"

"And free," both boys spoke at once.

"And free," continued Mari-Car, "and she has the right to meet someone and be happy—and he's hot, by the way."

"Who?!" The question came in unison.

"Your mother's boyfriend," she said, smiling from ear to ear, and then, seeing their intention, quickly got up and got away.

Both boys got up at once and began chasing her around the apartment; they caught her and brought her back to the couch and tickled her until she screamed, "Stop, stop."

"OK, what do you say?" asked Ozan.

"About what?"

"About what you said about that Luca guy."

"That it's true; he's hot!"

They began tickling her again.

"OK, OK, stop please!"

"*Tamam*, what do you say?" asked Ozan again.

"That he's hot…" They readied their hands to come down and tickle her again, then she quickly added, "but you're both hotter!"

They relented. All three dropped back onto the couch breathing heavily, exhausted.

Mari-Car was the first to talk. "Should we finish our discussion of the matter, boys?" Her breathing was still labored.

"Let's!" said Peter John. "I've got to get going."

"OK, in conclusion, Ozan is concerned that his mother is hiding something, but he does not want to speak with her directly. However, he will consult with his uncle Osman. Anyone wants to add anything else?"

"Nope. I'm off to be with Deniz-Mare. I can't wait, because I haven't seen her all day, so I'll let you guys continue with whatever it was you were doing." His last sentence was filled with mischief.

Ozan and Mari looked at each other.

"What do you think? You started all this." Ozan leaned toward Mari-Car, brought her mouth close to his, and ran his thumbs over her lips while staring deeply into her eyes.

"I think yes," answered Mari-Car, pushing him back on the couch, getting on her knees, and removing her top.

He brought her on top of him, held her face in his hands, brushed her hair away from her face, and brought her open lips to meet his. His tongue began its exquisite exploration of her mouth, her neck, her breasts…

"I think Peter John made me paranoid; I keep thinking that Ozan *Bey* might really walk in any minute."

Ozan got up and, without saying a word, picked her up and carried her to the bedroom.

CHAPTER 102
AMÇA, I'M SCREWED!

"Osman *amça*, I know that you are busy, but Mari-Car and I would like to talk to you. Maybe you can come to the apartment where they're staying; there's no one else here…"

"First of all, how are you, my favorite nephew?"

"Like I have a lot of competition!" retorted Ozan playfully.

Osman chuckled and added, "I'll send my assistant to get you and bring you to my office."

"No need. I know where it is," replied Ozan.

"No, I'm in my private office getting some documents ready for a trip. I'll send someone to get you."

Mari-Car walked out of the bedroom, showered, hair in a ponytail, wearing an earth-toned miniskirt and a blue, long-sleeved, turtleneck crop top that matched her eyes perfectly.

"God, you're beautiful!" Ozan came close and ran his hand through her hair.

"My uncle is sending someone to—" The knock prevented him from finishing. "And here they are."

He took her hand and stopped at the door so she could put on her just-above-the-ankle brown boots.

"Here, you lean on the door, and I'll do it."

At a deliberately slow pace, he slid his hand down her leg, picked up her no-show-sock-covered foot, placed it in the boot, and zipped it.

A second knock was heard.

"*Aspetta un minuto, per favore* [Wait a minute, please]," said Ozan from the inside.

"*Va bene* [OK]," came a female voice outside the door.

Mari-Car could hardly control her laughter; she covered her mouth with her hand to keep it from bursting out. Ozan continued the process of putting on her other boot at an even more painfully slow pace.

"*Buonasera*," they said one after the other when they finally opened the door.

"*Buonasera. Sono* Marcella. *Piacere; per favore seguimi*." They nodded and followed as instructed.

"Why did Osman *amça* send someone to get us? We know where to go," Mari-Car said.

"Evidently, we don't. He has another office that we've never been to, so he insisted on sending someone."

"You said that so cute," he added.

"What?" Mari-Car wanted to know.

"'Osman *amça*."

"Oh, that." She rolled her eyes at him.

"Yes, that. Say it again."

"No,"

"Please." He stopped in the middle of the hallway, looked at her, and brought his hands together to plead.

Mari-Car's cheeks turned red; she looked at Marcella and rolled her eyes. Marcella smiled and shook her head slightly.

"OK. 'Osman *amça*.' There!"

All three got on the elevator, which took a special key card. Ozan and Mari-Car exchanged curious looks.

Mari-Car leaned over and whispered, "What if Marcella turns out to be a serial killer?"

"I'll protect you," he whispered back and squeezed both of her cheeks together with one hand, forcing her to pucker her lips, which he kissed oh so lightly.

She got on her tippy toes and whispered in his ear, "that was so sexy it left me wanting for more." Then she went and stood next to Marcella.

"Marcella, do you speak English?" He asked in Italian.

"*Scusa, non parlo inglese,*" came the response.

Ozan then looked at Mari-Car and said, "you are so dangerous missy, you get me all hot and bothered and then go and take refuge next to the young lady, I'll get you back."

Mari-Car checked to make sure Marcella was not looking and blew him a kiss.

"But you don't need to speak English to figure out what's going on: "She," Marcella pointed her finger at Mari-Car, "whispered something sexy in your ear and then came by me, you" her finger was now pointing at Ozan, "were left to burn while she teased you from right here next to me."

They both covered their faces to hide their embarrassment. All three burst into laughter.

They arrived at the top floor and followed Marcella out. At the door to the reception area, she once again swiped a card, stepped back, and signaled the young couple to go in.

"*Prego*," she said.

"*Grazie*," they replied in unison. Marcella answered with a wink.

Marcella led them to Osman's office door, which opened before she knocked.

"*Grazie*, Marcella,"

"*Si figuri, Signore* [Don't mention it, sir]."

While Osman and Marcella exchanged formalities, Ozan and Mari-Car went inside the office. They looked around, then at each other in awe.

"Oh my God, Osman *amça*, do you need an assistant? I could spend days here!"

Mari-Car unzipped her boots as she talked and placed them neatly against the wall near the door. Then she walked around, stood by the glass wall, and finally went and sank onto the couch. "How can you get any work done in this place?"

"Osman *amça*, how are you?" Ozan embraced his uncle. Osman took his face in his hands and kissed his nephew's cheeks.

"Awww, you look so cute together. Like father and son."

Ozan extended one arm to Mari-Car. "Come, *Çanim*, come." She got up from the couch and came and snuggled between the two men.

For a few moments, they remained sheltered in each other's arms. Osman then gently came out of the embrace but still kept one hand on Ozan's shoulder and the other on Mari-Car's.

"What would you kids like to drink?"

Mari-Car stepped away from the men. "Do you have wine, Osman *amça*?" she requested. She went to stand before the glass wall; Osman went back to his desk.

Mari-Car could not contain herself. "This place awakens in me a desire to give myself over to beauty, to magnificence. Look at those mountains!"

"Poetic, aren't we?" Ozan had remained on the spot where the three had embraced moments before, about halfway between Mari-Car and his uncle.

"Yes, this place brings it out of me." She turned to face Ozan and held his gaze; for a few seconds, it seemed to him that they were the only people in the room. Mari-Car then turned to continue to be mesmerized by the magical view.

Ozan then turned to look at his uncle, raised his shoulders, and just said, "I'm screwed."

Osman walked over to his nephew's side and patted his shoulder before commenting, "Enjoy it, live it, don't think beyond that, *tamam*?"

Ozan nodded in response.

Uncle and nephew settled on the couch, and soon, there was a soft knock. The door opened automatically.

"*E permesso* [Do you allow me]?"

"*Per favore vieni*, Marcella," said Osman.

Marcella walked in with three wine glasses and a tray with an assortment of cheeses and crackers; she set it on the coffee table in front of Osman's desk. A young man soon followed with a beautiful, mirror-polished ice bucket and two bottles of wine immersed in it, a white and a red. He removed the bottle of red and placed it on the table.

"*Buon appetite* [Enjoy]," said both assistants before turning around and returning to their tasks.

Osman got up and went to pour the wine. Mari-Car went once again to stand in front of the glass wall. Ozan observed her from his spot on the couch—he was so immersed in her that he didn't notice his uncle walk to his side holding two glasses of wine.

The scene of the three of them in the same space but in worlds of their own was frozen for a few minutes. Osman pondered the moment, wondering what awaited the two young lovers. He realized how much he wanted to spare them pain. He looked at Ozan and, for the first time, understood, or rather felt, fatherhood. It was good, it was bitter, it was sweet, it was scary.

"Osman *amça*, this is like paradise, this wall!" Mari-Car spoke with her hands, her eyes, her whole body. "It's like you're in the countryside without actually being there…is this your place of refuge?"

"It's one of them, *Kizim*," answered Osman, handing her a glass of red wine. "Very few people know of this place. I can count them on one hand, including you two."

There was silence, comfortable silence. Mari-Car sipped her wine, standing in front of the window, dreaming. As she stared at the landscape below, she wondered about the inhabitants of Como long ago. Did they think it was magical like she did now? She turned around, looked at Osman, walked up to him, and hugged him; it surprised him.

"Thank you, Osman *amça*. Thank you for sharing this place with me too."

He returned the embrace. "Your reaction tells me that I did the right thing; you felt my intention and purpose for creating it."

"And here is some wonderful accompaniment to this incredible wine."

Ozan was holding before them the tray with the variety of cheeses and crackers.

They both reached for some. Mari-Car savored the combination of her *tinto* with a bite of Beaufort *fromage*. She threw her head back. "Mmm. Does it get any better than this?"

Osman and Ozan exchanged knowing looks and smiles. Osman patted him on the shoulder.

"You're right," whispered Osman in his nephew's ear.

"About what?" Ozan whispered back.

"You are screwed."

"You two are up to something, I can tell!"

Mari-Car's index finger wagged from one man to the other as she spoke, holding her wine in one hand and a piece of cheese in the hand with the wagging finger.

"We might be, but it's all good, *Kizim*." Osman hesitated for a short moment before continuing. "Speaking of being up to something, you two seem to have something on your mind that you want to talk to me about." He went and got the wine and refilled both of their glasses. "Should we sit at my desk, or is the couch appropriate?"

"Definitely the couch!" answered Mari-Car immediately.

Osman turned to his nephew and asked playfully, "*Oğlum*, do you have any preferences?"

"I do, *Amça*, but when I'm in the presence of this girl"—he encircled Mari-Car's waist— "I either forget what they are, or they become the same as hers." He looked down at Mari-Car and kissed the tip of her nose.

"*Oğlum*, you're—"

"I know, *Amça*, I know…"

"OK, the couch it is!"

Mari-Car settled on the couch, legs bent at the knees and feet tucked behind her. Ozan sat next to her. She scooched closer, one arm wrapped around his neck; in the other hand, she held her glass of wine. She rested her chin on his shoulder. He kissed the top of her head. Osman sat facing them, leaning against the wide, comfortable arm of the couch, one foot up, knee bent, and the other on the floor to prop himself up. He, too, held a glass of *tinto*.

"I've never seen you so relaxed, *Amça*," Ozan commented.

"I don't do it often," Osman answered before moving on to what they wanted to discuss. "I'm listening, *cocuklar* [kids]."

Mari-Car, still resting her chin on Ozan's shoulder, raised her eyes toward him and smiled. "Go, *birtanem*, tell him!"

Osman shook his head, "I know, *Amça*, I know."

"What?" Mari-Car's charm lay in the fact that she lacked knowledge of the power she wielded.

Ozan cleared his throat. "Anyway, *Amça*, it's about my mother." He waited a few moments to see if his uncle displayed any reaction, but in typical Osman form, none came. He listened. "We think—I think—that she is seeing someone, a guy named Luca. I'm not sure, but it's OK. I mean, she is free to date, of course, but she's hiding it from me! That's mainly what's bothering me… she could've introduced him to me, asked me what I thought…I don't know, it feels weird. We've always been close, plus I'm her son! It should matter what I think." At the end of his faltering, incoherent speech, Ozan's eyes filled with tears.

A few moments of silence passed.

Mari-Car turned his face toward her and placed delicate, tiny kisses on his eyes until she dried his tears. He smiled down at her tenderly and caressed her cheeks.

"*Oğlum*, have you asked your mom about it? Have you told her how you feel?"

"See?" Mari-Car sat up straight. "I told him, *Amça*; I told him to talk to his mom. So did Peter John!" Osman looked at her confused. "My best friend, my cousin from North Carolina, Deniz-Mare's…eh…eh…close…friend? He has moved here to be with her until she gets better. He—"

"I'm sorry, of course I know who he is; you two grew up together, and the three of you went into town a while back, I remember. Dr. Nuñez told me about Deniz-Mare's happy reaction when he showed up. He's also staying with you and your mom in the apartment here in the hospital. I'm sorry, it's just that the name was not on my radar at that moment, but I know how important he is to you and to my niece."

"Thank you, Osman *amça*. Anyway"—her excitement returned— "we, Peter John and I, both told Ozan to talk to his mom about her boyfriend!"

"I am going to share with you a little bit about Luca, who indeed has been seeing Meryem, *Oğlum*."

The two young people sat up. Mari-Car brought her legs down, and they both leaned forward to better grasp whatever it was that Osman was going to say. They knew that he was a man of few words; none would be wasted, and they didn't want to miss a single one.

"Luca is not just my best friend, but my *fratello*, my brother." Osman brought his hand to his heart when he spoke the words "*fratello*" and "brother."

"He was present in the darkest, loneliest, most vulnerable moments of my life, and he continues to be central in my life. Luca covers my back when I need it; he is one of those few people with whom I share not only this space but all my special places, and he does likewise. The wine that you're now drinking comes from his vineyard…the rest, *Oğlum*, is for you and your mom to discuss."

He finished too soon, Ozan felt, but he knew it was all he was going to hear from his uncle—at least for now.

The silence was long but, again, comfortable.

"Can I meet him?"

"After you talk with your mom, *Oğlum*. I'll be gone for three or four days at a symposium in Istanbul; on my return, we'll arrange something, provided you have had that conversation with your mother, *tamam*?"

"*Tamam, Amça*."

CHAPTER 103
A FAVOR FOR OZAN

"Are you the speaker at the symposium or the student?"

"I'm the speaker. To tell you the truth, I have so much going on that this trip comes at a bad time, but I made the commitment long ago." Osman seemed tired. "Anyway, I have to be there. It's for students from Istanbul University specializing in cardiology; I will be speaking about minimally invasive cardiac surgeries. I'll be lecturing and possibly assisting in some of the surgeries."

"Sounds fascinating. My mom will be in Istanbul also; some of her designs are in a fashion show…her representative there couldn't make it, so she had to go instead."

"Probably against her own wishes," commented Ozan with a roll of the eyes. "Then a little light bulb went on inside his head. "Osman *Amça*, I'm about to ask you a huge favor. Mari *Hanim*, Mari-Car's mom, is very wary of our culture, very distrustful; I think she's believed everything portrayed on films about terrorists, et cetera—"

"No," Mari-Car interrupted. "She has personally known a lot of beautiful and talented Muslim women whose husbands and boyfriends have forced them to give up their careers in the fashion industry! That's why she is so guarded—she doesn't want me in a similar situation. And yes, she's probably going to Istanbul against her wishes—"

"I think she's a bit judgmental and displays a stereotypical attitude, *Canim*, especially for someone as well-traveled and well-known in her industry."

Mari-Car opened her mouth, and through her body language, Osman could see that she was about to lash out at Ozan, so he quickly intervened. "I think Mari *Hamim* has reasons for concern, *Oğlum*. You know my story. Think of my Zoey—may God rest her soul. What would her mother—may God rest her soul also—what would she say or think about her daughter moving to Istanbul with a Muslim guy? And unfortunately, the worst happened."

"Osman *Amça*, but we're not all like that!" Ozan seemed mortified.

That's what I used to think, when I brought Zoey into my family home, thought Osman, but he saw how distraught Ozan was and sought to console him instead.

"You are right, *Oğlum*, we are not all like that. You and I know that."

"And me!" Mari-Car raised her hand like a schoolgirl.

"And that's all that matters for the moment," added Osman.

Ozan was not convinced and insisted. "Osman *Amça*, can you take some time and please show Mari *Hanim* around, take her to the nice places in Istanbul? That's the big favor that I wanted to ask you. I just want her to see us as normal people. I had to pretend that I was Italian…"

"*Oğlum*, you are!"

"Yes, but my roots are Turkish…anyway, I had to pretend that I was Catholic for Mari-Car's sake!"

"Now that's bad! Does she still think you're Catholic?"

"No, I was pretty clear about that and told her about my views on religion."

"That's my boy!" Osman put his hand on the back of Ozan's head and brought him close; they embraced.

"I'll take time for Mari *Hanim*, *Oğlum*. Don't you worry—I'll show her the Istanbul that you and I know." Ozan hugged him tighter. He felt a weight lift that he didn't realize he'd been carrying.

Mari-Car stood back, observing the display of love before her, her eyes flooded with tears. She longed for her dad.

CHAPTER 104
WE'VE MADE YOU SAD

"Murcia was just a random place on the planet. María José was just another name in the baby book of names. Today, I am indebted to the place from which such beauty originated and to the name that has now become poetry on my lips, because it gives form to the essence that is you."

Mari repeated the words again before giving an explanation to her *abuelo*, Dr. Alberto, and Carmela, who had been looking at her with concern.

"Those are the words that Kurt wrote to me on my eighteenth birthday." Her tears seemed to gush out of a spring that never ran dry. "He sent me a Murcian lunch with the same delicacies that you've so beautifully displayed on the table for me."

"We've made you sad, *mi niña*."

"No, *Abuelo*, on the contrary. You've brought me back wonderful memories that I never want to forget, and you have given me the gift of reliving one of the most special days of my life, which Kurt made unforgettable."

"In that case, sit, *mi niña*. Let's enjoy it."

They sat and reminisced about her summers and holidays in Murcia; she told them about her life in New York, and they listened with fascination. She even told them about Milan and Deniz-Mare, the bone marrow transplant, et cetera.

"I'll make sure that I light a candle in her name to the *Virgen de la Fuensanta*," said Carmela, wiping her tears.

"Thank you, Carmela." Mari placed both hands on her heart. "I'd be very grateful."

"*Mi niña*, it's my *granito de arena* [little grain of sand] added to what you all are already doing for the *niñita*'s recovery." She crossed herself.

"*Amén*," responded everyone else.

"If you don't mind, I'd like to rest for a while. I still have a conversation pending with my *abuela*, but I'm exhausted, and my flight leaves early in the morning."

"Another conversation?" asked her *abuelo*.

"No, the same one. We haven't finished."

"María José, *mi niña hermosa*, I'll say goodbye to you now; I don't like *adios*, and at my age, who knows if we'll ever see each other again."

Dr. Alberto got up and came and hugged Mari. They both wiped tears from their eyes, and without saying another word, he left.

In her room, lying quietly on her bed, Mari was unable to sleep. Too many thoughts and emotions occupied her mind. She pondered what her grandmother had shared with her earlier; she had so many questions. Then, a light bulb went on inside her head: She needed to record whatever her grandmother was going to reveal to her. Otherwise, she'd miss important details. She wanted Mari-Car, but even more so her brother—yes, her brother José María—to someday hear her *abuela*'s account, because it also affected them directly.

She quickly got out of bed and began getting the video camera ready. It always traveled with her—it was how she captured the fashion shows, focusing on what she wanted, not only what the professional cameraman considered worthy.

She took the tripod out of its protective pouch, unfolded it, and adeptly set the video recorder on it. She wanted to avoid taking time to set up when she went to see her *abuela*. She relaxed. Maybe that was why she had been so anxious in bed a few moments before—because something remained incomplete, something that she needed to do, and this was it.

That happened to her often. She became agitated inside until she accomplished a task that was pending, even if she didn't know what it was; it eventually, somehow, made itself known.

CHAPTER 105
IMPOSSIBLE CHOICE

"*Abuelita bella*, are you awake?"

"I have been waiting for you, *mi niña*. Come, come." Her *abuela* motioned her with her palms facing down. "What all are you carrying there?"

"This, *Abuelita*, is a video camera; that way I won't forget any details of what you'll relate to me tonight." Mari quickly set up the video equipment.

Then she brought the large, comfy cushion and placed it in front of her *abuela*'s chair; she settled comfortably on it, rested her hands on her *abuela*'s lap, and waited patiently for the conversation to start.

Abuela looked at the camera, then at Mari, and asked, "Will *mi niño* José María see this someday?"

"I hope so, *Abuela*, I hope so."

Abuela seemed pleased and quickly got into the narration of the story that she was so anxious to tell and Mari so anxious to hear.

"*Pués* [So], *mi niña*, in this very room, your mother announced to your *abuelo* and me that she was pregnant and was going to marry the father of her child, your biological father, Samuel Levy. We were opposed, of course, because of the difference in cultures. They were a well-known Jewish family in the area. We were…well, *us*—a not-so-well-known Catholic family. María Victoria accused us of being racist people who lacked historical knowledge."

Her *abuela* went on to give details of the conversation she had had with her daughter before Mari was born.

"We basically consented to all of the demands of the Levy family, hoping that by doing so, we'd save the relationship with our daughter. It worked—she stayed home, we took care of her, and we anxiously awaited your arrival. Then, toward the end of the fourth month of the pregnancy, your mother went in for the ultrasound that would determine the sex of the baby."

Mari straightened up to listen to this part even more attentively. "I accompanied her to the hospital; Samuel met us there. She asked me to go in with them so I would be one of the first to hear the good news. I felt happy that she wanted to include me in their special day…we had become very close during those months but avoided talking about the wedding or the Levy family."

"So you heard the beats of two hearts, *Abuela*?" Mari asked impatiently.

"Not at first. The first sign that something was different was the doctor's facial expression. He strained to look closer at the screen but did not say a word for a few minutes. Then, after an interminable silence, we heard, 'Congratulations, you'll be parents,' then he looked at me and continued, 'and grandmother of two.'

"The three of us looked at each other and froze in place. Then I went to your mother's side and hugged her and Samuel. We were overflowing with happiness!" *Abuela*'s eyes teared up as she relived the happy moment. She continued, "Then, *mi niña*, just as we began to settle down, while we were still wiping tears of joy, we heard, 'A boy and a girl.' Mari, *mi niña*, I can't explain to you the joy that came over us. At that moment, I forgot about all the hurtful exchanges that had taken place between María Victoria and me; I no longer cared whether the wedding took place at a *sinagoga* or a church…all that mattered was what I had seen inside that screen: two tiny babies that I would soon hold in my arms. I began to plan in my head a room with two cribs for when your parents brought you for visits."

Abuela again became emotional while remembering that incredible day so many years ago.

"The next few months flew by with preparations of the nurseries and countless shopping trips. They got a nursery ready at the Levy's' home, where supposedly your mom and dad would live with you and your brother; we got one ready here for when you babies came to visit. In fact, the room where you're staying now and have stayed in during all your visits used to be the nursery that *Abuelo* and I got ready for you and our José María…" She hesitated, then added, "I'm sure that's not the name they kept for your brother, but to me, he'll always be my José María—Jochy, we said we'd call him." She wiped tears away.

"We saw the number two everywhere, or so it seemed, so we bought two of everything: two cribs, two armoires, two bathing and changing tables, each equipped with its own bath accessories—blue and pink washcloths, blue and pink baby soap, blue and pink bath towels. I embroidered your initials on them myself, J. M. and M. J. Anyway, we bought blue and pink pajamas, and I crocheted lots of blue and pink booties…" *Abuela* seemed to have a sudden flash of recollection and stopped her recounting. "Go, *mi niña*, go to that trunk next to the *armario* and open it." Mari quickly got up and did as her *abuela* had asked.

"It's locked, *Abuela*," Mari said with a concerned look.

Her *abuela* reached into her pocket and pulled out an old key chain. It was in the shape of a house with a large ring hooked onto it; at least ten keys hung from the ring. Mari had seen that key chain all her life. Her *abuela*'s dresses all had large pockets on the sides, and she always carried her keys inside. Mari, however, had never paid much attention to those keys; it was a normal occurrence to see her *abuela* reach for them in her pocket to get something out of the China cabinet, the armoire drawers, or the kitchen pantry—although she had noticed that in later years, the pantry remained unlocked—but even the nightstand on the abuela's side of the bed had a lock. As for the rest of the keys, she had no idea what they were for. But on this night, at least one of those keys would unveil to Mari something wonderful.

"It's the heart-shaped one, *mi niña*," said her *abuela* as she handed Mari the keys. "Open that trunk and look inside."

Mari felt wrapped in delight and wonder. She brought her hands to her mouth and just stared at the trunk for a few moments before she began to slowly pull out its contents: two blankets, a blue and a pink one; two bath towels in the same colors; stuffed animals; and booties—so many pink and blue booties! She held them tenderly and brought them to her cheeks.

"I made the booties. They were quick and easy, so I began right after we saw you kids on the sonogram."

She pulled out two baby books. They only had the initial data: names, weight, place of birth, breastfeeding schedule, then nothing.

She looked at her *abuela*, surprised. "What happened, *Abuela*? Why did my mother stop writing?"

"We only had you together for eight days, *mi niña*." She wiped away more tears.

"Why?!" Mari could not hide her astonishment.

"That is the saddest part of this story, *mi niña*…"

"I want to know what happened, *Abuela*. *Dime* [Tell me]!"

"At the birth, only your doctors, your *abuelo*, and I were present. We immediately notified Samuel when we suspected that your mother might be in labor and told him to meet us at the hospital. We expected to see him and his family there, but that wasn't the case; we did not see them until you and your brother were eight days old.

"Samuel's family announced that there would be a circumcision ceremony for your brother—a *bris* they called it. It made your mother, María Victoria, very nervous; I was anxious but didn't want to make things worse, and I wanted to allay her fears. 'Think of it as a baptism,' I told her. But what bothered her and made her nervous was that they didn't ask her if José

María could be circumcised; they just told her that he would be. 'You were right, *Mamá*, it is a different culture,' your mother confessed to me apologetically and anxiously."

"And how about my father, Samuel, *Abuela*? Where was he? What did he say?"

"That's why I told you that your father was…is, I assume, a good man but weak; he would not go against the wishes of his elders, his parents. He never said anything, never even came by to see you and your brother after we brought you home from the hospital. *De hecho* [in fact], we didn't see him at all until the eighth day, at the *bris* ceremony.

Everyone was well-dressed. All the friends of the Levys, plus some of the extended family, attended the ceremony. I think the *sinagoga* was reserved specifically for that private event; it wasn't during a regular service. Anyway, from our side, only your father and I, and your mom of course, went. Since we didn't know much about the ceremony, we didn't know who to invite."

Abuela raised her shoulders and turned her palms up, indicating helplessness.

"When we walked into the *sinagoga*, all the front rows were taken by the Levys' crowd, so your *abuelo*, your mom, and I, feeling somewhat awkward and not wanting to attract attention, found some empty seats midway from the front. I held you, and your *abuelo* held your brother. Your mom, who was shaking from nerves, sat between us…"

Abuela had a hard time continuing; her breathing became labored. Mari worried.

"Maybe this is enough for now, *Abuela*…"

"Nonsense! This story will get out tonight if it's the last thing I do, *mi niña*, and after this, you will go and find your brother, wherever he is. Find him, *mi niña*, find him! So your mother became more and more anxious. 'I'm afraid, *Mamá*, I'm afraid. Please forgive me.' She looked at your *abuelo* and pleaded, '*Papá, perdóname por favor, perdóname.*'"

Mari's eyes flooded with tears; she could feel her mom's desperation of long ago, but she remained silent at her *abuela*'s feet.

"I think, *mi hija*, María Victoria, sensed something, I think she had a *premonición*, because she couldn't stop crying…or shaking." She reflected for a moment before continuing. "So an elderly woman, who we assumed to be Samuel's grandmother, came to where we were and said that she was the *sandek*; at the time, we didn't know what exactly that was—"

"It's the person who holds the baby during the ceremony, like our version of a godparent," interjected Mari. "I have Jewish friends, and I have attended circumcision ceremonies, so I'm familiar with the ritual, *Abuela*."

"Well *mi niña*, this *sandek señora* took your brother gently from your *abuelo*'s arms. The rest of us attempted to get up to follow her, but she signaled us to sit down, so we stayed behind. We were like fish out of water, trying not to offend while trying to figure out what our role was in the unfamiliar setting."

Abuela shook her head slightly, still confused about what had happened right before their eyes years ago.

"Your *abuelo*'s empty arms now held your mom's tremoring body. He embraced her with one arm, brought her head to his chest, and caressed her wet cheeks with his free hand. That scene has remained ingrained in my memory all these years; it was heartbreaking. Hearing your brother cry made your mom go from quiet tears to sobs, to the point that the people near us turned to us to find out what was happening. That cry was the last we heard from our José María, your twin brother."

Mari was not expecting that ending.

"What?" she said in bewilderment.

"After that, the *sinagoga* emptied. We waited patiently for Samuel and his parents to tell us where the reception was; we thought there would be one. Instead, a well-dressed middle-aged man came to us and asked us to follow him; we did. We entered a small office where he handed us a document to sign that would give complete custody of your brother to Samuel, your father. We were all stunned. Your mother let out a wail and crumbled onto the floor. The man panicked and called an ambulance while your father picked her up and took her out of the stuffy room. You were still in my arms and started crying, so I began pacing and rocking you in my arms. I couldn't do much else. You were a newborn, and Mavi had been nursing both you and your brother, so we didn't even have a bottle."

Mari could tell that it took her *abuela* a tremendous effort to tell the story, because telling it caused her to relive each heart-wrenching moment. However, she knew she couldn't stop her, so she allowed her *abuela* to continue the narration. Still, hearing it became as heartbreaking as telling it. She could feel the helplessness that they all experienced at the time.

"Your *abuelo* rode in the ambulance with your mother. The lawyer gave you and me a ride; I still carried you in my arms. Once there, you wouldn't stop crying, so we explained the situation to the nurses, who quickly brought a bottle with a special formula for newborns. You sucked almost with desperation. I felt guilty that I had kept you without food for that long, but once your little belly got full, you stopped crying."

Abuela took a few minutes before continuing. Mari remained quiet.

"The nurses wanted to take you to the hospital nursery to care for you, but I wouldn't let them. I held you to my chest tightly for fear that the Levys would come and steal you from there. They were not just rich, but also powerful. I was so afraid. Your mother spent weeks in the hospital, only being fed intravenously. 'It's like she's lost the will to live,' the doctors would say. Your *abuelo* and I were desperate. We thought we were going to lose both our daughter and our grandson. I can't remember darker days, *mi niña*.

"We contacted the best lawyer we knew: your father, José Felipe. He had loved Mavi since they were kids, and I think he kept the hope alive that she would someday return his love, but when Samuel entered the picture, José Felipe, like the gentleman that he was and still is, stepped aside. He was very successful, had his own law firm, and loved your mom, so we were sure that we could win your brother back."

Mari hardly dared to breathe for fear of missing a word, especially at this crucial part of the story.

"José Felipe, your father, had all the documents drawn, and he and his team of lawyers were ready to start the process… but your mom's health continued to deteriorate. She refused any food, became lethargic, her look became fixed, and her hair began to fall out. The doctors warned us, 'Your daughter might not survive the stress of going through a litigation process of that magnitude. We are doing all we possibly can, medically…but beyond that, it's out of our hands; it's your choice.' It seemed that we had been given an impossible choice: save our daughter or bring our grandson back."

At this point, *Abuela* burst into sobs.

"*Abuela, abuelita querida.*" Mari threw herself onto her *abuela* and clung to her neck. "Don't suffer for the decision you made when facing an impossible situation…at that point, we all do the best we can."

"*Gracias, mi niña*. I wanted you to know what happened. It's important that you know and that someday your brother knows what happened…that we fought for him, that we did not abandon him."

"He will know, *Abuela, tranquila*."

She took Mari's face in her hands and kissed both cheeks. "Let's continue, *mi niña*. I know I won't have another chance to tell this story."

Mari sat back down on the cushion at the feet of her beloved *abuela*.

"So…*mi niña*, your *abuelo* and I spent one entire day agonizing over what to do. We finally told ourselves that even if our grandson grew up far from us, he would be alive and, more importantly, safe. The Levys were selfish, hateful, even cruel, but they would not harm him. Our Mavi, on the other hand…well, we were at the verge of losing her. So, in deep sorrow, mourning the loss of our grandson, we opted to step back from the litigation process and began the long and difficult road that would eventually lead to our daughter's recovery. We refused, however, to sign any papers that said that we would give custody of your brother to the Levy family. 'We just won't fight for custody,' your *abuelo* made clear to the Levy family's lawyers, lips tremoring as he spoke. I remember that day like it was yesterday." Her *abuela* again began to reminisce. But this time, rather than sorrow, Mari spotted anger on her *abuela*'s face.

"Thank God that their team of lawyers had agreed to meet at José Felipe's office," *Abuela* continued. "During the meeting, José Felipe, hearing your *abuelo*'s faltering voice and seeing his anxious state, placed a hand on his shaky one and restated what your *abuelo* had said: 'My clients will not pursue custody of their grandson José María Levy Cortés; on the other hand, they will not sign any document giving the Levy family complete custody of their grandson.' Your father spoke with force and reassurance; we felt safe for the first time since the whole horrific process had begun. The other lawyers consulted among themselves, made a few phone calls, and we waited. They complied; however, their compliance came accompanied by a threat: 'Our clients agree not to require the signatures of Ms. María Victoria Cortés Fernández or the Fernández Cortés family on the document demanding complete custody of their grandson'—no name was given for the child, unfortunately—'but his birth records will remain sealed, and at the slightest attempt on your clients' part to reopen the case, we'll pursue full custody of their granddaughter also.' That's when I let out a wail, and I woke up here, in my bed."

At this point, a long period of silence ensued; neither Mari nor her *abuela* moved. Then she resumed her narrative, naturally and serenely.

"Your mother remained in the hospital another two weeks. The doctors wanted to see some physical and emotional improvement before they released her. We took you in every day. At first, she remained lethargic, but slowly, the light in her eyes began to appear. Dim as it was, it was an improvement from the lifeless skeleton she had become. Your father never left her side, nor yours. When we took you to the hospital for visits, he held you in his arms, walked you in the hallways, placed you in your mother's arms. It was a joy to see the small family of three begin to emerge.

"Once your mother was home, your father continued to be an integral part of our family. I don't know what we would've done without that rock of a man, José Felipe, to support us. The hospital psychologist made weekly visits to our home; your mom spoke to her about your brother, and to José Felipe, but not to us. I think she knew that we too were too weak with pain—mourning does that to you—and she wanted to protect us. You were six months old when José Felipe came to ask for your mother's hand in marriage and for permission to adopt you. We weren't surprised. For the first time in many months, we saw a semblance of happiness on your mother's face. We saw their love burgeon into something beautiful, pure, and serene. '*Gracias, Papá, Mamá*. I'll never forget what you have done for me,' she said to your *abuelo* and me on the day of their marriage, '*Hija mía*,' I told her, 'What *gracias*? We just did what parents do: love and fight for their children. We just wish we could've done more.' We all knew what I meant to say—that I wished we could've gotten our grandson back."

Abuela threw her hands up in the air in helplessness as she expressed her wish to have done more at the time.

"*Abuelita*, you are one of the strongest women I know. Now I realize it even more—you did an amazing job of handling an impossible situation."

"Anyway, *mi niña*, we are almost finished with you and your brother's story, and I can die happy. The wedding took place here in the back terrace. It was simple but beautiful: the parish priest, two of José Felipe's law firm partners, who were also witnesses, Dr. Alberto, your *abuelo* and I, and you." So Dr. Alberto knows the story, Mari whispered thoughtfully. A new sense of admiration and love for the old doctor began to rise in her heart.

Her *abuela* pulled her keys from her pocket, singled out a key, and handed them to Mari. "Here, *mi niña*, go to my nightstand; open the small door below the drawer there."

Mari went to the nightstand next to the *abuela*'s side of the bed and got on her knees to open it.

"Done, *Abuela*."

"Take out the jewelry box on the top shelf."

"Here, *Abuela*, this one?"

"Yes, *mi niña*. Open it—there are wedding pictures there, of your parents' wedding."

"But I've seen their wedding pictures…"

"Those pictures didn't make it onto the wedding album, *mi niña*, because you're in them."

Mari looked at the pictures, fascinated. "These are priceless, *Abuela*."

"Yes, they are, *mi niña*. That's why right now I'm entrusting them to you."

Mari looked up and gave her *abuela* a surprise look. "You want me to take them right now?"

"Yes, *mi niña*. I want you to take them now—and the jewelry box."

Mari hugged the pictures and carefully placed them back in the box.

"*Mi niña*, now that the jewelry box and its contents have found their rightful owner, lock the door back up. *En fin* [Anyway], *mi niña*, not much more left to tell. We would've preferred that you and your parents remain close to us, but your father never forgot the threat that the Levys had made, and he and your mother feared losing you too. So, I don't know what deal José Felipe made with his partners at his law firm, but he said it was a good deal, and he asked for our blessing and permission to take you and your mother to New York."

"*Abuela*, do you know why they chose New York and not California, or…I don't know, Miami, for instance?"

"All he said was that it offered direct flights to almost anywhere in the world and that it had good schools and universities, so I didn't ask anymore."

Mari remained pensive for a long time. *Had my father chosen any other place, I would not have met Kurt,* she thought. Her tears began to flow as she reminisced.

"*Mi niña bella*"—her *abuela* reached down and used her withered fingers to wipe her granddaughter's tears— "I know how much you've suffered. I know, *mi niña*, I know."

Both women then allowed their tears to flow; sobs followed.

After they subsided, Mari embraced her *abuelita* and squeezed her tight.

"*Ay, Abuelita*, I wish I could bundle you up and stuff you into my suitcase. I never want to let you go."

"*Mi niña*, one last *consejo* [piece of advice]." *Abuela* held her granddaughter's hand in one of hers and patted it with the other. "Don't close yourself off completely to the idea of finding love again. You are young, beautiful…don't be alone. Life is easier when lived with someone you love. Look how beautiful your life turned out, in spite of everything, because your mom chose to love again after your father."

"My story is different *Abuela*; my first love was *grande y bueno*."

"Then he wouldn't want you alone and sad."

Mari thought of mentioning that some other wise person had given her similar advice but knew it would be best to avoid bringing up Ozan *Bey*'s name.

"By the way, *mi niña*, where is it that you are going tomorrow?"

A sudden war broke out inside Mari's head. She hadn't forgotten the reaction that hearing the name Ozan had triggered in her grandmother. She took a deep breath, however, and went for it.

"My designs will be in an important fashion show in Istanbul—"

"*Turquía?*"

"*Sí, Abuela, Turquía.*" Mari held her breath.

Her *abuela* reached for the keys in her pocket and singled one out, as she had done before. "This is to the front drawer of that small table where I have the statue of *la Virgen de la Fuensanta*. Open it, *mi niña*."

Mari obeyed. "*Ay, Abuela*, you have lots of rosaries here."

"Take out the red one; that is the Rosary of the Blood of *Jesús*. When you pray it, the blood of *Jesucristo* will protect you. Also, take the Rosary of the Holy Wounds; that one will hide you from danger in his holy wounds." Mari took the two rosaries out one by one. "There is a smaller one also—that's a chaplet."

"A what?"

"A chaplet. It's smaller, fewer decades. That one is to pray to San Miguel, for his protection. Take it, *mi niña*. Also, there should be a small book of prayer in the same drawer."

"*Sí, Abuela*, there is."

"Take it. It'll instruct you in how to pray all the rosaries. You'll be fine in Istanbul, *mi niña*. Only, don't go falling in love there!"

"*Abuela, por Dios*, that's impossible! I'm only there for three days—tops! Then I'll be back in Milan for a while and finally, back home to New York."

"*Está bien, mi niña, está bien.*"

Mari locked the drawer back up and brought the keys to her *abuela*. Once again, Mari clung to her neck and kissed her cheeks. Tears flowed, but no words were uttered. Mari just turned around, grabbed her camera and tripod, and left the room.

CHAPTER 106
WE FOUGHT WITH ALL OUR MIGHT TO KEEP YOU

Before going into her bedroom, Mari went in the back terrace where she knew she'd find her *abuelo*. He was seated in a worn, but comfortable recliner that had been there since as far back as Mari could remember. The night was chilly, but he seemed oblivious to it and only wore a light cardigan over his shirt.

"*Abuelo…*"

"I was expecting you, *mi niña*; come close," he said gently; his eyes were blurry. Mari went to him, got on her knees in front of him, and leaned back on her heels, her hands resting on his lap, hiding under his.

Her *abuelo* tightened his grip around her hands. "I know that your *abuela* finally revealed to you the secret that we had held inside for many years. I have never been very religious in the traditional way, *mi niña*, but I sense that there is something beyond that is superior. All my life, I've been faithful and prayed to that Superior Being that I believe is God. I've prayed that we will die in peace and that you and your brother will someday be reunited. My only request is that when you find our José María, your brother, you will let him know that we loved him and fought for him…" *Abuelo* remained silent for a short while, but Mari knew that he hadn't finished. "*Mi niña*, don't hold a grudge against the Levy family. After all, they are your flesh and blood. Don't hold them to account; that is God's job, *mi niña*."

"*Abuelo*, wait." Mari ran inside and grabbed the video camera that she had left just outside her bedroom door. "*Abuelito*, you tell my brother what you want to tell him."

The *abuelo* looked into the camera, as instructed by Mari, and spoke. "*Mi niño*, José María…" He choked up and grabbed his handkerchief to wipe his tears and face. "The last time I held you in my arms, you were eight days old…" He choked up again, and Mari could not hold her tears back either.

He continued, "I'm old and probably will not meet you in person, but I want you to know, *mi niño*, that we have always loved you. Not a day goes by that your *abuela* and I don't think of you, and we fought with all our might to keep you…" He was overtaken by emotion and signaled Mari to stop recording.

She put the camera down and went to embrace her *abuelo*. They remained in that position for a long time. She finally spoke.

"*Abuelo*, this is my goodbye. I don't want to do it again tomorrow. Besides the fact that it will be very early, I couldn't stand to say goodbye to you." They hugged again, but just as had happened with *Abuela*, no more words were exchanged.

CHAPTER 107
A RECEPTIVE HEART

When Mari entered her bedroom, she checked her cell phone and noticed a bunch of missed calls from Mari-Car. She worried. The first thing that came to her head was, of course, Deniz-Mare. She immediately called.

"*Mamá*, where have you been? I've been calling all night."

"Is Deniz-Mare OK?" Mari asked, feeling a lump in the pit of her stomach.

"Yes. All is the same. She's in good spirits." Mari let out a sigh of relief. "It's just that Ozan's uncle Osman will be picking you up at the airport tomorrow when you arrive in Istanbul…"

"Mari-Car, I don't need anyone to pick me up. I'll do what I always do when I travel—get a taxi and go to my hotel until it's time to go to the event, and then—"

"Mari *Hanim*, it's Ozan." Mari rolled her eyes. Who else would call me Mari *Hanim*? she thought. "You'll be in our city. You've done so much for our family. Please allow my uncle Osman to pick you up at the airport, and please let him show you our city when you're done with your event...it's the least we can do."

A long silence followed. Mari was very hesitant and terribly nervous. The astonishing story of deception her *abuela* had told her had made her even more wary of people who came from drastically different backgrounds from her own. In fact, an unexpected feeling of anger seemed to creep up out of nowhere as she heard Ozan's voice. All she could think of was the nefarious deception that her own mother, María Victoria, had been subjected to so many years before.

Mari did not want Mari-Car to undergo such suffering, and maybe, she thought, having learned at this particular time about the devastating deception that her own family had experienced was a warning, a sign, so that she wouldn't make the same mistake that her *abuela* had—giving into her daughter when she accused her of being intolerant. Mari-Car has done the same thing, Mari thought. She felt confused and nauseated and instinctively held her stomach.

She was bewildered, even felt guilty that such thoughts were running through her head. She truly loved Deniz-Mare, Meryem had become a close friend, and she was getting used to Ozan, but she just could not push away the terror that was gripping her at the moment.

Countless anarchistic thoughts crowded her mind, and she began to shake. She thought she was having a panic attack, which brought her into more panic, so she quietly began doing breathing exercises.

Suddenly, she realized that her relationship with her daughter might suffer because of her possibly unfounded fears. *My God, I sound just like my abuela all those years ago,* she thought.

"Mari *Hanim*? Ms. Mari?"

"*Mamá*, are you there?"

"Yes, I'm here; I'm sorry. I'm just going over my itinerary in my head and…yes, OK, it looks like it's going to work out," she answered, her heart pounding.

"*Gracias, mami linda.*" Mari-Car's voice was cheery.

"*Gracias,* Mari *Hanim.*" Ozan's sounded subdued. But Mari still harbored some anger. *So now the guy speaks Spanish,* she thought and rolled her eyes.

Mari was a bundle of nerves when she got in the taxi before dawn; the feeling continued during the train ride to Alicante, and it got worse when she boarded the flight to Istanbul.

On the flight, she remembered that she had not talked to her parents as she was accustomed to doing before going on a trip. But Mari-Car's call had put her out of sorts, so she had decided to text her mom from the plane, glad she didn't have to call and expose her nervousness with her shaky voice.

"*Hola Mamá.* On a flight to Istanbul for a fashion show. *Bendición, Mami.*" It was short and sweet. She heard back almost immediately.

"*Dios te bendiga, mi hija.* Remember to pray the Saint Anthony Rosary. He is the patron saint of lost things. Don't get lost in that strange city, *mi hija*. People there are very different from us."

Her mother's text had done nothing to calm her fears; if anything, it intensified them. Now she understood, after her *abuela*'s revelations, what her mother meant by "people there are very different from us." More than anyone, her mother had a right to speak those words; they carried credence and found a receptive heart in Mari.

CHAPTER 108
MARI ARRIVES IN ISTANBUL

"Ladies and gentlemen, we have begun our descent into Istanbul. Please turn off all portable electronic devices and stow them until we have arrived at the gate. In preparation for landing in Istanbul, be certain your seat is in the upright position and your seat belt is fastened."

The familiar noise of clicks was heard throughout the plane, and then the captain's upbeat voice came on the speaker.

"Ladies and gentlemen, welcome to the beautiful and fascinating city of Istanbul, where the current temperature is a very pleasant twenty-two degrees Celsius. For our American friends aboard, that is about seventy-two degrees Fahrenheit. We wish you a pleasant stay and thank you for choosing to fly with us."

Mari usually didn't mind flying, but she found herself gripping the arms of her seat during descent; she felt her head encased in pain. The flight attendant noticed her discomfort and brought her a glass of mineral water.

"You'll be fine," she added.

"Thanks," Mari mustered.

After landing, Mari grabbed her garment bag and small carry-on suitcase. She followed the crowd through immigration, still feeling that she could faint at any moment. Her stomach had been so tied up in knots that she was unable to eat during the flight.

"*Hosgeldiniz*! Welcome!" said the young immigration officer in both Turkish and English. His admiration of Mari was obvious, but she remained oblivious.

She was grateful for the friendly luggage handler that appeared before her upon entering the baggage reclaim area.

Mari had decided to check a small suitcase with all the things she had previously packed in her carry-on bag, which now was filled with the wooden box of memories, plus her tripod and video recorder—things that she could not afford to lose.

She spotted the unassuming bright-yellow suitcase that she had found in her bedroom closet the night before. She pointed at it, and the young man grabbed it off the carousel and loaded it onto the cart.

He signaled her to place the carry-on and the garment bag on the cart also, but she politely refused, tightening her grip on both items.

She went through the security checkpoint without incident and into the waiting area for arriving passengers.

Her head and heart were pounding, her vision became blurry, the stress she felt affected her breathing, but she tried to hide her discomfort.

Mari gave the luggage handler a generous tip and asked him politely, in what she hoped was universal sign language, to go and leave the cart next to her.

Mari then placed her carry-on on the cart, draped her garment bag over everything, and began pushing the cart herself while scanning the crowd, trying to see if she recognized Osman.

This would've been so much easier if Mari-Car had let me do what I always do—grab a taxi! she thought, annoyed.

Along the way, Mari noticed some women wearing tightly wrapped head scarves and long robes with long sleeves and a few women wearing burqas; her anxiety level increased. It also blinded her: she missed the fact that most people were in Western attire.

By now, she had almost reached panic mode.

Suddenly, Mari was surrounded by a group of men wearing white robes and slippers. Her head began to spin; the strange sounds around her seemed to intensify. She left the cart and got ready to run, but she suddenly found herself on top of a stranger.

A confused look emanated from piercing blue eyes that penetrated her wide-open dark ones; the two remained intensely fixed on each other. The look emitted by the striking azure eyes felt vaguely familiar. Her forearms rested on his chest as he lay flat on the cold, hard floor wondering what had just taken place in what seemed like microseconds. One minute he was standing, stretching his neck to try to spot his passenger by following Ozan's description and the picture he had sent him, and the next minute, he had found himself in this awkward position.

Mari was the first to break the uncomfortable, albeit intense, moment. "We cannot be too careful; you never know what these people will do."

Osman tried to look around, but he was barely able to raise his head. "What people?" he finally said in slightly accented English.

"The extremists," she replied, turning her head to look at the group of men in white robes and slippers that had made her so afraid just before she had run into the man that now lay beneath her.

One of the men was pushing the cart with her luggage toward them. "Hello. You left your possessions behind," he said, smiling.

To be continued.

ABOUT THE AUTHOR

Tina Muñiz Steimle is first and foremost an educator who believes that teaching takes place not just in the classroom but anytime you have before you a willing learner. She holds a Bachelor of Arts in French and a Master of Education from Grand Valley State University in Grand Rapids, Michigan. Tina drew her inspiration for her novel, *Bir Zamanlar—Once Upon a Time—* from visiting the magnificent cathedrals and castles of Europe; the charming colorful villages of Tuscany and Como; the French Alps and their breathtaking beauty; Parisian sidewalk cafes and their laissez faire atmosphere. The alluring and fascinating traditions of Türkiye, admired by the author, inspired the title of the book.

Tina was born in the Dominican Republic and grew up in Holland, Michigan, which, after many years of absence living in beautiful and far-away places, she still considers her hometown.

www.ingramcontent.com/pod-product-compliance
Ingram Content Group UK Ltd.
Pitfield, Milton Keynes, MK11 3LW, UK
UKHW040746120225
454989UK00014B/78/J